OF SCARS AND SCALES

OF SCARS AND SCALES

THE LEGENDS OF ANTICUUS
BOOK TWO

ROBIN WINCKLER

Published in the United States of America

Cover Designer: Sarah Penney (sarahpenneydesigns.wordpress.com)

Editors: Laine and Aria Nichols (avadel-ink.com)

ISBN: 979–8-9867747-3-2 (paperback)

First Edition: April 2025

10 9 8 7 6 5 4 3 2 1

*For those who are willing to wait
no matter how long it takes.*

PART ONE
SHADOWSLAYER

"There is a myth about a man consumed by dark magic—so
much that he *became* it.
Little else is known, but some believe this man to be real:
a ghost that haunts our lands."

I

A CHANCE ENCOUNTER

The castle of Sheniir had become the center of myths and legends since it fell to Selini's Draconic forces many years ago. It was once a powerful and prosperous kingdom that proudly displayed the might of humans without magic's blessing. Pride had ultimately amounted to nothing, and the kingdom swiftly collapsed beneath the power of the Golden Head Dragonborn, Aurum. Now, the castle lay in ruins. Its walls were crumbling, its great doors hanging loosely on their hinges. Shards of glass were scattered across the dusty floors. It was a hotbed for rumors, and Nari was no stranger to the stories that emerged from it.

Some said the castle was haunted by the spirits of those who were slaughtered in the battle with the dragonborn, clinging desperately to their hatred as their bodies turned to dust. They said the ghosts whispered to any who came, leading them deeper into the castle until there was no escape and death claimed them, too. They said the souls sought to stain the halls with more blood.

However, Aviva always had a different view of the castle. *"It is filled with dark magic,"* she used to say, her forest-green eyes dim with worry. *"You must never go there, Nari, or you could face the corruption of your soul."*

Doubt lingered in Nari's mind when her mistress spoke of such things. For a purification specialist, Aviva was uniquely afraid of corruption. *If there's anyone who should not fear forbidden magic, it's someone who knows how to get out of it,* Nari reasoned.

She didn't know how many of the rumors were true—if any. But now, as she stared up at the looming archways of the castle's entrance, shivers trailed her skin. Gripping her staff so hard that her fingers began to ache, she swallowed her fear. Though the air was clear of the thick, tainted feel of dark magic, though there was most likely no evidence of ghosts wandering the halls, something had occurred at the old castle of Sheniir. Something that forced Aviva to reach out to her. Something that cut the thread of Aviva's life in the tangled web of magic.

Death swallowed the place where her mistress's touch should have been; it was cold and foreign as it brushed against Nari's senses. If Aviva had been killed—

"Does it lead inside?" a soft voice asked.

Nari jumped at the touch of a hand against her shoulder. Spinning around, she came face to face with the curious stare of her brother, Ronan. He lifted his hands and stepped back, his boots scuffing against the dirt-covered stone. In the moonlight, he looked as pale and fragile as the ghosts she couldn't seem to get out of her mind. It didn't help that his eyes were underlined with deep, dark circles and his red-brown hair was matted and tangled from weeks of non-stop travel.

It took her a moment to piece together what he was asking about. She stiffened and turned back to the castle, letting her gaze rest on the thin, emerald trail that wound through the shadowed halls. "Yeah," she murmured, her shoulders drooping. "It does."

He rubbed the back of his neck. "Sorry. I wasn't trying to

scare you. We don't have to go in while it's dark if you would rather wait."

"It can't wait." She raised her staff and brushed a hand across the crystal situated at its top end. It glowed against her palm, humming as magic crawled to the surface of the glass. She pulled away. Light bloomed from within and expanded until it enveloped a wide circle around them, brightening their path. "Aviva's call was urgent, and I sense death here."

"You don't think…?"

"I don't know what I think, Ronan!" Nari snapped, whirling to face him. The surge of anger that clawed at her throat sent her magic spiraling into a fit, swirling around her fingers as she fought to keep it down. It couldn't find release, suffocated beneath the spell Aviva cast over her training staff. If anything, it only dragged more frustration to the surface. With a heavy sigh, Nari turned away once more. "Just stay close to me. I don't like this place at all."

"Sorry," he said again. "I don't want to fight with you. What kind of Mage Guardian would I be then?"

"Let's get this over with. I don't know how long before the Summoners will be snooping around this place, and I don't want to be here when they arrive." She couldn't help but recall Aviva's constant warnings. *"You're an unregistered Mage practicing magic without their consent. Do not let the Summoners catch you. If they do, they will seal your magic away."* At the moment, Nari wasn't sure which was worse: having her magic sealed or accepting the death that lay in front of her.

Her legs were like lead, each step like wading through a knee-deep puddle of mud, but she fought to move forward and slunk through the entryway. The light from her staff spilled over the floor, illuminating muddy footprints that trekked to and from the castle entrance. Deep gashes scarred the stone, and blood dried in dark blotches everywhere she turned. Scattered weapons littered the ground, blades rusted through as they fell to disrepair. The bodies they once belonged to were nowhere to be found. Nari clamped her jaw shut and swallowed the bile that burned the back of her throat.

Just follow the thread. She locked her gaze on the thin thread of Aviva's magic, winding deeper into the hall and disappearing around a corner. *Don't look at anything else.*

"It smells foul here," Ronan whispered, brushing up against her shoulder. His hand found its way to the hilt of his sword, hidden beneath his cloak. "How deep do we need to go?"

Nari followed the trail around the corner at the end of the hall and stepped through the arched doorway into a large throne room. Like the rest of the castle, it was sad and broken, forgotten by the world save for the haunting myths of its misery. Moonlight shone through multiple openings in the roof, and rubble cluttered the space beneath the holes. At the far end of the room, there was a throne seated upon a raised dais. Torn shreds of a tapestry hung on the wall behind the throne, turned a pale auburn from exposure to sunlight and a lack of care. A splotch of blood stained the floor—fresher than what she had seen in the hall that led to the room. It had darkened and dried but lacked the same muddy tint as the older patches. There was otherwise nothing notable about the room.

The emerald thread fizzled out as soon as they reached the center of the room, dispersing into tiny green sparks. Nari gasped, fumbling to catch the sparks as they faded. There wasn't even a touch of warmth as they brushed her fingers, nor did they cling to her like living magic would. Cursing, she spun around to examine the room again.

"I don't get it," she muttered, extinguishing the light in her staff. She moved toward the throne and dismissed her staff into a shower of sparks, grateful to be rid of its weight in her hands. "Aviva's trail vanished. What are we supposed to find here?"

"She didn't give you any hints?"

Nari shook her head, folding her arms. "There's nothing

here. What's more frightening is that she's *gone*. I can't even sense her spellbook or Iila, her familiar."

Ronan pursed his lips. With a sigh, he jerked his chin toward the exit. "We should leave then. The Summoners could be here any minute. Maybe it was some kind of false alarm."

"Yeah…" Nari remained rooted in place, her fingers creasing her sleeves beneath their grip as she wrapped her arms around herself. Wary, she swept her gaze around the empty room.

The throne before her was carved from solid stone, as cold and unwelcoming as the rest of the dead castle. Yet, in the moonlight, the air around it shimmered with life. It was faint, but there was magic swirling around the throne, tinged gold and flickering with a will of its own. It left no imprint and hardly bore a presence at all, but it was there.

She frowned, studying it. Slowly, she approached the throne. It loomed over her as she stood at the foot of the dais. *Is this what you were trying to show me?*

Frost bloomed across the surface of the throne, swiftly encasing its back in frozen waves. The air turned frigid, and Nari shivered, her breath fogging in front of her face. Magic spiked around the throne, blue with the imprint of someone unfamiliar. Its presence was enough to send Nari stumbling back; she shrank in on herself to keep out the invasive touch of ice.

Ronan was at her side in an instant. He snaked one arm around her protectively, drawing his sword with the other. The distinct scrape of metal against its sheath rang through the air. "Who's there?" he called. "Come out and show yourself!"

A crash echoed through the room behind them. Nari stiffened, summoning her staff as she spun around, her back pressed to Ronan's. A large chunk of ice had shattered against the stone, throwing tiny particles across the room. One slid to where she stood and crashed against the toe of her boot. She scrutinized it. The shard glittered with the touch of ancient, powerful magic, one that raised the goosebumps along her skin.

"Ronan," she whispered, glancing at the throne again. "I think we should go."

He tensed against her. Together, slowly, they backed away from the throne, one step at a time. Nari stilled. The throne shrank as the distance between her and it grew, yet the hum of power resting in its seat still brushed against her. Its whisper spun around her, coiling like a snake as it slithered up her spine. It was there for a reason. She couldn't leave.

Her lips parted, a protest on her tongue. The air chilled and, with a sharp hiss, the light in her staff winked out. Darkness cloaked the room. Panic slammed against Nari's ribs like a bird in a cage, but no matter how hard she willed it, her staff wouldn't light.

Cold snapped at her skin. A small figure shot out from behind the throne, pressing close to the shadows as he slipped farther toward the back of the room. He left icy white foot-prints in his wake, fractals that illuminated his form just as he retreated into the darkness again.

Gritting her teeth, Nari gripped her staff in both hands, the harsh press of the bumpy wooden rod digging into her palms. Magic circled her fingers but refused to obey her command, leaving them cloaked in darkness as the figure fled from sight. She wanted to curse, but the rush of anger only made the connection more flimsy.

"Nari, bring the light back!" Ronan snapped.

"I'm trying!"

The threads of magic slipped through her fingers like water. Frustrated, she gritted her teeth and allowed the twisted, burning anger growing within her to take command of the power. It bent to her will, lighting the staff with a faint glow. As it slowly brightened, the shadows fled, revealing the blue-cloaked figure perched on the seat of a tall, narrow window in the far back wall. His gaze snapped toward her as the light fell over him, staring right through her soul with piercing ice-blue eyes that glowed dimly in the dark. Long, pointed ears poked out from beneath sandy blond hair, and a pair of azure horns curled up from the top of his head. The dragonborn flinched and pushed out the window, vanishing into the night. Gone, along with the chill in the air.

Seconds ticked by, but Nari stared dumbly at the empty window, frozen and quivering with fear. Her ears roared, and her breath came in shuddering gasps when she tried to ease the trembling in her hands. A *dragonborn*, far outside the boundaries of Hybrid Territory. They weren't supposed to be able to come this far. They were banished from Sheniir and the rest of the human kingdoms, yet her eyes couldn't have deceived her.

She wet her lips, pausing to try to mask the growing knot of panic in her chest. "D–do you think that was what Aviva called us here to see?"

"I don't know." Ronan sheathed his sword. He slid his cloak from his shoulders and wrapped it around her, pinning it in place with the blue badge that named him as her Guardian. "We should go. There's no telling if that *thing* will come back—and what he'll do to us if he does. We got lucky."

"Maybe the Summoners will catch him when they show up here," she muttered.

"Maybe."

With one last glance back at the window, Nari left the throne room with Ronan beside her. Confusion twisted her mind, and fear cut every thread of logic that tried to put things together. She had only one choice, and that was to return home, to Aviva's forest. To face the corruption she was told to run from.

2

THE BOY WITH RED EYES

13/1/X/xx-68

TOBIAS WAS no stranger to tension. Novelists were proud of their abilities to write it—or so he assumed from the number of manuscripts he had scanned that featured the crackling discomfort between characters. History was flooded with tension between people and dragonborn, mortals and gods, men and the land, and so on. More than that, Tobias himself had experienced quite a lot of tension in the few short weeks since leaving home to chase down the thief who stole his precious book.

But there was nothing like the razor-sharp glares that Oliver threw at Eira every few minutes. They were looks painted with malice, weathered by hatred, and consumed with anger. It never failed to send a shiver down Tobias's spine—despite that the younger boy was *always* pointing his weaponized gaze at the former thief beside him and never at Tobias himself. Even from the other side of the market, separated by the bustling crowd, Oliver's amber stare found its way to them. Nothing could shield them from his judging look.

Eira cleared her throat and shuffled behind Tobias, the

scrape of the beaten dirt road against her soles filling the thick silence.

They stood at the edge of the market, shaded by the eaves of an old building, its brick facade scribbled with words Tobias couldn't read. It was in a town not too far from the castle of Sheniir. The name escaped Tobias's mind, but he found that he didn't care. It didn't matter; it was cold, far from home, and left him feeling as painfully empty as the castle they had left behind.

Oliver glanced up at them again, clutching a bright red fruit in one hand. Arayna leaned forward to sniff it but caught herself as the shopkeeper regarded her curiously. Her ears and tail were both hidden beneath the coat she borrowed from Oliver—one that hung too loosely over her frame—and he had advised her to "act as normal as possible," as though this was something she could do. He seemed to trust her more than he trusted Eira, however.

The tension was uncomfortable, painful even. Tobias's hands ached from how tightly he curled his fingers into fists, his back ached from standing so rigidly, and his jaw ached from how tightly he clenched it shut. His *everything* ached.

More than anything, Tobias hated tension. He was a victim of it this time, and Oliver's pettiness knew no bounds.

Pettiness, he echoed, tugging the collar of his coat up to shield his neck from the bite of cold air that whirled past him. Was it petty of him to miss his family, to blame Eira for the betrayal that led to the death of his friends?

"It's going to take him a hundred years to find all the supplies he wants if he doesn't cut that out," Eira grumbled. "What, does he think I'm going to stab you and run off? I don't even have my knives; he took them all." She threw back her head and groaned. "We'd get through this faster if he let us help."

"Give him some space," Tobias answered. "He just lost someone very important to him—two people, in fact." *Three if you want to count Uriah.* But no one ever did.

Uriah's name had become a taboo subject. No one spoke even a whisper of him, as though it were better if he didn't exist at all. It was a strange thing; Eira had committed the same offense of betrayal. The only difference was that she found herself freed by the end while Uriah was killed, yet Oliver wouldn't hear a word about Uriah. If Eira was a subject of hatred, Uriah was ten times worse. An inkling of pity diluted the muddy waters of Tobias's mind—but it was quickly cleared by the echo of Kase's last words: *"Uriah is not who you think he is."*

Tobias still wasn't sure who he thought Uriah was.

"He acts as if I didn't lose someone too," Eira snapped, forcing Tobias back into the present conversation. She folded her arms over her chest and leaned against the wall, throwing her gaze at the ground. "Kase and Aviva were precious to me, and I…"

Again. No Uriah. Tobias fiddled with the loose thread that hung from the seam of his tunic. "I know. It hurt all of us, but don't expect him to welcome you back with open arms so easily. You destroyed his family."

Eira sucked in a sharp breath. A pause. Then, quietly, "You know that wasn't me."

"It doesn't matter what I know or don't, what I believe or don't," Tobias said calmly, tugging on the thread. "Oliver isn't me. He holds different ideas and different opinions. Even if it wasn't you who killed Kase, it was you who sent everything spiraling into place for the…" The last word caught in his throat like a stone, heavy as it sat on the tip of his tongue. He licked his lips and dropped his voice to a low murmur. "The dragonborn."

Another heavy silence. Eira pushed away from the wall, wiping her dirty hands on her skirt. "I would have preferred the Shadowslayer that Uriah told you about."

"Me too." Tobias dropped the thread and lifted his head. Again, Oliver was looking at them from across the marketplace, though he had gone so far that he was difficult to see among the crowd. Tobias waited until he looked away again before continuing. "But a dragonborn is what we're up against."

"And we still haven't decided what to do about it?"

"Oliver wants to wait on the High Summoner's response."

"Why is Oliver in charge of you?"

Tobias sighed, rubbing his temples. A headache was beginning to form there. "Eira, please, it's been a long day and we still have a lot of it left to go."

"Sorry," Eira muttered. She rubbed her arm, pressing her lips into a thin line. "I'm not keen on getting involved with the Summoners. As you can probably imagine, I doubt they're fond of me. I don't want to get arrested for attacking High Summoner Maven and using magic without a..." As her sentence trailed off into a confused sputtering, she flapped her hand around as if to help the words come to her. Finally, she snapped her fingers and straightened, a light in her eyes. "Mage license—that's what it's called—or whatever."

"Some of that can be waived. Maybe." Tobias tried to sound optimistic, but his last run-in with Maven left him with little hope. Though young and still learning how to fill her position as High Summoner, she was a stickler for rules with hardly a shred of mercy for those outside of her view of what was right. The only reason Aviva had been let off the hook was because of the larger problem at hand: the corruption that was sown by the dragonborn. Aviva had claimed there was only so long before Maven returned to deal out punishment to her. He had no doubt she'd been right about that. *In one sense, I suppose death was an easy out for her.*

He shook his head. No. That wasn't fair to her.

"Tobias?" Concern twinged Eira's voice, and her hand brushed his arm as if to comfort him. When he met her eye, she quickly withdrew, threading her fingers through her long, brown hair instead. "Um, you alright? You seem off today."

Sighing, he looked away and slid his hand into his pocket,

where the small, round pin from Kase was tucked safely away with the scrap of Aviva's spell. It had become something of an anchor for him, like the key hidden beneath his shirt. He couldn't depend on Kase's strength anymore, but the memento offered a sense of closure. He assumed that was what it was meant to do for Calix, if he ever found him.

"Same reason everyone is off," he murmured. "I'm over-whelmed, and I miss them."

He didn't think the yawning, empty ache in his chest would ever diminish, nor did he expect the cloud over his mind to clear with it. There was a void in what remained of their group—one that yearned for Kase, Aviva, and Uriah to fill it. It was harder to laugh without Uriah's stupid jokes, harder to focus and plan without Aviva's calm demeanor, harder to press on without Kase's never-ending encouragement. For someone who suffered so much, he was always smiling, always optimistic that things could get better.

Now, he was gone, and the world darkened. Even Smoke, old and detached as he was, seemed pained by it. He rarely stayed with them anymore, and when he came around, he never opened the bond to speak to them. There was sadness in his old eyes; Tobias could only imagine the pain he felt.

How am I supposed to find Aviva's apprentice and ensure Calix's safety like they asked when I can barely convince myself to focus on the world in front of me?

A figure bumped his shoulder as it hurried by. It was a young boy, buried in a black cloak that was too large for his scrawny form. He paused, spinning on his heel to face Tobias. Light rippled over his expression as though there was a thin veil that concealed it. "Sorry!" he called, dipping his head politely. Unruly dark hair poked out from the hood of his cloak. "Please excuse me." When he lifted his head, his gaze lingered for a moment, searching Tobias's face before he turned and sped off to join a white-cloaked figure a few paces ahead.

Tobias froze, his mouth part way open to call to the boy again, but the words died on his tongue. A chill trailed down his spine, and he snapped his mouth shut, pulling back.

The boy's eyes were red like blood.

Eira gasped, gripping Tobias's shoulder as she pulled herself to his side. "Did you see that?" She pointed the way the boy had gone—however, the surprise in her voice was laced with excitement rather than the nervous fear that thrummed through Tobias's veins. He followed the tip of her finger to the young girl cloaked in white at the boy's side. "That's a Calistian, I'm sure of it!" Eira went on. "Do you see her hair?"

Tobias frowned and pried Eira's hand away, still trembling from the sudden rush of adrenaline. "Why would I care about some girl's hair?" *Why should that be more important than that boy?* Red eyes haunted his nightmares, glowing in the dark as their beastly owners prowled through the shadows. Only dragonborn and their hybrid offspring had red eyes. The only thing he needed to focus on now was the pounding of his heart in his chest and the feel of his nails pressing into his palms to ground him in the present.

"Just look, please!" Eira insisted, oblivious to the fear that gripped him.

Pressing his lips into a thin line, Tobias focused on the girl as she and the boy wandered deeper into the crowd. She was easy to spot among the colorful wraps worn by the townsfolk. White cloaked her form like snow on the tips of the distant Aurora Mountain Range—that in and of itself was a very Calistian trait, but he followed Eira's finger and took in the girl's hair instead. She was studying the red-eyed boy at her side, her long cinnamon-brown ponytail swishing behind her as she walked. It fell to midcalf, despite that it was pulled up and out of her face. From a distance, it was difficult to tell, but he thought he could make out tiny braids among the silken waves of her hair. She cast a quick glance over her shoulder before leading the boy away and vanishing in the crowd.

Eira nudged Tobias's side. "Only wealthy and influential Calistians grow their hair out that long," she said. "Must be someone pretty important in the court. She might be able to help with our dragonborn problem!"

Tobias stiffened. Before the seed of hope in his chest had a chance to bloom, he quickly stamped it out. "Eira, she's a kid. And how do we know she can actually kill a dragonborn and isn't just some spoiled rich girl?" His skin crawled. He doubted she was *just a spoiled rich girl*, judging from her choice of company. Sighing, he added, "Our best bet is to report the dragonborn sighting to the Summoners and let them deal with it." But even as he said it, the words didn't fill him with any hope. Traditionally, it had been the Calistian people who dealt with dragonborn sightings before the Summoners took over everything.

Many Calistians were said to be dragonborn slayers, desperate to avenge the elves of their kingdom, Calistie, that were slaughtered by Selini's people hundreds of years ago. Perhaps the girl was one who followed the vengeful footsteps of her people, but Tobias couldn't shake the legends that circled the dragonborn they chased —the one who dragged them all into this tangled web together and wrenched three of their friends from them. He was Aurum, the servant of the goddess's Golden Head. He had spearheaded the slaughter of the elves, the ancestors of the Calistians—but even if he hadn't, Tobias was wary of pitting a young girl against a Head Dragonborn. It was a death sentence; no one deserved that.

Red eyes, his mind whispered, pulling him back to the glimpse of the young boy in her company. *A Draconic trait.*

Tobias's fingers curled into a fist. Suspicion chewed at the edges of his thoughts. Calistian or not, dragonborn slayer or not, he had no reason to trust her yet. Draconics and Calistians were never seen together. On the rare occasion that they were, one of them was always dead.

Oliver saved him from whatever argument hung on Eira's lips. He approached as soon as she began to open her mouth, and she quickly shut it once he and Arayna came within earshot. Confusion darkened his gaze as he glanced between Eira and Tobias. The murderous look had dampened for the moment, allowing them to breathe without being choked by tension.

"Back to the inn?" he asked. "Arayna and I are finished."

"Yeah. Let's head back. It's cold out here," Tobias muttered.

AFTER THE UNFORGIVING icy wind outside that slashed Tobias's resolve to bits, the hearth's steady warmth was a welcoming release. He sighed as he sank into the stiff-backed chair, enveloped in the comfort of home—or at least, some semblance of it. When his shivers began to subside, he tugged his overcoat away from his shoulders and draped it across his lap. Dragging his fingers through his hair, he leaned against the table, desperate to shake the tiredness that clung to him. It stuck as the spike of nervous energy began to fade, leaving the red-eyed boy to his memories.

Eira dropped into the seat beside him, while Oliver and Arayna slid into the booth across from them a moment later, having first gone to drop the supplies in their room upstairs. Dim candlelight cast long, flickering shadows across their faces, painting them with weariness that was difficult to see in the sunlight. Oliver in particular seemed marred by exhaustion, his eyes underlined by deep, dark circles. Arayna studied him and leaned against his shoulder. He remained stiff and unresponsive, gaze fixed on the table instead. Tavern chatter filled the room; it was more comforting than the silence that haunted them.

Tobias lost count of the minutes that passed. Somewhere in the uncomfortable silence, a server girl came to ask if they wanted anything. Only Oliver responded. He was given a cup of water after that, which he drank without a word.

Arayna cleared her throat. She shifted awkwardly and sat on her hands, her wolf-like ears flattened against her head. "So… what now? Do we have any plans? How long are we going to stay here?"

"Until we know what to do next," Oliver muttered. "I don't want to stay in Faruu for long but—"

"Wait," Tobias interrupted. "What's Faruu?"

Oliver frowned, narrowing his eyes. His pointed, judging stare returned, making the hair on the back of Tobias's neck stand on end. "This town, Tobias. This town is Faruu."

Eira rolled her eyes and flopped against the back of her seat. "These stupid Sheniirian towns and their stupid double consonant names."

"That's a vowel, actually," Tobias corrected her. He picked at the hem of his tunic until another thread came loose, glad to keep his hands busy and his mind engaged in meaningless chatter.

"Same thing!"

Arayna screwed up her face. "What's a vowel?"

"A promise," Oliver said. "You know. A vow."

"No that's—" Tobias sighed, pinching the bridge of his nose. "Never mind."

"Right." Eira cleared her throat and lifted her chin. "*Anyway,* can we discuss something important, please? I have a suggestion —one that may produce faster results than trying to contact Maven ever would, and one that doesn't hold the threat of arrest over my head."

Oliver snorted. He folded his arms over his chest and leaned back against the booth. "I'm listening. What could you possibly have come up with, oh wise one?"

Eira frowned at him, which only made him smirk. With a huff, she looked away. "Tobias and I met a girl—"

"Saw, Eira," Tobias corrected with a glare. "We *saw* her. And for the record, no. This is a bad idea."

"—saw a girl at the market today. A Calistian." This time, it was Eira's face that took on a proud smirk, while Oliver's darkened into a sulk. She rested her elbows against the table and put her chin in her hands. "I think she could take care of our dragonborn problem. We just have to find out where she went and ask her."

Arayna wrinkled her nose with a snort. "Weren't you born in the kingdom of Calistie? Using that logic, *you* could take care of our 'dragonborn problem.'" She made sure to mimic Eira's tone as she threw the flimsy phrase back at the thief. Mischief glittered in Arayna's eyes, but it was edged with something darker.

"I was born on the outskirts," Eira said. "This girl must have been raised in the inner cities—you know, the places where the dragonslayers come from?"

Laughter cut off the end of her question, dry and humorless. Surprised, Tobias snapped his gaze toward Oliver, who was smothering his laugh behind his hand. The dark look in his eyes had brightened with amusement, but there was something mocking about the way his shoulders trembled and his smile curled.

When he caught his breath, he straightened and cleared his throat, but a flicker of a smile still remained. "Eira, we're not chasing the dragonborn. Aviva tasked us with finding her apprentice, and Kase asked Tobias to find Calix. They didn't ask us to hunt this... Shadowslayer or dragonborn or whomever."

"But we can't let him get away!" Eira snapped, gesturing vaguely. An angry flush darkened her cheeks. "Who knows how many other people he'll hurt? Who knows how many others he'll trick and control?"

"The spellbook is gone. It's not our problem anymore."

"Not our problem? So you would let him go free and destroy someone else's life because it's *not your problem?*"

Oliver slammed his hands against the table, rattling his empty cup. Arayna jumped, and Eira shrank back. Even Tobias's fingers curled, his hand sliding to the hilt of his sword as he kept a watchful eye on Oliver.

"He's a Head Dragonborn," Oliver hissed. "A servant of a god —basically a demigod, if that's easier for you to understand. Chasing him is a death sentence; you know this! We did that once and look where that got us!"

Eira pushed her shoulders back. "But I—"

"It's your fault we're in this situation." Oliver shoved to his feet and threw his arm out in a gesture around them. "You and Tobias both—it was his idea to go to you, and it was *you* who baited us into facing Aurum. It's your fault we lost so much. It's your fault that things can never be what they once were!"

"What, you liked it better when we were at each other's throats? When we didn't speak to each other?" Eira shot from her seat, eyes narrowed and her hands trembling at her sides. "You liked it better when we were separated?"

"Kase is dead!" Oliver reached over the table and grabbed the collar of her blouse, yanking her toward him. "Aviva is dead, even Uriah is dead! They're dead *because of you!*"

The tavern quieted. All eyes turned to their corner, sending a shiver down Tobias's spine. The server girl who had spoken with them before fiddled with her tray and ducked into the kitchen. No one dared to breathe, their stares burning with curiosity.

Tobias straightened and stood, gently prying Oliver's hands free. "Oliver," he muttered. "Watch yourself."

His gaze flicked around the room, and realization quickly

dawned in his face. He pursed his lips and shook Tobias off. Silently, he dropped back into his seat, folding his arms over his chest. "Sorry," he murmured, but he refused to meet Eira's eyes. He hid behind his unkempt, coal-black hair to avoid her.

As soon as Eira and Tobias were seated, the general chatter began to pick up around them once more. It was quiet at first, as if the other tavern patrons were waiting for them to start a fight, to flood the room with their thick tension, but it quickly returned to its usual murmuring rhythm. Arayna ducked her head, combing her fingers through her hair absently.

"What did Kase die for?" Oliver whispered, broken and trembling. He hung his head, pressing the heel of his hand to his eyes as he sucked in a sharp breath. "What did we gain from losing him and Aviva?"

His question was left hanging in the air between them. Tobias shrank back, attempting to hide from it. Though unspoken, he knew the truth. It sat on the tip of his tongue, bitter and heavy; speaking it would be so freeing. And yet, he said nothing.

"That's right," Oliver spat. When he pulled his hands away and dropped them in his lap, his eyes glistened with unshed tears. "They died for nothing."

Tobias's fingers curled tighter around the hilt of his sword until they began to ache, as if begging him not to voice what they already knew. "It wasn't for nothing," he said. "Someone gained something from their deaths, but it wasn't us. That's how it always is."

Oliver flinched as if he had been struck. Arayna reached to comfort him, but he brushed her away and rose to his feet. Without a word, he left with his back straight and his head high, as if to hide the brokenness that lingered in his eyes.

"Oliver!" Arayna called. She shoved herself out of the booth and bolted after him, catching up before he made it to the stairwell. They shared a quick word, and Oliver cast a glance back at Eira. Then they disappeared around the corner of the stairs.

Once they were gone, Tobias let out a long sigh and sank against the stiff back of his chair. His cloak felt heavy in his lap, pressing down on him. As cruel as ever, his mind drifted to the round, silver pin Kase had given him, tucked safely away in his pocket. His fingers twitched, and he curled them into a tight fist. *I made a promise. I'm going to find Calix. But...*

"Eira," he murmured, shifting his gaze to her. She inclined her head, puzzled. "Why don't we go find that Calistian girl?"

Eira's lips curled in a smile. "I thought you'd never ask."

3

ENEMY OF THE DRAGONBORN

Only after he had stepped back out into the cold did Tobias remember they had no way of knowing where the girl had gone. That was enough to plant the seed of doubt in him and uproot his resolve. If it weren't for Eira, who grabbed his arm and forcefully pulled him along, he would have ducked back into the tavern, sat down, and let it all go.

If you find that girl, his mind whispered, *you may find a hybrid with her. The boy with red eyes. What then?*

The question fell flat, unanswered. It was as heavy and baited as Oliver's questions about death, but unlike that, he had nothing to say. *What then indeed.* If he were honest, he would freeze with his hand against his sword, always thinking back to the monsters that ripped his mother from his childhood. He turned his focus elsewhere to keep his thoughts quiet.

Fading rays of twilight soaked the now empty marketplace in a soft, golden glow. The crowds had dispersed as the day settled into late evening and most vendors were closing up shop for the night. Only a few stragglers still wandered the market, but even they were already leaving when Tobias and Eira arrived. The white-cloaked girl was nowhere to be found. Eira cursed and paced, pressing a fist to her lips.

"If I were a rich Calistian girl, where would I go for the night in this town?" she muttered, her face creased with a thoughtful frown.

"Well…" Tobias tucked his hands into his overcoat to keep them warm. His breath fogged in his face when he sighed. "How many inns are there? This place is pretty big. We can't search all of them."

Eira stopped, the click of her heel against the cobblestone echoing in the stillness. She turned her head slightly, glancing at him out of the corner of her eye. Tucking a loose strand of hair behind her ear, she returned to his side. "Can I ask you something?"

His lip twitched as a sense of déjà vu came over him. "You just did," he said.

The only reaction she gave his subtle reference to their meeting was the roll of her eyes. "Come on, be serious. This is important to me."

"Go ahead."

"You trust me, right?" She bunched her skirt in her fists, her face downcast. "You don't blame me for what happened?"

Her question didn't come as a surprise, but the fact that she asked it still caught him off guard. He paused, searching for the right words. Like shifting sands, the answer slipped through his fingers, and he fumbled in the dark to grasp it again. Finally, he managed to piece something together.

"There's no point placing blame because we're all at fault," he said flatly. The harshness of his tone made him wince. "I split us up in the first place—in fact, Oliver is right that I begged everyone to go back for you. You were under the spell's control, bound by someone else's will and not your own. Oliver was supposed to protect Kase, Arayna was supposed to protect Aviva. Do you see the problem here?" He dragged his fingers through his hair. He didn't even bother trying to explain how much they screwed up with Uriah. "It's never ending. I'd rather focus on what can be done now."

"Sure. Right." Eira turned away and continued down the road. "Let's try the inn on the other side of the market. That's the last direction we saw them heading in."

Tobias stuck close to her side, matching the rhythm of her quickened steps. "There's something I think you should know before we meet up with this girl," he said. "Something important."

"No need to draw it out then. What is it?" Eira waved her hand, not even looking at him. She kept her eyes locked ahead.

A chill slithered down Tobias's spine. He sucked in a sharp breath and grabbed Eira's hand, pulling her to a stop. She snapped her gaze up to meet his, her brow furrowed in confusion. As soon as he opened his mouth to speak, the courage withered away. What if he imagined the red-eyed boy and there was nothing to worry about? *There's no reason to make her panic.*

"Never mind," he murmured, dropping her hand. "Just be careful."

"Okay...?" She rubbed her wrist, eyeing him as her frown deepened. The look softened, and she tipped her head. "You sure you're okay?"

Rather than struggle to form words from the chaos of his thoughts, Tobias shrugged halfheartedly and continued down the road. His fingers trembled at his sides, and he curled them against his palm to hide it. Cold nipped at his cheeks, as merciless and icy as it had been during their entire stay in the town. Deiah had long since ended, taking with it the last lingering threads of the warm season. What followed was Xenah, which should have brought a slight chill and the golden-red tint to the leaves in the trees. Instead, the full force of cold had already settled over the land. Tobias hated the cold; it was bitter and evil, slicing him to bits each time the wind blew.

But it was nothing compared to the chill that wracked his bones. *What am I doing out here anyway? I'm going to get killed by some half-breed kid, or I'm going to fumble my way through an explanation of our problem to this girl—if we can even find her.* The rhythmic, repetitive slap of his boots against packed dirt quickened—he didn't even remember leaving the cobblestone behind. He could only assume Eira was following, but he didn't stop to check. He wasn't even sure where he was taking himself. Urgency dulled beneath the anxious buzz of his thoughts. Over and over, the same whirlwind of thoughts circled in his mind. *Give the pin to Calix, find Aviva's apprentice, stop the dragonborn, undo the corruption, give the pin to Calix...* His nails bit into his palm. *Where's Talia when I need her?*

Without thinking, he took a sharp turn and found himself at a dead end. Two walls rose up on either side of him, and a third blocked his path forward. They were constructed out of smooth stone, sturdy when he rested his hand against one. It was cool against his palm, void of any markings or scars. Frowning, he pressed his hand flat against it. It was too cold, too smooth. It almost seemed to hum beneath his touch. Almost like...

"I told you already, he definitely saw me. People don't let that stuff slide—he's definitely going to come after me. Maybe he'll bring a whole hunting party."

"Honestly, I doubt that. He didn't look like that kind of man. I'm sure you're still on edge because of what happened."

Voices whispered back and forth from the other side of the third wall directly in front of Tobias. One belonged to a young boy, broken apart by the heavy drawl of a foreign accent. The other belonged to a girl, who spoke softly yet carried confidence through her tone. Despite their figures being hidden behind what looked like solid stone, the banter was clear and unmuffled as if there was no wall there at all. Frowning, Tobias crept forward, putting his hand against the hilt of his sword.

"There you are!" Eira cut in. Her hand landed against his

shoulder, jolting him out of his thoughts. He spun around to face her. Eira grinned. Though it didn't quite reach her eyes, there was a playful, teasing look to it. "You went a little too far. We were headed to the inn, remember? It's back this way."

The voices behind the wall came to an abrupt stop. Anxiety pricked Tobias's skin, spurred on by the silence that fell. He stiffened and grabbed Eira's hand. "We should go."

"Yes, that's what I was saying. This is a dead end, you know."

Tobias opened his mouth to explain, but the cold touch of metal against his neck turned the words to ice on his tongue. He clamped his mouth shut and reached for his sword. Eira jerked back, the teasing glint in her eyes replaced with a steely glare as her gaze settled on the figure behind Tobias.

"On your knees," the girl snapped, firm and unwavering. Confidence had shifted to authority, ringing with surety that didn't fit her young voice. "Take your hands away from your weapons. Now."

The command rippled over him. He found himself sinking to his knees and raising his hands above his head before he could think better of it. The press of the knife lifted from his skin as the girl stepped away. Eira, however, remained standing, her mouth hanging open in shock.

"She told you to get on your knees," the boy's voice growled. He appeared behind Eira in a flash of blue sparks and threw a kick to the backs of her knees. She crumpled easily with a startled gasp. Flecks of ice danced around the boy's fingers, diluting the air with their chill.

"Wait a minute!" Tobias cried, twisting around to peer at the girl behind him. Her glare was pinned on him, sharp and icy like the first frost of Sefah. It didn't match the soft, round shape of her face. She lifted the knife, its onyx blade glinting in the evening light. Tobias forced himself not to flinch and instead lowered his voice. "We don't mean any harm. We only want to talk."

"Did you follow us?" the girl bit back. "Who sent you?"

"You're a Calistian, aren't you?" Eira shoved up from the ground. The boy put a hand against her shoulder to shove her down again, but she shrugged him off. "We have a problem. A dragonborn problem. We think you can help us."

A flicker of recognition darkened the girl's eyes. She hesitated, her brow furrowing. "A dragonborn problem?" she repeated slowly. Her gaze flitted between the two, and the ice in her glare melted slightly. Sighing, she tucked the knife back into its sheath and helped Tobias to his feet, waving a signal to the boy. Obediently, the boy skirted around Eira to rejoin his companion.

Behind them, the wall had vanished, revealing an alley that led all the way back out onto the opposite street. Beyond the street, the outskirts of the town could be seen in the distance. In place of the wall, there was only the slightest haze of a mirage that flickered like heat waves rising off a stone. It was as though there had never been a wall there at all. Tobias's skin crawled with wrongness. Immediately, his gaze shifted to the boy. The *hybrid.*

However, when their eyes met, the boy's were a warm brown instead of the striking blood-red he had seen before. Gone was the look of a hungry, half-draconic beast. Now, he appeared as small and innocent as the girl he stood beside, albeit a little scrawny and glaring fiercely. Confusion twisted Tobias's gut, and his hand quickly found its way back to the hilt of his sword.

"Here's the thing," Eira began, oblivious to the storm that clouded Tobias's mind. She fiddled with her hands, sliding her fingers together before pulling them apart again. "There's this dragonborn on the loose. He had me under a spell for a while and hurt a lot of people. I managed to get free thanks to Tobias here, but... well, the dragonborn got away. I... I don't want him to hurt anyone else. I want to deal with him."

"*Deal with him?*" the girl echoed, raising a questioning brow. "You didn't think to raise this to the Summoners?"

"I can't." Eira dropped her hands to her sides. "If I alert the Summoners, they'll probably arrest me for what I did. Besides, I think this is beyond a Summoner's skill. I think this needs a Calistian—a dragonborn slayer."

The girl narrowed her eyes and pursed her lips. "Right. Where did you see this dragonborn last?"

"The castle of Sheniir," Tobias said. Just the mention of it sent a chill down his spine. Memories of it came back with a vengeance, flooding his mind with images of the crumbling castle and the bones that littered its halls. With trembling fingers, he reached for the pin in his pocket—the one Kase had left in his care until he could find Calix. *Kase's dying wish,* he reminded himself. As if he needed to be reminded.

"Sheniir?" The boy stiffened. He shot a look at his companion, but she only laughed lightly.

"If it was at the castle, it's probably not a dragonborn," she said. "Maybe you saw the Shadowslayer, a local legend."

"Kiara," the boy hissed.

"It wasn't the Shadowslayer," Tobias snapped, fixing the girl —Kiara, it seemed—with a firm stare. "There is no such thing as the Shadowslayer. That's just a myth. The dragonborn, however, is very real."

"I have reason to believe that he's real." Kiara didn't waver under his glare nor did she return it. She regarded him calmly, her stance relaxed and her gaze clear. There was no hostility in the way she carried herself; even her hands were kept at her sides, away from the weapons at her hips, visible beneath the hem of her half-cloak. She slid a glance to her companion. "There's something we have that might interest you."

"We're not interested in the Shadowslayer!" Eira cut in. She marched forward and made a grab for the front of Kiara's cloak. The boy snatched up her wrist and shoved her back. Eira groaned and yanked free. "Listen! The dragonborn is Aurum. We don't have time to babysit your fantasies when *he* is running loose!"

Tobias liked to think of himself as calm, level-headed, and logical, someone who wasn't prone to panic the way that so many were. In this instance, however, he found himself siding with Eira. The calm look in Kiara's eyes made his blood boil. Of all people, she should have understood their fear. Aurum destroyed the ancestors of her people and ravaged her kingdom. She was a Calistian, she was born to be his enemy, yet she didn't so much as flinch at the mention of his name. Even her companion shrank away when Eira spoke. *Perhaps he isn't a hybrid like I thought. Wouldn't he be excited to hear news of Aurum if he was?*

Kiara crossed her arms. "Yes," she finally said, "that's why I think you'll be interested in what I have to offer. Caerul, if you would please." She nodded to her companion.

Caerul went rigid, eyes wide as they flicked to her. His mouth opened and closed in a silent argument before he stuffed his hand into his cloak and pulled out a scrap of aged paper. Its edges were yellowed, and the writing that covered the face of it was smudged. Kiara accepted it from him and held it up for Tobias and Eira to see.

"Recently, Caerul and I uncovered this scrap of a letter," she said. "It's written in Draconic script, and we've only been able to translate pieces of it, but we know it references the Shadowslayer and the castle of Sheniir." She pointed to a word separated from the body of the letter, penned in more complex shapes like a signature. "It's signed *drekisn diem a, Aurum.* Literally, it's 'servant of the goddess's head, Aurum.'" Her gaze shifted to meet Tobias's. "Head Dragonborn Aurum."

Ice gripped Tobias's heart, freezing him with dread. His breath snagged in his throat as he stared blankly at the letter. "If they're connected..." Uriah wasn't trying to throw them off. He wasn't pulling the Shadowslayer out of nowhere. He *knew* something.

"*If* they're connected," Kiara began, pressing the paper back into Caerul's hands. "I believe hunting the Shadowslayer will be much easier than hunting Aurum himself. If you would be willing to help us catch the Shadowslayer, we will help you with your dragonborn hunt. Besides, catching the Shadowslayer may bring Aurum out of hiding—at least, that's what we think."

"We?" Eira wrinkled her nose.

"We work together." Kiara gestured to herself then to Caerul beside her, who only acknowledged them with a stiff nod. "We were sent to put the Shadowslayer's spirit to rest. We can't delay our mission any longer." Her repetition of *we* became more pointed each time she said it, and she kept her gaze fixated on Eira until the point was painfully obvious: there was no arguing this condition.

Eira planted her fists against her hips. "Okay, I get it. No need to be so pushy."

"Who sent you?" Tobias frowned. He couldn't imagine who would send a pair of children to hunt a monster, who would be that desperate to get rid of a ghost from the past. And yet, the irony was almost laughable, considering he and Eira were trying to talk Kiara into helping them with their own monster. Even that twisted his gut and drove a thorn into his heart.

"Head Dragon Rider Talia," Kiara answered plainly. "This is our final test as student Dragon Riders."

4

FORK IN THE ROAD

"Talia?" Shock laced Tobias's voice, pitching the question a little higher than he intended. "My sister Talia?"

Caerul frowned, his brows knitted together as he looked Tobias up and down. "You do kind of look like her." He gestured to his face, circling it with his pointer finger. His gaze flicked away, as if he were trying to recall something, before his attention snapped back to Tobias. He pointed decidedly at him. "Same face," he said plainly.

"Same face...?" Tobias echoed. He had always been told that he and Talia looked quite similar—it used to bother her when they were kids, and she would complain that it was *an insult to be compared to her baby brother.* Tobias shook his head to clear the thought. With a sigh, he pinched the bridge of his nose. "Listen—"

"That. Talia does the same thing," Caerul interjected with a sly smile at Kiara. "The nose pinch."

"—I can't imagine my sister giving out this kind of test to a couple of children, Dragon Riders or not. This is foolish and dangerous, and she would never have you risk your lives for something as trivial as your Rider license. In fact, most students don't even have a chance to take their final test until they're eighteen or maybe twenty."

"If you don't believe us, you can ask her yourself." Kiara fished a pendant out from beneath her cloak and held it out to him, dangling the smooth, round gem from a black cord. The jewel sparkled in the moonlight, glowing with a faint green light. It hummed with the presence of magic, which made his skin prickle.

Eira snatched it from her. "Where did you get this?" She glanced at Tobias. "Does your sister even have one?"

Kiara shrugged as she tucked her hands behind her back. "Who knows? There's only one way to find out. However, if you ask her about the Shadowslayer, you'll have to tell her how you found us. You'll have to tell her you want me to hunt down Aurum for you. I can't imagine she would like that idea, either, if what you believe about her is true."

Tobias pinched his lips into a tight frown, his brow furrowing as he gently accepted the communicator from Eira. It was cool to the touch, a pale green like the vibrant leaves of a forest in Deiah, the summer season. He had only seen communicator gems from a distance, hanging from the necks of wealthy patrons in the taverns of Floridus. He had never seen one in the hands of his sister, which would make it useless unless he got one to her. Though there wasn't any sort of mockery in Kiara's eyes, and she kept her face flat and void of emotion, there was something about the way she held his gaze that was a dare, like she was baiting him. He had no way of knowing if what she said was true unless he went back to his sister himself; by the time he did that, he would likely have lost Kiara and whatever she could offer him.

And if he went to his sister, he would, as she said, have to explain why he was working with Kiara in the first place—that he was hunting the most deadly dragonborn in all of Anticuus, and he was dragging a child into the midst of it all. It would put a wedge between them, one that was built on cruelty if he learned Talia had not, in fact, called for this hunt.

She's lying to you, he decided. *But... she can be useful. Whatever her reason, we have to work with her for now.* His gaze shifted to Caerul at her side, who was equally as blank and unreadable, though more fidgety than his companion. *But I won't let them out of my sight.*

"I'll pass on the opportunity for now," Tobias said, hating how small his voice was as he held the priceless relic out for her.

A pleasant smile graced her lips. She dipped her head to him and accepted the gem. "If you're certain."

Nodding, Tobias cast a sideways glance at Eira, whose tight frown and narrowed eyes portrayed that she was just as concerned by Kiara's words as him. "Thank you. Are we in agreement then? We will help you catch the Shadowslayer if you will help us defeat Aurum?"

"For now, I suppose." Kiara tilted her head back, fixating on the sky for a moment. When she looked at him again, she gave a firm nod. "That is the deal."

"And... Caerul, was it? He comes with us?"

"I go wherever she goes," he spoke up. He pressed his side to Kiara's. "Our dragons go with us, and we go together."

Dragons. For the first time, a bit of the wariness that pierced Tobias's lungs melted. Again, he found himself working along-side those who were blessed by a dragon's approval—once, that had been enough for him. Now, he wasn't quite sure. Smoke had left them, and Kase was gone. A hollowness had been left in their absence, one that ached with grief and loss. Maybe it wasn't for his sake that he should think twice; it was for theirs.

"Fantastic!" Eira clapped her hands together and replaced her disapproving frown with a charming grin. "Let's report back to Oliver then. We've found a solution, and he doesn't have to sulk anymore."

"Oliver?" Caerul echoed. He sucked in a sharp breath and

took a hasty step back as he shook his head. "Never mind, actually. We should… think about this some more. Consider our options."

"Oh, come on," Eira said, turning on her heel. "He's not that bad. Besides, what could you have even heard about him? Ruber is small, as is its influence."

Caerul made no reply—he didn't even look at Eira as she walked away with her head held high. He only inclined his head to Kiara, who paused for a moment as if lost in thought. Finally, they shared a look and followed Eira. No words were exchanged between them, and yet they seemed to have reached an agreement. Tobias hesitated a moment longer, glancing back at what had once been a wall that hid them from sight and was now an open alley. At the far end of it, almost invisible except for when he stared too long, a pair of bright blue eyes glowed in the darkness. When he spared a second look, the light was gone and the hum of magic that tinted the air had vanished. A shiver raced down his spine, and he quickly turned away.

THIS TIME, when they entered the inn, a hush fell over the tavern. Men set down their drinks and looked up from their card games. The women, who were leaning over the men's shoulders, turned lazily to the open door. Instinctively, Tobias's body seized up under the watchful gazes of the patrons. However, their eyes were not locked on him. Instead, they followed Kiara as she strode toward the far end of the tavern, the curled end of her long ponytail swishing behind her. She kept her chin high, her jaw clenched, and her steps purposeful. Dressed in all white, sporting her silver sword at her waist, she stood out like blood in snow.

"A Calistian," was the whisper that drifted through the quiet air. "Who called for a dragonslayer so far out here?"

"Are you sure? What business could a Calistian child have?"

"She seems too young to be a dragonslayer."

Eira crossed straight to Kiara's side, pointing her to the staircase that was almost hidden around a dark corner in the wood-paneled walls. Caerul followed, speeding up the stairs and disappearing from sight before Kiara could even get her foot on the first step. Tobias waited for Eira to go up before following.

It wasn't until Kiara was gone that life returned to the room below. Cautious and slow at first, but when she did not return, it turned boisterous once more. Tobias marveled at the effect that one girl could have on a room full of people, but he wasn't oblivious to the reasons. Everyone in Anticuus whispered about the Calistians. They were the only ones who ever stood up to the dragonborn and lived to tell the tale. The only reason the Summoners could implement their control over the border was because of the Calistians. Descended from the elves, a race so lost to the pages of history that no human properly understood them anymore, Calistians were revered for their strength, their beauty, and their knowledge of the dragonborn. They were mortals, humans like everyone else, but they had earned their place on a pedestal above the rest.

And yet, Kiara's presence didn't fill him with a sense of relief like he had assumed it would. If anything, having her there only made his skin prickle with anxiety.

Knowing better than to ignore his instincts, Tobias filed the feeling away until he could sort it out. There was something off about her and Caerul. It was only a matter of time before he unraveled their secrets.

Eira led the two companions to the room at the far end of the hall, where Oliver was pacing in the middle of the floor while Arayna sat perched on the edge of the desk, swinging her feet. Her ears pricked when they entered, chin jerking in their direction. Curling her lip, she shoved off the table, landing with a thump that wrenched Oliver out of his reverie. When he turned, there was anger burning in his eyes, but the flame diminished as his gaze slid over Kiara and Caerul, replaced by confusion.

"Tobias," he said, "what is this?"

"A solution!" Eira cut in. She shoved Kiara and Caerul forward, ignoring the way that Caerul flinched. "This is Kiara. She's a Calistian dragonslayer—she's going to help us defeat Aurum!"

Kiara dipped her head awkwardly—albeit politely—but Oliver didn't so much as glance at her. His focus had landed on Caerul beside her, disbelief and anger etched into the lines of his face. They stared at each other, stiff and unmoving. Caerul was the first to look away, hanging his head. Oliver schooled his features and cleared his throat.

"That's not a solution, Eira. That's a child," he said, brushing the moment aside.

"You're a child," Eira grumbled back. She folded her arms and stared him down, one brow quirked in a dare for him to argue back.

"Adult working age was declared seventeen a long time ago," Oliver stated, never one to back down from Eira's challenges. "I'm seventeen. Therefore, I'm an adu—"

"That doesn't count."

"Kiara has offered to help us deal with the dragonborn in return for our help putting the Shadowslayer ghost to rest," Tobias interjected, careful to use Kiara's words when speaking of the Shadowslayer, the mysterious myth that Uriah had insisted he and Eira were working for. It directly conflicted with Eira's account of the dragonborn, something Tobias was growing increasingly wary of. How do you defeat a creature older than time itself, whose hands are stained with blood and thrumming with magic?

He wasn't sure Kiara was the solution either. *Oliver's right. She's a child.*

But so was the Summoner, and that was who Oliver intended to run to.

Oliver swiveled to face him, already seething despite that the conversation had barely started. "We can't be *dealing* with either of those things," he snapped. "Aviva asked us to find her apprentice—to stop the corruption taking over her forest, remember? We have to escalate the problem back to the Summoners if we want to accomplish that. We don't have time to deal with Eira's victim complex or Uriah's deluded fantasies of the wandering ghost of Sheniir."

The reminder of Aviva's final words crashed down on Tobias, snatching the air from his lungs. She entrusted him with a spell and a task—to find her apprentice, Nari, and work with her to purify the darkness that was seeping into the land. The darkness that was taking up other Mages, draining their life, and leaving their corpse to rot until it was discovered by those who knew nothing of the problem. Magic-users were being crushed beneath the shadows, but...

"I don't know where to begin with Aviva's problem." Tobias met Oliver's cold glare and held it. He squared his shoulders under that unwavering icy look. "She had many, it seems, and holding her spellbook for a time does not make me qualified enough to fix all of them. Magic is something I don't understand, and I wouldn't be able to help Nari anyway, much less explain what's wrong to a Summoner. That is, if they even listen to us at all considering their issues with Aviva's disappearance." He gestured toward Eira, Kiara, and Caerul with a sweep of his arm. "But the dragonborn is a physical problem, a viable threat. Something I can face with my sword. I can't do it alone, but I know it's something I can help with. It's a problem we can fight."

Oliver scoffed, rolling his eyes so hard it was a wonder they didn't drop out of his skull. "So you want to go to war instead, sure. Fine. Alright, do as you wish. But what about the Shadowslayer? He's not even real, Tobias. He's a story, a myth. You know that."

"But my sister wants someone to deal with him, and Uriah was convinced that he had something to do with our tangled web of golden threads."

"He's connected to the dragonborn you seek," Kiara interjected, stepping forward. She hesitated, brows drawn together as an uncertain frown settled on her lips, and moved back again. "We have a letter—"

"You believe a letter that mentions a *popular myth* is proof of conspiracy?" Oliver snapped, shooting a razor-sharp glare her way. "You're just as dumb as the rest of them."

Caerul balled his fists. "Leave her alone."

"Why don't we split up?" Arayna pushed away from the desk she had been leaning on. It was the first time in a while that Tobias had heard her voice; it brought a strange sense of relief rolling over him. She clasped her hands behind her back, rocking on the balls of her feet as all eyes turned to her. Shrugging, she said, "We'd get more done if we went our separate ways here, and you would finally stop arguing. Oliver and I will go back to Aviva's forest to look for Nari."

"Then Eira and I will go with Kiara," Tobias murmured, frowning. It did make sense. They had struggled to get anything practical done under Oliver's disapproving frowns and death glares, and he had a differing opinion on what should be done at all.

For the second time, Tobias was shocked by Arayna's wisdom. For all her bickering and oddities—and her mysterious beast magic, which she generally took great care not to use—she had moments that completely disrupted the image he had constructed of her. He thought of Oliver as the one who said intelligent things, despite that most of the time, Oliver simply said pessimistic things. Sometimes they were legitimate concerns, but he was often too wrapped up in his own frustration to see anything clearly. Arayna was more his pillar than he was hers.

He glanced at Eira, then at Oliver. "I think that's fair."

The Beast Master merely smiled at Oliver, her fangs poking out beneath her upper lip. She scooted closer and nudged his arm with her elbow. "What d'ya say? You and me against the world again?"

There was a softness in his amber gaze when he looked at her, but his hand still drifted to the scar on his shoulder, hidden beneath his tunic. "Fine," he muttered. His hand dropped, and his attention returned to Caerul, who stiffened under the scrutiny. "I'll warn you, though: you don't know what you're getting into."

Caerul's lip twitched, and he pushed his shoulders back, chin high as his expression quickly hardened. "There's no choice anymore. There is only retaliation."

"Big word for a scrawny thing like you." Oliver turned away. "Arayna and I will leave as soon as the sun is up. So goodnight and goodbye."

5
WEAVER OF ILLUSIONS

True to his word, Oliver left the next morning before Tobias had a chance to see him again. Arayna had gone with him as agreed; the idea of them traveling together offered some inkling of comfort to Tobias, but even that was quickly darkened by worry. It wasn't too long ago that they were at each other's throats. Tobias could still remember the fear in Oliver's voice when he and Kase first approached him about seeing the Beast Master. He wouldn't even speak of her then. Though they seemed to have made peace, it could be such a fragile thing at times.

Take care. Tobias closed the curtains, cutting off the sun's light as it rose above the mountains in the distance. *Be safe, and watch each other's backs.*

Turning back to the empty bedroom, he breathed a small sigh and dragged a hand through his hair. A weight lifted from his shoulders, but it left an emptiness behind. Though mind-numbingly frustrating, Oliver's constant banter and berating had brought him a distraction for so long. In its absence, his heart began to ache again. He clenched his jaw against the tightening in his throat and fished for the round silver pin Kase had left him. It wasn't much larger than a coin, its edges smooth as he ran his thumb along them. He had cleaned the blood from its face, but the memory of it haunted him. It almost seemed to glow in the dark, pulsing with a faint red light.

Give it to Calix... Tell him I won't be able to keep my promises.

"I'll find him," Tobias murmured—as if the pin was Kase himself, safe and cradled in the palm of his hand. As if he were still alive. "But let me chase this dragonborn first. Let me put an end to this nightmare."

A soft knock sounded against his door. "Tobias?" Eira called. "Kiara and Caerul are already waiting outside. Are you ready?"

"I'll be right out." Pocketing the pin, Tobias slipped into his coat.

As he made his way to the door, he snagged his satchel from the back of the desk chair and his sword leaning against it. Wood creaked beneath his boots. His hand settled against the door knob, and he hesitated, casting one last glance at the tiny bedroom. Typical of an inn, it had everything a person would need to be comfortable for the night—a warm bed, a desk to write at, a closet to stuff his clothes away in, a set of candles to light when the sun went down. It was by no means a home, but it was safe. Safer than the world outside would be.

If he left the inn, he would face a dragonborn: the deadliest creature in the world, created solely for destruction and bloodshed. He had already lost so much to such creatures. *But how many more will suffer and die if I run back home with my tail between my legs, or stay here and stick my head in the sand?*

Steeling himself, he opened the door and stepped out.

Outside, the cold seemed to have worsened from the night before, despite the sun shining brilliantly overhead. The air nipped at Tobias's cheeks, prickling his skin with its bitter, icy breeze. He shivered and wished he could fold into his coat completely.

Beside him, Eira shivered, her face scrunched in displeasure. Her knives, returned to her before Oliver left, were once again sheathed in the pack around her waist. "This wind is kind of awful."

"It's worse than awful."

"Come now. Don't be so bitter. I'd like to appreciate some of the hard work Sefah puts into his season if I can."

"Yeah? It's Xenah, Eira. Your winter spirit needs to back off and let me enjoy autumn a bit longer."

"The Seasonal Spirits are not confined to the wishes of man." She wagged her finger, a playful smile on her lips. "Best learn to trust their wisdom."

"What wisdom is there in cutting out the warm seasons in favor of ice and snow?" Tobias muttered, tucking his chin into the collar of his coat. "Nothing grows in the winter."

"I thought you were a writer, not a farmer. What does it matter to you whether it's warm or cold when all you do is stay indoors?"

Kiara cleared her throat, cutting off the retort forming on Tobias's tongue. Both he and Eira straightened and turned to the young girl, who was staring at them with one brow raised and a frown on her lips. Today, her long hair was pulled back in a tight braid down her back, though the length was just as striking as it had been in the ponytail. She folded her arms and shifted her weight to one leg. "If you're done discussing the weather, can we move on to more important things?"

"Yes, of course." Eira beamed, lifting her chin high. "I believe my point has been sufficiently made, so let's get on with something else."

"Right," Kiara muttered dismissively as her gaze slid to Tobias.

He shrugged. There was no point arguing with Eira over

useless things. Otherwise, she would run him ragged with her almost-constant chatter.

Kiara turned on her heel, braid swinging behind her. "This way then." With a wave, she led them down the town road, weaving in and around alleys and markets barely beginning to buzz with early morning activity. The scent of freshly baked bread wafted through the air; it reminded Tobias of Floridus, and his thoughts briefly strayed back home before he grounded himself in the present again. The letter, Kiara's promise to rid them of Aurum, her strange companion with the red eyes he could have sworn he saw. There was no time to reminisce. He had made his choice already.

It wasn't long before they emerged on the outskirts of the town, where Caerul stood waiting with two young dragons. The mountains were distant silhouettes behind him, and the sun had just barely crested their peaks, casting the fields in golden light. The scene almost brought a sense of calm rolling over the anxious chatter of Tobias's thoughts, but he couldn't shake the unease that crawled down his spine when he looked at Caerul. That hazy mirage had not faded. If anything, it was stronger when he stood next to the dragons.

One was a white dragon, a female as evident by the lack of spines around her jaw, giving her a sleek and distinctly snake-like face. Sunlight sparkled through her scales, revealing an iridescent shine to her pearly body. Her legs were long and slender, perfectly matching her body and gifting her with an aura of grace—even the way she folded her wings at her sides was delicate and purposeful. The horns atop her head were small, curved backward in the beginning of the traditional crown of a white dragon. She bowed her head as Kiara approached, a soft purr rumbling in the back of her throat.

The second was a blue dragon, cerulean like the endless waves of the sea. Glittering patterns of swirls curved through his scales, a trait Tobias had never seen in a blue dragon before.

Though young—his head rose barely two feet over Caerul's own —there was a maturity in his blue eyes which flickered with the touch of magic. Spines stuck out from the sides of his head, framing his face in a fan of graceful blue spikes that curled up toward his horns. An icy blue mane tumbled down his neck in a mess of fluffy curls.

Blue dragon. Tobias frowned. What was Talia always telling him to be wary of? They possessed a power, an affinity for something. It sat at the front of his mind, yet he couldn't grasp it. He clenched his jaw in frustration.

"This is Faiera." Kiara reached for the white dragon, stroking her small snout. "The blue one is Stiria."

"Very Calistian names," Tobias remarked. "Do you both come from Calistie?"

Kiara shook her head. "Just me. Cal—"

"Floridus!" Caerul interrupted, a sheepish smile on his face. He gave Kiara a pat on the shoulder, leveling her with his gaze. "I come from Floridus."

Tobias's fingers twitched, inching slowly closer to the hilt of his sword. "Is that so? I come from Floridus as well."

The haze over Caerul's face flickered as surprise lit up his expression. "Really?" Then he paused, drawing back. "Oh, I guess that makes sense. Talia is your sister."

"What a coincidence!" Eira chirped, grabbing Tobias's arm and shaking it. "You're both from Floridus, Kiara and I are both from Calistie. A perfect split!"

"Some Calistian you are." Tobias pulled his arm from her grasp, pinning her with a glare. "Falling prey to a dragonborn? Aren't you supposed to be above that?"

Though he kept his tone light and teasing—and Eira's smirk assured him she knew it—something darkened in Kiara's expression. Her hand fell away from Faiera's snout and she looked away with a heavy sigh. "Calistians are not higher beings," she murmured. "We were just lucky enough to inherit territory from the elves."

An argument formed in Tobias's mind, but he clamped his mouth shut and buried it. Though it disagreed with every legend and whisper he had heard about the Calistie kingdom, it was ultimately the truth. Their reputation had eclipsed their humanity to the point that even looking at someone as young and as small as Kiara gave him the idea that she was some kind of savior.

Eira, always brave to voice the thoughts he could not, asked plainly, "But you *are* able to help us, right?"

"I want this world to be freed from Aurum's clutches just as much as you do." Kiara straightened, fixing Eira with a firm stare from her unwavering blue eyes. "He has destroyed far too many lives already. I'm not going to let him have his way. Head Dragonborn or not, he's a monster."

"As long as there's no confusion, I don't care whether you consider our people lucky or not." Eira shrugged. "Just don't forget what we've agreed on."

Caerul bristled, curling his lip back in a decidedly inhuman manner. "Kiara is not your tool, and you will be certain not to treat her as such." He drew his words out slowly, each one carefully fashioned into a knife aimed at Eira. Tension crackled in the air between them, but it wasn't as striking as the cold aura that gathered around Caerul's fingertips. When the magic shifted, the haze over his face wavered again—for just a moment, Tobias caught a glimpse of something glowing beneath it.

Red eyes.

The blue dragon. Eira's retort blurred to the background as Tobias shifted his attention to the dragon standing beside Caerul. Stiria was elegant and poised, almost as if sculpted from ice. It was barely perceptible, only visible when the light glinted off it, but there were blue threads surrounding him, binding his aura to the mirage over Caerul's face. An illusion weaver. Talia's words came back to him in a rush. Blue dragons had the power to create illusions.

Distrust slithered down Tobias's spine like a snake. His hand flashed to the hilt of his sword, gripping it so tightly that his knuckles ached in protest. He wasn't wrong. He truly did see red eyes that day.

Caerul was a hybrid.

6

TRUST OVER TRUTH

"Eira." Tobias slid his sword from its sheath, flooding the air with the bone-chilling scrape of metal. "Step away from him, he's a—"

Don't.

The warning froze on Tobias's tongue as his whole body went rigid. A tingling sensation settled in his mind, warm like the embers of a flame. It was a single word, spoken directly into his mind—small, yet it boomed with power. Familiar warmth coursed through his veins as an old presence settled heavily over him, a weight that pressed against his back. He sucked in a sharp breath. *Smoke.*

He couldn't see the old red dragon, but he didn't have to. One as powerful as Smoke could establish links from far away, though how he knew the right moment was beyond Tobias's knowledge. Even without seeing him, Tobias could feel the hostility brewing in the link between them, edged with desperation and oozing with sadness.

Please do not expose him, Smoke said, his voice softening as he went on. *It will only bring pain.*

Tobias gritted his teeth. *Like his people brought to me? Why should I care—in fact, why do you care? Why do you choose to speak up* now *on behalf of this strange hybrid?*

Smoke paused for a moment. *He is not as distant and "strange" as you believe,* he murmured. *All I ask is that you trust in me, and the truth will be revealed in time.*

Anger burned in Tobias's chest. *I'm sick of your cryptic warnings!* he snapped, but his words slammed into a dead end. The link had already been severed, sealing away Smoke's ancient, fiery presence once more.

"Tobias."

Eira's hand landed on his shoulder and jolted him back to attention. She frowned, searching his face with concern glittering in the depths of her azure eyes. "You okay? You were saying something?"

Behind her, Caerul and Kiara were staring at him as well. Kiara's hand rested against the knife at her side, and she held one arm in front of Caerul protectively, eyes narrowed like a beast waiting for the other to attack. Caerul, however, had stiffened and drawn into himself. The moment Tobias looked at him, he glanced away, awkwardly rubbing his right arm, which was wrapped tightly in a white cloth. The haze of the illusion remained intact, perfectly concealing his blood-red eyes—probably pointed ears and fangs as well. *But...*

Tobias released the pent-up breath he had been holding. "It's nothing," he muttered. "I… thought I saw something, that's all." Cryptic as he was, Smoke always had reasons for the things he did. Dragons didn't live as long as he had without a wealth of wisdom and at least a little bit of cunning as well. *I'll trust you for now, but I'm not going to trust Caerul.* He directed the thought toward the severed bond, though he knew he had no way of getting it across to the dragon unless Smoke chose to receive it.

Eira shrugged. "If you say so." She released him, but her

puzzled gaze lingered on him a moment longer. As much as he liked to poke fun at her, Eira was no fool. He had no doubt that she saw right through his words, but he wasn't sure she could land at the same conclusion unless he shared it with her. If she had seen what he had, she would have ratted Caerul out long ago.

But he could hold his tongue. As long as the old dragon lurked in his mind, his lips were sealed. All he could do was wait for the truth to reveal itself.

Kiara relaxed and dropped her hand back to her side, narrowing her stance so that it was no longer defensive. "We believe the first place we should go is to the Aurora Range: the mountains far north of Calistie City." She pointed to the distant forests that surrounded Calistie's capital, then slowly dragged her finger across the horizon to the cloudy, white-tipped mountains that loomed over the earth like sleeping giants. "It's a snowy realm populated by blue dragons and other cold-dwelling magical creatures. The magic is dense there."

"And why do we believe the Shadowslayer would go there?" Eira asked, folding her arms over her chest. "That's far outside the realm of Sheniir—and it's Calistian territory. Aurum would be stupid to go there, or to send his ghost partner to snoop around."

"Stiria has a connection to that place," Caerul added, moving to stand beside his dragon. He rested a hand against Stiria's cool blue scales. "His power is closely tied to Sefah, the winter spirit. Those mountains are said to be—"

"The last resting place of Sefah, yes I know." Eira huffed.

"—which is why Stiria could sense something off. Dark magic is growing there. It's worth checking out."

"It's too cold for us to travel there." Tobias could only imagine how bitter it was atop the mountains of Sefah, the realm that belonged to the winter spirit. If he was cold in the outskirts of Sheniir, where there was no ice or snow, he couldn't imagine the kind of agony he would experience in the icy waste of the Aurora Range.

"Stiria can shield us from the cold," Caerul said, gesturing again to the blue dragon. "We wouldn't be warm per se, but we would be protected from the worst of it."

"How do we plan to get there?" Tobias prodded.

Reasonable as ever, Kiara had an answer. "Stiria and Faiera can each take two people. Since Oliver and Arayna left, it won't be a problem."

Tobias scrutinized the two dragons. They were significantly smaller than Smoke, who could fly several people without problem. *Two per dragon* might have been pushing it, especially for Faiera. Her back was slightly arched, making it awkward for whoever sat behind the Rider. She also had a smooth body, easy to slip off of during flight. The more he thought about it, the more his stomach twisted with dread. There were too many problems for almost no guarantee that they would find anything useful at all.

And what you might find if it is a useful endeavor is a blood-thirsty, murderous Head Dragonborn, his traitorous thoughts reminded him.

He glanced at Caerul. Even knowing about his Draconic features now, the illusion held firm. Innocent brown eyes, small round ears, scrawny, unassuming body. Like this, he didn't appear to be a threat. *All I ask is that you trust me,* Smoke had said.

It was becoming increasingly harder to trust anyone.

But there was always that small part of him that foolishly sought out the danger he was faced with. Talia called it his curiosity; she said it would be his undoing. It had always been a joke they shared, but now he couldn't find the will to laugh for humor. He sighed and dragged his fingers through his hair, a dark chuckle escaping his lips. "Oh, Talia, what have I gotten myself into?" he muttered.

"So… is that a yes? Are we going?" Eira swung back to his side, hooking her arm around his.

"Do we have a choice?"

"Of course you have a choice," Kiara said. "But this is our only lead. If we don't go, we'd have to start with nothing. This is the best option we have if we want to catch the Shadowslayer and get to the bottom of what Aurum is doing."

"I understand." Tobias took a deep breath, packing away his panicked thoughts of what lay in wait in the snowy wasteland. "We should go."

Kiara nodded and turned to Faiera. She whistled, and the dragon came to her side. Stiria followed, bounding circles around the graceful white dragon and chittering with excitement. Caerul grabbed Stiria's reins and tugged until the dragon stilled. *Reins*, Tobias echoed, taking note of the thin leather bridle clamped around the dragon's snout. He noticed the same was true for Faiera. *They're still learning to control their dragons. They haven't been Riders for very long at all.* Unease pricked his skin.

"I don't want to force discomfort on anyone by splitting us up unfairly," Kiara said, leading Faiera to Tobias. She held the dragon's reins out to him. "You and Eira will take Faiera. I will go with… Caerul." She paused for a moment, something else forming on her tongue before she corrected it with *Caerul*. She glanced at where he stood beside Stiria. "Faiera knows where to go. She's a well-behaved flier. It shouldn't be difficult."

"I understand." Tobias accepted the reins. There was a subtext underlying the surface of her words, one that almost seemed to echo with hostility. He could still recall the press of her onyx blade against his neck, the cold look in her eyes when she glared down at him. Perhaps it was in his best interest to not voice what he knew about Caerul if only to remain on her good side for a little while longer.

She didn't wait for further confirmation. With a quick pat to

Faiera's neck, she turned sharply on her heel and rejoined Caerul and Stiria. He greeted her with a smile, and they shared a few quiet words before climbing onto Stiria's back.

A soft hum rumbled in the back of Faiera's throat. She lowered her head, her clear, iridescent eyes fixated on Tobias's face. Unlike Smoke, she did not speak, nor did she have a presence to open to his mind. The faint whisper of a breeze brushed his cheek; that was the mark of her power and a sign of her approval. When she lowered her head and closed her eyes, he placed his hand against her, stroking the smooth white scales between her horns.

"Tobias," Eira called in a singsong voice, already perched on the dragon's back. She grinned down at him. "Stop making friends so we can go. You'll have time to pet the dragon later."

"It's appropriate to first introduce yourself to dragons and be sure to gain their approval before you go around jumping onto their backs," he informed her. He waited until Faiera lifted her head again before he climbed onto her back, sliding into the seat of Kiara's saddle.

As soon as he was seated, Stiria took off with Kiara and Caerul. Faiera watched him leave before she unfurled her wings and leapt off the ground after him. Wind knocked Tobias back, and he had to grip the front of the saddle to keep from flying off. Eira shrieked and grabbed hold of his shoulders, her fingers digging into his coat. As soon as Faiera stabilized herself, the pinch of Eira's fingers lessened. The world spread out like a map beneath them, distant and small when they were among the clouds. Tobias inhaled the fresh air, relishing what little warmth he could find before it was sucked away by the Aurora Range.

This is what you wanted, he reminded himself, reaching to grip Kase's pin again. *If you want to be rid of Aurum, this is the first step.*

The more he said it, the less he began to believe it. No matter how much he tried to trust, the truth had never felt so far from his grasp. *Maybe I should have listened to Oliver.* But there was no turning back now, not when he was too high in the air to make sense of the scattered landscapes below. This was the path he had chosen. He had no choice but to stick with it now.

7

LEFT TO ROT

COLD SLICED TOBIAS'S SKIN. Wind whipped through his hair and clawed at his clothes. Flecks of snow drifted through the air like dandelion puffs, harmless as they latched onto him. Blotted out by thick, gray clouds, the sky had turned darker since they left. The white-tipped peaks of the Aurora Mountain Range stuck out like a scar against the darkness. Without the sun's light, they seemed dull and lifeless.

Ahead, Stiria's glittering body dipped and fluttered down to the frozen landscape. He gave a sort of chirp, communicating something to Faiera. She folded in her wings slightly, allowing her body to drop steadily after him. Tobias's breath caught in his throat as they plummeted back to the ground. Body tensed, he clung to her neck until his muscles ached. Behind him, Eira gasped. Her hold around him tightened, arms digging painfully into his ribs. The ground rushed at them. Tobias squeezed his eyes shut.

Faiera slowed long before they reached the rocky, snow-covered mountainside. She and Stiria parroted another call to each other. They landed together between two of the peaks, where the land dipped into a valley that was somewhat shielded

55

from the harsh winds. The thick mounds of snow swallowed Faiera's legs, pressing against her belly as she sank into them. She growled deep in the back of her throat, lip curling to expose her sharp teeth. Stiria, however, looked at home in the powder. He sank deep into it, stretching out his neck to bury his chin in the snow. A purr rumbled through his body, his eyes closing like a pleased cat.

Tobias quickly dismounted from Faiera's back, a slight smile pulling at his lips. *Stiria is an ice dragon after all.* The Aurora Range was the home of blue dragons, so it was no wonder he seemed to enjoy it so much. Shivering, Tobias wrapped himself tighter in his coat. *Me, however? I might freeze to death.*

"S–Stiria." Caerul climbed out of his saddle and bundled himself in his cloak, his teeth chattering from the cold. "The protection spell p–please. You know it doesn't take much to fall prey to Sefah's wrath in a place like this."

"This place in particular," Eira added with a murmur. "He *died* here. The mountains are cursed with the wrath of winter."

"The spirit of Sefah lives in the season of winter," Kiara corrected, swinging down from Stiria's back with a swift, graceful movement. "It was just his original body that died. Actually, some believe—"

"Alright, I get it," Eira snapped. She made a show of rolling her eyes. "Sorry I don't make a habit of memorizing every bit of Calistian history."

"Not like you had that many books to read anyway," Tobias quipped. *Being a thief and all.*

Eira turned to him with a glare so heated he couldn't believe it didn't melt the snow around them. He returned it with a smug smile. The normalcy of their banter kept the anxious gnawing at the back of his mind at bay. It was strange how quickly he had come to depend on her company when keeping watch over her had originally been a chore Oliver had thrust on him.

At Caerul's coaxing, Stiria hauled himself up out of the snow and swiveled to face the group. The swirling patterns that traced his scales began to glow as the air hummed with magic. When the dragon leaned forward, he exhaled a puff of air, glittering with flecks of blue. It twirled around them before settling into Tobias's skin. The vicious nip of the cold subsided. Although the chill remained, it no longer sapped his breath away and paralyzed him with tremors. He sighed as the tension slowly ebbed from his body.

Eira rubbed her hands together. Her breath clouded in front of her face when she sighed. "Better. I don't mind the cold so much when it isn't threatening to kill me."

"We need to head east of here. Stiria and I saw a camp when we were looking for a place to land." Caerul pointed deeper into the valley where the cliffs rose higher on either side. "It's on the other side of the ravine. I didn't want to fly us any closer in case someone is there, but I think it's worth checking out."

A camp? The idea that anyone would come to the mountains and set up camp with the intent of *staying* made Tobias's skin prickle. "And you think it's the dragonborn? Or the Shadowslayer, I suppose."

"I think the disturbance Stiria can sense is strongest there," Caerul answered. He rubbed his arms, exhaling a shuddering breath. His gaze flicked away, shoulders hunched beneath his cloak. The mirage wavered again, like a flame in the wind that was desperate to keep itself lit.

Tobias rested his hand against the hilt of his sword, drawing comfort from the familiar leather beneath his palm. Fear settled at the back of his mind, a pressure that slowly built into a headache that pierced his skull. It thrummed through his veins, and his fingers tightened around the hilt until his knuckles began to ache. Hunting a ghost and a dragonborn was already disturbing enough on its own; doing it with a hybrid who was trying so hard to hide what he was only made things worse.

~

THE SNOW WAS SO thick that they clambered onto the backs of the two dragons and rode them like horses down to the camp Caerul had seen. It was a slow walk. Faiera trudged through the packed ice with quiet, disgruntled groans. Tobias tucked his feet up on her back to avoid getting caught by it as she moved. In contrast, Stiria bounded through the mounds like a fox hunting for prey buried beneath the powder. He flung chunks of snow up into the air as he landed into it, trilling in delight at the cold. Caerul clung to the dragon's wild, ice-colored mane, eyes narrowed though he didn't argue. There was only so much control an inexperienced Rider could have over their dragon.

By the time darkness had begun to settle over the frozen landscape, the modest camp came into view, just a silhouette against the sky. A large tent was set up along with several other small, scattered structures that Tobias couldn't make out from a distance. The thick mounds of snow thinned as they approached the camp, now barely covering Faiera's feet. He slid down from her back and walked ahead. The crunch of snow behind him announced Eira doing the same. She appeared at his side moments later.

"It looks empty," she said. There was a slight tremor in her voice, perhaps a lingering effect of the cold despite Stiria's spell.

Tobias nodded. "That works in our favor." *I don't enjoy the idea of getting caught snooping around.* His father used to scold him for it when he was a kid, but that didn't bar him from trying. He only learned to get better.

Kiara jumped from Stiria's back. Snow crunched beneath her boots. "Stay close," she said as she crept ahead. Her hand drifted to the hilt of the sword at her side, one that was decorated in swirling, unfamiliar letters—Calistian, he guessed, or old elvish. Like her dragon, she was almost entirely hidden, swallowed in her pure white cloak. If it weren't for her long braid of dark hair, twisted in intricate waves down her back, he could have lost sight of her entirely. Caerul trailed after her. In his black cloak, he was her opposite, the dark to her light. *The hybrid to her dragonborn slayer.*

It still didn't make sense. Why would a Calistian willfully travel with and *befriend* a dragonborn hybrid? Unless he was lying to her too and she was also a victim of Stiria's illusion powers, unable to see him for what he really was. Tobias shuddered to imagine what that meant for Talia. There was no way she would willingly teach a hybrid. *Right?*

"Tobias." Again, Eira brought him back to the present with a hand against his shoulder. He jerked away, and she lowered her hand, her gaze darkened with concern. "Are you okay?"

"Let's keep moving." He turned sharply away and plodded after Kiara and Caerul, his boots already heavy with snow. Or maybe it was his mind that pulled his limbs down like they were piled beneath hundreds of large stones.

As they drew closer to the camp, a rank stench wafted through the air. It was sour with rot, sharpened by the metallic scent of blood. Tobias recoiled and pressed his hand to his nose. His stomach flipped, throat tight with unease. Caerul jerked his whole body back as if struck by the smell. Only Kiara pressed on, lips pursed and chin high.

Rows upon rows of cages came into view, scattered across the campground and positioned a good distance away from the large tent. Some housed a crumpled form, others a small lump, all of them concealed beneath shadows. All of them reeked with the stench of death. Tobias slowly approached one of the cages, jaw clenched and palms slick with nervous sweat. He knelt down and peered inside.

There was barely any light with the sun gone. A painful sense of longing for Aviva's magic and how quickly she could summon light overtook him. His chest twisted painfully. At the same time, he was almost thankful for the darkness. He didn't know if he truly wanted to see what lay rotting within.

As if to spite his conflicting wishes, a sliver of moonlight cut through the clouds and fell over the frost-covered metal bars of the cage, illuminating the figure inside. A body lay curled on the floor of the cage, as still as a rock. Lifeless, glassy eyes stared emptily ahead. The pale skin had turned white as snow, sucked dry of all color and shriveled against the bones beneath. Blackened scorch marks stained the white skin, a stark contrast to the lifeless coloring. A Mage's staff lay across the body's outstretched hand. The other clutched a small pin to the chest. Empty. Crumbling. All life and magic pulled, leaving only a husk of a person behind. Left to slowly rot away in the unforgiving cold of the Aurora Range.

Tobias jerked, swallowing hard against the bile that crawled up the back of his throat. Mouth open, he swung to face Eira at the cage beside him, his report ready on the tip of his tongue. It died at the look of horror in her eyes as she surveyed a similar sight.

"Mages," she breathed, shaking her head. She stepped back, arms wrapped around herself. "Are they all Mages?"

"And magical creatures." Kiara stood by one of the smaller cages a little ways away, a tiny light illuminating the form huddled inside. It was a small cat-like creature with a tail that split in two at the end. The fur had peeled back from its body, exposing bone beneath. It had been there longer, but bore similar symptoms to the Mage—dull, drained of all magic.

Whispers and rumors drifted through Tobias's mind. He had read manuscripts, articles, and other stories that depicted a similar image: Mages going missing and later turning up dead, sapped of magic and life. It was amusing to read when it was nothing more than a distant story, the line between superstition and news blurred by the outlandish retellings and embellishments. Now, the truth lay before him, warped as death pulled the bodies apart piece by piece, slowed by the eternal winter of the mountains.

"The dead Mage plot," he blurted out, scrambling away from the cages. Caerul and Kiara swung to face him, their faces cast in sharp shadows that warped their appearance into ghastly mimics. Luminescent scales, the tiny lights in their hands, flickered.

"The what?" Eira asked, breathless and bewildered.

"The dead Mage plot," he echoed as he turned to her. "Mages go missing only to turn up dead. It's connected. It has to be."

Kiara's gaze hardened. "Split up and search the camp. We need to uncover who was here and what they were doing—more importantly, we need to know if it truly *is* connected. I'll check the cages for any survivors." Without waiting for anyone's agreement, she left them to simply do as she had commanded.

8

GOLDEN SEAL

Determined to put as much distance between himself, the bodies, and even Caerul as possible, Tobias marched off toward the large tent, its cream-colored tarp waving in the wind. Gold trim lined the edge of the door flap. It was strikingly modest otherwise—unassuming, like it belonged to some lower middle class researcher from the Navaric kingdom. For all he knew, it did, but the unsightly scene outside twisted that reason into nothingness. Surely, no human could be so cruel.

He lifted the flap of the tent and ducked inside. Candles lit the space, casting dancing shadows across the fabric walls. A cot sat tucked into one corner, almost entirely hidden beneath thick pillows and padded blankets. Rich fur pelts covered the floor and trapped the warmth within the walls of the tent. Across from the bedroom area, a small desk stood with a thin chair set up beside it. Papers littered the surface, paired with pens, crudely bound books, and several other writing utensils. Beneath the chaos, a map of Anticuus stretched across the surface of the desk. Black X's and red circles marked several areas on the map, but the scribbles meant nothing to Tobias.

"Whoever this camp belongs to must be a man," he muttered

as he picked up one of the papers from the desk. "What kind of Sheniirian ghost needs a bed and a place to write?"

Perhaps it's the dragonborn, some small, dark part of him whispered. It squirmed in his mind like a pile of worms. *They write, they read, they scheme. I suppose that means they must sleep too.*

"Find anything?" Eira chirped.

He jumped and swung around to face her with a glare. She only grinned mischievously, hands clasped innocently behind her back. The vicious nip of the cold air had turned her nose red, making the rest of her skin strikingly pale in comparison.

With a sigh, he swung his arm toward the desk. "I've found a lot here. I could be telling you whether it's actually useful or not if you hadn't interrupted me."

She hummed and stepped lightly toward the desk, trailing the pad of her finger along the edge. "If it's out here, it's probably all important. Who would want to come to this cursed place to do pleasure writing, hm?"

Pursing his lips, he tilted his gaze down to the paper in his hands. The writing was scribbled hastily, too warped for him to read. "Eira, does any of this seem familiar to you? From the time you spent with…" He faltered, tongue frozen as the name leapt to his mind along with the image of monster. "With Aurum?" he whispered.

This time, she didn't freeze. She shrugged, gaze pinned on the desk. She snatched up another paper from the pile, holding it to the lantern light as she squinted at the jumbled words. Splotches of black ink had ruined the page, and the writing was shaky, as if the hand that made it had been trembling at the time. Tobias assumed it was likely a reject.

"I still don't remember much," Eira finally said, though she hid her face as she spoke. "It's all in pieces, fragments. I don't remember ever seeing him write. The most I can remember is how he would lounge on that throne in the castle of Sheniir, limbs spread like he owned the place. How he would sneer down at me, always ready to pounce if I made one wrong move." She lowered the paper and frowned, a flicker of remembrance stirring in her eyes. "He would talk to himself, pace sometimes. I think there was one time I caught him eyeing his reflection in a mirror somewhere, o–or maybe a pool. He seemed so… dissatisfied." She turned distant, the muscles in her face going slack. Finally, she slammed the paper down and turned away. "If he wrote, it wasn't in front of me—or I've forgotten."

"I see." Tobias set his paper aside. His mind spun. The reason they came was because of a letter, one signed by Aurum himself. Even if Eira never saw him write, perhaps it was something he did regularly. Due to the conflict between humans and dragonborn, Tobias never bothered to learn about the finer details of their culture. It hadn't even occurred to him that such violent creatures would pen letters at all. Who could they possibly hope to send them to? Who would take the time out of shredding the flesh from bones and bathing in blood to read such a delicate, personal document?

Eira fiddled with a loose thread on her blouse. "Tobias, be honest with me. Are you okay? You seem distracted lately—more so than what I assume is normal for you." She spared a quick side glance at him before looking away again. "I know I'm not really your friend. I mean, it wasn't that long ago that I was trying to kill you." A nervous laugh slid from her lips, and she dragged her fingers through her hair, raking it back from her face. "I guess I'm trying to say that you can tell me if something is bothering you. I know how easy it is to take advantage of you when you're like this. I don't want that to happen again."

He snorted, leaning on the edge of the table. "You think I'm easy to take advantage of?"

That trademark grin of hers returned as she lifted her hand. Kase's silver pin was caught between her pointer and middle fingers, the red gem glittering in the dim, warm light. "I know you are."

Mouth agape, he patted the pocket where the pin had been. "When did you—"

"I'm a thief, remember? It's what I do." She waved the pin around before flicking it back to him like a coin. He fumbled to catch it against his chest. With a huff, she folded her arms and raised her brows at him. "Pickpocketing's not the worst thing, but you get my point. I'm worried about you."

His skin crawled, and he couldn't help but glance past her at the fluttering tent flaps. Between the two, he could see Caerul's small, black-cloaked figure as he wandered across the camp in search of other clues. Even when he disappeared from sight, the tension in Tobias's jaw remained. "I don't know how well a dragonborn can hear from a distance," he murmured absently.

Confusion knitted Eira's brows together. "Are you worried Aurum will hear you? I don't think being overheard should be your greatest concern now."

"No." Tobias shook his head and sighed. He sank into the small desk chair. "Something isn't right, Eira, but I can't tell you what it is."

"Oh." She dipped her head, twisting the loose thread around her fingers. "I understand. I don't expect you to have any reason to trust me yet."

"What? No, no. It's not about trust. It's about Smoke. He stopped me from sharing the truth with you."

"Kase's dragon?" She wrinkled her nose, that damp look of sadness quickly replaced by one of bewilderment. "He left us. How would he even know what we were doing?"

All he could offer her was a shrug. Being a Celestial Class dragon and one who had lived as long as Smoke had, there were understandably many mysteries that surrounded him. He held a connection to the mind; perhaps it allowed him to hear thoughts and *feel* intentions over a long distance. Or maybe he hadn't gone as far as they had assumed and lay in wait somewhere nearby—only to take the hybrid's side rather than

Tobias's, a friend of his late master. Everything he knew about dragons seemed useless when it came to the old red one.

"All I can say is be on your guard," Tobias answered after the quiet became unbearable and Eira's piercing stare threatened to cut right through him. He turned his gaze back to the desk. A small drawer was visible now, pushed back from the edge of the desk and hidden by the surface when looking at it from above. Curious, he pulled it open. Something inside rattled against the wooden walls.

Stacks of envelopes were neatly packed away inside the drawer. Gold sticks of sealing wax lay beside the envelopes, glistening as the light fell on them to reveal a shimmer effect set into the wax. A seal rolled to the front of the drawer, its handle made of smooth wood and painted with tiny gold runes. Tobias plucked the seal from the drawer and lifted it to the light. He turned it to inspect the face, and a gasp wrenched from his lips.

The carved image on the seal bore the emblem of the five-headed dragon, each adorned with a different set of horns, like five crowns. If it was painted, he knew each head would be a different color: gold, black, green, red, and blue.

The image of the dragon goddess, Selini.

He slammed the seal against the desk. Swallowing hard against the rising fear that slowly sank its claws into him, he grabbed a stack of the enveloped letters. All the lips were stamped with the gold seal. Unbroken, untouched since the letter was hidden away within. All of them left unsent.

"Eira." Tobias jerked the strap of his satchel over his head and held it out to her, his gaze locked on the glittering golden seal. "Stuff as many things in there as you can. We need to figure out what's going on here."

She snatched the bag from him with a snort. "Now you're speaking my language."

While Eira busied herself shoving papers into the satchel, Tobias broke the seal on the first letter and wrenched its contents free. Three sheets of parchment came loose, each one completely covered in writing on both sides from top to bottom. The swirling letters were packed closely together, too condensed to read properly. He flipped to the final page. A signature had been penned at the very bottom of the back of the third paper. It perfectly mirrored the one Kiara had shown them from the scrap she had found. Though he couldn't read the Draconic script, he knew exactly what it said. Ice crept into the tips of his fingers.

Drekisn diem a, Aurum.

Head Dragonborn Aurum.

9

PROOF

"It's the same," he murmured. A roaring filled his ears, his heart thudding wildly in his chest. Fear constricted his throat, and the air became too thick to breathe. Aurum, *the* Aurum, was close. They were closing in on him. He swallowed hard and tensed his body to keep from trembling.

Eira's shuffling came to a stop. "What does the rest of it say? Is the Shadowslayer part of his plot?"

"I don't know. I can't read Draconic. But here"—he pointed to the signature, leaning toward her so that the light fell on it—"this is the same as what Kiara showed us."

Eira swung his satchel over her shoulder and closed the flap. She folded her arms and paced a few steps away. When she came to a stop, the toe of her boot tapped anxiously against the padded ground. "I don't know what to make of it. Do you have any thoughts?"

The proof of Aurum's meddling had grown, now a mountain that loomed over him like the peaks of the frozen Aurora Range. And yet something was missing. What did he want? What was he doing? How did he connect to Shadowslayer? Tobias's gaze trailed back to the letters, to the swirling, elegant writing. Suddenly, he was home again, hunched over Aviva's spellbook as he tried to rip out its secrets. Back then, he was alone. No one could help him: his sister's wisdom was useless in the face of magic, his father's words fell short of the situation, and there was no one else he knew to turn to. Now, the spellbook was gone and he was faced with a new puzzle, but he wasn't alone. He didn't have to be.

He took a deep breath and exhaled slowly to calm his frazzled nerves. "Kiara and Caerul managed to decipher one of these letters before. We should take what we can and leave this place. They can translate the letters once we're out of here." A shiver trailed down his spine, and he turned, half expecting to find someone watching him. There was only the tent flap, still waving in the wind. He clenched his jaw. "I don't like this place."

"You and me both," Eira murmured.

They fled the tent without a glance back. Tobias didn't need to look, anyway. The map, marked by glaring, red circles, was burned on the inside of his eyelids. It meant something. He just had to figure out what.

The moment he stepped out of the tent's shelter, his boots sank into the snowdrift. Piercing cold nipped at his skin in spite of Stiria's protection. He tensed, sucking in a sharp breath. Eira drifted past him, unbothered by the cold, it seemed, though the wind tore at her skirt and snagged her hair as it whisked by. She clung to Tobias's satchel, draped over one shoulder, and paused until the gale passed.

"Kiara!" she called. Her voice echoed back to her in the eerie quiet. Caerul and Kiara were nowhere to be found, but their two dragons were perched at the outskirts of the camp. Eira huffed. "We need you to take a look at something!"

"Not so loud." Tobias crinkled the letter as he closed his fingers into a fist. He nudged her shoulder. "We don't know—"

"Relax." She waved a hand at him. "There's nobody out here.

Just the ghost of Sefah, and I think he's tortured us about as much as he's going to."

"You don't know that," he hissed. His skin crawled, and a pressure lingered on his back, like the weight of someone's gaze had settled there. To add to that, he still didn't know what to make of Caerul, nor was he wholly convinced that Kiara was no threat either. *I don't even know for certain that I can trust Eira, do I?* Maybe ghosts and dragonborn should have been the least of his concerns.

"Eira, Tobias." Kiara rounded the corner of the tent, her long braid swishing behind her. Caerul, who was usually at her heels, was nowhere to be found. "What did you find?"

"Letters," Tobias said.

He held out the one he had opened, and she took it, frowning at the Draconic script. She moved closer to the light that flooded out from the tent and held the papers in its warm glow. The wind howled, clawing at the pages, but she held firm. No one spoke a word as she shuffled through the writings. Finally, Eira heaved a sigh and dragged a hand across her face.

"Well?" she prompted. "What does it say?"

Kiara hesitated, eyes wide when she turned to them. "I–I need more time. This writing is complex. My knowledge of Draconic is—"

"Kiara!" Caerul's cry rang through the still air, tight with fear. He appeared around the tents a second later, the illusion over his face flickering weakly. "Someone's coming."

Tobias stiffened and grabbed the hilt of his sword. "We need to go."

"No time." Caerul shook his head. He scratched incessantly at his arm beneath his black cloak, his wild gaze flicking around them in search of something. "The dragons can't run fast enough in the thick snow, and we'll be too visible if we take to the sky."

"It's dark," Eira snapped. "No one will see us."

"There are creatures that see better than we do in the dark," Kiara murmured as she stuffed the letter into a small pouch hanging from her waist. "Scatter and hide. We'll wait until it's clear to leave."

Eira's arm hooked underneath Tobias's before Kiara could even finish her statement. She pulled him away toward a stack of rotting wooden crates on the far side of camp. A foul stench hung in the air around the crates, but Eira shoved him down behind their cover before he could complain.

"This isn't splitting up," he hissed as she settled beside him, knees tucked against her chest. "Nor is it a good place to hide if he comes from this way." He gestured to the open stretch of snow-covered ground in front of them.

"Well, you'll protect me then, won't you?" She winked.

"You're insufferable."

"It's a miracle you still put up with me." Shifting, she peered around the crate, one hand creeping toward a knife strapped to her waist. "Caerul and Kiara aren't in my line of sight anymore."

Tobias sighed and glanced in the direction of the dragons, who had also fled. "Probably for the best."

The wait was agonizing. Cold sank deep in Tobias's bones, piercing his core with icy talons. He shivered and gripped the hilt of his sword. Darkness pressed against him, as thick as the air he struggled to breathe.

Eira jerked back against the crate with a gasp, her shoulder bumping his. "There's a man," she whispered. "Black cloak. He has no face."

"What?" Tobias went rigid, a sickening mix of surprise and fear churning in his stomach. Curiosity slithered beneath the surface of his skin and coiled tightly around his heart, squeezing until the world began to spin. He glanced out the corner of his eye, but all he could see was the edge of the rotting crate and the white snow beyond it. As he began to move, Eira gripped his shoulder and yanked him back, shaking her head.

Stay put, she mouthed.

He clamped his jaw shut until it began to ache. There was nothing to do but wait until he passed. *He has no face,* his mind echoed, droning on until the words became slippery and lost their meaning. A feeble explanation wriggled to the surface, one that left his muscles tense and uneasy. *A ghost,* it said. *The Shadowslayer.* His fingers tightened around the hilt of his sword. Perhaps the legend was true after all.

Eerie quiet consumed the still air. There was no crunch of snow beneath boots, no clink of weapons or armor, not even the subtle shuffling of clothes that came with movement. Was he standing still? Tobias leaned around the crate again. Eira's nails dug into his arm, a warning he ignored.

A tall figure glided gracefully across the snow, moving too smoothly to be walking. He seemed to float just above the ground, carried by the darkness that rolled off him in waves. Shadows coiled where his feet should have been, rising up to his middle before fading into puffs of smoke. A black hood hung over his head, its edge pulled low to obscure his face—or lack thereof if Tobias was to believe what Eira had seen. His back was to Tobias; all he could see was the man's broad shoulders, hidden beneath his cloak.

He moved purposefully, silently, as if he were looking for something. The shadows pooling around him spread across the ground like waves stirring up the ocean's surface. Tobias held his breath, but still the cloaked man didn't turn their way. Rather, he seemed intently focused on something out of Tobias's line of sight, on the other side of the sand-colored tent.

Kiara and Caerul, he realized with a jolt. Pulling back with a gasp, he turned to Eira and held her gaze firmly. *I think he knows we're here,* he tried to say with the look. She drew her knees closer to her chest and covered her mouth with her hands, eyes wide and trembling. She seemed to understand.

"I wondered how long it would be before someone discovered me here," a distorted voice said, ringing in Tobias's ears as it drawled from beneath the black hood. "To what do I owe the pleasure of this visit?"

The wind answered unprompted, moaning like the spirits of the dead still caged not far from where Tobias crouched. Everyone else remained silent. Tobias didn't dare to breathe, afraid he would alert the ghost to their position. His heart thudded in his chest, fear turning the tips of his fingers to ice, numb from the cold.

The ghostly man hummed; it quickly blended into a low chuckle. "I can feel your presence. Your fear. Your... *magic.*"

Eira squeezed Tobias's arm. Pain flared beneath her iron grip, but he bit his tongue to keep from lashing out. *I have no magic. Maven said I was completely devoid of it. Unless...* Dread swallowed him as he recalled the thin slip of paper stuffed in his pocket, the one Aviva had left him with. Had her spell given him away?

No. He bit the inside of his cheek. He had to trust Aviva's spell would be hidden. If the man was sensing magic, he wasn't looking for Tobias and wouldn't find him. He didn't know exactly what his magical emptiness entailed, though, and if it would be enough to shroud both Eira and the spell. Kiara could protect herself. Calistians were born to fight.

Caerul's shout cut through the air. It cracked with pain and quickly dissolved into a growl as he was dragged out from his hiding place. A scuffle broke out beyond the edge of the crates, accompanied by the hard crunch of snow. Magic oozed into the air, thick enough that a suffocating pressure built in Tobias's lungs, and he pressed his back against the crate with a stifled gasp. It was choking and *wrong,* smothering him like a hot blanket wrapped around his head. It wasn't like the static brush of Aviva's spells. This magic's aura was twisted.

"You're—" The distorted voice wavered, surprise putting a

chink in its eerie, threatening lull. It lasted only a second before a growl replaced it. "Why have you come to this place?"

"I don't have to explain myself to a dead man's curse," Caerul gasped.

Tobias peeked around the edge of the crate. The shadow loomed over Caerul, an inky black hand clenched around the boy's neck as it pressed him into the snow. Caerul clawed at the man's grip, the illusion over his face flickering to reveal the fear beneath. Tendrils of darkness rolled over him, and he squirmed away, eyes wide and teeth bared. All his efforts were wasted on the creature. Fear pricked Tobias's heart, and he grasped the hilt of his sword. He shifted to crawl out from behind the crate.

"Let him go!"

Kiara's voice rang out from somewhere beyond Tobias's line of sight. The command rippled through the air with a bite that promised vengeance. He shrank back from it, even knowing he wasn't the target of such wrath. The shadowed figure moved, revealing Kiara standing a few paces away, her silver sword drawn and poised to strike. She lifted her chin.

"If you want to fight someone," she snapped, "fight me."

IO

SHENIIR'S GHOST

KIARA'S SKIN CRAWLED, icy both above and beneath the surface. The taste of bile coated her tongue but she quickly swallowed it, cringing as it burned the back of her throat on its way down. Her hands trembled as she gripped her blade tighter. Fear thundered in her pulse until the ground began to rock beneath her and her ears started to ring. Caerul stared up at her with pleading eyes, flickering between the true red of his irises and the deep, chocolate brown from Stiria's illusion spell. Snow all but consumed his face, smothering him, choking him, yet still she could hear the protest as clear as day: *Illémine, don't.*

She had to. She was a Calistian—the warrior Tobias and Eira sought hope in, the friend Caerul depended on, the girl who could slay the dragonborn. A ghost from Sheniir was not enough to deter her.

The Shadowslayer's white-masked face jerked toward her, neck bent at an awkward angle, and she flinched. His black hood draped eerily over his head, concealing his form beneath rolling shadows that caressed the thick blanket of snow. Something akin to a laugh slipped out, muffled and distorted like a broken music box. He shoved away from Caerul, shoulders still shaking as his mocking chortle continued. Like a wild animal, he tilted his head and prowled toward her, moonlight glinting off his mask. Shadows licked at her boots. She held firm and pointed her silver blade at his chest.

"Fascinating." He leaned in until he was mere inches from her face, his body contorted to avoid the end of her sword. His clawed hand reached out from beneath the cloak, brushing long fingers down her cheek. Blood stained the tips. He reeked of decay. "It is as she said," he drawled, voice curling up with the hint of a vicious grin. "*She* told me you would come. Yes, you just couldn't stay away. You Calistians never stay away."

Her heart leapt to her throat. Her skin burned where he touched her though he was deathly cold, harsher than the wind that nipped at her cloak. The scent of rot choked her. His mask stared blankly back at her, but if she let her eyes linger long enough, a new face appeared in its polished surface: dark eyes that wandered, a smile that oozed with lies, a neediness that trapped her beneath his claws.

"Kiara!"

Caerul shoved her aside and thrust himself between her and the creature looming over them. Thin streams of blood oozed from the bruises in his neck and snow clung to his matted dark hair, but he was upright and steady on his feet. A sword of ice appeared in his hand and, in one fluid movement, slashed across the Shadowslayer's inky black form. Frost exploded along the path of the cut, glistening with the same swirling patterns that traced through Stiria's scales. The ghost let out a guttural roar and stumbled back as the ice ate away at his form.

Caerul spun and grabbed Kiara's hand. "Go!" he cried. The ice sword vanished from his grasp but it left behind bits of frost on his skin. He sprinted away from the scene and yanked her along behind him.

Her legs moved of their own accord, though shaky and numb. He held her steady, but he didn't look back. An itch pricked the back of her mind, wriggling until it sparked into a memory. "Tobias and Eira—"

Caerul cut her off with a sharp whistle, his fingers pressed to his lips. Stiria's cry responded from a little ways ahead behind a snowdrift. In the dark, it was difficult to spot the dragons until Faiera's white head lifted from the mounds of powder. Caerul changed their course slightly and headed straight for the dragons.

"They're smart. They'll follow," he finally said, twisting to look at her over his shoulder. His voice came out hoarse, choked raw from Shadowslayer's attack and rough as if he had screamed for hours. Red gleamed in his eyes, his pupils narrow slits like a dragon's. The scar cut across his nose and down one side of his face flickered into view before disappearing again. Drawing ice through his bond with Stiria must have weakened the illusion.

Her heart skipped, panic clawing its way up her throat until her jaw clenched painfully, teeth pressed hard into each other. She squeezed his calloused hand. Despite the chill around them, despite the lingering touch of Stiria's magic, his skin burned like a fever. If his illusion fell, the Shadowslayer would be the least of their concerns.

"Kiara!" Eira appeared beside her and jolted her out of her muddied thoughts. She kept pace with Caerul easily on her long legs. "What's the plan?"

Ever the cautious one, Tobias kept up the rear, though his gaze constantly strayed back to the camp as it shrank into nothing but a nightmarish memory. Darkness swallowed it, and the Shadowslayer, who was likely almost consumed by Stiria's ice, disappeared in turn.

Exhaustion dragged Kiara's limbs, a weight that crushed her shoulders and threatened to break her. She took in a breath and opened her mouth to respond, but the words snagged on the tip of her tongue. Her mind spun, stuffed with thick cotton that buzzed like a hive full of bees. *What's the plan? What* is *the plan?* Death hung over the camp like a storm cloud—it clung to her skin and sank deep into her core until it settled in the pit of her stomach. What plan could withstand such force? Anything she pulled together would crack the moment she was faced with that echo in the reflection of Shadowslayer's mask. Fear chilled her to the bone, cutting deeper than the crisp mountain air. She gripped her sword tighter and jerked her gaze away from the desperate look in Eira's eyes—they always looked at her that way as if she were some kind of saint, a holy knight who could purge all evil from Anticuus. Dragonborn slayer, Calistian, Dragon Rider, savior, protector, warrior. Her tongue stuck to the roof of her mouth and her words fled. "I…"

Caerul tugged sharply on her arm to ground her in the present again. Her steps faltered, boots caught in the thick snow, but he was quick to pull her back on course. She glanced at him, but his gaze was locked on the dragons, who were only a few feet away now, rising to stand as they grew closer. Even without looking, he always seemed to know when she was slipping, sometimes better than she did.

She gave a subtle nod and steeled herself, locking away the buzz of her anxious thoughts in the depths of her mind. When the pounding headache began to subside again, she ran her tongue over her lips and gathered her words. "Get to the dragons," she ordered. "We have to leave before he recovers."

"Recovers?" Eira gasped between breaths. "You mean he's not dead? That was quite the hit."

"He's already dead," Caerul murmured. "Stiria's magic won't be able to get rid of him. Since he's, ah… *created* by evil magic, he can only be killed by the light. Something that cancels out his power."

Kiara's hand flicked to the dagger at her waist and she pursed her lips. *Something that cancels evil magic.*

"The ice won't do that?" Tobias questioned.

Caerul scoffed. "That ice will barely hold him for long. If we don't hurry and get out of here, he's going to—"

"Catch up to you?" The Shadowslayer's distorted laughter rang out all around them like the howl of the wind.

The shadows shifted at their feet, growing thick and inky, oozing with tainted magic. A hand shot out from the darkness and closed around Tobias's ankle. He cursed as he tumbled to the ground. Eira went back for him, knife at the ready. Cold slithered up Kiara's leg and, with a sharp yank, pulled her down. Her hand wrenched from Caerul's, robbed her of the safety and security he promised. A gasp fled her lips just as her face met the snow, a harsh frigid greeting that snapped against her skin. She shoved upright and yanked her dagger from its sheath. The onyx blade glittered in the moonlight, humming as she settled it in her grip. She sliced through the shadows coiling around her with ease. The knife sang as it greedily drank in the evil magic. Once free, she scrambled to her feet and whirled to find the Shadowslayer's cloaked figure looming over them once more, his empty white mask boring into Caerul.

"Cal—"

"Go help Tobias!" Caerul cut her off with a fierce glare, his lips pinched in determination. "Get to the dragons. I'll be right behind you."

He was right; she knew that. And yet, she remained frozen in place, clinging to the onyx dagger and waiting for the monstrous shadow to make a move. The blade trembled in her hands. It begged for magic to consume, hungry after being sheathed for so long. Her mother warned against its use. *It's a blade that destroys and consumes magic,* she said. It was made to fight corruption, but it could just as easily become corrupted itself. It could destroy the ghost of Sheniir, but at what cost?

The Shadowslayer shuffled forward; Caerul took a step back. Tensing, Caerul summoned his ice sword again, swinging it through the air to shake loose flecks of snow from the blade.

He lunged at the ghost's shadowy body, cutting a path with his sword straight through the darkness and leaving sharp crystals in its wake. This time, the Shadowslayer only laughed at his efforts, a dark, muffled sound that rumbled behind his mask. He took hold of Caerul's arm before he had a chance to escape to Kiara's side. Bloodied claws sank into Caerul's cloak, and his jaw clenched.

The knife hummed in Kiara's grip, suddenly warm against her palm despite the ice in her lungs. Her legs were like lead, or perhaps the snow had become a shackle that chained her. *Move!* she begged, but her body refused.

The Shadowslayer dragged Caerul in close and grabbed his face, tilting it to get a better look. "Your face," the monstrous shadow sneered. "Where is your *true* face? Show it to me."

Caerul jerked his head free and spat. Cold wind stirred around him, whipping up the loose snow around the shadow into a storm of ice. He curled his lips into a sneer. "I have nothing to show the likes of you."

"So be it." Inky black threads shot out from the Shadowslayer's fingers and wound tightly around Caerul's arm. He withdrew his clawed hands, letting Caerul dangle by the threads. With a swift, fluid motion, he pulled hard on the threads, jerking them in different directions. A gut-wrenching snap resounded through the air, pierced by Caerul's raw scream.

Kiara's heart skipped. Fire blazed in her chest. She shot toward the monster and cut the threads with her onyx blade. Caerul collapsed, his bloody arm bent at an sickening angle. Kiara's stomach churned at the sight, and she turned away, taking another swipe at the Shadowslayer with the knife. He vanished before the blade could touch him and reappeared in a puff of smoke once her swing had passed. A growl tore from his throat as he lunged for Caerul again.

A flash of shining blue scales whisked past Kiara and tackled the masked monster to the ground. Stiria bared his teeth, his fur ruffled and his pupils narrowed like slits as he towered over the Shadowslayer. His talons sank deep into the man's cloaked shoulders. Shadows leaked out from the wound like smoke, but they were soon choked out by the encroaching frost that burst from Stiria's touch. The Shadowslayer grunted in effort as he struggled against Stiria's hold, but even he was no match for the power of a dragon.

Faiera bounded over the snowdrift and curled around Caerul, her white scales hiding him in a protective shield. Kiara nodded to the dragon, catching a flash of understanding in her pale eyes, before rushing to where Tobias was still pinned. Her knife sliced the tendrils of darkness away easily. He muttered a quick thanks as he pushed to his feet.

"Get to the dragons." Kiara shoved the onyx blade into its sheath. "We can't stay." *Not if the Shadowslayer knows who Caerul is.* As his friend, it was her duty to guard his secret, to protect him from those he was fighting tooth and nail to escape. Once the illusion was broken, there would be no safe place. *Either the Shadowslayer will kill him or...* She glanced uneasily at Tobias, almost certain she would find the burning anger and hatred in his eyes that she had seen in the faces of so many others.

She shook her head. There wasn't time to dwell on the what ifs. All that mattered was getting everyone out safely with the letters. Bringing her fingers to her lips, she whistled sharply—both dragons looked her way. If Faiera spoke to her through their bond, the voice fell on deaf ears—not even a discernible whisper made it to her—but Kiara knew the dragon understood her in other ways. She motioned to Faiera. The white dragon scooped up Caerul and dropped him haphazardly over her back. Her wings fluttered as she leapt gracefully into the air before landing in front of Kiara. Stiria followed once Shadowslayer was safely pinned beneath a coating of thick ice. The blue dragon let out a chortle as he snagged both Tobias and Eira, slipping them into the saddle, and broke into the air.

Kiara climbed onto Faiera's back, carefully situating Caerul against the base of the dragon's neck. His eyes fluttered, and he slumped forward with a groan, his broken arm dangling uselessly at his side. The scent of blood clung to him like a ghost. If she were looking at him in the sunlight, its stains would no doubt be obvious; the moon, however, couldn't shed enough silvery light to reveal the truth. Her heart twisted. "I'm sorry," she murmured.

He didn't move. She wasn't sure he could hear her as Faiera took to the skies.

Wind roared in her ears, and the cold nipped relentlessly at her face. The snow-covered grounds of the Aurora Range shrank beneath her until the Shadowslayer was nothing more than a speck, a distant nightmare that could no longer touch them.

Just as relief began to sink into her bones, a spear of darkness hurtled up from the ground and struck Stiria's side. He howled as he plummeted from the sky, taking Tobias and Eira down with him. Darkness swallowed them, and they vanished from sight.

Caerul convulsed as if he was the one shot down, a strangled cry pulled from his lips. He heaved in a gulp of air as he trembled all over, his good arm wrapped around his side in the same place Stiria was struck.

Kiara steadied him, her fingers digging into his shoulders. "Close your connection," she cried. Panic made her voice tight. "Cut him off, or you'll die!"

"I can't leave him," he moaned. "I can't..."

"Remember what Talia said. If you leave the bond open with a wound like that, it will kill you. Close it off right now!"

Faiera suddenly veered, twisting so sharply in the air that Kiara was almost thrown from her back. Gritting her teeth, she clung to the edge of the saddle with one hand while the other pinned Caerul's limp body against hers. When they steadied again, a dark void yawned in the open air before them, leaking shadows like a cup that overflowed. The Shadowslayer emerged from within, his head twisted at an angle that made Kiara's stomach drop. If it weren't for his mask, she would expect to see a wide grin etched into his face.

"You have nothing to hide behind now." He stood in the air as if it were solid ground, his dark cloak billowing around him. "Let me see your true face. The face of the *ah tetiahl*!"

Fear sank its claws into Kiara's skin, as icy as the winds that swirled around her. She clapped her hand over Caerul's eyes, concealing their brilliant red shade. The tiny point of his ears stuck out beneath his wild, choppy hair. If it weren't for his cloak, the iridescent blue scales that dotted his broken arm would be visible as well. Without Stiria's power, he was completely exposed.

"I must have him." The Shadowslayer reached for them, the scarred hands of a man showing beneath his dark shroud of crackling magic. "I must have *Selini'ea ah tetiahl.*"

Magic snapped in the air, wild as it crackled around her. At her side, the knife began to hum, wriggling in its sheath like a wild beast begging to be set free. She grabbed its hilt. It was hot against her palm, almost burning. "Over my dead body," she hissed.

In one fluid movement, she pulled the knife from the sheath and flung it at the Shadowslayer. It struck him in the chest, the black blade buried deep in his shifting form. The dark magic hovering around him vanished instantly. He dropped from the sky like a discarded doll.

Shivers wracked her body as she sat back in the saddle. "Caerul?" she whispered, slowly removing her hand from his eyes. His breath puffed against her palm, but it had grown shallow. She chewed her lip and glanced back at where the others had fallen. Uncertainty weighed within her, a scale tipped by fear. Her knife, their one defense against the Shadowslayer, was gone, and she had trouble believing the ghost would die with it. Not to mention, Stiria's wound had broken his hold on the illusion spell. If she went back, she had no idea what she would find, or if Caerul would last long. *Without Stiria, I can't bring everyone back either.*

Steeling herself, she turned away. "I'm sorry, but I'm no savior." With a light tug on Faiera's reins, she guided them away from the mountains and left the others behind. "May the winter spirit protect you."

PART TWO
RUIN

"The shadow mourns the person he used to be.
Every night, he dreams of shining gold, cracked and oozing an
inky, corrupted black.
When he awakes, he tastes the rot in his soul."

II

WOUNDED AND FORGOTTEN

THE WORLD HURTLED toward Tobias at an alarming rate. He wasn't sure exactly when he had been thrown from Stiria's back, or when he had pulled Eira close enough to muffle her scream against his chest, or when Faiera's white form had disappeared into the shadows overhead. Everything was a blur until he slammed into the cushion of a snowdrift with Eira atop him, pinned against his chest with her arms wrapped firmly around him. He sank deep enough to be crushed in the embrace of bitter cold, and he could almost taste a curse against Sefah or whoever created such an abomination on his tongue. Instead, he let out a groan, but he was too numb to tell if anything was broken. Only his head ached, his temples throbbing as his skin warmed with the heat of panic.

Stiria crashed seconds later, a wild shriek torn from his throat that quickly died out. Eira shot to her feet first before grasping Tobias's arm and hauling him out of the snow. Together, they raced to the dragon's side, ice crunching beneath their boots. The white powder around them was steeped in a crimson that oozed steadily from a wound in Stiria's side. Whatever had struck him was strong enough to shatter the scales around his belly and leave the soft skin beneath utterly exposed. His head flopped against the ground, eyes staring unfocused and empty.

"What do we do?" Eira's voice trembled, her hands shaky as she picked loose bits of broken scales from the skin around the gaping wound. Darkness licked at the edges, humming with a strange, distorted energy that made Tobias's skin prickle. She inhaled sharply and pressed her fists to her eyes. "Where's Aviva when you need her?"

"Gone," Tobias murmured. He reached for the pin still tucked away in his pocket, and his fingers brushed the paper with the last resort. His throat clenched. He should have used it when he had the chance, though he had no idea what it would do. "You still have the letters?"

"Yes."

Hopelessness choked the breath from his lungs, pushing against his efforts to take a deep, calming breath. His jaw ached from clenching his teeth. *Don't lose your head,* he could hear Talia's voice echoing in the recesses of his mind. The ghost of her hand brushed his shoulder, steadying him the way she used to when he was a kid teetering on the verge of a fit. The way their mother used to do to both of them before she was killed. *Stay calm, no matter the situation,* Talia's memory echoed. *Panic distorts the mind, and it has never once solved a problem.*

This time, he was able to take a long breath of freezing air. He held it for a moment before releasing it, watching it cloud in front of his face. The anxious buzzing in his mind calmed, and the world seemed quieter. He glanced at the sky. The dark shroud was beginning to disperse, just enough to see another body fall from the sky far from where they were, a man cloaked in black. The Shadowslayer. A small, white form fled the scene. Faiera—and with her, Kiara and Caerul.

He tapped the hilt of his sword. "I think we're going to be on our own getting back."

"What?" Eira shot to her feet and followed his gaze to the sky. "No way. She didn't! Isn't she worried about Stiria? Not to mention us. We'll freeze out here without his spells and we can't go back if he can't fly! There's miles of snow in every direction —even the camp is too far away to see. I wouldn't even know where to *start*."

"It can't be helped. She can't cart us and Stiria back with just Faiera." Already, he could feel his teeth beginning to chatter. The effects of Stiria's anti-cold spell were quickly wearing off. "I think she's weighing Caerul's life against ours."

Again, his hand slid back into his pocket and brushed the cool silver of the pin. He gripped it tightly, feeling the ruby inlaid in its center press against his palm. The spell paper scraped his knuckles. If Aviva was there, she could heal Stiria easily and they would be on their way. If Kase was there, he would have come up with a plan. But they were gone. Both left him with a task, and he had failed to do what they asked. He hadn't given the pin to Calix. He hadn't found Aviva's apprentice. He hadn't even been strong to cast the unknown spell. *Oliver was right. This was a stupid idea.*

Defiance pricked his skin until, burning beneath the cold, he released his grip on the pin. They were close to uncovering something important, something that could shed light on why a dragonborn had been so invested in Aviva's spellbook, why he had manipulated Eira and slaughtered their friends. Regardless of what Kiara had decided, he wouldn't let Eira die. *Calm. Be rational. First...*

He knelt beside Stiria and smoothed a hand through the tangled mane down his neck. "Hold on," he whispered. "We'll get you out of here."

Stiria's eyes slid closed, and he gave a snort of acknowledge-ment. It would have to do.

When Tobias rose to his feet again, he was met with Eira's puzzled stare. "What do you plan to do?" she asked, her breath clouding in front of her face. It curled like smoke as it faded into the air.

Smoke. Red scales flashed through his mind, burning with a heat strong enough to rival the sun itself. Before he could stop it, excitement pulled a grin to his face. Eira's confusion sharpened, but he didn't answer her. She would find out for herself soon enough.

Closing his eyes, he blocked out the world around him, searching for the thread that would connect him to Smoke. The rush of wind in his ears and the snap of cold around him was replaced by a steady warmth. It was faint, barely even a thread at all, but it was still there, spiraling far out of his mind's eye. *Smoke,* he called, taking the thread in his hand, letting it curl around his fingers. *You're still there, aren't you? I have no right to ask this of a dragon that isn't mine but...* He paused, fumbling for the words. Kase's agitated half of his regular conversations with the dragon raced to the front of his mind, and he sighed. *Come make yourself useful.*

Why should I? the old dragon answered immediately, his deep voice rumbling down the length of the thread like echoes in a cave. *I have no bond with you. My master lies dead and buried, so there is no reason for me to answer the calls of this world anymore.* Laughter crawled from the other end of the bond, powerful and edged with mockery. *Do you even know who I am?*

You still protect that half-breed, don't you? Tobias reasoned, praying his rationale was correct. For whatever reason, Smoke was connected to Caerul, deeply enough that he refused to let him be killed at Tobias's hands. *He was injured, and his dragon was struck down. You know better than I do that separating a Rider and his dragon is more painful than anything else in the world. At the very least, take Stiria to him.*

This time, Smoke paused thoughtfully. When he spoke, his voice turned soft. *Do you not even wish to beg for your own life?*

I can't imagine you would find that a convincing argument, but if you wish to hear it, I don't want to freeze to death. I don't want to learn what might kill me first out here: the beasts roaming the mountains, the Shadowslayer, the weather—whatever. Eira doesn't either.

You do not need to argue your case for me, Smoke said, bemused. His words drew up as if in a smile—though the image of a smile on a dragon's lips was hardly comforting. *I would disgrace my master's memory if I refused his friends in their time of need. You need only ask, and I will always come.*

Even if I don't know who you are?

"Tobias!"

Eira jolted him out of his trance with a sharp yank to his shoulder. The thread slipped from his fingers, and his connection plunged into silence. Still reeling, he blinked several times to allow his vision to settle on her face. With a grin on her lips, her eyes wide, she pointed to the sky, where the sun had risen above the horizon to chase the darkness away. With it came Smoke's shimmering red body, illuminated by the sun's light so that he shone like a ball of fire, flying straight for them. Already, the crisp mountain air seemed warmer against Tobias's skin. Neither the darkness nor the frigid air could stand against the old dragon's flames.

Smoke's powerful wings buffeted Tobias with wind as the dragon slowly settled in the snow. Once his feet touched the ground, he folded his wings gracefully against his back and stretched his neck toward them. Friendliness warmed his amber eyes. Eira's hand shot out to touch him, and he lowered his head. Giddy, she pressed her palm to his smooth scales.

"He's warm!" she announced.

Tobias brushed her comments aside. Marching up to Smoke's side, he gripped the dragon's scales and hauled himself onto his back at the base of his neck. His arms burned at the effort, and his hands smarted where the sharp scales bit into his skin. He wiped them on his pants and settled into the heat of Smoke's back, relishing the way it banished the chill in his bones. Clearing his throat, he asked, "Can you take us back to Kiara and Caerul?"

Smoke nodded and bent lower so that Eira could climb up behind Tobias. *I will know where they have gone.*

"And Stiria?" Tobias jerked his chin at the little blue dragon, who didn't seem any more impressive than a horse in the presence of such a massive beast as Smoke. Being wounded—fighting to even take a breath—didn't help his case.

Wings unfurled, Smoke lifted himself off the ground and gently scooped up Stiria in his talons. Once the smaller dragon was settled, Smoke veered away from the mountains and climbed higher into the sky. *He will make it,* he finally answered. *The wound is not too deep. To him, it is of no great consequence. To his master, however...* He trailed off.

A sudden rush of fear and grief spilled through Tobias, dragging up memories almost forgotten. If strong enough, a bond between Riders and dragons could reflect injuries onto the other. Caerul's small, fragile body came to mind, already beaten and broken from his brief fight with the Shadowslayer.

Kiara is not going to let him die, Smoke murmured as if he knew—and perhaps he did. *He will fight. However, without Stiria's power, the illusion will be broken. You know the truth, but it will be laid bare before you. Are you able to keep from acting out against Caerul?*

When the image of dragonborn hybrids came to mind, it was always attached to violence, fear, and blood. They had been marked as monsters all of Tobias's life and for good reason. The Draconic people killed without mercy. They had always been monsters, and that was all they could ever be.

As long as Caerul is able to make peace with me, I will do the same for him, Tobias answered the dragon, sticking to their bond to avoid tangling Eira in the conversation. He settled his hand against the hilt of his sword, drawing comfort from the closeness of the blade. Back at the camp, Caerul had fought to protect them from the Shadowslayer, to give them chances to escape. He wasn't the bloodthirsty beast that lurked in the back of Tobias's mind, painting his memories with blood. He wasn't the creature that had destroyed his family. He was Caerul, and for whatever reason, he was hiding. It was almost as if he was more human than dragonborn.

He assumed Smoke's silence meant his answer was sufficient and settled into the long ride with his thoughts. Slowly, as Sefah's mountains faded behind them, the quiver of fear in his hands diminished. His body relaxed, and he slumped against Smoke's neck. Though the hot scales pricked his cheek, his eyes drifted shut, and sleep came for him.

12

LUMAS

The flight down from the mountain stretched on in an eternity, a slow trickle of time that oozed past Kiara like sludge. Yet, somehow, the sprawling town at the base of the mountains came into sight much too quickly, as if it were a wild beast racing to snatch her up in its jaws. Dawn had come and gone by the time she spotted it beyond the mountains, and the sun was now nestled firmly in the blue sky dotted with wisps of clouds. So far above the ground, Kiara could see the distant shape of Calistie City sparkling on the horizon. Her heart fluttered, sweat coating her palms as her gut squirmed with anxiety. For the first time in nearly two years, she was back within the borders of her kingdom.

She remained tense the whole way until her muscles were screaming in protest, but she couldn't relax even if she wanted to. One arm hugged Caerul's limp form against her chest while the other kept firm hold of Faiera's reins. It gave her some semblance of control, though she knew the dragon could fly perfectly fine without her guidance. Faiera had always seemed more intelligent than other young dragons. She knew exactly where the nearest town—a small settlement named Lumas—

would be and how to get there as quickly as possible, even if Kiara recoiled at the thought.

If it weren't for Caerul's condition, she would have taken him somewhere far away where she could tend to his wounds on her own. She would never have dared to return to a place that could risk destroying everything she had built.

Caerul, she repeated, rolling the name around in the back of her mind. It was heavy on her tongue, foreign and awkward even after knowing and using it for so long. She spared a glance down at him, but all she could see was his wind-tossed hair and the tiniest tip of his slightly pointed ears. It was the name he asked her to call him in front of others, all part of Stiria's disguise. Caerul was a mask, a lie. She hated using it that way.

"To me, you'll always be Calix," she murmured. "I don't want you to have to hide forever." As she spoke, however, the words felt heavy and wrong. How could she judge someone who ran from his past when she couldn't escape the looming guilt that clung to her as she returned to Calistie's borders?

A faint presence brushed the edges of her consciousness, friendly and pleasant like a summer breeze. Wordless whispers drifted into her mind. Glancing at Faiera, she found the dragon staring back at her with pale eyes. She looked away before Kiara could press further and folded in her wings to begin their descent—softly, carefully, so as not to jostle Calix. For a moment, they were falling. Once, the wind tearing at her face and the ground below growing closer and closer would have been enough to make her body numb with fear. Now, she clutched the saddlehorn and leaned into Faiera's neck until the dragon caught the wind again. Graceful as ever, her talons brushed the tall grass, stark white against the dry brown, as she landed safely on the outskirts of the town. The snow was thinner at the bottom of the mountain, collected in random clumps across the landscape, but the air still carried an icy chill that made Kiara shiver.

They were far enough away that they wouldn't be spotted easily by the guards—she hoped they would mistake Faiera for the snow if she remained still—and they were likely not to attract attention. At least, not until Kiara dragged a healer out. If they even had one.

She had never been to Lumas, but there were whispers that it held connections to the long-dead lord of winter, Sefah. Some reported having seen his ghost wandering the streets at night. *That had better be nothing more than a rumor,* she thought sourly as she dismounted. *I've had enough of ghosts to last me a lifetime.*

Faiera pressed her belly to the grass. Calix laid against her neck, his eyes squeezed shut. His arms dangled limply at his sides, the injured one twisted in such a way that made Kiara's gut wrench. She had no doubt it was turning a gruesome shade of purplish black beneath his cloak like the bruise on his neck, and she thought she saw the bloodstained white of a bone jutting out from his skin. Pain twisted his expression, putting wrinkles in his brow that made him appear many years older.

Tears pricked her eyes, but she quickly blinked them away before gently sliding him off of the dragon's back. His head lolled against her shoulder, and his lips moved soundlessly as if he were trying to speak. She stretched him out in the grass beside Faiera, pressing his arm against the dragon's pearlescent scales, which glowed slightly on contact. White dragons were known for their healing, and though Faiera was too young to mend any wound yet, she had the ability to nullify pain and keep the injury from worsening, like freezing it in time.

Kiara stood and took a deep breath. She yanked her hood over her head, tucking her hair into her cloak to hide its length. "Stay here," she said as she caught Faiera's eye. "Keep him safe. I'll be back soon."

No voice answered, as always, but Faiera dipped her head in response. Warmed by her dragon's quiet support, Kiara turned and hurried to the road that led into the town. Being a small settlement, Lumas had no gates nor a thick protective wall like the capital. Two guards were posted at the outskirts on either side of the worn dirt road, their uniform blue cloaks bearing the emblem of Calistie's soldiers. She smiled at them, hoping it didn't look too much like a grimace. They didn't stop her as she passed, but they exchanged a puzzled look. Swallowing hard, she pulled her hood further down and sped up. She hoped they had been stationed at Lumas long enough that they knew little about the affairs of Calistie City—and wouldn't be able to recognize her face.

"Miss!" one of the guards called. His steps were clipped as he made his way toward her. "Please wait a moment."

Kiara halted, heart pounding. Slowly, she turned to face the guard, her hand inching toward her sword hidden under her cloak. She wet her lips before addressing him. "Yes, sir?"

His eyes slipped from her face down to the front of her cloak. Concern knitted his brow. At the same time, realization dawned on Kiara, and the heat drained from her face as she followed his gaze. Deep crimson stains marred the front of her snow white cloak—Calix's blood. Her breath hitched, and she stiffened.

The guard seemed at a loss for words. Judging from his smooth skin and cropped curls, she guessed he was quite young. He fidgeted with the neckline of his coat. "Did something happen? Are you in need of assistance?"

He doesn't recognize me. A little of the tension in her chest lifted. She let out a breath, but the awkward air between them still lingered. Even a skillful silver tongued liar couldn't weave their way out of this mess. The second guard had turned her way. His face was pinched and betrayed his suspicion more clearly than the younger guard's. She touched the front of her cloak. It was still damp and smelled sharply of blood. "I—"

"There you are, miss! I was beginning to think I'd lost you after we got separated by those wolves."

A third figure in a thick brown cloak lined with tan fur at the neck made his way past the guard at the road, who spared him a look that was reminiscent of a parent's disappointment in their most tiring child. The third person didn't seem to mind, his eyes trained on Kiara. As he ran to her, he unfastened the cloak and, pushing past the young guard, wrapped her in it. The scent of fresh herbs clung to the heavy garment. "Come on. Let's get you cleaned up. I hope you aren't injured?"

Under so many watchful eyes, Kiara froze, her nails digging into her palms. When the guard began to scrutinize her with narrowed eyes, she cleared her throat. "N–no. I'm fine. I… got into a little scuffle is all. It's wolf blood."

"As expected of you, miss." The third man smiled warmly and squeezed her shoulder. She stiffened at the contact, her throat tight with fear. His skin was ice against her, almost as pale as the snow. When she met his gaze, his eyes were a striking shade of azure. Soft, sandy blond curls framed his round face like ocean waves. "That's why I hired you to keep me safe out there." His words were slow, writing a script for her to follow if she wished to get out of the trouble she had walked into.

She nodded numbly, mind distracted by the ringing that consumed her ears. Her eyes didn't linger on his face—they drifted instead to his elongated pointed ears, a sight she had only seen in the figures of the old tapestries of history hanging in the halls of her home. Her heart dropped. They weren't like the subtle curving point of a dragonborn's ears. They were ethereal and distinctly not human: the ears of an elf.

The young guard scoffed, rolling his eyes—seemingly unperturbed by the piece of ancient history in their mix. "Seriously, Unda? A man should not depend on a young lady to defend his safety. You have a sword for a reason. You should use it." He gestured sharply to the silver blade sheathed at the elf's side.

Unda chuckled and slid around to stand by Kiara, his hand

still perched on her shoulder. "You've never seen her in action. If you did, you too would seek her protection. She's quite the fighter!"

"Where did you see these wolves?" the older guard asked as he approached them, a stern look on his face. "We will want to dispatch a team to ensure they don't stray too close to the town."

"Oh, yes, of course." Unda pointed off into the distance, farther down the road. "We ran into them out that way. Near where I like to pick herbs. If you could take care of them, that would be much appreciated. Thank you."

The guard nodded. "Very well, Hayden here will take a report to the officers. You may go. Have a good day, miss, Unda." He dipped his head in a polite farewell before returning to his post. The younger guard lingered a moment longer before he scooted off to report the supposed wolf attack.

Though they weren't looking, Unda spared the guards one last smile before he led Kiara away. She shot a glance back at the retreating figures of the guards, torn between the prickle of fear and the budding relief in her chest. They seemed to trust him, but that didn't mean she should yet. However, if she parted ways with him, she doubted the guards would fall for the same scheme twice, and she couldn't risk being found out. Not when Calix needed her.

Gritting her teeth, she followed the elf with her hand against her sword.

He dropped her shoulder once they were a good distance from the guard post. "Sorry about that," he murmured. "I didn't want you to get caught and risk exposing your friend."

Kiara stiffened. "I'm here alone." Though the instant the words left her, she regretted it. It was never wise to admit she was traveling alone—even to an elf.

"I saw you fly in with your dragon." There was a smile in his voice when he spoke, and though his words tripped up with the beginnings of an accusation, there was no threat behind them. Even if there was, he was barely taller than her, and without his heavy cloak, his thin, frail frame was painfully obvious. It was no wonder the guards were so quick to believe he had gone out with hired help, and why their scolding about his lack of swordsmanship seemed like a usual occurrence. Yet, there was something *old* in the way he watched her, something that seemed to know what she didn't. It was this that sent a shiver down her spine. If he truly was an elf, she was looking at someone who had been around for centuries, though he didn't look much older than his early twenties.

As if sensing her discomfort, his tone lightened into a joking manner. "Besides," he continued, "is that what you planned to tell the guards when they questioned you about the fresh blood on your clothes? That you came here on your own?"

Her face warmed with shame at the insinuation she was a murderer toting a victim's blood. She tucked the fur-coated edges of his cloak closer together to hide the stains on her own. For someone so old, he was surprisingly shameless. Wasn't wisdom supposed to come with age? *In fact...* She stopped and blocked his path, meeting his calm gaze with a steely glare. Her trembling fingers itched for the security of her blade in hand, but she kept them at her side instead. "The elves are dead," she snapped. "The dragonborn made sure of that, yet you're here. Who *are* you?"

He searched her face with an irritating calmness, completely unruffled by her accusation. One of his ears twitched—proof that they were real and not some sort of elaborate costume. "I am Unda," he said. "I'm the healer of Lumas."

13

OF ICE AND SNOW

LEGENDS CLAIMED THAT SEFAH had the world's bluest eyes. None could rival their intensity, nor the brilliance of the color with which he was blessed. They were said to be like a pair of rich jewels, one stamped with the symbol of a snowflake that glowed a snowy white like his hair. Staring at Unda's face, drowning in the depths of his gaze, Kiara almost began to question the truth of the legend.

His eyes were blue like the sea for which he was named, a deep and unending pool of azure, cerulean, and ultramarine that sparkled in the sunlight like the rolling waves of the ocean. *Unda* was a distinctly Calistian name, evidenced by its soft *ah* ending which so many repeated in the modern day out of love for the elvish culture. It was a ghost of a bygone age, an old name with its roots in a time long forgotten—just like him.

Kiara's lip twitched as she fought to conceal her surprise. Though the fact that he was the healer wasn't that shocking. He fit the image: a fragile build like a twig—weak and drenched in the scent of herbs. What struck her was the idea that an immortal, one of the only survivors of the massacre, would be serving as a healer for a small, backwater town at the very edge of

Calistie instead of the capital. There was no way he would be turned aside at the gates, as many in Calistie City practically worshiped the elves. Wouldn't he rather seek the protection of the royal family in the capital city?

The slightest hint of a smile lifted the corners of his mouth. "Does it surprise you that much? I believe you of all people should know that appearances are not everything, Crown Princess Kiara Ateléaria."

Her breath caught in her throat and she flinched, hand flying to the weapons concealed beneath her cloak. "How did you—?"

He nodded to something behind her. "I happen to be quite good at reading."

Part of her didn't want to see whatever he was pointing at. Panic seized her lungs and the world seemed to rock beneath her. If not for her tightly clenched jaw, she was certain she would have lost her last meal right there at his feet. Instead, she braced herself and turned. They had come to the center of the town where a letter board was posted with various announcements on scribbled slips of paper. The most glaring was the poster bearing her name plastered on it in big letters, along with a surprisingly accurate sketch of her face. Calix's likeness was posted beside hers, the word "wanted" etched in eerily threatening script. The rest of the information blurred as she stared back at her likeness in horror. It was a wonder no one had recognized her yet, but her travels must have obscured some of her regality.

"Please understand I do not intend to harm you." His voice was dangerously close to her ear this time. Something tugged her hood farther down, almost completely obscuring her vision in white. "I want to help. We must treat your friend and get you on your way before the guards figure out who you are."

"Why should I trust you?" she ground out, her shoulders tensed.

"That's up to you to decide. If you choose to run, I won't stop you."

The temptation to bolt pulled at her and whispered sweet promises of escape in her ear. Her legs trembled beneath her, just waiting for the order to carry her away from the scene. No one could blame her. She had spent so long trying to bury the past, to resist the call to come home though she was duty-bound to her people and her country. If she wished to escape, she could. But Calix would not survive if she left him, and she couldn't convince herself that he would make it to another town either. The outskirts of Calistie were sparsely populated, and she couldn't think of a village within a day's flight. Defeat sank into her bones.

She let out a sigh. Her shoulders dropped and she relinquished her hold on her weapon. "Okay." Turning to Unda, she pursed her lips, feeling a tightness well up in her chest once more. An old custom came to mind, one exchanged between elves with something to lose. Without sparing it a second thought, she bowed her head to him as she took his hand and squeezed. "Please, if you can, you must heal Calix," she said.

He withdrew from her grasp and cleared his throat, the first sign of awkwardness she had observed in him. "There's no need for you to lower your head to me. It will be done."

As she straightened, her father's words echoed in her mind: *You are a princess, Kiara. You do not lower your head to another.* The harshness of his words dwindled as he had searched her face. *The burden of the crown is one that must not be given an excuse to break you. Stand tall and straight; people will respond to your will accordingly.* At one time, she had clung proudly to his words, holding fast to his teaching. But her pride was broken. It wasn't more important than Calix.

By the time she thought of something to say in response, Unda had already moved on. He slipped past her and ripped her "missing" poster down from the board. He tore it to unrecognizable shreds before disposing of it with the wave of his hand and a flash of magic. He turned to her with stiffness that rivaled a soldier's. "Come on, then. We need to hurry back to my clinic. Can you have him brought there?"

Her heart skipped, and she quickly ripped Calix's poster down and shoved it into the small pouch at her waist. "I would rather not risk having him seen." *And I can't reach out to Faiera to ask anyway.* Her unease simmered and brought the steam of confusion rising to the surface. "But you have magic, don't you? Can you not heal him with that?"

"Complete healing takes a great deal of strength from the user." His jaw clenched, and he looked away in shame, the elongated tips of his ears drooping. "Currently, I do not have that kind of power to offer. I cannot completely restore him, so I'll need some supplies to aid me."

Guilt suddenly left a foul taste on her tongue as she regarded his fragile appearance once more. There was a sickly look to his pale complexion. His wrists were so thin she could wrap her whole hand around them. Magic took a great toll on its user. If he was not careful, he could lose his life to its call. *Or worse.* Her mind took a sharp turn, hooked on the horrifying image of the Shadowslayer. Magic could take far more than any person should give.

Unda ushered her away from the scene and guided her to the far road that led down the market street. As they walked, she explained Calix's injuries as best she could, holding back on noting his hybrid nature in case it frightened Unda away. Nothing seemed to faze him. Calm wrapped him in a cool air like the first fall of snow. Her steps were clipped as she made her way deeper into the bustling afternoon crowd, her fingers bunched into fists beneath Unda's heavy cloak, but he glided gracefully at her side. Like Unda, many of the other towns-people were dressed in thick cloaks to combat the cold. They shuffled past and paid Kiara little attention. However, they greeted Unda with pleasant smiles and warm hellos to which he always responded with the dip of his head. Kiara looked away from him before she could fall too deeply into the comfort of the safety he offered.

The market was smaller than it would be in more central towns, but its sellers were no less boisterous. They boasted thick wool coats in preparation for the vicious winter storms to come and bitter-smelling herbs that were supposed to keep people warm. She caught sight of boots for hiking in the snow as well. Perhaps the only connection Sefah had to this town was his oppressive winter, but that was certainly not unique to Lumas.

Guards patrolled the streets with their hands casually resting against their sword hilts. Kiara ducked her head as she passed them, biting her lip and keeping her shoulders stiff until she was certain they hadn't taken an interest in her. One stopped to talk to Unda, but he quickly waved the matter away before the guard could take notice of Kiara huddled beside him. When they were gone, she snapped her head up and returned to scanning the stalls for something that looked like a healer's setup, itching with impatience to return to Calix's side. It seemed like an eternity would pass before they made it to their destination, much less got back to him.

The market street ended. Icy fear sank its claws into her skin. Calix's pained expression and broken arm flitted through her mind and sapped her of the patience she had worked so hard to build. *I still don't know if he shuttered his bond with Stiria,* part of her whispered, crawling up from the recesses of her mind, *nor how badly it hurt him before he did.*

A soft, comforting presence brushed against the back of her mind and hovered there until her anxiety's edge diminished. It came with no words, but the warmth was reminiscent of Faiera. Touched, Kiara brought a hand to her chest, resting it just above her heart. *Trust,* the dragon seemed to say. *Calm.*

Kiara took a deep breath, but the tension in her muscles refused to relax. Calm was a stranger to her restless heart, even more so when Calix was involved. As long as he was with her, she would never be able to grasp the serenity that Unda held.

FAIERA'S PEARLESCENT SCALES glittered in the soft rays of late afternoon sunlight as Kiara approached with Unda at her side, a bag stuffed full of medical supplies slung over his shoulder. The dragon had folded her wing protectively over Calix and laid her head down with her eyes closed. As they drew nearer, she cracked one eye open. It shifted warily to Unda, and her lip curled slightly.

"It's okay," Kiara said, putting her arm in front of the healer. Faiera's eye settled on her face, her pupil still narrowed to a tiny slit. Kiara forced a smile, hoping it would mask the tension in her limbs. *Confidence. Let her know you're truly okay, or she won't believe your words.* "He's here to help. Let him see."

Faiera released a heavy sigh—acceptance, Kiara assumed— and folded her wing back to reveal Calix still resting like a corpse at her side. His face was pinched in pain, his twisted arm sprawled out at his side. Splotches of blood stained the ground beneath him, but the flow was considerably slower than it would have been without Faiera's healing ability. He was stranded in sleep, suspended from his agony, and unaware of the elf Kiara had brought to aid him: the man who now knew Calix's most closely guarded secret. His deep blue scales were visible on his arm, marred with scars and scratches. Kiara watched Unda's reaction carefully, her hand inching toward her weapon again.

Unda glided to Calix's side and knelt, legs folded under him. His expression was placid, void of the sneer of hatred and disgust that contorted the faces of those who knew the real

Calix. With gentle hands, he lifted Calix's arm and examined the broken bone jutting out from his flesh. Nausea twisted Kiara's gut. She looked away sharply.

"Forgive me," Unda murmured, sending a jolt of nervousness racing along her skin like lightning. Frost crawled across his fingertips, blue as his eyes and swirling with a sudden chill. The sharp pull of magic flooded the air, a pressure that pounded against Kiara's head. Threads of azure wound around his hands, and his palms began to glow. Taking Calix's arm firmly in both hands, he twisted and snapped it back into its right form.

Calix awoke with a scream, voice raw with agony, and thrashed in Unda's grip. Kiara rushed to his side and pinned his shoulders down until Unda could finish healing his arm. Wild red eyes turned to her, wide and rimmed with tears. Calix heaved a ragged breath, hiccuping through the sob that escaped him. Weakly, his other hand gripped her cloak. Sweat plastered his unruly tangles to his forehead.

The white glow from Faiera's power sharpened, and the pain in Calix's eyes dulled. Slowly, he stilled, his chest heaving as he took in a long, deep breath. As his eyes fluttered shut, his head lolled to the side, and his fighting stopped.

Kiara released him and the breath she had been holding. Her shoulders trembled, skin prickling with unease. Anger simmered in her chest. She glared at Unda and the blue threads of his magic that stitched Calix's wounded flesh back together. She blinked away her tears. "You could have warned me!" she snapped, her voice pitched high with panic.

One of Unda's pale, pointed ears twitched, now tinged blue with ice like his fingers. "I'm sorry. This wound is best treated with magic. It will take much too long to heal otherwise."

"That's not the problem!"

He blinked at her with innocent eyes, shining in the light and round as though he were far younger than he truly was. No malice or evil intent lay hidden in that face. "Then I'm very sorry that I have offended you," he said honestly. The glow in his hands vanished before he laid Calix's now healed arm at his side. The bruising was gone, as was the disfigured, broken appearance. It was whole and clean, save for his old scars.

Awe and wonder were two things Kiara had done her best to stamp out as she had grown older. There was little place for such childish fancies in the life of a princess whose sole duty was to serve and lead her people. And yet, despite her efforts, those feelings bloomed within her, choking out her earlier frustration. She took Calix's arm. The skin was smooth, warm beneath her touch, completely healed. Magic was beautiful, and the sight of it at work quickly melted her frustration.

"You're amazing." She looked wide-eyed at Unda.

Frost still clung to his skin, the tips of his fingers now white like in the old paintings of Sefah. When he exhaled, his breath clouded in front of his face from the cold, but it couldn't hide the proud smile that curled his lips. Rather than respond to her compliment, he pried open his bag and began to pull out his supplies. "I'm sure Calix would appreciate it if we would finish up here."

Together, they cleaned and dressed the rest of his wounds—though Kiara did little more than watch, occasionally handing cloth or bandages to Unda as he worked. Calix's body was in poor shape, bruised from his fight with the Shadowslayer, but Unda reassured her that the wounds would not take his life as long as he had time to recover. Not even the wound in his midsection implanted on him by Stiria would be enough to snatch his life away.

"He will be in great pain for a while and likely won't be able to move well tonight. Tomorrow, after my magic has had a chance to regenerate, I'll tend to him again," Unda explained as he gently wrapped Calix's arm in a sling. At Kiara's curious glance, he shrugged sheepishly. "I've done what I can, but the arm will be sensitive and weak for a time. He should refrain from using it recklessly."

Kiara pursed her lips. "I'm sorry to say it's impossible to keep him from being reckless."

Unda laughed, but there was an undertone of melancholy in his tone. As it faded, he gestured at Calix. "We need to carry him back. If you would, please."

She lifted her brows, flushed at the suggestion that she should be the one to lift him. She started to protest, but his weariness had etched deep lines beneath his eyes and the way his hands trembled was unmistakable. Though she doubted he could lift much of anything with his skinny arms at full strength. Nodding, she rose and carefully lifted Calix onto Faiera's back.

"I'm sure you're exhausted," Unda said. "Shall we head back to the clinic? I will prepare a room for you to rest as well."

At Kiara's signal, Faiera stood, careful with Calix draped against her neck. All at once, Kiara's exhaustion caught up with her. She steadied herself against Faiera's side, grateful for the dragon's strength. "Yes," she said. "Thank you for your hospitality."

His smile was fleeting, but she caught it before it disappeared. "I'm glad I was able to help in time." He led the dragon away in silence, leaving Kiara to match his pace as they plodded back to the town where the chance to rest awaited her.

14

A RELIC OF THE PAST

ALTHOUGH TOBIAS HAD PROMISED NOT to act rashly, not to consider Caerul the same as the monstrous hybrids that haunted his memories, he was becoming more restless the closer they got to the small town below the mountains. Smoke explained it was called Lumas and that Kiara seemed to have fled there with Caerul and Faiera. From above, the buildings and snaking roads seemed unbelievably small, packed closely together into a town that would have been tiny even compared to Floridus. Night had fallen before they reached the outskirts. Slowly, tiny flickering flames lit the streets and windows below. Tobias shivered against the vengeful evening wind, his face nipped by the chill in the air. *It's no wonder no one wants to live in this awful place.*

If they knew what one Calistian girl had brought into their midsts, even the people of Lumas who had weathered so many brutal, wintry storms would flee. A hybrid. Half dragonborn, half human. A monster that should never have existed.

Tobias clenched his jaw. He had promised not to think that way. He had promised to be rational and calm. He had promised not to be blinded by years of fear. The nightmarish visions that lurked at the back of his mind, stalking him like a hungry beast, could be subdued if he fought to take control.

You are overthinking this task, Smoke grumbled, his deep voice pushing through the thick wall of anxiety that had surrounded Tobias.

If I don't think about it now, I won't think about it at all. Next thing I know, my sword will be at his throat.

And then, you will be dead.

Tobias wrinkled his nose. His bones ached with cold and dread, or perhaps from his fall. Numbness had crept through his limbs, and he didn't even realize his hand had reached for the key resting against his chest until the chill from the metal nipped his skin. He quickly dropped his hand. *Are you threatening me?*

I have no reason to.

You seem bent on protecting Caerul, Tobias noted, shifting his gaze so that it rested on the approaching town below them. *He has a connection to Kase, doesn't he?*

Smoke beat his great wings. Heat rolled off his ruby scales. He dipped slightly and angled himself down toward the town. Eira squeezed Tobias's midsection, reminding him of her presence against his back.

I believe you know, Smoke finally answered, a hint of melancholy to his voice. It hung heavy with sadness, an ache that resonated deep within Tobias. It was grief, he realized after a pause, deeply rooted in Smoke's mind and winding down the length of the thread that connected them. Beneath his ornery exterior, the old dragon was broken inside—his heart still ached for the loss of his closest companion. He stretched his neck and tilted his head so that his amber gaze settled on Tobias. *Who do you think he is?*

Tobias stiffened, shrinking back into himself to avoid Smoke's piercing, soul-searching stare. It bored straight through him. He wasn't even sure he needed to scrape an answer together for Smoke to know what was on his mind. However, before he could reply, Smoke's accusing glare turned away as he began their descent. With the change in action came a change in subject—or lack thereof—and Tobias breathed a sigh of relief before the air was ripped from him.

The dragon surged down against the wind. Tobias gripped Smoke's scales until his knuckles ached as they raced toward the ground. Eira tightened her hold around his waist, her forehead pressed firmly against his back. There was little he could do but hope she had the strength to keep herself from flying off, though Smoke was no novice at carrying passengers. They stopped a safe distance from the earth and landed gracefully in the sparse grass with the powerful beat of Smoke's wings. Lumas sat on the horizon, just within walking distance but out of range of the great winds stirred by the dragon.

I will not go any farther, Smoke said, bending down to lay Stiria's wounded body in the grass. *This is a Calistian town. I do not want to risk their wrath—though their blades can do nothing to me, so you need not worry for my safety.*

Your confidence is so reassuring, Tobias quipped as he eased himself free of Eira's iron grip and slid down Smoke's ruby back. His legs, numb from sitting in place for so long, buckled beneath him, and he steadied himself against the dragon's side.

Eira jumped down with a yelp, promptly toppling into a sizable clump of snow as soon as she touched the ground. Tobias snorted. Red in the face, she scooped up a ball of dirt and snow and flung it at him. It pinned him square in the chest with a dull thump. "Not a word of this to anyone," she said with a pointed look as she got to her feet and straightened the front of her blouse. His satchel still dangled from her shoulder.

"I would never dream of it." Tobias nodded stiffly but his lips twitched with a smile. "You are as agile as a cat in my mind, a thief who always lands on her feet and whose claws never miss their target."

Another muddy snowball clipped the side of his face, leaving a dull sting in its wake.

Do not let your guard down, Smoke advised, a hiss of fire peeking out from his jaws. *A pair of cold eyes watch over this place. They have likely spotted my approach.*

A shiver trailed slowly down Tobias's spine. The warning brought an old myth to mind, a legend that spoke of Selini's servant spying on the world through a small pond. *A Head Drag-onborn?* he asked, suddenly feeling small and insignificant.

I cannot say. I do not sense danger from this place, nor have I fore-seen that disaster has befallen your companions, so I am certain it is safe. Smoke flattened his belly to the grass to meet Tobias's eye with one of his. *You must seek out the healer of Lumas. That is who Kiara and Caerul have gone with. He is a... strange man, but you should find it in yourself to trust him.*

"Trust him?" Tobias pushed upright, frowning at the old dragon. "What are you saying?"

Smoke fixed him with another one of those burning stares of his, the fire in his eyes almost enough to consume Tobias in its depths. *I am saying he is odd.*

Eira cleared her throat loudly, now standing poised at Tobias's side with her hands clasped behind her back. She tilted her head to the side. Her wind blown hair, now falling out of its circlet of braids, spilled over her shoulder. "Care to fill me in on your secret conversation?"

Tobias hesitated, a rush of awkwardness climbing to the surface at the reminder that Smoke had not established a connection with Eira. His mind reeled as he tried to put the pieces of his conversation with Smoke back together, weeding out what he could and couldn't tell her. However, before he could answer, a white dragon appeared low in the sky, flying straight toward them. Recognition flickered, and Tobias pointed at the dragon. "It's Faiera. She's coming this way."

Eira turned, the matter forgotten. Faiera's talons skimmed

the tall grass as she dipped lower. Her form became clearer the closer she got, and Tobias noticed on her back a figure draped in a thick, brown cloak. Once she was within a few feet of the group, Faiera's wings fluttered, and she settled herself on the ground, her small body nearly swallowed by the grass. Moonlight sparkled iridescently as it slid along her scales, and the elegant curve of her horns appeared more ethereal under the silver glow.

The figure swung down from Faiera's back with a practiced motion. A fur-lined hood obscured his face, but from his small stature and the bitter tang of herbs that followed him, Tobias guessed he was the healer of Lumas. He dipped his head low. "Caerul told me he could sense Stiria nearby. I'm glad you made it here safely," he said, his voice as small as he was.

Straightening himself, he brushed past them and made his way to Stiria, where he knelt with his hand against the dragon's mangled side. A faint blue light emanated from his palm, enveloping the wound in its icy glow. It shrank immediately, fading to nothing more than a faint scar where the scales had been torn off.

Eira stiffened, knife in hand and pointed at the healer's cloaked back. "Did Kiara send you out here to meet us in her place? She left us for dead!"

The healer turned to her, the milky pale skin of his nose visible beneath the hood. If the knife bothered him, he didn't show it. He didn't so much as flinch. "Yet you made it here safely," he said, a pleasant smile evident in his voice. "I am relieved to see that you both appear to be unharmed despite your fall. Perhaps the winter lord Sefah protected you."

Tobias's lip twitched at the thought. Protection offered by the cruel winter spirit was the last thing he wanted, especially in a place as vicious and cursed as the Aurora Range. Even though he knew very little of Calisitian legends, he had heard of the wrath of winter, which claimed that Sefah unleashed a plague upon the land that took the lives of countless innocents. "I'm not sure I want his help," he muttered.

"Either way, you shall have mine." The healer pulled his hood down, exposing soft blonde curls and a boyish face graced with a subtle smile. He had the pointed ears of an elf and a look of wisdom that didn't match his youthful appearance. With another quick dip of his head, one hand resting over his chest, he spoke again. "I am Unda, the healer of Lumas. It is as you guessed: I was sent by Kiara to meet you here and heal Stiria's wounds. If you would follow me, I will see that you are reunited with your companions."

Tobias's jaw went slack, his mouth left hanging as he stared in wonder at the relic of ancient times standing before him. The elves were said to have been slaughtered by the dragonborn, completely wiped out in the war waged against Selini's forces, yet here was one, alive and well, hidden away in the little town of Lumas. Thousands of questions raced through his mind, but his tongue froze in place. Dumbfounded, he could do nothing but stare in wonder. Eira held the same starstruck look in her wide eyes, her knife now laying forgotten at her feet.

I did say he was strange, Smoke mumbled. His tone resonated with arrogance and pride, as if he were taking credit for the elf's appearance.

Tobias ignored the old dragon's voice in his head. "You're an elf? But I thought that—"

"You're supposed to be dead!" Eira cut in. Though she voiced exactly what was on Tobias's mind, her bluntness made him cringe.

"I've heard that many times," Unda said plainly. He waved the subject away and turned his back on them casually, like they were discussing nothing of importance. "There were some that survived the slaughter, but I'm not sure how many besides me still live today. But that is all in the past."

Tobias opened his mouth to argue but thought better of it

before anything more than a strangled "uh" came out. He clamped his lips shut again and lowered his gaze. No, it didn't matter, and it was cruel to dredge up things that were painful to others. Never in his life did he imagine meeting an elf in person —it was childish to even dream of such a thing. They were little more than myths, fuel for the stories he used to spend all day reading and marking up. The tragedy had become so distant that it hardly seemed *tragic* to most people anymore. And yet it was a threat the dragonborn left hanging over their heads. Should they ever manage to swarm the human kingdoms again, to break free of the Summoners' enchantments holding back their numbers, they would ensure the same fate befell the humans.

Hesitantly, Tobias risked another glance at Unda, who was preoccupied with easing Stiria back to his feet. The fears racing through his mind did not seem to concern the elf. Serenity rolled off him like ripples over a pond, a calmness that was almost intoxicating. It was similar to the aura of Summoner Maven but less oppressive.

Once on his feet, Stiria gave off a low whistling sound and spread his wings. He bounded circles around the group, leaping over to Faiera and showing off his healed injury. She answered with a snort, seemingly unimpressed. Her reaction didn't deter Stiria, who continued prancing around, his fur-tipped tail whipping through the dry grass and patches of snow.

"Well then," Unda said, "we should get going." A thin layer of white frost covered his fingers, and his hands trembled ever so slightly when he reached to pull his hood down over his head again. He took a step forward and paused before glancing up at Smoke, who raised his head in turn. A moment of silence passed as they stared at each other. Finally, Unda dipped into a respectful bow before he spun away. He approached Faiera with clipped steps and climbed onto her back with the same practiced precision he had used to dismount.

Stiria sat waiting. Eira was already on her way to him, though she kept shooting puzzled looks at Unda. Tobias hung back, the warmth from Smoke's presence still pressed against him. The old dragon shifted, scales rustling against the earth as he moved. *It is safe to go,* he said. *Remember what I said before. You must not press Caerul.*

"I know." He couldn't remember grabbing the pin in his pocket, but the red jewel now bit firmly into his palm as he closed his fist around it. He tucked his chin into the neck of his coat, his gaze trained on Unda's small frame. "I feel coming to this place with an elf survivor was no coincidence."

Perhaps it is the will of the lord Sefah, as they say in Lumas. Smoke gave a snort as he rose to his feet. *I must leave.* With that, the thread connecting the two snapped. Smoke took to the skies, his brilliant red scales quickly swallowed by the darkness.

Tobias waited until he was out of sight to join the others. While he was reluctant to believe it was Sefah's will that his fate had been so twisted, he could concede that it was the will of *someone.* He could only hope that whoever was pulling the strings was not spinning them into some complicated trap.

15

CALIX

THE HEALER'S CLINIC WAS a modest building constructed of wood and stone, situated deep within the town near the administrative buildings. All was quiet, save for the murmur that floated from the guardhouse a little further down the street. Though the windows of the clinic were covered by white curtains, the warm light inside leaked out onto the street, casting long shadows across the ground. Due to the late hour, the roads were mostly empty, save for the patrolling guards who gave polite nods as they passed Unda. They didn't stare much at the dragons, but Tobias wasn't sure how long Faiera had been there already. Perhaps they were used to her presence, and one more of the same size was no big deal. *Or maybe they completely trust their healer. Their* elf.

Unda guided them to a stop outside the clinic and slid off Faiera's back. Eira and Tobias followed at his suggestion, and once they were on the ground again, Unda took the dragons' reins. He didn't even have to tug for the dragons to start following him. There was no hesitation or uncertainty in either of them. Tobias assumed that meant their Riders were safe as well.

"The two of you can head inside," Unda said, pausing by a corner of the clinic. "I'm going to show the dragons to the keep." When he met Tobias's gaze, the moonlight glittered in his crystal clear blue eyes. Though there was a softness to his expression, Tobias couldn't help but notice the predatory gleam that lurked beneath. His face was youthful and kind, the picture of an elf's grace, but his eyes were slit by vertical pupils—eyes of a dragon.

Tobias clamped his jaw shut, biting down on his tongue until he was certain Unda had left. He wracked his brain for some scrap of knowledge that would explain what he saw. Did the elves also have the menacing eyes of the dragonborn? He had never heard any detailed descriptions of the elves, and he hadn't had the chance to view any of the art that had passed down, as most of it had been destroyed in the war. What remained was stored in Calistie City, where a nobody from Floridus couldn't hope to see it. He did know, however, that a hybrid could possess those eyes, like Caerul did. But Unda had no other Draconic features.

Tobias's head was beginning to spin. *Smoke.* He reached for the thread that connected him to the dragon, but it was gone. Chilling silence lurked where Smoke had been, and it held no answers. Tobias's breath hitched. Unlike with Caerul, there were no illusory veils over Unda that Tobias could see, nothing that attempted to hide something about him. If he was a hybrid or a dragonborn in deep disguise, someone would know. Even if the people didn't, the dragons would know.

Smoke's words were ringing in his mind again. *It is safe to go... you should find it in you to trust him.* Though the old dragon was cryptic, his agenda had never been one that posed a threat to Tobias. He hadn't been wrong about Caerul. Was it unfair to think he was wrong about Unda, who had yet to do anything malicious?

All this because of his eyes. Tobias touched his forehead where a headache was beginning to form. *When did I become so fearful of little things?*

"Tobias." Eira touched his arm. "Looks like your mind is drifting again. We should go inside."

"Do you still have the letters?"

A puzzled frown settled on her lips. She reached for his bag and opened it, exposing their stash. "Of course. Why?"

"No reason." He turned with a shrug that did little to tame the nervous energy buzzing beneath his skin nor the suspicious quirk in Eira's brow. Still, he kept his thoughts to himself as he approached the door to the clinic. Voices drifted out from behind it—Kiara and Caerul, he guessed, and they were deep in conversation. Sighing, he swung the door open as loudly as possible to alert them to his presence. He couldn't be bothered to wait on them.

They stepped into the front room of the clinic, where the walls were lined with shelves of herbs and other medical supplies. It was a modest room, sterile in every sense, from the sharp scent to the obsessive neatness. Nothing was out of place. Even the row of cots against one wall was perfectly straight, blankets folded in such a way that there was not a wrinkle in sight. If it weren't for the fact that there wasn't a speck of dust to be found, Tobias might have assumed everything had gone untouched for some time. At the back of the room, a curtain hung over the entrance that led deeper into the clinic.

Both Kiara and Caerul were in the front room, with Kiara perched on the edge of a chair pulled up beside the cot where Caerul was seated, his back facing Tobias and Eira. A lone lantern on a table next to the cot kept the room lit.

As soon as she spotted them, Kiara jumped out of the chair, clutching a poster to her chest. Her hair was loose, spilling down her back in tangled waves that nearly touched her ankles. A loose gray tunic replaced her riding clothes. Her aura of authority seemed dampened, and she instead appeared like a small, frightened animal.

Caerul shifted on the cot to face them. His arm was wrapped in a white cloth, no longer broken. His piercing red eyes settled firmly on Tobias. A disdainful look twisted his features into an unpleasant frown and wrinkled brow. The haze of the illusion had completely fallen away, but it was still difficult to see the slight point of his ears beneath his unruly hair. Innumerable scars littered his exposed arm, however, and the back of his bare left hand was dotted with iridescent scales. If Tobias squinted, he could see the outline of scales peeking out beneath the bandages on Caerul's other arm as well.

Kiara stuffed the poster into her pocket. "Tobias, Eira. Welcome back." Her smile was strained as she searched their faces. She put one arm in front of Caerul in an attempt to shield him from prying eyes.

Tobias steeled himself and straightened his spine. Caerul's blood red eyes were almost sharp enough to pierce his heart. "That's it, then. You're not covering up the truth anymore."

"Stiria's too weak for illusions," he muttered. He shoved Kiara's arm away and pushed himself off the cot, ignoring the worried look she threw his way. He swayed a bit on his feet and steadied himself against the edge of the bed. "If you want to kill me, now is the best time. I'm tired, Kiara's tired, the dragons are gone. Don't waste your lucky shot."

"We can explain!" Kiara interjected, leaning over the cot to put herself between Caerul and Tobias. Caerul gently touched her shoulder and eased her out of the way. She clenched her jaw, her eyes wide with fear as they shifted to him, but she moved anyway. An understanding seemed to form between them, unspoken but something they both recognized.

Behind Tobias, Eira tensed. Even without looking, he knew her hand had gone to her weapons. "He's a—"

Tobias held up his hand, and surprisingly, she stopped

herself. Her words dropped off, but the whole room knew what it was she wanted to say. It was no secret anymore. Caerul was a hybrid, and everyone knew it.

He was right. It would be easy—too easy if Tobias was honest with himself. The blade at his side was more than sharp enough, and his feet were more than quick enough. He even wondered if Aviva's last resort spell could settle things, though he had no idea what it would do and what it would cost. If he listened to the whisper of fear in his ear, he could kill the hybrid and be done with it. And yet, reason breathed calm into his limbs and pushed out the burn of adrenaline that threatened to take control. Instead of reaching for his weapon, he pulled Kase's pin from his pocket. "I made a promise," he said, holding it up for Caerul to see. "To both Kase and Smoke that I would find you and that, when I did, I would make peace with you, not violence."

Caerul perked up, ears pricked as he leaned forward to examine the pin. It glittered in the candlelight, a ghost of something they both clung to. The tension in his shoulders visibly loosened.

Tobias took a deep breath. The small room suddenly seemed too small, the walls closing in on him the longer the silence persisted. Cautiously, hesitantly, he asked, "You're Calix, aren't you? The kid Kase was trying to protect?"

Kiara stiffened, more unnerved by the accusation than Caerul—or Calix—himself. She opened her mouth, an argument burning in her eyes, but held her tongue. Defeat crushed the vicious spark in Calix's expression, and he looked away, head hanging in shame. With his shoulders hunched, arm bandaged and pinned against his chest, he did appear small. He was still a child, despite his bond with his dragon, despite his half-breed blood, despite everything. Pity snagged Tobias's heart. He was no monster. He was a kid.

"Kase gave me that name," he whispered. He ran his thumb

absently over the hidden scales on his arm. "*Calix.* He told me it was something to treasure, but I don't deserve it."

"Why did you lie about your name?" Tobias crept closer, keeping his steps light and his hand away from his sword. Calix didn't look up as he approached, but he could feel Kiara's stare digging into his skull. "I've been looking for you. Kase told me to find you."

When he was mere inches away, Calix lifted his head. His mouth was set in a thoughtful frown. He and Kiara shared another glance, and he took one of the posters from her pocket. The thick paper was wrinkled from being stuffed away, but he carefully unfurled it and held it up to the light for Tobias to see.

An unflattering rendition of Calix's face was sketched onto the paper beneath the word "wanted," which was scrawled in bold text at the top. *Wanted,* it read. *Former apprentice* Draconis Aitlas (*Dragon Rider*) *Calix, a dangerous young male hybrid, for the capture of Crown Princess Kiara Ateléaria. All information should be reported to Lord Cassius Vyrn and the Calistian Guard.* The rest of the words blurred into meaningless scribbles the longer Tobias stared. A dull headache formed at the base of his skull, and a sinking sense of dread settled in his gut. He ran his tongue over his dry lips to collect his thoughts. "So you're… a wanted criminal in Calistie?" The words were too heavy even as he spoke them, and they seemed to drop like a stone between him and the two. His gaze slid to Kiara, who was still standing rigid and fearful beside Calix. "For kidnapping the princess…?"

"It's not true!" she snapped. She snatched the paper from Calix and tore it straight down the middle. "He didn't *kidnap* anyone; we fled together. He was being hunted. I chose to leave with him." For once, her voice was trembling. There was genuine fear in her gaze as she met his, a pleading look that begged for her words to be heard. Yet she quickly looked away, her voice dropping to barely more than a whisper. "You must understand. Cassius is lying. We couldn't risk Calix or myself being exposed for anything. If they catch us, they'll kill Calix and I'll…"

"So you admit you're Princess Kiara." Tobias sank onto the cot. The world was spinning, and his mind was racing to keep up with it all. Calix's secrets were one thing; hybrids were known for their ability to sneak into human towns on the rare occasion, and the news that the Calistians wanted his head on a pike for something he had done—or not done—was nothing new. But the idea of the heir to the Calistian throne standing a mere breath from him, the idea that he and Eira had plotted to throw her into battle against an almost unkillable monster, the idea that they had dragged her to Sefah's frigid grave in search of a nightmare and had almost gotten her killed… that drove a blade straight through his heart. Guilt took hold of the hilt and twisted it sharply.

He was waist-deep in secrets now, and the waters were steadily rising. It was only a matter of time before he was drowning in them.

Eira's knife clattered to the ground. She was still standing dumbfounded by the door, her mouth agape. It opened and closed several times, working to form some sound which never came out. Instead, she dropped into a low bow, bent at the waist. "Your Highness. I–I had no idea." Her words tumbled into one another in a rush to get out. "All this time, you never told us?"

Kiara winced. "I had my reasons. I couldn't be sure we could trust you."

"And why are you telling us now?" Tobias pressed. The pin dug into his palm as he closed his fist around it. "You're the one that left us out there. I can't say that was a gesture of trust, so I don't believe much has changed."

"Because I advised her to."

Tobias swiveled to face the front entrance just as Eira scrambled out of the way. Unda stood in the doorway, a cold wind blowing in from outside. He stepped in and threw the door shut, sealing out the frigid air. As he entered the room, he carried himself with an air of assurance, instantly quelling all the warring confusion and betrayal swirling in Tobias's mind. Though his voice was small, so soft it was easy to miss, it carried the weight of the world. He slipped out of his cloak and hung it over a hook by the door. Without it, he suddenly looked vulnerable and fragile. When he turned back to them, he folded his hands in front of him, ears pricked and waiting for a response.

Tobias's tongue froze to the roof of his mouth. Even if he wanted to give one, his mind was blank, filled only by a low buzzing that rang in his ears.

When no one spoke, Unda shifted, closing one hand tighter around his wrist. "Kiara and Calix are being hunted by Calistians. However, Calix is also hunted by another. They have survived this long on their own, but they can't continue this way forever. It is logical to assume that they will need assistance and protection. The four of you are already traveling together, so you might as well be open with one another."

"Who else is hunting Calix?" Tobias asked, but some part of him already knew the answer. The image of the dragonborn burned itself into his mind, and his gaze slid to the letters hidden in his satchel at Eira's side. There were too many pieces, but he could feel them slowly beginning to slot together.

Eira cleared her throat awkwardly, fiddling with her skirt. "Aurum," she said. "He told me killing Kase would bring the hybrid out. So…" She lifted her face. The horror in her expression was clear as day. "*You're* the one he's looking for."

Calix shrank back into himself and sank onto the cot. His head bobbed in a tiny nod, the smallest hint of agreement. Nothing more was needed. He was the dragonborn's prey.

"That's why we must continue our search for the Shadowslayer," Kiara said, and she sat beside Calix. "We must get to the bottom of this plot and stop Head Dragonborn Aurum before he kills Calix. If you want to report our activities to the guard, I won't stop you, but please let us see this through to the end."

In spite of himself, Tobias looked again for Eira's approval. Her lips were pinched, her brow furrowed and wrinkled as she lost herself in thought. When she finally met his eye, she gave a small nod. They wanted to stop Aurum just as much as Kiara and Calix, and the Calistian princess was their best shot at killing him. Turning her over to the guard would only put them back where they started but now without Oliver's support. They couldn't do it alone—no one could.

Taking a deep breath, Tobias released the sharp threads of anxiety that tried to cut his skin. The pin in hand glittered with lantern light, a warm reminder of the promise he had made to Kase. "Alright," he sighed. "Let's focus on the dragonborn."

16

PROMISES KEPT

BEFORE BEING USHERED to bed by Unda, Tobias stopped Calix to give him the pin. He froze at the sight of it, his beastly red eyes turning watery. Gingerly, he accepted Kase's dragon keeper pin and studied it under the lantern light. A faint, shaky smile settled on his mouth. "I miss him," he whispered, and his voice broke. "He didn't deserve to suffer."

"I know." An ache formed in Tobias's chest, the weight of grief crushing his shoulders as he tried to straighten and face Calix evenly. "He was a good man. I only knew him for a short while, but I could tell he cared about you. I promised him I would give this to you. He never mentioned that you were…" He trailed off, fumbling for a polite way to phrase the truth. He had never considered what to call a hybrid—he had never spoken to one at all.

Calix snorted with laughter and wiped his eyes, his sadness dispelled as he managed a sly smirk. "You can say it. Half-breed, hybrid, it doesn't matter. I've heard it all, but I'll always be Calix."

Calix. Tobias rolled the name around in his mind, testing it on his tongue. It wasn't Draconic by any means, taking root in something else. "You say Kase gave you that name. What about Caerul?"

He froze. When he looked at Tobias again, there was a touch of something else in his eyes, something frightened. "Caeruleus is what my *parents* named me." His lip curled and he spat the word with venom, teetering on a snarl. "I don't remember when it started, but Kiara called me Caerul. It… stuck around, but only for her. I never meant for anyone else to use it."

There were countless things Tobias wanted to ask, and he could have spent the whole night grilling Calix about his past: how he met Kase, why Aurum wanted him dead, how he ended up at Talia's school and how he left, how he met Kiara, and so many other things. However, exhaustion was etched into Calix's face almost as clearly as if the word was written on his forehead.

"You should get some rest." Tobias reached to touch Calix's shoulder and thought better of it, glancing at the scars that decorated his arms. No child should have that many, and they didn't have the same rhyme or reason that battle scars did. Instead, he stuffed his hands into his pockets. "I think Unda is preparing a bed for you."

Calix only nodded. With a lazy wave, he shuffled to the back of the room and disappeared behind the curtain.

Only after he, Unda, and Kiara had left did Eira approach him. She slipped the satchel over her head and held it out. Anger and disappointment twisted her features into a sharp frown, her glare like daggers turned against him. "You knew and you couldn't tell me?" she snapped. "Do you know what his people have done? He's a monster, Tobias—and a criminal at that!"

Her tone was painfully accusatory, and it threatened to break the more words she spat at him. He bristled, a retort forming automatically on the tip of his tongue. *Of course* he knew what the dragonborn had done. Everyone in Anticuus knew that they were called monsters for a reason. If it hadn't been for Smoke's intervention, he would have outed Calix the moment he realized the truth. If it weren't for his promise to Kase, he would have told Eira back in the mountains. It hurt that he couldn't, it hurt that he was forced to bury his fears, to see past the nightmares that haunted him. His mother's blood was on the hands of hybrids. They were the reason his sister was forced to grow up so fast, leaving him in the dust. They were the reason he took up the sword even after dreaming that his only weapon would be his words and his pens. All at once, everything he'd worked so hard to ignore was dragged to the surface again, and he burned with the need to correct Eira's perception of him.

But he didn't. Instead, he snatched the bag from her outstretched hands. Paper crinkled inside as he pinned it against his chest. It was their key to understanding Aurum's plot, and he wasn't going to let it go—not until he forced the puzzle pieces together.

"You don't have to stay," he reminded her. "You've done your part. You deserve to be free of this mess. But I can't let go yet." He glanced at the curtain through which the others had disappeared. There were still people he could protect. "Besides, do you really think he kidnapped the princess?"

"I don't know anymore. That's the problem." Eira folded her arms and chewed her lip, her brow creasing as she took on a more thoughtful expression. "I had heard the princess went missing some time ago, but I was..." She trailed off, and it seemed a realization dawned on her. Quietly, she added, "I was with Aurum at the time. The political concerns of my homeland meant nothing to me, and I couldn't even remember having cared about the princess either—personally or otherwise. It's not as if I grew up in the capital where she was on display."

"I think there's more to the story, and we can afford to offer a little grace," Tobias said. He offered a small smile when she met his eye. "Just like there was more with you. For now, however, we should get some rest."

She searched his face in silence, a guarded frown on hers. Finally, she nodded. "You're right." The words fell flat, void of any real belief in him. However, she left it at that and ducked behind the curtain before he could say any more. Unda's voice greeted her on the other side. They spoke briefly before their footsteps trailed off down the hall.

Tobias hesitated a moment longer. The scent of herbs was overpowering, burning the back of his throat with a myriad of bitter smells, but it brought back memories of his brief stay in Aviva's cottage. The letters crinkled again—he hadn't realized he was holding them so tightly until his arm began to ache. As it always did when he was finally alone, that nagging wriggle of doubt returned. *Am I making the right choice?*

The empty room gave him no response, nor did his cruel mind bring up any of Talia's wise words to fill the silence. She was too far for even his subconscious to reach, oblivious to the puzzle before him. For once, he was left alone with his thoughts.

Shaking his head, he swiped the curtain aside and stepped through the doorway.

Sunlight streamed through the window and fell upon Tobias's tightly shut eyes. It was only a gentle brush, the barest kiss of light against his skin, but it managed to wrench him from the threads of sleep. He groaned, throwing his arm over his face and rolling over to block out the light. But it was too late. Sleep had already been snatched from him by the brightness. With a heavy sigh, he resigned himself to his fate and sat up.

Unda's home had been dead silent when Tobias had crawled

into bed. Now, lively chatter drifted down the halls along with the pleasant smell of freshly baked bread. Tobias's empty stomach growled in anticipation. He untangled from the blankets and practically tripped over his own feet getting to the door.

After taking a moment to comb his fingers through his hair and at least pretend he looked presentable, he stepped into the quaint hallway. Kiara's voice was the clearest as she prattled on about ancient Calistian history, readily spilling a famous story about the elves and dragonborn racing to catch a unicorn. "It was the spark that started the second war," she was saying. "The unicorn was claimed by the dragonborn after Aurum brutally beheaded the elf queen's representative."

"Do you really believe that old story?" Eira chimed in, spoken around a mouthful of food. Even the rolling of her eyes was obvious in her voice.

"It's true. The palace has records—no, there's a living record right here. Unda, tell them it's true!"

Unda gave a laugh, awkward and a little strained, but he didn't interject.

"It's not a guessing game. The answer is pretty obvious," Eira continued. "Aurum is cruel and deranged, and he'll do whatever Selini asks him to do. If she says the elves have to die, he'll be the first in line to start killing. That's all there is to it."

Tobias found his way into the kitchen and adjoining breakfast room just as Unda sank to a seat at the table. His pointed ears—still real and not a stress induced hallucination Tobias had dreamed up the previous night—were turned down. His smile faltered. "I wonder," the elf said, "if that is truly the end of it."

Eira was seated across from him, her plate full of bread and various meats, cheeses, and fruits from all over the table. She raised a questioning brow in response but kept her mouth shut.

Kiara was perched in the seat next to her, leaning forward with wide eyes like a small child being told the most fascinating story. Calix sat beside her, his chair pulled close to hers as he carefully braided her long hair. He was already halfway down her back and seemed more interested in his task than in the food in front of him. Some of the color had returned to his skin, and he sat straighter than he had yesterday. His bandages were gone—it seemed the healer had made quick work of him. Yet, despite the kindness he had been shown, his gaze was sharp any time it drifted back to Unda. Something accusatory and uncertain lurked there, but he turned back to braiding before it could linger long.

None of them seemed to notice Tobias's presence in the entryway, so he hung back for a moment longer.

"Do you know something else about the unicorn hunt?" Kiara asked. "Something the records don't say?" She leaned so far forward that it was a wonder she hadn't yet face planted into her breakfast. Maybe it was her royal grace that protected her, though it was hardly evident from the scene.

Eira nodded slowly. "It could even help us better understand what Aurum is planning. Or at least how he thinks."

"That is ancient history," Unda said. His tone was gentle, but there was an immovable firmness in his gaze, a darkness that lurked beneath that sea of blue. "Some things are best left in the past. There are facets of history that would do well to be forgotten. I won't go digging them up for your amusement."

Defeated, she slouched back in her chair, her royal grace forgotten. "If that is best." Her words were accepting, but her tone was rife with disappointment.

Eira stabbed her fork into a chunk of apple, a sly smirk on her lips. She wiggled the apple at Kiara. "You need to get your head out of those old legends. How many do you have stored up there? Is there even any room for anything else?"

Kiara sat up, jaw hanging open in an argument that never came. She shut her mouth, her eyes narrowed at Eira. Instead of taking the bait, she turned to her own plate of breakfast, which was mostly empty. "It is my duty to recall the rich history of my country, and much of it is not something I wish to see repeated."

"Duty this, duty that." Eira rolled her eyes and shoved the apple into her mouth. "You make it so un-fun to argue with you."

"Unentertaining?" Kiara supplied.

"Don't patronize me."

Tobias cleared his throat, which startled both Eira and Kiara. He smiled awkwardly when they turned to look at him. The level of comfort and familiarity that had developed between the group in such a short amount of time was striking. It seemed to be completely void of the hostility that lingered the night before, but perhaps he was only gleaning what was on the surface. Calix had yet to look up from Kiara's braid in his fingers, his movements slow and awkward as he worked with his newly healed arm. He hadn't spoken a word and seemed so small in his seat that it was too easy to overlook him. Perhaps that was the cause of the peace in the room—he was almost forgotten.

"Tobias, so glad you could join us." Unda stood and greeted Tobias with the quick dip of his head. Today, he wore a blue scarf wrapped around his neck, pinned in place by a small silver clasp. "I hope you slept well."

Eira tilted her head back to look at Tobias, scrutinizing him. "Must have since it's almost noon."

Tobias's face warmed. "I was tired." Maybe that would explain the familiarity that wasn't there when he went to sleep —he had missed several hours of conversation.

"If you're hungry, help yourself to anything you like. I'm sorry for the odd assortment of things. I must admit that I'm not familiar with what humans normally eat and when." Unda cleared his plate, which he had barely touched, from the table and offered his seat to Tobias. "Though, if you don't mind, would you bring your satchel to me so I can take a look at the letters you collected?"

"Letters?" Tobias looked pointedly at Eira.

She shrugged. "I asked Kiara if she would look at them, and he overheard. He just wants to see them."

"I'm curious about this connection you have drawn between the shadow ghost and Aurum." Unda smiled, but it looked broken and forced. "It's pure curiosity, that's all."

If there was one thing Tobias understood, it was curiosity. He could never resist its pull and had found himself in many troubling situations because of it. An inch of understanding formed between him and the elf, a connection that he hadn't expected to see in someone so alien. "Of course," he said. "I'll go get them."

He left the room in awkward silence and returned with the satchel in hand to the same stifling quiet. All eyes were on him as he cleared a spot at the crowded table and spilled the sealed letters, scrolls, and other stolen things onto the surface. The wax faces of Selini stamped onto the letters sneered at him, and he looked away before his mind could wander too far. With an awkward gesture, he stepped back so that Unda and the others could examine their loot. Calix gingerly lifted a paper from the pile, but quickly dropped it as if it had burned him. He returned to tying off Kiara's braid with a cord, but his hands trembled as he worked this time, his eyes glued forcefully to what he was doing. Unda took one of the sealed envelopes and turned it over, examining the old, yellowed paper.

"Eira and I thought these might be useful, so we grabbed as many as we could from the camp," Tobias explained. "They have the seal of the Head Dragonborn and the same signature that Kiara showed us, which we believe is Aurum's. It would be useful if they were translated though." With that, his gaze slid to Calix, who stiffened but refused to look up.

Following Tobias's lead, Eira also looked to Calix, but she

lowered herself so that she was within his field of vision and put on her best, most convincing smile. "Please? It would put that dragonborn blood of yours to good use—a noble cause."

He shook his head fiercely and pulled the knot in the cord tight. "No," he snapped, dropping the finished braid.

Eira rolled her eyes and straightened. "Don't be like that. You want Aurum dead as much as we do, don't you?"

"Of course he does!" Kiara interjected, twisting to put her body between Eira and Calix. The show only made Eira raise her brow in a condescending question, but she said nothing more.

Chewing his lip, Calix met Tobias's gaze with an apologetic look rather than an angry one. He ducked his head, his shoulders hunched. "It's not that. It's just that... I can't read," he murmured. "No one ever taught me. Kiara and I translated the last one with Stiria's help, but he hasn't woken up yet."

The silence that stretched between them this time was thick with awkwardness. Eira's cheeks slowly turned red. She shot out of her chair, mouth open in either an argument or apology, but neither came. The sound of a wax seal breaking was enough to banish the subject.

Tobias jolted and swiveled to face Unda, who was holding the opened envelope in one hand and unfolding the letter that had been inside it with the other. He scanned the page. His face slowly fell, an unmistakable, heavy sadness darkening his eyes the longer they lingered on the text. After a moment, he looked up and, in the blink of an eye, wiped his expression clean and dragged up his usual smile. He held out the opened letter to Tobias; it was decorated with the same Draconic text as the rest —signed at the bottom by Aurum as always.

"Thank you," Unda said. Frost bloomed across his pale skin in a thin layer. "I can't make sense of this text. You should have Stiria read these to you when he is ready." He left as soon as the letter was out of his hands, a trail of icy footsteps behind him.

Tobias watched him retreat until he was out of view. Though he wanted to offer the elf the benefit of a doubt, there was something about his words that rang false. For someone who couldn't understand what he was reading, he had lingered long on the letter, letting his eyes scan the whole page before he discarded it.

His eyes, which were eerily similar to those of a dragon.

17

THE WINTER SPIRIT

WAITING FOR STIRIA seemed to take an eternity. Due to the severity of his wound, he had been sleeping ever since Unda took him to the keep. Calix had gone out to be with him following their simple lunch and promised to return when the dragon awoke. Tobias and Eira, restless after Unda's strange behavior, had gone out to wander the town, claiming that they were going to buy supplies. Kiara wasn't sure what supplies they needed. They didn't even know where they would go from here, but she was glad that they were the ones going out and not her. The more she appeared on the streets, the more likely it was that someone would recognize her and her appearance in Lumas would reach the ears of Cassius. She was grateful for a moment to be alone with her thoughts.

Or at least, she thought she would be. She sat against the wall of Unda's clinic while he busied himself with a new patient. Her knee bounced restlessly, and her fingers tapped incessantly against her arms. She shifted to try to keep still, but somehow she always found herself repeating the same mindless action.

If Cassius found her, she would be forced to go home. If Cassius found her, she would be forced to listen to his sickly sweet words of flattery, his constant pressuring and praising and... She shifted again, this time wrapping her arms around herself and tucking her feet onto the edge of the chair to make herself as small as possible. A shiver trailed down her spine.

If Cassius found her, he would kill Calix and destroy any hope she had of stopping Aurum's plot, yet for some reason, that was not the thought that filled her with fear.

Across the room, a little girl from the village sat swinging her legs over the edge of one of the cots, filling the silence with the occasional soft tap of her heel against the wood floors. She and her mother—who stood at her side as still as a statue, lips pursed as she cast nervous glances at Kiara—had come in several minutes ago. The little girl boasted a large scrape up her forearm, one that dribbled blood but was mostly just angry and red. She couldn't have been much older than six or seven, and her face was puffy from crying, but her worries seemed to be forgotten the moment Unda knelt and took her scraped arm in his hands.

He cleaned her wound gently before spreading a thick salve over the affected area and wrapping her arm in white bandages. He tended her small wound with the same care and attention that he had offered Calix's, though there was no glow of magic in his pale fingers this time. For someone so powerful, he guarded his power religiously.

When he was done, the girl stood, testing the bandages with a wide grin. "It doesn't hurt!" she exclaimed, waving her arm excitedly.

The girl's mother touched her back. Even her expression had softened once the sight of blood was gone. "What do you say to Unda?"

She bent into an awkward bow and quickly added, "Thank you."

Unda smiled. He inclined his head to them in a silent acceptance. As the little girl hurried to the door, he exchanged a few quick words with her mother and pressed the small jar of salve into her hands, but their conversation blurred into the background.

The girl had stopped by the door and now stood staring directly at Kiara with curious dark eyes. She didn't break contact until her mother steered her away. It was barely audible above the creak of the hinges, but Kiara caught her whisper as she left: "That girl is familiar, Mama."

Kiara snapped her gaze down, shoulders tense until the door shut again. Lumas would only be safe for so long. Her time was running out.

"Is something on your mind?" Unda asked. He was watching her from across the room, pity etched so clearly into the lines in his face that her heart sank with shame.

She hugged her knees to her chest. Some of the hair around her face had slipped from Calix's careful braid and now hung awkwardly in her eyes. Sighing, she shoved the flyaways behind her ears. "I'm okay." Desperately, she scrounged for something that would change the subject and dissuade him from prying. "That girl seemed like she's been in your care before."

"Children are prone to injuries. It's a natural part of play."

"Were you a reckless kid?"

He laughed lightly. "My siblings were. I was often caught up in their troubles accidentally."

Kiara picked at a stray hair caught in the fabric of her pants. It came free easily, and she twisted it in her fingers, carefully avoiding his piercing blue gaze. "You left in such a hurry after asking for those letters. Is something wrong?" *And if you can read them, why didn't you offer to help?*

He let out a breath as he crossed to the island and wiped his hands on a small cloth that had been sitting atop the counter. In no rush to answer, he faced the shelves and reached for a small wooden box tucked away on the middle shelf. The lid creaked as it opened. He set it down on the counter with a decisive thud that rattled the contents inside. "I remembered I had work to attend to. I apologize if my reaction startled you. I was unnerved by the reminder of Aurum's violent behavior." His voice dropped into a low mutter, letting the end of his statement trail off with shame. He tucked his chin into the scarf around his neck to hide the frown that had settled over his lips. "It's hard to imagine someone can be so cruel."

"Oh," Kiara said, scrutinizing his back as he turned away from her. She flicked the strand of hair from her fingers. "I'm sorry to remind you of such things."

"The past is the past. It's my fault for clinging to it." He took a deep breath and straightened. "If I only choose to dwell on the things that hurt me, I'll never learn to move on from them."

Kiara stretched her legs, tapping the heel of her boot against the wood-paneled floors as she pondered his words. The way in which he said them sounded almost mechanical, like he had heard them a thousand times over and couldn't help but repeat them. She would have sounded the same if she were to speak of the many rules that guided her life at the castle. *Keep your head high, speak politely but firmly, do not let yourself be swayed too harshly by another's words, always be sure that your mind is your own*—even now, the words were ringing in her ears. If she hadn't locked her jaw, they might have slipped from her tongue and Unda would be subjected to their monotonous, repetitive drawl. Eventually, he too might have found himself saying those things in that defeated voice.

She fiddled with the hem of the gray tunic he had lent her. "You could read those letters, couldn't you?"

"I know a few words. It's not enough to convey anything meaningful to you."

"From your reaction, I assumed..." She let her sentence trail off, the rest of it choked from her by the thorns that pierced her heart. It wasn't her place to question an elf, especially not one who must have gone to great lengths to hide himself for so long.

But if he knew something else, why didn't he share? The letters were important not just to her and Calix, but to anyone who was running from Aurum. It could explain the missing Mages, the fact that Aurum wandered free outside of Hybrid Territory, and what the Shadowslayer was.

Unda was watching her again with that old, knowing look. If he searched hard enough, she was sure he could uncover all her secrets. "I think we could both use a distraction," he said and gestured for her to join him at the island where he had laid out small wooden boxes, neatly wrapped paper packages, and jars of medicinal supplies.

She hesitated, suspicion worming its way into her mind as her thoughts of Cassius were stirred once again to the surface. *He's not here,* she reminded herself firmly. *He doesn't even know you're here.* After she was able to take a deep breath, she shook her fears away and pushed out of her chair, straightening the front of her loose fitting tunic. She strolled cautiously over to Unda's side. "What can I help with?"

"If you could help me pull supplies off the shelves, that would be much appreciated. Things have gotten cluttered here and I need to take the time to reorganize."

Kiara frowned and surveyed the shelves. "Cluttered" was not the word that came to mind as she took in the neat rows of supplies, most of which were labeled precisely and dated to make it easier to manage his stock. Nothing seemed out of place, but she knew better than to argue. Instead, she simply agreed with a nod. She turned and reached for the shelves but stopped short, her outstretched hand hovering in front of the closest shelf. The holes where he had already taken things down were scattered randomly across the rows. Rather than starting on one end and pulling everything off as he went down the line, he seemed to be cherry picking items based on some imaginary list that she didn't have.

"Is there a specific order to the things you're pulling out?" she asked.

"Oh." He paused and examined what he had laid out on the island countertop. "Dry herbs."

Kiara pursed her lips.

"Those with a sweet scent?"

The muscles in her face ached from how tightly she was scrunching her expression in a very obvious show of confusion. He met her squinting stare with an equally confused look, though his was more graceful, with one brow raised and his lips pinched in the tiniest frown. With a sigh, she shook her head. "I really don't know what I'm looking at here."

She had never spent lengthy amounts of time in the castle healer's office, much less learned anything about medicinal materials. The only times she could remember having gone to see the court healer was when she had scraped her knees as a child or the one time she spilled hot tea on herself and ruined her favorite lavender colored gown. Calistie castle's healer dealt only in magic; his assistant handled all the non-magic procedures as it was a less requested service in the court. He always seemed displeased to see her, one of the only royal servants who wasn't falling over himself to eagerly meet her needs. On the off chance she visited him, she itched to leave as quickly as possible, and he seemed just as restless to get her out of his wing in the palace.

Even during her short time at the Dragon Rider school, she couldn't remember ever having visited the infirmary, and her class on first aid and healing was one she often dozed off in—though admittedly, the memory made her cheeks warm with embarrassment and shame. She placed too much confidence in Faiera's natural gift of healing, assuming back then that she would never need it anyway.

Unda swept past her and ushered her to the island. "Why

don't we switch jobs then? Check the dates on the items I hand you. If anything is older than a few months, set it aside."

"That I can do."

Time passed quickly as she examined the small jars of herbs Unda handed to her. They were marked with a date scrawled on a piece of paper stuck to the lid. His handwriting was delicate and near-perfect, and she envied its beauty. He had the slender hands of a writer or a scribe, and she wondered if he was used to working with paper more than he was with medicines. Since he was a being who had lived a long life, perhaps he dabbled in more than one job.

She turned one of the jars over in her hand. It was marked from two winters ago, so she added it to the small collection of older herbs. "I thought it was too cold near the Aurora Range for much to grow," she said. "Do you travel to collect most of this?"

"There are a few traders who come here on occasion with the plants that won't grow in the cold, but I do travel some." He gave a small laugh. "I travel more than the people would like, but they are well protected in my absence. Despite the weather, there is not much sickness here. The people of Lumas believe they are blessed by the winter spirit, Lord Sefah."

Kiara perked up at the mention of Calisite's seasonal spirits. She spun to face Unda. Excitement fluttered in her stomach like thousands of butterflies. "Are they?" she breathed.

The tiniest hint of a knowing smile was all the pale elf offered before returning to the wall of shelves. Two silver rings, one on each hand, glinted in the lantern light as he reached for another small box. It opened with a squeak. After a quick look at its contents, he closed it and put it away. "It is hardly my place to say for sure. However, if nothing is protecting this place, how is it that the Shadowslayer has never come here despite being holed up within the mountains?"

"He's hunting magic, but there's nothing of significant power to attract him here," she said. "Besides..." She wrapped her arms around herself and threw her gaze to the ground to avoid that piercing stare. Uncertainty squirmed inside her, and her hands itched for the comfort of a weapon that would protect her as the shadowy ghost's masked face surged to the front of her mind. *I killed him,* she wanted to say, the words on the tip of her tongue, yet her mouth remained shut. She'd thrown the knife at him, pierced him with the magic-sucking black blade, and he'd fallen from the sky and disappeared into the shadows. But how could you kill something that had already died?

She steeled herself and met Unda's waiting gaze. "Besides, if Sefah is protecting this town, why did he let the Shadowslayer settle in the mountains in the first place? Aren't they the heart of the territory he controlled when he was alive?"

"It was the people Sefah loved, not the place." Unda fiddled with his scarf again. His voice dropped to a murmur as he added, "It is the people his spirit would protect. It is natural for beings to want to protect others." He paused, his eyes distant. "If the dead are also trying to protect something, what do you suppose the Shadowslayer is protecting?"

Kiara bristled, disgust curling her lip. Sefah, like the other seasonal spirits, was made to serve Anticuus by its creator. His physical death was a tragedy in the history of Calistie, but he was immortal and thus it was supposed that his spirit lived on in the icy cold. He wasn't like the dark magic that swirled endlessly around Sheniir's monster. Despite the myths, despite the unforgiving nature of his power, Sefah was a force of good. The comparison left a bitter taste in her mouth. "The Shadowslayer is a curse created from the evil of a dead man," she spat. "He doesn't have the same autonomy nor heart that Sefah's spirit does!"

Unda remained as eerily calm and composed as ever, save for the crackle of ice spreading across his fingers. Kiara shivered at the sudden chill in the air.

"All magic has a purpose." Unda curled his fingers into fists. The ice snapped against his skin and fell away, turning to glittering blue sparks before it hit the ground. "Consider the purpose before you rush headlong into conflict with it."

"You're defending the Shadowslayer?" she sputtered.

"I'm saying that you must see past the obstacles in front of you if you want to unravel the truth."

She stared at him blankly until the chill died down, but even then her mind was painfully empty. All she could remember was the way her grandfather used to complain about the strange way in which the elves spoke of things, always dodging the point of what they were saying. Ancient dragons were much the same; immortals were said to love puzzles because they had an eternity to unravel them. It was why the records written by the seasonal spirit Xenah were hated by so many historians—he never spoke plainly about the things he wrote. Similarly, Unda felt no pressure to be frank with her. He was already returning to work before she could string together a response.

Luckily, she didn't have to come up with anything to say. Calix barged in from the back door, flinging the curtain out of his way. He leaned against the wall, bent over to catch his breath. Excitement shimmered in his ruby eyes, and a wide grin split his lips when he tossed his head back. "Stiria's going to read the letters."

Kiara was already halfway to the doorway before she remembered she had left her work unfinished. She paused and glanced at Unda apologetically. His usual smile had returned. Gone was the strange, cryptic stare, the abyssal depths that threatened to drown her. "Go," he said in that soft voice. "I'll be fine here. I'll send Tobias and Eira your way when they return."

With a nod, Kiara hurried to Calix's side. His smile was brighter than the sun, and the warmth in his hand when he took hers was more than enough to banish the cold creeping through her bones. The truth was within reach. All they had to do was grab hold of it.

18

DEAR TENIREL

Excitement, anticipation, and dread drove Calix from the clinic the moment Kiara's hand was safely nestled in his. He couldn't get away fast enough, especially not when he couldn't shake the nagging sense of familiarity whenever he looked at Unda's face. But even escaping that for a time was not enough of a promise to bring his thoughts to harmony. His whole body thrummed with the cacophonous melody of fear and a pinch of eagerness. Heat rose to the scales on his arm, hot enough to singe the skin around them. He bit the inside of his cheek to keep from mentioning it to Kiara.

The truth. You need to know the truth, and so does she. You have to know what Aurum is doing. The prickle of *wrongness* that crawled through his skin had lingered long before the death of Kase and remained even after. Something was coming. He had to know what it was.

His skin itched. He gripped Kiara's hand tighter to keep his nails from raking his flesh. A ringing settled over his ears, drowning out the sound of his boots slamming against the pathway as he ran, consuming even the sounds of the wind rushing past him and Kiara's measured breathing behind him.

Her fingers curled around his palm, returning the grip that he clung to her with.

"It's okay," she said. "I'm right here with you."

He tried to smile again, but his mouth refused to follow the motions. All he could manage was an awkward grimace. The need to smile was gone. His bond with Stiria hummed as the dragon brushed against the back of his mind, breathing a calming chill into his body that eased the pain in his scales.

I am here as well, the dragon whispered. His icy power settled over Calix in a comforting, protective blanket. Confidence seeped down the bond. Though he knew it didn't come from his own mind, it quickly eased the tremble of anxiety that wracked his bones.

They cleared the edge of town and came upon the keep together, both breathless from the run. Shaky, Calix clung to Kiara's hand until he found the strength to stand on his own again. She smiled at him, her pale blue eyes glittering like a pair of diamonds. Her braid was coming undone, framing her face in wild strands of loose hair. When she nodded at the open door to the keep, he flushed and quickly looked away.

The dragon keep was similar to the stables for the horses, only it was built with larger creatures in mind. It was constructed of stone on the outside, and the ground within was packed dirt. So far outside the town, the dirt was soft, untouched by daily traffic though a path connected to the keep. A large pair of wooden double doors closed it off from the outside world and kept the warm air in; they creaked as Kiara and Calix pushed them open. Beds of padded straw and cloth were laid out for the two dragons, scraped into nests that were the perfect size for adolescent dragons. Faiera was curled up in one corner, her nose tucked beneath her tail and her eyes sealed shut with sleep. Her pearlescent scales glittered in the faint evening sunlight that streamed through the open doorway, her sides rising and falling peacefully.

Stiria lay stretched across his nest in the middle of the room with his wings folded awkwardly over his side. Only a handful of missing scales and a pale scar marked where the wound once was. Calix had dumped out Tobias's satchel at the dragon's feet before he left, frozen in a moment alone with the haunting image of Aurum's signature stamped everywhere. Golden eyes burned the back of his neck, always watching. They seemed fiercer when he had sat with the letters and papers which were spread all around Stiria. Among them had been Kiara's letter opener, a tiny blade he'd clung to for protection as he'd cut the seals.

Hesitantly, Calix strode forward now and picked his way through the sea of words, bending to collect the knife first. He handed it off to her in silence, grateful the moment its faint weight left his hand. The longer it stared back at him, the more his scars would burn. "It served me well," he said when the silence began to stretch.

She ran her thumb along the flat edge of the blade, tracing intricate patterns in its face. Inhaling deeply, she tucked the small blade away in a hidden pocket. It was always with her though there were few uses for it on their travels. "My father will be glad to hear it got some use."

"If we both live long enough to tell him, that is." Calix shuddered. Despite himself, his fingers found their way to the softness of Stiria's mane. He fell against the dragon's side, trembling with anticipation. The letters glared at him from the floor. Their glimmering gold seals sucked his newfound confidence out in one glance. Swallowing hard, Calix shut his eyes and buried his face in Stiria's mane.

Maybe he didn't want to know. It was better to live in ignorance, to let the ghostly masked man run wild and to pray to Taiyo that Selini's wrath would fade and he would be overlooked.

It was a fool's hope, a dream he could never have. Aurum

wouldn't stop until he was dead, and if Calix wished to kill him first, he had to know the truth.

Kiara's hand settled against his back. His breath hitched at her touch, and she quickly withdrew. "You don't have to do this, you know. If I find the right books, I might be able to translate them, but it will take me some time. No one is forcing you to—"

"Aurum won't wait, and I don't want to be clueless the next time I run into him." The thought of holding knowledge over Aurum's head lit the excited fire within him, but it was always fear that snuffed it out the moment he was able to taste it. Aurum's merciless sneer loomed over him, his black scales gleaming in the golden light of his power. What good did knowing his plan do if he was still too weak to overcome him? How did he even know there was anything worthwhile in the letters? His skin itched again, and this time, he dragged his nails across the burning flesh on his arm.

"Calix." Kiara grabbed his hand. Her pale eyes bored into his, her lips pursed and her brows knitted together with concern. She knelt beside him, still cradling his hand in hers. "I'm right here. Take a deep breath with me." She searched his face, and after a moment, she drew in a long, deep breath. He mimicked her. They held it for a moment before both exhaled slowly.

He took several more deep breaths before his mind began to still and the crawling anxiety receded. The ringing in his ears finally died down, allowing him to take in the sound of Faiera's light snores. Something cool touched his lap. Stiria had draped his tail over him, its fur-covered tip streaked with mud and dirt. A soft purr rumbled in the back of his throat as he stretched his neck and brushed against Calix's forehead. The ridges of his scales dug into Calix's skin, but not painfully so. It grounded him. He took another long, shuddering breath and sank against the dragon's side. "Thanks," he murmured.

Kiara let go and sat back on her heels. Sheepishly, she tucked one of the loose strands from her braid behind her ear. "You seemed excited earlier. When you came to get me."

"I thought I was." Calix rubbed absently at his arm. His scales were bound, hidden beneath a white cloth, but he could still see the faint outline of them against the fabric. They were the mark of his imperfection, a curse that garnered Selini's rage. The urge to swear inched its way to the tip of his tongue, but he clamped his jaw shut to keep quiet. There was no point in cursing out someone who wasn't there, nor his scales which he could not be rid of. He had tried to cut them out, and so had his father once or twice. The scars were all that remained as proof of their efforts. It was a sin he could not cleanse except with his death.

The words echoed with Aurum's voice, teetering on a mocking laugh. They swirled around him. No doubt, the letters would speak of the disgusting half-breed child who had slipped through his clutches, the blight who deserved to die to keep the blood of the dragonborn pure and strong.

Sighing, he began to comb his fingers through the fur on Stiria's tail—anything to keep them from digging into his arm. "I *thought* I was," he muttered. "But then it all came rushing back to me. I can't kill him, Kiara. He's a monster, and I'm his prey. Kase died because he tried to protect me. If I dig too deep, I..." The words caught in his throat as he lifted his head, and he bit his lip.

She was staring with the slightest frown on her lips and a little wrinkle in her brow that betrayed her thoughtfulness. The cogs in her mind were turning, always trying to decipher what he was trying to say before he said it, but it wasn't that which made him pause. It was the honesty in her gaze, the soft way that she looked at him. Kindness and loyalty were traits he had seen in very few others, but Kiara was a wealth of both. There was strength in the way she fought the Shadowslayer to protect him, in the straightness of her back and the grip she held over her sword. There was gentleness in the way she spoke to him, the way she held his hand when he was drowning and guided him out of the depths of his fears.

His mouth was bone dry, and he quickly shut it, wondering how long it had been left hanging open. *I'm afraid I'll lose you too.*

You can tell her, Stiria nudged.

"Caerul?" Kiara leaned in, her hand landing against his. The old nickname sent a shiver down his spine.

The huge double doors swung open, flooding the keep with dust and sunlight. Calix and Kiara startled and jerked away from each other. Eira and Tobias stood breathless in the open doorway, their forms silhouetted by the evening light that spilled over the snowy plains. Both of their faces were flushed as if they had run the whole way.

As usual, Eira found her voice first. She straightened and stepped farther into the small room. "Well? What do they say?"

"Sorry, nothing yet." Calix made a point of clearing his throat under her watchful stare and quickly scooped up one of the letters. Its seal had already been broken, and the paper was weathered and old. Some of the writing was smudged, but it was still readable—or so he assumed. The squiggles and lines meant nothing to him. The only thing he was able to recognize was the signature because Kiara had shown it to him before. Holding the paper firmly in both hands, he reached into his bond with Stiria and twined the dragon's magic around his senses. Icy cold sank beneath his skin, and he focused the power on his eyes. The frigid air stung, but he blinked his tears away. Through Stiria's eyes, the squiggles became recognizable. A faint whisper flooded his mind, offering up their meaning. His head began to spin.

Calix licked his dry lips. "It opens with 'dear *tenirel.*'"

"Tenirel?" Eira wrinkled her nose and turned to Tobias. "Who's Tenirel?"

"It means little brother," Calix offered. "I've heard it said before. It's like a show of respect. A title? No. What's the word?"

Instead of helping, Stiria shifted to look at another letter. *They all open the same way,* he said. His voice floated through the chaos in Calix's mind as easily as a leaf drifted along the currents of a stream. He prodded one of the pages with his talons, dragging it closer to Calix's leg. *They are all signed the same and addressed to the same person.*

Cold dread settled heavily in the pit of Calix's stomach as he relayed the information to the rest of the group. He didn't know anything about Aurum's personal life, but he doubted *tenirel* referred to an actual brother. Instead, it brought to mind the fuzzy image of the other four Head Dragonborn, and his palms became slick with nervous sweat. He shuddered.

"But then," Tobias added, his fist pressed against his chin as he frowned at the ground in deep thought. "Why haven't any of these been sent out? Why does the Shadowslayer have *personal correspondence* between Aurum and his brother?"

Calix blocked out the question. The answer burned his tongue, branded on the back of his mouth, but he swallowed the urge to voice it. It went down his throat with the nauseating taste of bile, thick and sticky. He shrank closer to Stiria's side and looked at the paper again. It trembled in his hands, so shaky it was almost difficult to read. He skimmed the words, quickly absorbing the information through the whisper of Stiria's voice that brushed against his subconscious.

Slowly, it dawned on him. The letter detailed reports of kills made, magic drained from Mage corpses, progress made on an unnamed spell, and lastly, the hunt for the escaped imperfect hybrid: Calix himself.

The world closed in around him, pressing tight against his shoulders. His throat clenched, too small for the amount of air his lungs demanded. He thrust the paper away from himself and pressed closer to Stiria's side, fighting for a breath as his vision tunneled. Fluttering panic raced through his veins, and all that kept him from spiraling was the press of his nails against his scalp, the sting as he raked his fingers through his hair. "I can't," he rasped. "I can't. I can't do it."

Golden eyes loomed over him, boring into his soul with their piercing glow. Phantom cold nipped at his skin. The confused shouts around him dissolved into ceremonial drawl. Someone's hands closed around his, hot like burning coals with a grip strong enough to break his bones. He shrieked and thrashed until he broke free.

Calix. Stiria's cool snout brushed his cheek. His leathery wings closed around him, the thin membrane stretched between his bones just enough of a cover to shut out the visions that danced in his eyes. The dragon wrapped him in a protective embrace and held him still until order came to the world once more. *You're safe. I'm here.*

"These aren't conversational letters." Calix curled against Stiria's side, burying his face in his knees as he pulled in on himself. Tears slicked his cheeks—he couldn't remember crying —and his breath came in shuddering gasps as he struggled to breathe calmly like Kiara had shown him. "He's making reports to one of the other Head Dragonborn. They're coming for me. They're coming for me, Stiria."

19

UNINVITED GUEST

IF IT WEREN'T FOR STIRIA, who quickly wrapped Calix in his wings like a mother hen, the hybrid child probably would have bolted in his onslaught of panic. Tobias had tried to stop him, but Calix fought blindly and struck him in the jaw. The punch smarted, and Tobias flinched as he tried to rub the pain away, but it was already fizzling out as the weight of Calix's confession, quiet and muffled beneath Stiria's wings, slowly dawned on him.

A Head Dragonborn reporting to another Head Dragonborn. They weren't dealing with a rogue acting on his own—under the goddess's orders or not. They were dealing with a plot, one that involved more than a single dragonborn. It was no longer just them against Aurum and the strange ghost of Sheniir. It was them against Aurum, the ghost of Sheniir, and potentially all of Selini's forces.

Tobias's gut sank. Only Calix's erratic breathing could be heard above the stunned silence, and even that soon began to quiet. No one dared to speak. Tobias couldn't even lift his gaze from the letters, which had been scattered during Calix's fit and were now half-buried in dirt and straw. *Dear tenirel,* every one of the documents began, though Tobias didn't recognize the Draconic script. *Drekisn diem a, Aurum,* they finished, and this signature was burned into Tobias's mind.

Oliver was right. It was more than they could handle alone.

Kiara spoke up. "It's getting late. We should go back to the clinic." Though her voice was soft, it still carried that edge of importance and command. She bent down and gently brushed Stiria's wings aside.

Calix was curled into a tight ball against the dragon's scales, his face tucked into his knees. A slight tremor shook his shoulders, and he flinched when she laid her hand against him. Only when Stiria nudged him gently did Calix lift his head. The blue glow from his eyes was gone; now, they were wide and fearful, his slit pupils narrowed so small that they were almost lost in the blood red of his irises.

Tobias turned away and began to collect the scattered papers. He shook the excess dirt away before stuffing them in his discarded satchel. A thick stack of old letters appeared at the edge of his vision, and he looked up to meet Eira's shaky smile. She thrust them into the open satchel before stalking outside. After checking to make sure he had picked up everything, he slung the bag over his shoulder and hurried after her. The shuffling of footsteps behind him told him Calix and Kiara were following.

"We should talk to Unda." Eira shot a glance over her shoulder as she walked. "He might know something useful, like which Head Dragonborn it could be referencing and what that means for us. I don't know much about any of them besides Aurum."

"Aurum is the eldest," Calix muttered. He sniffled and wiped his face. Though he set his jaw and spoke slowly and firmly, it couldn't mask the slight tremor that still hung on his words. "The second is Stellae, the servant of the black-scaled head who acts as some sort of seer. Then there's the two girls, Foliis and

Ignis, one of which is dangerous for her beauty while the other is chaos in fleshly form. Since the letter is addressed to a *tenirel* instead of a *tenias,* it has to be Stellae or the youngest."

Tobias had no faces to match with their names, but a shiver raced down his spine all the same. His tongue stuck to the roof of his mouth, afraid to voice the question that rose steadily to mind. Without his sword to take hold of, his hand found its way to the strap of his satchel instead. He gripped it tight enough that the edge of the leather dug into his palm. "And the youngest?" he finally managed to ask in a whisper.

Calix chewed his lip and dipped his head, shaggy bangs hanging in his eyes. "No one knows anything about him anymore. At one time, he was the one blessed with the power of the goddess's eyes, but he seems to have... gone away?" He paused for a moment, taking another shaky breath, before he added quickly, "Vanished. He seems to have vanished."

Confusion stirred in the back of Tobias's mind. He stopped, boots scuffing the dirt path, and turned to Calix. The first question that he wished to ask was whether or not the myth was true, but Smoke's warning that a pair of cold eyes were watching him gave him pause. Instead, he shoved that question down and strung together another, one that was more pressing. "So which one do you think is the *tenirel?*"

"I don't know." Calix rubbed his bandaged arm, the heel of his palm digging into the scales hidden beneath. "I don't even know if the fifth—the youngest—still exists. It's not like I was —*desika,* the only one I got the pleasure of meeting was the great Aurum. If I'd stuck around for that *kahfl* ceremony, I'd have more to say, except that I wouldn't because I would be dead." He bared his tiny fangs at the toes of his boots, and it wasn't long before his explanation dissolved into a mess of Draconic that Tobias assumed was mostly swears.

Eira cleared her throat and grabbed Tobias's arm as she came to rejoin the group. "Are we assuming it's Stellae then?"

"No." Kiara cut in this time, her voice sharp enough to behead a man. "We aren't going to assume anything. We still need to figure out what role the Shadowslayer plays in all of this. Why would Aurum need some human legend-turned-real to do his dirty work for him? And if he's writing to Stellae, the second-most powerful of Selini's servants, why doesn't he ask for help? He wasn't asking, was he?" she added with a sideways glance at Calix.

He shook his head.

"It doesn't add up. I agree with Eira. We should talk to Unda." With a decisive nod, Kiara marched on ahead, her braid swinging behind her. She kept her head high, perched and ready for a crown, but her confident mask wavered as Tobias spotted the way her hands trembled at her sides.

The rest of the long walk back to the clinic was spent without a word. They stuck to the quiet backroads of the town to avoid unwanted attention for both Calix, who was slowly recovering from his panic, and Kiara, never far from his side. Knowledge made the satchel heavier, and it weighed down on Tobias's shoulder like a sack of dense rocks rather than letters. Though secrets were suffocating, nothing was quite as painful as knowing the truth. His whole body hummed with shock. An emptiness inside him yawned deep and wide to suppress the chill of fear in his fingertips.

Kiara led them to the back entrance of Unda's clinic. Her white cloak from the other day was strung up to dry on a line just outside the back door, along with other clothes and blankets. They fluttered in the crisp breeze, ghostly figures that howled at Tobias as he passed. Shadows stretched long over the back door. The sun did not touch the ground behind the clinic, and thick clumps of frost clung to the earth beneath their feet. Kiara and Calix approached the door, and it swung open without a sound as she took the knob in her hand.

She stepped through the doorway, shaking dirt and ice from her boots. "Unda!" she called. "We need to talk to you!"

Calix and Eira followed her inside, and Tobias shut the door behind himself to seal the encroaching darkness outside. The sun had disappeared behind the mountains; its last rays scrubbed out the blue of the sky with a deep crimson. It threw the empty kitchen into a wash of blood red. Voices drifted through the curtain that separated Unda's house from his place of work. One was a gruff man's voice, speaking in clipped, agitated phrases that blurred into the heat of anger before Tobias could make out the specifics. The other, quieter voice that answered belonged to Unda.

Confusion and intrigue twined into a mess of burning curiosity that banished the fearful chill in Tobias's hands. He motioned for the others to keep quiet and crept toward the curtain. The wooden floorboards creaked. He spotted Kiara close behind him, her face scrunched in concentration. Tobias pressed himself to one side of the curtained doorway and edged the cloth aside just enough to peer through.

Unda stood at the front door, his hand gripping it so tightly that his knuckles had paled to white. Ice locked the door in place, holding it to the floor at his feet and to his hand, his fingers covered in thick crystals of glittering frost. A tall, bulky man loomed over him, his dark hair crowned with a silver circlet. The blue cloak of the Calistian Guard hung over his shoulders, embroidered with the emblem of the crown over his heart. He shoved against the door, but it didn't move despite the powerful muscles in his arm.

Kiara's breath hitched. She pressed herself closer to the wall, her eyes wide. Tobias spared her a quick glance, but the conversation continued before he could address the growing fear in her face.

"I've told you already," Unda said calmly. The temperature in the room dropped to an icy chill that almost rivaled that of the

Sefah Mountain's air. "You cannot come inside. Your presence causes great stress for my patients."

The man sneered like some beast and leaned in, his other hand shifting to something at his hip—even without seeing the object, Tobias recognized the gesture. It was a sword. Instinctively, he reached for his own, fear sharply tugging his heart. His skin prickled when he remembered too late that his weapon wasn't with him.

"You have no right to keep me out," the man barked, self-importance creeping into his voice and raising it to a level that could be heard all the way down the street. He shoved the door again, but it refused to budge. "I'm the head of the Calistian Guard, overseeing the search for Princess Kiara and the monster that captured her, and I know you're keeping her here. You're nothing but a lowly healer from the slums. You have no right to bar me from her. I demand to see Kiara!"

Lord Cassius Vyrn, Tobias recalled from the posters he had seen around town.

A small gasp slipped from Kiara's lips, jolting Tobias out of his own thoughts. As soon as the sound left her, she slapped her hand over her mouth and backed away from the door on shaky legs. She shook her head, slow at first before it turned into a furious denial of what was said. "We have to go," she whispered, her voice breaking. "Right now. We can't stay."

"Go." Tobias pushed away from the wall. He met Eira's waiting stare and nodded firmly. "I'll catch up."

She hesitated, shoulders stiff and lips parted with an argument. As Calix and Kiara raced out the door, she shut her mouth and spun on her heel to follow. She had barely taken a step before she paused. Heaving a sigh, she wrenched one of her knives from her belt and marched over to him, pressing the hilt into his hand. "Don't do anything stupid," she said. When she turned this time, she left.

The press of the leather hilt against his palm lit a fire in his veins and bolstered his resolve. He waited until everyone was out and the door was shut before he flung the curtain back and stepped into the clinic, breathing in the scent of bitter herbs.

Wicked shards of ice had formed in the air around Unda, their razor-sharp tips pointed at Cassius. A blue glow surrounded the elf, tainting his sandy curls a deep cerulean. Though the lord towered over him, he regarded him calmly, his hands poised at his sides. Neither had noticed Tobias's entrance.

"Do you now?" Unda's voice dripped with barely concealed rage. "You *demand* to see her?"

One of the ice spikes grazed Cassius's jaw, and he flinched, pulling back away from the door. For a brief moment, his gaze flicked away from Unda and landed on Tobias behind him. A faint smile curled his lips as a flash of gold lit up his dark eyes.

Recognition and dread slammed into Tobias in a dizzying mix. He raced toward them in spite of himself and pried Unda away from the door. Standing face to face with the hulking figure of the lord, he could see the spiderweb of gold threads surrounding him. "Here!" he cried, slicing the magic threads with Eire's knife. "Cut here!" It passed harmlessly through them, but they shimmered as they reformed behind the blade's arc.

With the flick of his wrist, Unda sent one of his icicles flying through the threads. Magic clashed against magic, filling the air with a harsh crackling sound. The threads snapped, and Cassius's form wavered. As the ice spike pierced the porch behind him, he disappeared completely. A tiny, black dragon was left in his place, no larger than a small dog. It squawked at the spike and fluttered its tiny wings. Beady eyes swung toward them. The dragon let out a chortle before it flew off, its scales shining gold in the dying sunlight.

A black dragon, a beast that bore no magic of its own and was thus the perfect catalyst for spells—including a perfectly crafted illusion of a Calistian lord. An involuntary shiver shook him. The dragon's eerie black scales bore the same shadowy form as the Shadowslayer's cloaked body, and the flash of gold left in its wake spoke to the presence of the monster they were chasing.

Unda jerked free of the door, ice cracking as it released him, and spun away with a curse. "He knew if he frightened her, she would leave my protection and take Calix with her."

"I'm going after them." Tobias stalked back through the curtain and slammed Eira's knife on the kitchen table before he dashed back down the hall to the room where he had spent the night. His sword was still propped against the wall where he had left it, and the sight of it drew a sigh of relief from him. He snatched it up and tied the sheath to his waist before he ventured back out.

Though his heart hammered with fear in his chest and his mind was cloudy with the tumultuous whirl of information swirling inside it, he sprinted out the clinic's back door and left the freezing chill of Unda's icy magic behind. Gold threads lingered in the corners of his vision. It was unavoidable. Aurum had found them.

20

MESSENGER

AN ANGRY STITCH formed in Tobias's side. His legs burned as he ran. The world blurred around him, cold wind nipping at his face and whipping through his hair. It hadn't felt like such a long distance to the keep when he was racing Eira across the snowy plains, desperate to know the truth behind the letters. Now, it seemed like an eternity of road stretched between him and the end of it, and his muscles ached from being pushed to their limits. But the agony was nothing compared to the fear thrumming in his veins.

He burst out of the field of dry grass, stumbling to a breathless stop under the long shadow of the dragon keep. It took a moment to fill his lungs with enough air to find his voice. His tongue, dry as sandpaper, stuck to the roof of his mouth. He fumbled for his sword. Darkness swirled around his feet, licking at his pant leg. Swallowing a curse, he ran for the door of the keep. "Eira!"

The thief poked her head out the open doorway, brow creased with bewilderment. In the growing darkness, the lines of her face were hardened. "Tobias?"

Behind her, Calix and Kiara were busily saddling their dragons. Calix's movements were swift and precise, strapping the leather saddle to Stiria's back with ease. Kase's pin was attached to the saddle bag, half hidden beneath the flap. It glittered in the dim light.

Unlike her partner, Kiara fumbled with Faiera's straps, her shaky fingers struggling with the buckles and clasps. Gone was the powerful mask of a princess and a warrior, the one who could slay a dragonborn without mercy or fear. Instead, he was looking at nothing more than an ordinary girl. Whoever the real Cassius was, his mere presence was enough to break her.

"He was a fake. A spell put on a black dragon." Tobias slipped past Eira and took the saddle straps from Kiara's hands. He held them until she lifted her head and met his gaze with a wide-eyed stare. Trying to convey calmness and security, he took a deep breath to still the hammering in his chest. "He was never here, but Aurum is. If we flee now, we'll be leaving Unda's protection."

"There's no protection anymore," Calix said, approaching in clipped steps. When he snatched the straps from Tobias, his face twisted and he touched his arm—the one Aurum had broken. A muscle twitched in his jaw, but he tightened the straps and slid the buckles in place before Tobias had a chance to stop him. "If that dragon knows where we are, Aurum will, too. The elf's healing may be good, but he won't survive in a fight."

"He's sheltered us up until now. Smoke told me to trust him."

"You don't know Aurum like I do!" Calix snapped, and his red eyes flashed as he swung to face Tobias. "Nothing will stand in his way. We have to leave."

Tobias balled his fists. "He *wants* us to flee."

"We'll be gone before he gets here. I always slip through his fingers—that's why I'm still alive. If you want to put Unda in danger by staying, go ahead, but I won't have anyone else killed because they were protecting me." Calix's voice wavered. With a curse, he shoved away from Faiera's side and stuffed his hand into his pocket. Kase's pin, Tobias realized with a jolt, must have been hidden away there.

Kiara pressed her lips into a thin line, laying a hand against Faiera's side. She had stood by quietly while Calix argued for them to leave, and the fear had slowly bled from her features until she was able to school them again. Pushing her shoulders back, she gave a firm nod and tucked the loose strands of hair around her face back into her braid. Her now-pristine white cloak, which she had reclaimed from the clothes line, fluttered as she pulled it on. "I agree that we should leave," she said. Her hands were steady as she buckled her sword to her hip. "However, it's my duty to protect any surviving elves. We're not abandoning Unda."

Tobias let out a breath. It was fair enough. *Besides, if the elf comes with us, his protection will too.*

Calix, however, bristled at her suggestion and whirled to face her. "How do you intend to do that, Kiara? The dragons are small. They can't carry more people."

"We'll find a way!" Kiara argued, face flushed. She turned to study the dragons, and Tobias did the same. Both were watching inquisitively, heads bowed as they waited for a command.

No matter how much Tobias wanted to deny it, Calix was right. The ride was tight with just two people. Adding a third—even to Stiria, the larger of the two—would put them at risk. It would slow their pace as well, making it even easier for Aurum to catch them.

"Whatever we're doing, we need to leave," Eira said, still lurking by the open doorway. She glanced nervously outside.

Tobias raked a hand through his hair and released a sharp breath. The air between Calix and Kiara was tense, and it would take too long to come to a decision with both so high-strung. "We should at least tell Unda we're leaving," he said tightly, attempting to hide the uncertainty in his voice. "It's only fair to offer the choice to him. Maybe he'll flee on his own." Though he doubted that. The elf hadn't tried to follow him when he left, nor had he mentioned plans of escaping. He had a duty to Lumas. Tobias wasn't sure he would go even if he was the one being chased.

"I'll tell him. If he won't come with us, he should travel to Calistie City. They can protect him there." Kiara fished for a necklace hidden beneath her cloak and pulled the cord over her head. It was the green gem, Tobias realized with a jolt. The one she offered during their first meeting as a means to communicate with his sister Talia. It still hummed with magic, able to reach anyone who also possessed the spelled relic. When she caught him watching, she closed her fist around it. "Someone should escort him at least," she said. She motioned for Faiera, and the dragon flicked her tail as she sauntered toward the exit.

Something inside Tobias shriveled at the thought of leaving his only chance of connection to Talia in Unda's hands. *You'll see her again,* he reminded himself. *You know you will. But only after Aurum is defeated.* He would be able to face her properly then.

Calix was the first one out the door, right beside Stiria, who bounded along as if he had never been injured at all. In fact, both seemed completely restored, despite Calix's arm hanging awkwardly at his side and the tiny splotches of blood that were beginning to seep through the cloth wrapped around it.

As soon as Tobias stepped outside, the elongated shadows that blanketed the earth stirred and a figure rose from their depths. Wind whipped through his black cloak, tearing the hood from his head to reveal jet-black hair that fell in uneven, choppy lengths over his blank white mask. He came with the nightfall, darkness rolling from his form like smoke. The little black dragon from before swooped down from the starlit sky and perched on his shoulder. Kiara's necklace hung from its mouth, and it dropped it into the Shadowslayer's waiting hand, ignoring her cry of outrage. He crushed it in his fist as easily as if it were made of sand, scattering glittering flecks of green in the wind. The dragon's beady eyes flashed gold and it let out a hiss, baring tiny fangs that gleamed white in the moonlight—almost like it was smiling and laughing at them.

Stiria roared, scales lit with the glow of his magic as he summoned his icy breath. Threads of gold shot out from the darkness and bound his jaw shut before pulling him to the ground and tying him in place. Faiera shrieked and, in seconds, was tied down by the magical threads as well.

Blood roared in Tobias's ears. His hand shot to the hilt of his sword automatically. Stiffness consumed his limbs, crushing him from the inside out. His hand hovered mere inches from his weapon, and he strained against the invisible force pinning him in place. A quick sideways glance told him the same imprisonment had been forced upon the others as well. His heart leapt to his throat, and a wild panic sank its claws beneath his skin.

The Shadowslayer glided toward them, one hand stretching out from the folds of his inky cloak and reaching up to his face. It settled over his mask, which he pulled away. The moment it left his skin, twin black horns appeared on his head, curling up from his unruly black locks. Matching onyx scales covered the sides of his narrowed face and dotted the bridge of his nose. His lips curled into a malicious grin, fangs at the edges of his mouth. His eyes glittered gold like a pair of lavish rings, each dotted with the narrow slit pupil of a predator. His tall frame towered over all of them, a wall of strength and power that they quivered before.

Tobias's breath seized. Red flickered at the edges of his vision as he focused on the monster standing only a step away. He didn't need to ask, nor did the creature need to introduce himself. The signature that marked every one of the letters in his bag flashed through his mind. *Drekisn diem a, Aurum.*

They were never searching for two separate entities. Aurum *was* the Shadowslayer.

"Aurum," Eira gave a nervous laugh, the sound teetering on

the edge of tears. "I never knew you left the castle. Well, I mean, I guess I knew since you weren't there that day. I've been wondering where you went. I guess you like masquerading as local legends in your free time. You really could have told—"

Aurum was on her in the blink of an eye, grabbing her chin and jerking her toward him. She yelped but quickly swallowed the cry as his eyes flashed dangerously, glaring down at her. "I misjudged you," he said, voice rumbling from the very back of his throat. "I mistook you for a spineless coward, but I should have known you were a traitor, too. Is this how you think to repay my kindness? Stealing from me and siding with the *imperfect?*"

The heat of anger burned Tobias from the inside out. He begged his limbs to move, forcing his hand toward his sword. In his pocket, Aviva's paper charm burned. With an audible snap, his body lurched out of the magic's hold. All at once, his palm met the hilt and ripped his blade from its sheath. His body moved of its own accord, and in a blur of motion, he brought the blade down on Aurum's wrist; it sliced through with sickening ease. Tobias tasted bile on his tongue. The dragonborn's hand dropped to the ground at Eira's feet, limp and useless. Eira fell back with a shriek, scrambling away from the severed limb. The heel of her boot kicked one of the hand's fingers, and her whole body recoiled. Grabbing her arm, Tobias hauled her to her feet. Shaking, she clung to his back and hid her face in his coat, bunching it in her hands.

Tobias lifted his sword and pointed it at Aurum, despite the obvious trembling in his arm and the dizzying panic that had taken firm root in his mind. "Let us go. I'll return the letters, and we'll stay out of your way."

Calix's blood red eyes swiveled to him, and though frozen by Aurum's magic, he could almost see the desperate shaking of the boy's head. It was useless, that much Tobias knew. Dragonborn could not be reasoned with—especially not violent spirits such as Aurum who bathed in the despair of his enemies as well as their blood. He was the spearhead of the elf slaughter, the most revered and powerful of all five servants of Selini's heads. The letters were the least of his concerns; he came to kill those that had crossed him.

However, the flame of anger in his eyes diminished as he glanced down at the hand lying at their feet. His lip twitched, and a low chuckle escaped him as he bent down. Tobias shuffled back, never dropping his blade even as Aurum righted himself, the hand poised in place over his wrist. With a jolt, Tobias realized there was no blood on his sword, nor pouring from the severed wrist. Instead, it oozed with shadows. Aurum calmly reattached his hand, stitching the wound closed with gold threads as he laughed to himself. He flexed his fingers, now fully healed, and admired them with childlike wonder in his golden eyes. The same look turned to Tobias, and his grin spread wider.

"Fascinating!" he breathed. "Truly fascinating. No human has managed to wound me since—" He paused, frowning deeply. Then, with a shrug, he waved his newly-healed wrist as the lines of his frown slowly diminished and that wide, unsettling grin returned. "Well, since Kase! And before that, who knows." Casually, as if it were nothing more than a toy, he touched the tip of Tobias's sword and pushed it out of his face. He leaned in close enough that the smell of decay overtook Tobias's senses, and he choked, vision blurring as his eyes watered.

Gagging under the smell, Tobias looked away and fumbled for the spell, the last resort. It sang in his hand, and already the air began to clear. He lifted it, allowing its light to shed the darkness from Aurum's form. "Stay back!" he cried.

Aurum's face twisted. With the wave of his hand, an arrow of gold pierced straight through Tobias's palm, its head emerging on the other side. Agony ripped through his flesh, and he doubled over with a scream as Aviva's spell dissolved and its light faded. The arrow disappeared just as quickly as if it had never been there at all.

"Your Mage is dead," Aurum sneered. "Her leftover magic won't save you again."

Tobias blinked away flickering black spots, heaving in sharp breaths as he cradled his shaky hand close to his chest. Searing pain ripped along the path of the invisible wound. There was no blood, no hole, yet everything was on fire.

His sword was ripped from his other hand, and the force yanked him forward. While he flailed, Aurum's fist connected with his gut. Pain exploded in his midsection, the wind forced from his lungs. Wheezing, Tobias collapsed.

Eira cried out, but the ringing in his ears drowned out her voice. A slender hand settled against his back—hers, no doubt—but he didn't dare look away from Aurum, who was slowly approaching the frozen Calix and Kiara. He couldn't tell if the spell still held them or if they were pinned down by pure trepidation.

"And you." Aurum summoned a long, slender blade from a shower of gold sparks, swiveling to point the tip at Calix. Moonlight glinted off the polished sword, illuminating its wickedly sharp edges. He leveled it against Calix's neck. "May the goddess forgive your sins in death."

"Stop it!" Kiara cried, finding the strength to move again. She leapt between the two of him, shielding Calix with her own body. Generations of hatred and fury burned in the depths of her penetrating glare, but Aurum didn't flinch.

Instead, he sighed. "Oh, you naïve Calistians. Always in the way, just like she said you would be." He withdrew the sword from Calix and, in one fluid movement, brought it down across her body.

Kiara collapsed, a bloody mess as she writhed in agony. Not even a scream left her lips, only a pained, shallow gasp. Calix stared down at her in horror. He whipped around to Aurum with a guttural roar and charged him, barehanded. Aurum threw a blow to his head, and the sound of his fist connecting with Calix's skull echoed in the still air. Calix crumpled at his feet. Pride gleamed in Aurum's gold eyes, the slit of his pupils narrowed by the glow of his magic. His sword turned again to gold flecks of magic and disappeared from his grasp.

Mouth agape in a silent scream, Tobias struggled to right himself. He fumbled for his own sword, which he had lost in the sea of withered grass. Eira's hand, once a steady support against his back, curled tightly around his coat again with quivering fear. The edges of Aurum's black cloak appeared in his vision, and his head jerked up to meet the dragonborn's waiting stare.

The dragonborn sunk to his eye level in a crouch, obscuring the carnage behind his shadowy form. Though the cloak obscured much of his body, his broad, powerful shoulders were only accentuated by its folds. "Humans are such incredible creatures," he said. "The terror in your eyes is marvelous." With a gleam in the depths of his brilliant golden gaze, he shifted to Eira. "Do you see now what I was trying to teach you? It wasn't so hard." He sighed before rising to his full height again. "The plans have changed."

With the snap of his fingers, the little black dragon appeared once again, flitting around him with a myriad of nonsensical whistling chortles before it shot to the ground and folded in its leathery wings. A pool of darkness expanded around them from within the dragon's scales until it swallowed the world entirely. Grass tickled Tobias's cheek, but he couldn't remember when he had collapsed, nor when the feeling of Eira's hand against his back had disappeared. In seconds, the world was swallowed up and him along with it.

PART THREE
CORRUPTION

"Lost in the sea of his despair,
the man of shadows wanders the land.
Whatever he touches turns to corruption and ruin,
and only death is found in his wake."

21

DESPERATE PLEA

The world was sinking into a pool of shadows, and all Eira could do was watch. Tobias's head disappeared beneath the surface. She lost count of how many times she called his name with no response before he was gone. Aurum faded into the blackness, leaving her with the ghost of his mocking smile and his laughter running circles around her frantic thoughts. Even Calix and Kiara were taken by the yawning pit, consumed by the dragon's void. In mere seconds, her world was gone. The pool began to shrink while she stood still in the grass, untouched and untaken. She lunged for the edge and shoved her hand into the depths, reaching for Tobias or Kiara or anyone. An electric shock rattled her bones, and she was forced out. The portal closed.

Alone, Eira sat back against her heels, staring numbly at the place where Tobias had been. Cold ripped at her exposed cheeks, and she shivered, wrapping her arms around herself to keep out its vicious bite. If she had taken up her weapons instead of hiding behind him, maybe their one chance at stopping Aurum wouldn't have ended in such disaster.

A mournful, hollow cry shattered her reverie. Her heart

leapt to her throat, and she turned to find both dragons still caught in Aurum's web of magic threads. With a gasp, she fumbled for one of her knives and scrambled to the blue one's side—she couldn't keep their names straight. She pressed the blade to the thread, but her knife passed through without snapping it. A curse slid from her lips as she tried again. And again. Frantically, she tried another thread with the same result. Again. And again.

No thread would cut.

Hot tears welled in her eyes and her throat squeezed so tightly that she couldn't get out another sound. Her chest burned with anger. She slashed at the threads. Her knife hit the blue dragon's scales instead and bounced off harmlessly, flying out of her grip and disappearing into the grass.

"I'm sorry," she choked. She sank to her knees, staring into the dragon's pleading eye. Ice crackled across the swirling patterns in his scales. She shook her head. "I can't do it. I can't cut the threads."

Even after all this time, she was still a prisoner of Aurum's sick game.

No. Defiantly, she shoved to her feet again. Aurum was not undefeatable, nor was it impossible to overcome his magic. Tobias had done it for her—she could do the same for him, for Princess Kiara, for the dragons, and even for their strange half-breed companion, who was always watching with those freakish red eyes. Even he didn't deserve to be hunted down and slaughtered by Aurum.

"There has to be something. Do you have some sort of magic knife?" She gestured vaguely for the blue dragon, begging him to understand. Kiara had wielded an onyx-colored blade back in the mountains, the only weapon that worked on the Shadowslayer's—or Aurum's—magic-infused form. If she had something similar, Eira could cut the threads. Or at least, she assumed she would be able to. Uncertainty cracked her resolve.

The blue dragon gave a dejected moan, his one visible eye sliding shut so that she didn't have to look at the sadness within it anymore. She took that to mean no, he didn't have a magic knife stashed away in his equipment.

Behind her, the white dragon thrashed restlessly in her bonds. She let out a feral roar and twisted to snag one of the threads in her mouth. The air around her shimmered with magic, but the thread rejected her attempts. She screeched again and thumped her tail. Eira didn't even have the courage to approach her, much less ask if she had anything to help.

Light footsteps rustled through the tall grass. Eira stood to attention, reaching for a second knife only to find her collection empty. Her fingers tingled with unease, but as she focused on the figure, she breathed a sigh of relief.

Unda was coming toward her, his blue scarf billowing in the cold night winds. Though darkness had fully set in over the outskirts of Lumas, he carried no light with him. Dressed in grays and blacks, his skin pale as moonlight, he looked like a ghost floating across the barren land. In one hand, he held a knife—Kiara's black knife, she realized, as he breezed past her and easily cut the blue dragon free. A shower of sparks rained at their feet with each cut. The dragon got up and shook himself like a wet dog.

"Thank goodness you're safe," Unda said breathlessly.

A flash of anger cut through Eira, and she balled her fists. "Where have you been? We needed you! You have magic. You could have done something!"

His expression shifted, something caught between hurt and fear. He held up the knife. As the light shifted across the blade, it glittered as if it were inlaid with thousands of tiny jewels. "I went to fetch this."

"You went back to the mountains for a *knife*?" She narrowed her eyes, though her frustration was already giving way to something else—a foolish hope. It was the very knife she had been wishing for. Somehow, he had magicked it into his possession, and the thought of that sent a shiver down her spine. How did he manage to find it?

Unda lowered the knife. "Kiara mentioned it was the only thing that could hurt the Shadowslayer. I also have this. Tobias left it." He produced a second knife from his belt—one of hers.

"He's Aurum," Eira murmured, accepting her knife back gratefully and slotting it in its place. She watched numbly as the elf, followed by Calix's dragon, moved to the other dragon's side and cut her free with the same ease. "This whole time, we've been wondering what the connection is. Now, I wish I didn't know."

Unda hesitated. She couldn't see his face, but the way his ears drooped betrayed his heavy expression. "I see," he said, bending down to cut another thread. It crackled and hissed as it came into contact with the knife before it gave way with a loud snap. "There are no bodies here and very little blood, so I'm assuming he took them alive?"

"What should I do?" she blurted out, wringing her hands. She tapped her foot, but even that was not enough to rid her of the bundle of restless energy steadily growing inside her. With a frustrated huff, she began to pace. "He's a monster. What does he even want with them? He's never taken people alive before. He always..." She trailed off as her memories shifted from Aurum to the Shadowslayer, focusing on the cages of corpses they had found in the mountains. Nausea twisted her gut, and she slapped a hand to her mouth.

Once the white dragon wriggled free and bounded away, Unda turned. There was a grave seriousness in his expression, his lips pinched firmly and brows knitted together. Even his eyes had grown colder, glowing with a faint blue light. "You have to rescue them before they are lost to his corruptive power or he gives up his interest and kills them. Stiria and Faiera will be able to take you to their Riders, but you will have trouble rescuing your friends without help."

Eira filed their names away, careful to remember this time. "Aren't you coming with me?" She glanced at the broken shards of Kiara's enchanted necklace, the one she had been intending to give to him. She didn't have the same startling sense of Calistian duty as the girl, but she wasn't quick to deny his protection now.

Unda brought up one of his usual sad, bittersweet smiles—the one that didn't reach his eyes and seemed to dull their light. "I cannot go, but I can give you this." He held out the knife, which was laid across both open palms. The way he bowed his head slightly made it appear as if she were being offered a sacrifice or an important relic.

The knife hummed with a strange power, pulsing with magic imbued deep within the blade itself. Its hilt was simple, wrapped in leather and with a golden cross guard that protected her fingers from the blade's sharpened edges. When she lifted it gingerly from his hands, it settled in her grip with more weight than her other daggers. The black blade was slightly longer and wider, too.

"It will keep you safe," Unda said as he straightened. Only then did she notice the silver sword strapped to his hip. A teardrop jewel dangled from its hilt. It flickered with power, keeping time with the pulse of the black blade. "If you decide to return it to Kiara when you get the chance, tell her it is best not to be discarded. An object such as this should be treasured."

Eira tore her gaze from the weapon and forced herself to meet his sad eyes. "But I can't go by myself. Even with this, Aurum will crush me." *I need Tobias.*

Unda didn't offer any shred of ancient elf wisdom this time, but his silence let the cogs of her mind turn. Something clicked, and she let out a gasp.

"Oliver!" she cried, stuffing the black dagger into one of the pockets of her belt. "Oliver went to find the apprentice—if I can catch up to him, he has to help me!"

"Then I wish you well." With the wave of his hand, Unda summoned both Stiria and Faiera back to his side and offered their training reins to her. Moonlight trailed across his twin silver rings, one on each hand, and something flickered in his expression. When he was standing next to the scaled creatures, the beast-like appearance of his round, innocent eyes became more obvious. The longer she watched him, the more his eerie youthful appearance sent shivers down her spine.

Even the healer in a tiny Calistian town had his share of secrets.

But she couldn't dwell on that. With determination to strengthen her spine, she took the reins and tugged the dragons away. She mounted Stiria, whose calmness seemed more dependable than Faiera's restless pacing. Without looking back, she took the dragons to the skies and set off for Aviva's forest.

22

THE ECCENTRIC APPRENTICE

13/3/X/xx-68

IF THERE WAS one thing Oliver hated more than traveling, it was traveling with someone who didn't know when to stop complaining. It wasn't the first time he'd traveled with Arayna and, if he held true to his promises, certainly wouldn't be his last. Although he was about to make it his last time if she asked again if they were "almost there."

They had hitched a ride on a merchant's wagon, one that rattled along the road as if it were one misstep from falling apart beneath them. Most of the wares had been sold by the time the old man allowed them to climb into the cart, which left plenty of room for them to shift and for Arayna to get agitated. It didn't help that the wagon was open at the top, offering a view of the changing scenery around them. Once they got away from well-traveled roads and small towns, the rocky wasteland of Sheniir behind them, Arayna became restless. Her foot tapped constantly against the wood floor—a sound that was so slightly off rhythm with the tap of the horse's hooves that it grated on Oliver's nerves.

Much to his chagrin, he heard the sound of her telltale sigh. "Are we almost there?"

A muscle in his face twitched. "Like I said the last hundred times you asked, no. We're not."

She groaned loudly as she flopped against the bottom of the cart. Her groan morphed into a whine, and she kicked the air, her wolf ears drooping. "How far are we? We've been traveling forever!"

"It's been two days since we left the inn in Faruu, and travel takes a lot longer without Smoke to fly us around. Grow up, Arayna." He folded his arms and sank against the edge of the cart. "Also this was your idea. If you don't shut up, I'm going to stuff my dirty sock in your mouth."

"Ew!" she shrieked and sat upright, the fur on her tail standing on end. Her lip curled back, baring her pointed wolf teeth. She flung a heavy sack of luggage at him, knocking him square in the face.

He jolted back from the impact, hitting the wall of the cart. His nose stung where the sack had hit him, but not as much as his pride. Gritting his teeth, he threw it back at her. She dodged with ease, and the sack hit the opposite edge with a thud that rattled the wooden structure almost as obnoxiously as the gravel road they were traveling on. If the man driving the cart cared, he didn't turn around. He was so old that Oliver wasn't even sure he could hear their bickering, which must have been a blessing from the heavens.

"Ha! You missed!" Arayna jeered, jabbing her clawed finger at his chest. She grinned like a child who had just won the greatest victory of their life. Her simple-mindedness astounded him. She giggled and the mocking finger dropped as she tucked her chin into the collar of *his* coat, which he had gifted her when the air took on a more vicious nip because her shabby clothes of fur and cotton barely covered her arms and legs. It was a wonder she hadn't yet caught the world's most miserable cold and died.

His face flushed with anger. It had been the longest two days of his life, which said a lot because every day that he dealt with Arayna was the longest day of his life. Or with anyone, actually. But especially Arayna. *And Kase.*

In an instant, all the anger building up in his chest fizzled out and he found himself crushed beneath something else. It pulled heavily at his heart and pricked his eyes with moisture, which he furiously blinked away. Instead, he thought of how that lanky half-breed had come slinking into his room at the inn, following Tobias and Eira at the heels like some dog. *Kase's* half-breed: the dirty, starving, pitiful kid he had scooped up heroically from the border of Hybrid Territory and raised, nurtured, and protected like he was his own kin. Then, when he couldn't do that anymore because he had garnered the attention of Selini, he had the audacity to try to shove him into Oliver's life—into the home that was already crumbling because Arayna had lost her humanity.

Tobias could hunt down that dragonborn. He could have his fun with his newfound thief friend and their little gang of misfits. Oliver never wanted to look at that half-breed's miserable scarlet eyes again, even if that meant plunging himself headlong into Aviva's mess.

Kase was stupid. He lived a stupid life and died an even stupider death. What did Oliver have to be choked up over?

At least she's smiling and laughing again, he thought as he peered across the cart at Arayna, who busied herself by struggling with the buttons on Oliver's coat. She seemed to have forgotten her worries, if only for the moment. A moment was all he needed. She didn't deserve to be broken by the world, not when she was already in pieces.

His fingers tightened around his bow. Magic thrummed beneath his fingertips, a steady rhythm that mimicked a calm heartbeat. It was eerie how warm it felt in his grip, how it almost felt *alive* as it hummed with power just waiting to be released. It was as much of a curse as Arayna's hybridity, like the weight of Kase's duty to the *séti xenakri*—the glowing green sword that demanded to protect others even at the cost of its wielder's life. He may have forgotten its history and its curse, but Oliver never would.

Objects that lived and breathed magic should have stayed legends, buried in the rubble of an era long forgotten.

"Oliver."

He jolted at the seriousness in Arayna's tone. "What is it?"

She was sitting up straight, her ears pricked. The slightest furrow in her brow gave away the bewilderment that had put her on such high alert. Stretching her neck, she sniffed the air—he cringed but watched her curiously. Finally, she swung her gaze in the direction of the encroaching forest ahead of them, where the trees had grown so thick that the road they traveled on was almost entirely swallowed.

The cart rolled to a stop, and the horses at the front nickered discontentedly, tossing their manes. The driver turned to them with leaves sticking out of his white beard. "This is as far as I can take you two."

"Of course, sir. Thank you very much." Oliver scooped up his things and pushed himself over the side of the cart. Gravel and dirt scuffed against Arayna's boots as she leapt out behind him. He fished out a small pouch of coins from the depths of his bag and placed it in the old man's outstretched hand.

The man dipped his head as he pocketed the coins. "Be careful of these woods, boy. Something evil lurks here."

Oliver shared a look with Arayna, who shrugged. With a sigh, he slung his quiver and bow over his shoulder. "We'll be on our guard."

When the man had no more helpful advice to offer, Arayna waved farewell with a beaming smile and the two set off into the forest. Shadows passed overhead, engulfing them in a wash of darkness. Oliver shivered, skin prickling with unease at the heavy presence of corruption. Unlike the last time they came to Aviva's forest, they entered easily—no barrier stopped them, and no tiny reptilian eyes watched them pass through. However, darkness lurked in every corner, a beast that was just waiting for the chance to spring. Sunlight didn't reach the forest floor despite the plentiful holes in the canopy of leaves. The air was thick with magic, and it pressed heavily against Oliver's head until his ears popped. From the way Arayna scrunched her nose and flicked, pulled, and scratched at her ears, he guessed she was suffering the same problem.

Black marks scarred the faces of the trees lining their path. A rotting stench filled the air, and it took all of Oliver's willpower to keep his lunch down. He knelt beside a young oak, its trunk barely wider than his leg. Its spidery branches bore no leaves, and darkness had almost entirely swallowed its wood. Strips of bark peeled away to reveal rotted tree flesh beneath, gray and lifeless. He reached to run his hand along the wound.

"Don't touch it." Arayna grabbed his wrist, his fingers mere inches from the sickly darkness.

Rolling his eyes, he shifted to peer up at her stern glare. "I held bark of the corrupted trees last time," he said, but he made no move to wrench from her grasp.

"Aviva was here last time," she said. Her iron grip tightened. There was a pleading look in her eyes that he couldn't ignore. "Please leave it alone. It's dangerous to play with magic."

He shrugged off her grip and stood. "It may not even be magic. Maybe the forest is just dying." But the wrongness crawling beneath his skin, the prickle that raised the hair on the back of his neck, only came in the presence of thick magic. His body knew even if his mind was reeling—Aviva had not been wrong. Her forest was being corrupted.

Arayna stiffened, the fur of her tail standing on end again as she stood to attention. "Someone's here." She pointed farther down the path.

Oliver listened, shutting out all other thoughts, but he couldn't hear anything. He knew better than to ignore her senses, however. He nodded and raised a finger to his lips. Lowering himself, he crept down the path, hiding behind the thick foliage that didn't ooze with corruption. Arayna prowled through the flora with the stealth of a predator, eyes narrowed and ears flattened back.

Voices soon reached Oliver's ears, one the shrill voice of a young girl and the other the quiet—notably tired— murmur of a young man. They were bantering back and forth, arguing about something that seemed of great importance to the shrill girl. It wasn't long before he and Arayna reached the edge of the clearing and Aviva's small cottage came into view. Her garden of exotic flowers had all withered with corruption, and shadowy claws crawled up the ivy-covered walls. It was as if the forest was mourning the loss of its beloved Mage and, mad with grief and rage, was bent on destroying itself.

A sharp tug on his shoulder brought Oliver's gaze to the two figures emerging from the open cottage door. The girl was dressed in Mage garb, draped in a white cloak and carrying a magic staff. The taller boy who followed her must have been her Guardian, in a matching cloak but rather than magic relics, a sword poking out from beneath it. They erupted into another argument. Their talking never stopped. Oliver heaved a sigh.

He knew better than to hope he was looking at the wrong Mage. No one besides Aviva's apprentice or the Summoner would dare come to the forest, and she didn't seem nearly important enough to be a Summoner from the palace.

"...and I'm telling you there has to be something here," the Mage girl snapped, jabbing her finger at the boy's chest. "Aviva was cryptic, but she wouldn't leave a thread all frayed and hanging. Keep looking."

The boy sighed and waved her accusing finger away. "Nari, we've been through the whole house twice over. Her spell doesn't point to anything here. You have to—"

"I don't want to talk to those halfwits that got her killed! Not only that, but they destroyed her book. That was supposed to be mine when I graduated, Ronan! Now, all her best work is lost because a bunch of idiots had a little adventure. To Selini's jaws with purifying the corruption and stuff. I'm going to hunt down those morons and—"

"And have a nice conversation with them?"

"—and skin them alive!"

Ronan winced. "That's morbid and a little extreme. Don't you think you're being unfair?"

Their conversation continued, but Oliver drowned it out, his lip curling in distaste. He could almost feel his eyes glazing over. *What a pleasant apprentice you've got there, Aviva. Nice work.* Maybe it was a good thing Tobias hadn't come. He couldn't imagine that stick in the mud would take kindly to being called a halfwit and a moron or being threatened by a tiny girl waving a magic stick around. But then again, he was a pushover sometimes. Maybe he wouldn't say anything at all.

Grass rustled as Arayna came and crouched beside him, her lips pushed out in a pout. "I don't like that girl," she growled. "Is that really supposed to be Aviva's apprentice?"

"She was here to learn magic, not manners."

"Well, she should have learned both."

Oliver snorted. Aviva had the patience of a saint if she dealt with this Nari person every day for who knows how long. Her companion, Ronan, seemed more agreeable, however. Frankly, he seemed more like someone Aviva would take on as an apprentice, but teaching was useless if the person didn't have an aptitude for wielding magic. But if Aviva believed Nari was capable of dissolving the corruption, she must have had a reason. That was what forced Oliver to emerge from his hiding place, ignoring Arayna's warning hiss. He stepped out of the foliage, hands raised in an effort to look as innocent as possible to avoid being skinned.

"I hear you're looking for a halfwit."

Nari's shriek startled the birds from the trees. Ronan drew his sword and shoved her behind him, steely determination darkening his razor-sharp glare. Only a small flicker of light in the jeweled orb atop Nari's staff spoke to her own efforts to defend herself, but it winked out before any spells came to fruition.

"Who are you?" Ronan challenged, pointing the tip of his sword toward Oliver's chest. Several paces spanned between them, diminishing the threat of its bite.

"I'm Oliver."

Their only answer was a pair of blank stares.

He sighed, raking his fingers through his hair and pushing it out of his eyes. "Kase's cousin? He was Aviva's Guardian. We were friends."

"Oh!" Nari cried. She shoved past Ronan and scampered toward him, looking him up and down. She circled him like a vulture, one finger trailing down the length of his bow as she passed it. Her stormy gray eyes lit up, and she grinned, tiny sparks spitting from her fingertips. Choppy, jaw-length strands of red-brown hair fell in her face, and she quickly tucked them back behind her ear. "You are indeed. Aviva told me. You were at Sheniir?"

He frowned at her closeness and took a measured step back. "I was."

She turned to cast Ronan a beaming smile, apparently having forgotten her earlier threats. He didn't seem convinced but sheathed his sword and approached cautiously. They had the same red-brown hair and sun-kissed complexion—in fact, even the soft curve of their faces and the shape of their round eyes were similar.

Nari grabbed Oliver's hand and shook it, breaking his concentration before he could properly file the thoughts away. The motion was fierce and awkward, and he quickly pried himself free before his blatant dislike of her touch became too obvious. He could already feel his nose beginning to scrunch. He wiped his hand on the front of his sweater.

"It's so good to meet you," Nari cooed, taking up her staff in one hand again. Her smile oozed with lies—or maybe it was just her earlier tone echoing in his mind. "I was wondering when I would have the chance to be introduced to Aviva's old friends. Did you come here all by yourself?"

"There's another," Ronan said. He nodded at the bushes where Arayna was hiding.

Oliver turned and found her glowing blue stare half-hidden in the leaves. He dipped his head in a tiny, subtle gesture. *It's safe,* he tried to say. *But be on your guard.*

Whether she understood or not was beyond him, but she burst from the bushes the moment they locked eyes. Leaves clung to her tangled ponytail, and her ears twitched with barely concealed aggravation, which was reflected in the way her lips were pressed together and her unwavering stare burned a hole through his skull. He could only offer her a shrug. She always seemed ticked off about something. It was nearly impossible to keep track of her mood swings.

Nari's face contorted in disgust. Her gaze traveled up and down Arayna. The curl of her lip only worsened as she lingered on the Beast Master's dirty appearance. Nari's eyes went from her scars to her matted hair, her beastly ears and tail, her lanky build, and even to her tattered clothes barely concealed beneath Oliver's coat—she was not what anyone would call pleasant, much less attractive. People's first look at the wolfish girl always painted a similar expression, or worse. But Nari cleared her throat and wiped the look from her face, plastering a fake smile over it instead. "And this is?" she said, her voice a little shaky.

"Arayna." She lifted her chin and scooted to Oliver's side.

"Here we go again." Nari rolled her eyes. She cast a pointed look back at Ronan like this was a conversation they had shared many times before. "Another one of those Calistian *ah* names. Do you know how hard it is to keep them straight? They all sound the same. Arayna, Aviva—by the stars, if I ever meet a Calistian, I'm going to—actually, can I call you something else? How about Ray? Ari?"

"You can call me the Beast Master of Ruber," Arayna said.

The annoyance flitting across Nari's stormy gaze turned to mockery. As a sly grin found its way to her lips, she banished her staff with the flick of her wrist and a shower of sparks. She folded her arms across her chest and shifted her weight, taking on that stance that girls for some reason thought gave them the right to say something rude. "I've never heard of a Beast Master. What is that exactly?"

"A master of shapeshifting," Arayna said plainly and mechanically. Oliver had heard her give the same explanation a hundred times over. "To wielders of beast magic, it is the same as being recognized as a Mage."

Nari snorted and waved a hand vaguely at Arayna. "You don't seem to have mastered it since you're stuck in this form."

Oliver blocked Arayna's path with his arm. She hadn't even moved, but he could practically feel the anger growing within her. It hummed beneath his veins, almost tangible enough to be his own anger, but he knew it was passed from her to the bow and from the bow to him. He had spent enough time carrying the burden of the enchanted bow to recognize the cling of its presence on his brain.

"Ah." Nari's attention turned away from Arayna and instead settled on something between them that Oliver couldn't see. She reached out, one finger extended, and caught on a thin string wrapped around Arayna's finger. It was invisible until it caught the sun's light, shimmering faintly as Nari twisted it. She dragged her finger down the length of the thread. "I see. Something is suppressing your magic."

The other end of the string connected to the bow—that much Oliver knew without looking. He swallowed the rising fear in his throat and met Nari's eyes, which glittered with mischief. That smirk of hers didn't come from a place of innocence. She knew exactly what she was hinting at. Inclining her head to the side, she dropped the string. It wriggled, free of the tension, and vanished from sight again. With her hands tucked behind her back, Nari withdrew from the two of them.

"Seems like the Beast Master has a master of her own."

23

DECAY

FEAR WAS A WILD CREATURE, stalking Oliver and breathing down his neck. He could feel its stare on his back, and the anticipation of being struck by it made his skin crawl. When he turned to look at the beast, however, the pair of eyes that met him were Arayna's. His breath hitched. It took all his willpower not to run from the heat of her glare. A hunter did not run from a beast; he would never run from Arayna again. Hidden beneath his sweater, his old scar itched with a subtle warning of the consequences of testing her limits.

When the bow was enchanted, its wood woven with iridescent threads of magic that gave it its strange reddish color, he was told that she must never learn of her connection to it. If it was broken, she would become a monster once more, and he would lose her to the beast curse.

"Arayna," he started, but the argument was lost before it had even formed. *Please don't look at me that way,* was all he could think to say. *I didn't have a choice.*

Thankfully, Nari didn't know silence and was moving on before Oliver could drown in his shame or Arayna could demand to know more. "Well, now that your introductions are over with." The apprentice unclasped her cloak and, with a dramatic flourish, shoved it off her shoulders. It pooled at her feet, stark white against the dying grass, the brightest thing in the clearing, untouched by the growing darkness Aviva feared.

With a snap, Nari summoned her staff to her hand again and twirled it across her fingers. The strings of jewels bound to the top clinked as they bounced against each other. "I am Nari, apprentice Mage of the great Aviva, master of purification and light magic. I'm the world's only hope of defeating this evil corruption that is draining the life from our world." Sparks danced around her head, a display of light and magic that sapped the uncertainty and fear from Oliver's bones. Rather than the awe she assumed she would inspire, however, annoyance took root in his heart. For someone who had never graduated to being a full-fledged Mage, whose existence had been hidden from even Aviva's closest friends, and whose home was slowly being devoured by an unknown evil, she had an overabundance of confidence.

When her display was over, she gestured to her Guardian behind her, who was standing stiff as a soldier waiting for a command. "And that's my brother Ronan," Nari drawled. "You can ignore him. He's mostly for decoration because *obviously* I don't need his sword to protect me when I have magic."

"Right." Oliver crossed his arms. He didn't bother informing her that a Mage Guardian's other duty was to protect the Mage from their own desire for power and to stop them from using more magic than they were able. Or to just prevent stupid mistakes. Not that Uriah or Kase had been particularly good at that, as they were stupid mistakes themselves. Aviva, a young Mage who graduated too early because of her gifts, should never have been given protectors who were equally young and inexperienced. It was as if the Summoners had set them up to fail.

"And your purpose here?" Arayna asked. She didn't even look at Oliver as she shoved past him.

Ronan started to answer, but Nari shushed him loudly and waved him away. He remained rooted in place, but the displeasure twisting his expression was dark with frustration—though not surprise.

"We received a message telling us to go to the castle of Sheniir." Nari traced a lazy line through the air. "There was something weird about the throne, like this collection of magic was tied to it. Also a dragonborn was lurking nearby, but he fled before we could catch him. We totally could have though, don't you think?" She nudged her brother.

Oliver frowned, quick to stamp out the flutter of panic in his chest before it could take hold. "A dragonborn?" he asked before they could swerve off topic again. Eira claimed to have been under the influence of Aurum, but he couldn't imagine the goddess's favorite weapon fleeing from a fight, unless the destruction of Aviva's book had injured him. But even then...

"He was small," Ronan added, and the image of the great Golden Dragonborn Aurum was dashed to pieces. As he spoke, he bent down to collect Nari's discarded cloak and folded it over his arm. "He didn't look like much of a fighter. I think he might have been some kind of scout."

Oliver let out a breath of relief.

Nari huffed and elbowed Ronan in the side. "Would you stop interrupting me?"

He let out a pained hiss, massaging the place she had struck with annoyance in his brown eyes. She ignored him and, before anyone could interrupt again, continued with her version of the story. "After we answered Aviva's message at Sheniir, we came back to the forest to look for another hint as to what's going on because she was vague—typical Aviva. She charged me with stopping the spread of the corruption, and it looks like I have my work cut out for me."

It was a grave understatement of the problem. Oliver barely withheld the urge to roll his eyes so hard they would fall out of their sockets. After discovering the beauty that was expressing distaste through the roll of his eyes, it was a wonder he still had them so many years later. Perhaps Nari's oblivious behavior would be the end of them.

The sickly darkness in Aviva's forest had worsened considerably, with its blight reaching deep into the clearing where she had lived. During her life, her cottage was protected by charms and light magic. If it was so quickly overtaken after her death, it was only a matter of time before the whole forest was lost, drained of life and power. He didn't know if the blight would stop there, nor did he want to. Magic didn't act without purpose; it was always orchestrated by a wielder. He could only imagine what it was feeding as it stole the life from Aviva's home.

His gaze settled on a withered tree at the very edge of the clearing. Gray bark peeled from the trunk and collapsed into a pile of other chunks at its base, like leaves ripped from the branches by Xenah's chilly winds. Death and decay had taken over the place Aviva loved, the forest she said her late master had gifted to her. It twisted Oliver's insides into uncomfortable knots. "And how is your progress with that?" he asked.

Nari laughed, but the sound of it rang hollow with fear. Shoulders trembling, she leaned against Ronan until her fit of laughter passed. "Why would you even ask such a thing?" she teased. "Of course it's fine. It's all fine. It's going well—really well, some might say!"

"Really?" Arayna sneered. She swung her arm at the same tree Oliver had been staring at. "You would call *this* well? Don't you remember the light that used to flood this place? The air here used to be so clean you could taste it. Now, everything stinks of death, and the sun barely shines."

Nari refused to meet her eye, lips pinched. This time, she

didn't dare laugh—it was hard to do that under the ferocious wrath of the Beast Master. When she refused to even answer, Ronan sighed. "She hasn't been able to make any successful progress. She needs to find a stronger spell."

"Ronan!" Nari hissed through clenched teeth, whacking him in the chest. The blue jeweled pin holding the edges of his cloak together glittered, responding to her touch with a flash of magic. "Don't tell our enemies that."

"They're not your enemies. They're Aviva's friends."

"You don't know that."

A headache was beginning to form behind Oliver's temples. Their bickering was ringing in his ears, and he wasn't sure he would ever be free of its echo. He pinched the bridge of his nose and sucked in a sharp breath. Arayna's ears twitched with impatience. It was a wonder she had yet to snap. *Maybe she's more rattled by the bow than I thought.*

"Listen." Oliver sighed and forced himself to look at Nari and Ronan again. They paused in their argument, both fixing him with a curious stare as though they couldn't believe he had the audacity to interrupt their important discussion. He mustered up all the patience he had—which was little more than a sliver—and scrounged for the right words to make them stop. "I really don't care to earn your trust. You can think whatever you want of me, but Aviva asked us to find you, and I'm honoring her request. She said you were the one who could stop the darkness, but I can see you're going to need extra help."

Nari's cheeks flushed bright red, gray eyes alight with angry flecks of magic. Her indignation knew no bounds, and he almost wanted to admire it. Unfortunately, she was putting that persistence into her worst characteristics, so the only word that came to mind to describe being in her presence was *annoying.* He would rather listen to Arayna's travel complaints than listen to her parade her lackluster powers. What could Aviva have possibly seen in her?

"So, I have a plan," he continued. "I propose that we pay a visit to Summoner Maven. She promised to look into this darkness, and it's time we remind her of that promise."

Nari started to open her mouth to interrupt him again, but he stuck his hand up to stop her. "Before you argue about your unlicensed practice of magic, Maven offered Aviva a temporary pardon in light of the current predicament. I'm sure the same grace will be extended to you. Maven needs to know things have gotten worse. Either you go with us or we'll go without you and you can live with the knowledge that we turned over Aviva's last request of you to someone else. If you go, she may know a stronger spell that will help you overcome this challenge. I'm certain that's what Aviva wanted for you."

Nari pursed her lips, her brow furrowed at his challenge. In the brief span of their conversation, he had pinned her as someone who feared the blow her reputation would take should she back down, so it seemed like the right thing to dangle in front of her nose. The long, awkward silence that followed made his skin prickle with unease. Magic was a foreign world to him, and chasing shadows without a light was the last thing he wanted to do. However, his previous meeting with Maven had left a bitter taste in his mouth. It had taken great effort from Aviva to convince her that their plight was worth her consideration—more important than arresting and detaining Aviva for her crimes. But she was, by all standards, a powerful magic user. She had to have found something that would help save Aviva's world, the forest she loved, the magic she had cultivated.

And by extension, stop the unknown plot of Head Dragonborn Aurum and his dark power.

"Okay," Nari finally agreed. This time, when she met Oliver's waiting stare, her expression was deadly serious. There was no hint of laughter, mockery, or pride in the set of her jaw, only sheer determination. "If you think it's what Aviva would want.

But you have to promise you won't let my magic get taken away."

Smugness turned the corners of his mouth up in a smile. She was too easy to read. "I won't let that happen," he said.

With a firm nod, she took her cloak from Ronan's arm and wrapped it around her shoulders in one fluid movement. A jewel glittered on her cloak, a deep sapphire blue like the one on Ronan's. She stuck her hand deep within the white folds and produced a slim paper charm. The front of it was painted with old runes that glowed as magic lit the tips of her fingers. When her spell had set into the paper, she pressed it into Ronan's hands.

"Stay here," she said. "Keep watch over the forest. If something happens, this will instantly take you to my side."

"You're going with them alone?" His brows lifted in surprise, but it quickly flicked into concern as he took her hands. "Nari, I should be the one that goes with you. I'm your Guardian, your brother—I thought you said they were your enemies?"

"Someone must stay, and I trust you with this task. Besides…" A wide grin split her lips, and her eyes danced with mirth. "If they try anything, I can handle myself."

He didn't seem convinced, but he dipped his head to her respectfully and accepted her proposal. He slipped the charm into his pocket and wished her farewell with all the stiffness of a soldier. Oliver had witnessed many heartfelt, teary partings between siblings. He had watched Kase embrace his brother, sobbing his goodbyes into the younger boy's tunic as he clung to him desperately. Oliver had no siblings of his own, but he had been close enough with Kase and his brothers to consider them his siblings. The awkwardness in Ronan and Nari's goodbye was a far cry from what he had seen, but if the standard was Kase, perhaps it was skewed from the beginning.

Arayna cleared her throat, interrupting the moment. Her foot tapped with the familiar rhythm of impatience. Despite that and the fold of her arms, she said calmly, "We should at least rest here for the night. I'm hungry and tired. We can set out in the morning."

"You know, maybe I do like you, Ari."

"Arayna."

Nari shrugged. She was already halfway back to the cottage before she answered, "We'll work on it."

24

BEST KEPT SECRET

NARI LED EVERYONE BACK to the cottage, promising that the rooms were still prepped and ready to receive guests as they always were when Aviva was alive. Once again, she was droning on about frivolous things, but Oliver found it much easier to drown out the sound of her voice as he let his gaze drift to Arayna. The beast girl still refused to look at him, a far cry from how close she had been since the deaths they had witnessed at Sheniir. Slowly, she was returning to the distant and wistful girl he was trying to leave in the past. It was only a matter of time before she reverted back to the hungry beast that lay dormant inside her.

His fingers found their way to the smooth wood of the bow. It hummed against his touch, but for once he couldn't discern a sense of what was on her mind. All he knew was that the beast was suppressed beneath the usual haze, but she was beginning to figure that out for herself. If she learned the true nature of her "clarity" of self, would she destroy the bow and let the beast take over?

She won't let this die here, he thought bitterly as they crossed the threshold and entered Aviva's lavender-scented home. *She'll keep prodding until I break. That's how she is.*

Pain stabbed the pad of his finger, and he bit down on the hiss that rose to the tip of his tongue. A loose splinter had caught on his skin. The sight of it flared new irritation to life as he carefully pulled the sharp bit of wood from his finger. That stupid Mage was supposed to have enchanted the bow to keep it from peeling like that. Sanded to perfection, it should not have lashed out at him that way.

Maybe it was taking Arayna's side, directing her silent wrath toward him in the form of tiny splinters.

"...and if you need anything else, you can bother Ronan because I'll be asleep and, frankly, don't care," Nari was saying when Oliver finally tuned into the conversation again. He barely looked up before she waved flamboyantly and excused herself to another part of the house.

Ronan stood for a moment longer, looking after her until her form retreated into one of the rooms. When she was gone, her absence announced with the loud slam of her door, he heaved a sigh. "Please excuse my sister."

Oliver shrugged. "I assume she's rattled by Aviva's death."

"I guess so," Ronan murmured, his gaze dark. "I'll show you to your rooms. Is there anything else I can do for you?"

"Actually, we know where to go." Arayna stepped up to Oliver's side, an unusually thoughtful look on her wolfish face. "Go rest. You look like you need it."

His brow furrowed as he took in their weary appearances. There was an argument behind his brown eyes, but he seemed wiser than his sister and chose not to give it voice. Instead, he nodded. "Yes. Of course. Goodnight, then," he said decisively. With that, he turned and exited down the same hall as Nari, choosing the room next door to hers—both of which were across from Aviva's bedroom and study.

Arayna gave a decisive huff and spun on her heel. She shoved a stack of papers and books off a couch and plopped herself onto it, sending up a cloud of dust that tickled the back of Oliver's throat. Dim lantern light illuminated the messy room, casting long shadows across the floral wallpaper and carelessly strewn deskwork. In the mess, Arayna's beastly form looked right at home. If he hadn't come in with her, he might have assumed she had made it rather than knowing it was normal for Aviva's cottage to be disastrous on the inside.

Arayna glared up at him, lips pinched and ears flattened. "Wanna explain what she meant?"

The script unfolded instantly in Oliver's mind. First, he straightened. Then, he met her glare with a sharp one of his own, an amber blade that could cut through any opponent. Finally, he mustered his defensive tone and said flatly, "I don't know what you mean."

She threw a kick to his shins. Pain flared around the places she had struck and zipped up his leg. He set his jaw but remained firm. Her sapphire gaze was fiery, a hungry beast that was ready to rip him to shreds.

"I've known you a long time," she snapped. "Your little tricks don't work on me."

"Let's not be unreasonable, 'Rayna."

Another kick, striking the same place as before. "Don't start that."

"I have nothing to say to you."

"Yeah?" She lifted her foot for a third kick.

The slowly-forming bruise smarted, and Oliver stepped out of her leg's reach. "It's not something I'm ready to share."

With a seething hiss, she shoved to her feet. "So it's not my place to know? You think I shouldn't know that you put some kind of *spell* on me behind my back and have been lying to me about it for Taiyo knows how long?"

"You invoke the name of Taiyo now?"

"Stop avoiding the question!"

"Could you repeat the question? I forgot it in all this talk."

"Oliver!" She lunged for him, hands outstretched and aimed for the bow strapped to his back. He sidestepped and grabbed her arm, twisting it behind her back. Her momentum sent her crashing to the dirty wood floors with him pinning her in place. She screeched in protest, an indignant and squirming mess beneath his iron grip. With a growl, she twisted just enough that he could see glowing eyes behind her wild hair, splayed across her face in choppy locks. Her lip curled to reveal her sharp fangs, her face mirroring that of the wolf form she had barely escaped from. For a brief moment, something hollow and dark settled in the depths of her gaze, an emptiness that belonged to a monster and not a young girl—not his childhood friend.

Fear slithered beneath his skin, cold as ice when it settled in the pit of his stomach. The old wound in his shoulder suddenly ached. Though it had long since healed, leaving nothing behind but a slowly fading scar, it throbbed with the painful reminder of what that beast could do. Of why he bargained for the bow in the first place, and why its secret must remain hidden.

But while he held it, Arayna reverted to her normal self—or as much as she could be. In spite of himself, he released her and stepped back to allow her the space to stand. Once she was on her feet again, he took in a slow, deep breath before deciding to give up his script.

"Is this why I haven't really felt like myself since I've been around you?" she muttered, beating him to it. This time, she was the one who refused to meet his eye, instead locking her gaze on her wrist as she rubbed the spot where he had grabbed her. The skin had turned red with the imprint of his hand. "It's like I'm watching myself in a dream, not truly able to connect with what I really think and feel. It's because of the bow, isn't it?"

Hesitation flicked in the back of his mind. It wasn't too late to think of another excuse, but he swept the thought away and exhaled slowly. "I was trying to return at least some of your humanity to you," he said. "I didn't want you to stay trapped as a beast, not after you lost control and hurt so many people. The people of Ruber wanted to kill you. I had no choice." He hated how feeble the words felt as soon as they were spoken aloud. To her, they were nothing but petty excuses in a desperate attempt to justify himself.

Again, he found himself taking hold of the bow. This time, he slipped it from his back and held it between them like an offering. Its wooden body shimmered with the faint presence of magic—he knew the string Nari had pointed out was still visible to those who were more attuned to magic. Arayna spared it little more than a passing glance.

"And if it's broken?" she asked softly, voice barely above a whisper.

"You won't be able to change back—not to this form and certainly not to your human self. You'll be a cursed beast forever." The massive red wolf flashed through his memories, a monstrous creature that barely resembled the animal she adored. It was a disturbing, warped thing that knew only how to kill and destroy. That was the heart of the Beast Curse, the punishment for those who abused their shapeshifting abilities. Every time they changed form, they sacrificed their humanity until they had none left to give. Their evil magic claimed their body and soul, just as the long-dead druids designed the shapeshifting power.

If the bow was destroyed, that would be Arayna's irreversible fate.

As the reality dawned on her, her expression grew distant and cold. She folded her arms, shoulders hunched, and turned her back on him.

Something pricked his heart, stirring sparks inside his chest. He caught her shoulder before she could leave, fingers digging into his coat which she still wore. "Arayna, I promise, I won't let that happen. No matter what it takes, I will find a way to break your curse. You just have to let me protect you until then."

She shrugged out of his grip easily this time. Without looking, she shuffled out of the room, quiet and forlorn for once. "Goodnight, Oliver," she said before the shadows swallowed her.

25

THOSE WHO KEEP SILENT

OLIVER COULDN'T FALL ASLEEP. His mind was spinning too fast to find any relief, no matter how much he tossed and turned or how long he left his eyes closed so that the darkness enveloped him. Everything reminded him of the past—of the deal he struck with a Mage to keep Arayna's beast spirit at bay, binding her to the bow and keeping it secret despite how much it hurt; of Kase's promises, his infuriating need to be some sort of hero who buried his own fears beneath that grin; even of his fleeting childhood with Eira, Aviva, and the others, playing the part of adventurers on fantastic quests. But the most painful was when the sight of Kase's body flashed through his mind again. Like his childhood dream, those quests Eira used to lead them on, it all ended in a nightmare. Only this time, Kase was never to wake again, and Oliver was forced to wrestle with his absence.

He curled in on himself, tangling his fingers in his hair as he sucked in a sharp breath. An unfamiliar tightness welled up in his chest, along with a pressure behind his eyes. But he shoved it back down. He refused to cry. Not for an empty-headed fool like Kase.

When the sun finally broke through the line of trees again,

spilling through the window in pale beams, he was more agitated than he had been the night before. His eyes itched as he sat up, but he couldn't tell if it was from lack of sleep or something else. Gritting his teeth, he scrubbed at them until spots danced in his vision. It didn't help anything. He shoved out of bed and dressed quickly. He had wasted enough time already.

The cottage was quiet as he slipped out of his room, all except for the sound of snoring coming from the room Nari had gone into the night before. He barely made it a step out of his room before his boot caught on something outside his door— his coat had been folded neatly and laid in front of his room. His breath snagged. At some point during the night, Arayna must have brought it back. It was heavy in his hand when he picked it up, as heavy as the bow strung across his back.

I shouldn't have told her. He skimmed his thumb over a loose stitch in one of the coat's buttons. Beneath the simmering regret, he knew the truth. Nari hadn't given him a choice. She dredged up the secret without caring who it hurt. If he had lied to Arayna again, he would have lost her entirely.

However, standing alone in the empty house, he wasn't sure if she was still with him or not.

Fresh air. He needed fresh air. Throwing his coat on, he stepped outside to escape the stifling cottage.

Early morning sunlight kissed his skin with gentle warmth, enough that he could feel it against the ice in his veins but not enough to quell the autumn chill in the air. Despite the darkness lurking in every corner, the distant call of birdsong echoed beyond the tree tops. In the daylight, the golden leaves sparkled with dew. If he didn't know any better, he would have assumed Aviva's woods had been purified overnight, but the ashen trees at the edge of the clearing reminded him of the corruption rooted within. It wouldn't be that easy to shake off such a violent sickness. Especially not with Aviva dead and gone.

"...of course. I'll be sure to send them on their way soon."

Ronan's voice drifted back to him. The knight in the white cloak was standing off to the side among the wilting flowers of Aviva's garden, a rune-coated paper in hand. It glowed with a dim light, tainting the air with the thick hum of magic. As soon as he finished speaking, however, the light winked out and the paper crumbled to dust in his hand. Sighing, he shook the mess from his palm before wiping it on his pants.

Oliver folded his arms, grateful that he hadn't run into Nari. He wasn't sure he could stand to listen to her non-stop talking so early in the morning. Ronan at least seemed more reasonable than she was. "Selling us out already?"

He turned, hand resting casually against the hilt of his sword. As his gaze landed on Oliver, his expression softened. "I was letting the Summoners know you intend to visit. I imagine they'll be a little more lenient with Nari if they know she's coming at least." He looked away, picking at the leather on his hilt. "An escort will meet you partway."

That seemed like a good sign, unless the escort was there to put Nari in chains and seal her magic for her and Aviva's crimes against the order. It was impossible to tell with the Summoners, especially since Maven had taken over her mother's rule. Part of him hated the regulations for Mages, yearning for the ancient history in which the main focus of the Summoners was maintaining the border with Hybrid Territory, preventing those monsters from spilling out in droves and slaughtering the human race. The ability to contact them—to *summon* these great magic-users—was a remnant from that age. Turning their iron fist on their own kind, detailing rigid rules for a free and ever-changing art, seemed counterintuitive. If Mages were so busy bowing to the Summoners and the Summoners were so busy keeping them in line, who was watching the dragonborn?

Oliver schooled his features under Ronan's watchful stare. Though it was safe to assume Ronan didn't hold the Summoners in high regard either since he willingly worked under Aviva and his sister, Oliver preferred to keep silent. He couldn't risk being outed for carrying an unauthorized magical item either, though Maven had ignored him entirely the last time they met. There was no guarantee he would be safe from her scrutiny the second time.

"Are you sure you don't want to come with us?" he asked instead.

"Nari's right." Ronan folded his arms, his Mage Guardian pin flashing in the sunlight. Yet it seemed duller than Kase's or Uriah's had been, lacking the same sheen as an official sigil. "I have to stay. I'm going to continue searching the house for another spell that might help Nari clear this corruption, just in case the meeting with Maven doesn't go well. Besides…" He paused, his brow furrowed in thought and his lips pinched. When he spoke again, he lowered his voice to barely more than a whisper. "If things do go wrong, it's better if I'm not there to get captured as well."

Oliver snorted. "You would sacrifice me and Arayna instead."

"Of course not. I doubt the Summoners have much interest in the two of you. You're not *unregistered Mages* or whatever." He shrugged. "But if you would try to keep my sister out of trouble—"

"I'll do my best. She seems to attract problems the way a flame draws in moths."

Ronan looked away, breathing a quiet sigh. "I know she is difficult. I'm sorry for the trouble she has already caused you."

Oliver's hands itched to take hold of his bow, but he kept his expression flat and his hands still. He didn't need pity. His strenuous relationship with Arayna was nothing new, and it likely wouldn't be absolved until she was free of her curse. Until she was no longer teetering on the edge of being a full beast. "Don't worry about it," he said. "I'd be more worried about Maven's response to your sister than what poking and prodding she can do to me." *I may be able to dismiss Nari's behavior, but Maven is too rigid to even understand a joke.*

Much to Oliver's surprise, Ronan laughed. He muffled it behind his hand, but it didn't hide his smile. "Sorry. Arayna told me you would say something like that."

Instinctively, Oliver searched the line of trees for a sign of the eavesdropping hybrid girl. That was why the house was quiet—she must have already gone outside. "Where did she go?"

"Hunting." Ronan gestured to a game trail that crossed the edge of the clearing and disappeared into the depths of the forest. "I suppose she didn't approve of the empty pantry. I told her there's not much to catch here due to the spread of the darkness, but she went anyway."

The tiniest flicker of unease sparked in Oliver's gut. It was irrational, but he couldn't shake it. He dipped his head in a quick show of thanks before he sprinted off down the trail, not caring that his boots were crashing through the underbrush, loud enough to scare off any prey in the area. Aviva had warned him that the corruption didn't stop at plant life; it spread to fauna as well. He had tried to go off hunting while waiting for Kase to wake up from the poison, and she had stopped him, directing him to leave the territory.

"You must not eat anything in this forest," she had said, her green eyes dark. *"The more that is corrupted, the more at risk you are of being consumed by it."*

Arayna should know. She was more attuned to the ebb and flow of magic than he was, warning him against even touching the sickly black plants when Aviva hadn't. But she was also rash and irresponsible and even a tad foolish at times. If she was touched by the incurable corruption...

He burst out of the thick underbrush, emerging in a circle of tall trees with thick, ancient trunks. Their canopy of leaves was so dense that the sun was almost entirely blocked out. Arayna crouched near the middle of the circle, her wolf ears tense and upright. As he stepped out, one ear twitched and she turned to him.

"Arayna," he wheezed, breathless from his run. His side tensed painfully, and he paused to catch his breath. "You can't hunt here. I've got travel food in my bag, so I'll get you something."

"It's rotten here." She stood and shuffled out of the way, allowing him to see what she had been bent over.

The bones of small game littered the blackened ground, scorched and corrupted the same as the bark on the trees. Ashen flesh piled beneath the bones, dry as dust. An eerie chill permeated the air as if all life and warmth had been completely sucked from the place. Oliver jerked back as the stench of rot wafted over him. A similar sight emerged from the depths of his memories: a Mage woman's body had been discovered near Ruber when he was still a child, clinging to his mother's skirts at the wretched sight. It became a rumor, a legend, and a painful reminder of the cruelty of magic. The bones of prey and the peeling corruption of Aviva's forest bore similar marks to the dead Mage.

He swallowed hard against the taste of bile on his tongue. "It's—"

"Unappetizing." Arayna spun away from the sight, her expression twisted with pure disgust. As she passed, she hooked her arm around his and pulled him away. "I don't want to eat anymore. I want this place cleansed."

It was too long for Oliver's liking before Nari emerged from her room and graced them with her presence. Midday had come and gone before they had said their goodbyes to Ronan and set off on the road to Maven's palace. It was dark before they had made any significant progress. He had promised to protect Nari from trouble, but abandoning his promise was becoming more tempting by the minute. Would Ronan really know if he throttled Nari just a little bit?

You're better than that, he reminded himself, having lost count of how many times those words had echoed in his mind. Responding with violence would only diminish his intelligence. Not to mention he still—unfortunately—needed Nari's magical talents to fulfill Aviva's last wish. The forest had already deteriorated beyond what he expected. It was unfair to prolong the effect just to satisfy his annoyance.

In addition to that, Arayna had returned to giving him the cold shoulder. Once the initial shock of what they saw had worn off, she hadn't spoken another word to him. She barely even looked at him, not even when he offered her the last of his dried, smoked meat that he had packed for the journey. She accepted it, but with a pointed attempt to look at her shoes for as long as possible.

He sighed. She had always been difficult to deal with, but this was a new level of confusing. At least the violent, angry beast was something he understood. If it weren't for the scar in his shoulder, for the memory of what she could do when she lost control, he would have said it was better than the cold shoulder.

It wasn't until the following day that they caught up to their escort at the halfway point—a tiny town that wasn't even on the map, consisting of only a few cabins, an inn and stable, and the dirt road that cut through it. In the distance, the spires of the glittering Summoners Palace could be seen beyond the mountains, a grim reminder of their destination.

It was the cusp of the afternoon when they strolled into town. Arayna flattened her ears against her head, shivering without Oliver's coat to protect her from the harsh wind. There was no one to see her—no one but the tall man swathed in a rich lavender cloak who stood waiting by the inn's stables. As they approached, his eyes drifted over them. As soon as they settled on Nari, he paid the stable boy hovering near the entrance. He approached the group while the boy hurried off into the stables.

"I assume you are Apprentice Mage Nari and her traveling party," he said with the polite dip of his head, though his gaze was stern. He flashed a gold pendant that hung from his neck, the emblem of the Summoners etched into its surface. "I was sent to ensure you reach the palace safely. High Summoner Maven is waiting for you."

"Wonderful!" Nari beamed and clapped her hands together, the picture of an overeager apprentice. "And you are?"

The man cast a sideways glance at Oliver and Arayna, who he greeted with a haughty sniff. His salt-and-pepper hair along with the lines in his face betrayed his age. *So not everyone at the palace under the child ruler is a child.* Oliver took some comfort in the thought.

"I'm Kier," the escort said. "If there are no further questions, we should be on our way."

The stable boy returned at that moment as if he was waiting for his cue. Behind him trailed four horses, one of which was a mare whose spotted coat was almost as speckled as Kier's hair. The other three were drab and brown, following the stable boy obediently. Like the escort, all of them bore the Summoners' emblem somewhere on their saddles or equipment. They weren't magical like Maven's steed had been, but Oliver was grateful for them nonetheless. If he had to walk all the way to the palace while Nari rambled incessantly, Kier glared at him, and Arayna ignored him, he probably would have given up the journey entirely. Lying down and dying was more appealing than that.

Though he would still be dealing with the same issues, at least he could do it from atop a horse, who dutifully did all the walking for him.

Kier thanked the stable boy, who dipped his head politely before hurrying away. Respectfully, Kier offered one of the brown horses to Nari. She refused his hand and hauled herself into the saddle. "I've ridden before," she said confidently, but there was uncertainty in her eyes. "Just lead the way."

The escort shrugged before offering the other two brown horses to Arayna and Oliver. Oliver had barely taken the reins before Kier was already turning away to climb onto the back of his own horse. Arayna sniffed at his lack of manners, no doubt forming some kind of complaint in her mind—he could practically feel it simmering in her connection with the bow. He found himself agreeing, but Kier's rudeness made him wonder what the man had been told about them. Perhaps he had heard that they were friends of the rogue Mage Aviva and he was only polite to Nari out of formality. Or, as was often the case, he feared her ability to wield magic.

Desperate to break the ice, Oliver leaned in to Arayna and whispered, "Maybe he should have learned manners with Aviva as well."

Arayna bristled and quickly turned away. Without a word, she awkwardly climbed onto the horse's back and urged it to rejoin Kier and Nari, who had already started riding off.

Oliver sighed. It was going to be a long, tiresome visit to the Summoners.

26

LURKING SHADOWS

Despite Nari's best efforts to make the trip as miserable as possible, it somehow passed without Oliver wringing her neck. At first, she talked to cover how much she struggled with her horse. Eventually, Kier took her reins and began to guide her horse alongside his speckled mare. It was then that she tried to engage him in conversation, needling him for information that she never got and pestering him with prying questions that were never answered. As prickly as Kier was, Oliver admired his ability to keep his lips sealed.

After a while, Nari's constant chatter had dissolved into background noise that Oliver could easily tune out. Instead, he focused on keeping his horse steady with the group and mulling over his fractured friendship with Arayna. It was in his best interest to repair it before she was lost completely, but she didn't seem all that willing to help. Much like Kier, she dodged every invitation to conversation. She did little more than sulk as they rode during the day and pretended to sleep too heavily to be interrupted at night, which irked him more. She never slept as soundly as she did when she was putting in the effort to ignore him—her ears were too sensitive to allow for truly deep sleep, always alert to sounds that he could never pick up. During their last night before they arrived at the palace, he tossed and turned, too consumed with worry to sleep. He glared at her back across the camp. She was being unreasonable, and he was the only one that had to suffer her unfairness.

Finally, he sighed and turned over so he wouldn't have to see her anymore. Cold wind nipped him through his coat, but it was nothing compared to the growing emptiness in his chest. Frustrated and weary, he squeezed his eyes shut in a determined effort to force sleep to come to him.

At least Arayna ignoring him meant that she was the same as she had always been, even with her curse and the loss of Kase and Aviva hanging over her.

Morning came and went. Before Oliver knew it, they were riding through the gates with the glittering palace of the Summoners standing tall and daunting before them. Sunlight glinted off the spires like they were constructed of polished metals, blinding him with the brilliance of silver and gold. As they grew closer, he realized it was a hazy film over the entire palace grounds that sparkled—a magic barrier of some kind, one that tickled his skin as he passed through it with the rest of the group. Inside, the air was sticky with warmth, locked in an eternal summer and separated entirely from the harsh coming of winter beyond the barrier. It chased out the cold as if it had never been there at all. Not that he could complain. After extended months of frigid weather, he was becoming quite sick of the cold, even though the full wrath of winter had yet to come.

A stone path cut straight through the grounds to the front entrance of the elaborate palace. Gardens lined either side of it, and beyond them were various facilities that sustained the palace. It was far from any city or town and supported itself with a combination of workers and magic. Oliver spotted a rich farmland on the other side of the palace grounds, ripe with crops ready to be harvested. He had always heard the palace was self-sustaining, but he never knew if it was set up out of selfishness or fear.

"This way." Kier steered his and Nari's horses away from the central path toward a paved road that wound through the garden to the stables.

Nari allowed herself to be pulled along, her gaze wandering as she took in the sights. A pair of guards passed on foot by Kier's side, offering curt nods to him and paying no attention to Nari. She watched them go with a stupid grin, probably glad to not be arrested on sight for breaking Maven's magic rules.

Arayna followed close behind Kier, completely still atop her horse and keeping her eyes on the path ahead. Her rigid back was impossible to read, and the only hint that she wasn't completely checked out of everything was the slight twitch of her ears at every sound. Even the bow had given up offering hints to her emotions. He swallowed a curse. Arayna wasn't an idiot. He wouldn't be surprised if she had found a way to block the connection from prying into her thoughts. But he didn't care as long as it kept her from losing her mind.

They had barely made it to the horse-yard gates before four young boys in loose-fitting lavender sashes rushed out to meet them. Kier dismounted and, after a quick word, left his steed in their hands. One of the stable boys, with dark hair and a smear of dirt across the front of his sash, approached Oliver's horse, glancing about and twisting the hem of his tunic. He stammered something unintelligible, and Oliver cringed at the awkwardness of his attempt at conversation. With a sigh, he swung himself down from the horse's back and dropped the reins into the boy's freckled hands. There was no reason to force the nervous wreck to speak if he didn't want to.

As Oliver pulled away, the boy grabbed his hand. For such a fragile thing, he had an iron grip, ice-cold and slick with sweat. The scent of horses was all over him, but his eyes were wide with fear like someone who had seen something unspeakable. "Is it true?" he whispered, leaning in closer. His eyes darted back to the long shadows cast by the late afternoon sun. "Have you come to kill the monster?"

"What?" Oliver wrenched free of his grasp, furrowing his brow. "No, we came to—"

"Elias." Kier clapped the boy on the back, his face stern. Behind him, the other three stable boys had already left with the horses, and the girls were staring at Oliver impatiently like the delay was his fault. Kier steered the boy away. "Back to work. Don't bother the High Summoner's guests."

"Y-yes, sir." Elias hurriedly dipped his head to Kier before trudging off with the horse in tow. Before he disappeared, he cast a longing glance back at Oliver. Then, he slipped into the stables and out of sight.

Once he was gone, Oliver wiped his hands on his pants leg. Uncertainty twisted his gut into a painful knot. He turned to Kier. "What's he talking about?"

Kier's lips twitched. "We should hurry. The High Summoner is expecting you," he said. He was already setting off back down the road before Oliver could argue. Nari hurried to catch up with him, a carefree skip in her steps. Arayna went more slowly, ears pricked and tail fluffed like there was danger nearby, but she didn't stop to voice her concerns.

"Helpful, thanks," Oliver grumbled. He looked at the shadows pressed against the stable wall one last time, the same ones the boy had seemed so wary of. It was difficult to tell from a distance, but they almost seemed to be watching him. He shivered involuntarily and jogged to catch up to Arayna.

THEY WERE LED in silence through the halls of the palace, past elaborate tapestries displaying the Summoners' great victory over the dragonborn and the creation of the barrier that sealed their numbers within the borders of Hybrid Territory—or at least, that was the intention when it was created. One tapestry depicted the crown and scepter being passed down from one High Summoner to the next, securing their control over the magical border and their place as rulers of the Navaric kingdom, a position won through their efforts in the war. To have the Summoners rule was to solidify the era of peace, and their promise of protection was still maintained in the current day. They were not Calistian dragonborn slayers, nor would they ever be, but it was hard to trump their power. Only the best magic users could become Summoners, and even fewer had the talents to become the High Summoner.

Oliver tried not to scowl as he walked down the hall, skimming over the art, but his face began to ache after a while—a sure sign that his efforts were failing. The glittering tapestries failed to mention that the Summoners had been absent for most of the war, allowing the destruction of Sheniir and the loss of countless lives. Their "all-powerful" barrier was hardly worth the cost as hybrids and dragonborn alike still trickled through, and the manpower required to keep them back was dwindling. The war may have ended, but it wasn't the victory that the Summoners wished for it to be. For all that power, they couldn't crush Selini's forces entirely. They couldn't even keep their own people, the Mages of the Navaric lands, from going missing and being slaughtered.

And now, they're too worried about who has a license to perform magic to even properly deal with the darkness creeping into our world. As much as Oliver disliked Tobias and Eira's plan to dive headfirst into the disaster they witnessed at the castle in Sheniir, he couldn't deny his own reservations about returning for Summoner Maven's aid. He couldn't blame Aviva for hiding from her, but she had left Nari with an impossible task, one that could only be settled with the help of someone more powerful.

Unfortunately, Maven was the only powerful magic-user he knew, and the only one likely to know a strong purification spell.

Summoners whisked past them as they walked, always in a hurry with their arms full of spellbooks, faces ghastly as the light slid over them. Some of them glared down their noses at the ragtag group of visitors, but others seemed too enveloped in their own self-importance to even notice. Their glittering, star-covered cloaks made them stand out like jewels among the other figures in the halls. After a while, Oliver started purposefully looking the other way when they passed. It wasn't much, but he hoped his efforts would at least bruise someone's ego.

"Here." Kier stopped at a pair of huge double doors, both cut from smooth oak wood and inlaid with gold floral patterns—petals unfurling, vines of lush leaves curling around the frame, roses in full bloom. When Oliver tilted his head, the pattern shifted. It, too, was made of magic. Kier paid the ostentatious decorations no mind and pushed the doors, revealing the throne room beyond.

Careless as always, Nari went in first, tossing her head and strutting like she owned the place. Arayna hung back, arms folded and eyes darting around. Standing amidst the rich decor, she looked like a muddy dog that had snuck in when the portcullis was left open too long—an unwanted creature that didn't belong, and from the way she flattened her ears to try to disguise them in her unruly hair, she knew it too. Oliver waited until she finally looked his way and allowed himself to give her the tiniest smile. She froze, caught off guard, and turned away sharply. Without looking back a second time, she tramped inside. Her reaction stung, but he gritted his teeth and went in after her.

Once they had all gone inside, Kier bowed and left. Oliver watched him go before turning to examine the elaborate room.

The ceiling was high, curved into an arch that met in the

middle, where a chandelier hung from a thick chain. There were no candles in the chandelier's rings, only hundreds of untethered flames that cast dark shadows over the room. A plush carpet covered the stone floor, trailing down the hall to the raised dias, upon which a rigid-backed throne constructed of glass sat. Light filtered through the crystal, dotting the floor with shimmering iridescent spots. Only three figures stood in the room: two guards on either side of the doors behind them and a young girl in a pale pink gown that pooled at her feet in a long train. Black hair tumbled down her back in waves of midnight curls, woven with gold and tiny teardrop pearls. When she turned, the gold circlet atop her head caught the light. Her graceful appearance was spoiled the moment her metallic eyes settled on them and her face twisted into a mixture of panic and disdain.

"You," she hissed, practically spitting the word.

As soon as she spoke, the doors slammed shut decisively. The flames flickered, but even that force was not enough to snuff them out.

Instead of bowing, Oliver remained stiff and lifted his chin higher so that he was looking down his nose at her. "Maven."

From his left side, Nari cleared her throat—loudly, because she never did anything quietly. "That's *High Summoner* Maven."

"I don't care," he said, and he was already rolling his eyes before he could stop himself. Respect and titles only seemed to matter to Nari when she gained something from using them. She had been perfectly okay with dropping Maven's title before, but now she was going out of her way to make him look like a fool. *Go ahead,* he thought, folding his arms. *She can think what she wants.*

Maven's gaze flitted between the two of them and Arayna. Taking in a deep breath, she straightened and smoothed her features into that agreeable look of disinterest. As she turned, she swept the train of her dress out of her way and walked toward them, glittering like thousands of pink stars beneath the chandelier's light. Her jewelry clinked as she walked and filled the silence that stretched between them with the pleasant rhythm. Once she was within a few feet of Oliver, her calming aura washed over him, attempting to soothe his annoyance, but he steeled himself and blocked it out.

"To what do I owe the pleasure of this visit?" Maven asked. Though her tone was cordial, her gaze was sharp as it settled on Nari, cold and calculating—the same way she had looked at Aviva before lunging for her. Her hands moved, and Oliver tensed, but she merely folded them together. "Unless you've come to turn yourself in, apprentice, I don't have time to waste on you three."

"Turn myself in?" Nari laughed nervously and took a step back, wringing her hands. Her confidence had suddenly vanished, leaving her floundering like a fish out of water. "N-no, I... well, um..." Helplessly, she glanced at Oliver.

He sighed. For once, she was speechless, yet he couldn't even find relief in it. Like everything else she did, she only chose silence when it became a chore for him, of course. But he had made a promise to Ronan. He shielded Nari with his arm, snatching Maven's attention from her. "You already know why we're here," he said. "No need to terrorize Nari."

Maven twisted one of her rings: a gold band set with a small opal in the center. Her gaze flicked away, darkened with shame. "I simply believe all Mages should earn their right to perform magic under the law. But you're right. There are more pressing matters at hand."

The dirty servant boy and the shifting shadows outside the stables flashed through Oliver's mind. Uncertainty coiled in the pit of his stomach. "Like a monster on the loose?"

Maven inhaled sharply. When her eyes snapped back up to meet his, they were steely. The very air around her sharpened with the presence of magic, crackling at her fingertips. "How did you know about that?" She lowered her voice to a whisper, though her words were no less piercing.

Oliver fought the urge to smirk as he slid his hands into his pockets. "I have my ways."

The longer they spoke, the more obvious it became: something had already ruffled her long before they arrived, making it all too easy to get under her skin. Part of him didn't want to know what could frighten the great Summoner Maven, rumored to be the most powerful human magic-user in the last hundred years, but he couldn't let himself forget that she was still a young girl. Of course she would be frightened if there were rumors of a monster roaming the palace grounds—it was no wonder the other Summoners seemed to be in such a rush. However, if she was off her game, perhaps it would be easier to needle her into letting Nari walk away with a spell to stop the corruption.

Maven studied him, the cogs in her mind visibly turning. After a moment, her shoulders slumped in defeat. "I'm sorry," she murmured, hiding behind a curtain of black curls that slipped over her shoulder. "I said I would find a way to help you stop the spread of corruption, but something has come up. I have been unable to do as much as I would like. But if you're here without Aviva, that must mean..."

"She's dead," Arayna said. Her voice cracked, lips quivering as she pressed them into a thin line. She curled her fists at her sides. "And this time, we know it's true."

"I am truly very sorry for your loss," Maven whispered, like she thought speaking too loudly would break Arayna. "We didn't see eye to eye, but Aviva was a skilled Mage. I can only assume things have gotten worse in her absence."

Oliver narrowed his eyes. "Maven, don't delay things. What's on your mind?"

Maven hesitated, looking guilty like a kid caught red-handed. Noticing that he was still watching her, she wiped the look from her face, straightened, and summoned her staff to her side. The iridescent gem on top sparkled in the light almost as much as the throne behind her, only it hummed with magic. It was decorated with more tassels and jewels than Oliver remembered, but he attributed that to her being at home rather than on the road. She dropped the end of the staff so that it hit the floor with a resounding boom.

Nari jumped, but Arayna only looked more annoyed.

"You're right. I should not waste time," Maven said. "I believe there is some kind of monster lurking in the palace. Servants and guards have been found dead in the mornings, though no one has heard any kind of struggle or cry overnight. Last night, the locks on my door were tampered with, but nothing managed to get inside." She fiddled with one of the gold tassels dangling from the length of her crimson staff, gaze distant. "No one has seen it, but I feel an odd presence in the darkness sometimes. I've tried to draw it out, but it always seems to escape. I don't know how I'm supposed to fight something I can't see."

"You think we do?" Nari scoffed, her reverence and fear forgotten as she reverted back to her usual mean self. There was a mocking glint in her stormy eyes, and she moved closer to Maven to look down on the younger girl. "Sounds like we came at a bad time. Your hands appear to be tied."

The light in Maven's opalescent staff flashed dangerously. With a howl, a rush of air fluttered through Maven's floor-length gown and shoved Nari back a few paces before it disappeared entirely. Maven gripped her staff tighter, her jaw set with determination. "Do not forget that I am being quite merciful by allowing you to enter my palace, to speak face-to-face with me when I should be sealing your magic right away. I'm doing this out of respect for your master, so you would do well to find some respect for me before I run out of patience."

"Respect?" Nari summoned her own staff, ripping it out of the air in a shower of sparks. "Don't lie to me! Aviva had to go to the lengths she did because of your negligence as a Summoner—if there's corruption in our world, it's because you allowed it to fester. I have no respect for someone who invited death to my master's doorstep!"

Behind them, the sound of swords scraping their sheathes sliced through the air. Oliver tensed. The guards at the door had advanced, their expressions unreadable beneath their helmets, but their target was clear. Ronan's words rang in his mind, louder than the thundering pulse in his ears. Even if there was truth in Nari's words, there was a time and a place. This was neither, and Oliver knew Ronan would hate to see his sister skewered because she couldn't hold her tongue.

Gently, Oliver touched Nari's arm. When she tried to jerk away, he grabbed hold of her wrist and yanked her from Maven. Nari swung to face him, eyes wild with rage. The moment she noticed the guards, however, she released her staff—which disappeared again—and relaxed in his grip.

Once there was no threat, Maven lifted her hand and the guards halted. They quickly returned to their posts, weapons settled once more in their sheathes. Oliver let out a breath and dropped Nari's wrist.

"I don't wish to argue with you," Maven said. Gracefully, she turned and strode toward the throne, pink skirts trailing behind her. When she reached the seat, she sank slowly into it and leaned against one arm, chin resting on her hand. "Instead, I would like to offer a trade."

"A trade?" Oliver frowned, searching her face for a hint of what might be on her mind. She gave nothing away; her silver eyes were as guarded as the palace vault.

She dipped her head in a small nod. "Nari's Mage Guardian said that she was coming to learn a more powerful spell, one that would allow her to gradually dispel the encroaching darkness. Is this correct?"

"Yes," Nari muttered, though she wasn't looking at Maven. The floor suddenly seemed to be of great interest to her.

"Become my personal guards, kill whatever monster is lurking in my palace, and I shall teach you something." Maven sank against the back of the crystal throne, practically glowing in the light that reflected through it. "That is my offer."

Oliver was still mulling over her words when Arayna shoved her way to the front, her ears pricked at the idea of slaying a monster. "Yes," she said immediately. "We accept."

Maven's lips curled in a smile. "Very good. I look forward to your assistance."

27

THE TRAP

Maven had a grand plan for catching the monster. The moment Nari asked about it, a wicked grin split her lips and an excited gleam lit in her silver eyes. "We'll set a trap," she declared. "We'll station ourselves in an open room and wait for nightfall. Watch the hallway, keep an eye on the shadows, but don't be too defensive. I believe the creature strikes when it sees its prey will be caught off guard."

"Just the four of us?" Nari questioned. She twisted the hem of her shirt, lips pursed. "Don't you think that's a risk?"

"It's a risk I'm willing to take, but the guards will be on standby."

Just like that, the Summoner whisked them away to her private library—a small room packed with expensive-looking books and fragile scrolls. It was only a few doors from her personal quarters and faced straight down the uncharacteristically sparse hallway lined with windows on one side. She left Arayna and Oliver standing outside the room before dragging Nari inside. The sound of rustling pages and meaningless magic-user chatter filled the air, carefree and definitely unguarded. He couldn't tell if that was purposeful or if they were both so engrossed in their old books that they had forgotten the purpose of this task.

He propped himself against the doorframe, arms folded, and let his mind wander a bit. If he had known leaving Tobias and Eira to find Aviva's apprentice would mean getting roped into being Nari's temporary guard, then ending up doing the same for Summoner Maven, he would have stuck with them. At least they were getting somewhere, hopefully, with Eira's vague memories as leads on the rogue dragonborn. Instead of helping Aviva like he wanted, he was charged with staring out into a dimly lit hallway as the sun slowly sank behind the palace, waiting for a shadowy monster that may never come. He was a hunter, one on a mission that would determine the fate of everything Aviva left behind, and yet he was stuck babysitting. It was nothing new, truthfully. He was always getting dumped with the tasks no one else wanted, such as Arayna and her curse or Kase's half-breed rescue project.

He sighed and knocked the back of his head against the doorframe. Exhaustion pulled on his limbs, and his eyes were heavy with sleep. If he stared too long, the shadows lining the hall began to swim, and he could almost believe they were crawling closer.

"You can rest, you know," Arayna said. She stood on the other side of the open door to the library, head cocked to one side as she studied him with glowing eyes. It was eerie how much the darkness seemed to change her features. She became more beast-like once the sun disappeared, but that couldn't completely conceal her familiar mannerisms from him. Though she tried to hide it, her foot bounced nervously and her tail hadn't stopped twitching since Maven had left them at their posts.

He looked away, ignoring the warmth that spread through his chest. It was the first thing she had willingly said to him since the forest. Clearing his throat, he smoothed his features. "I'm fine."

She sighed—both out of annoyance and pity. "I know you haven't been sleeping. The dark circles under your eyes are really unbecoming."

"I worked hard to acquire them. Glad you've noticed."

"Would you cut that out? I'm trying to be sensitive."

"Yeah, right. You're about as sensitive as a rock."

Groaning in frustration, she threw up her hands. "What's your problem?"

Oliver bristled and shot her a steely glare. Already, the flames of anger had returned, and he was choking on them. "My problem? You're the one who won't speak to me because I didn't tell you about the bow!"

Her cheeks colored almost as red as her wolf-like ears. "Because you lied to me!"

"I didn't lie. I just wasn't telling you the truth."

"That's lying, you cad."

"It was to protect you."

Hurt flashed across her expression, the barest hint of something softer beneath her hard exterior. For a moment, her eyes watered, and he feared he had pushed her too far yet again.

But then her ears stood on end, and she jerked her gaze back to the shadows creeping along the carpeted floor. They had grown since Oliver last paid attention. All the lights that once lined the walls in glass lanterns had been snuffed out, throwing the hall into pitch blackness. Even the windows seemed clouded.

Oliver's hand inched toward his hunting knife. His skin prickled, and the hairs on the back of his neck stood on end. The heavy, static presence of magic pressed against him, threatening to burst his ears.

A pair of blood-red claws emerged from the darkness, poised to attack as they raced toward Oliver. Arayna tackled

Oliver out of the way, throwing the two of them inside the library and out of range of the claws. She kicked the door shut before helping him to his feet and flinging herself against one side of the door. Oliver took the other, heart hammering against his ribs as he shoved all his weight against it.

Across the small room, Maven stood from her plush armchair, a dusty blue spellbook still open in her hands. Nari sank further into the cushions of her seat as if she hoped to melt into them. She gripped the arms of her chair so tightly her nails dug into the fabric. No one said a word, but the message was clear: the monster from the shadows had finally shown itself.

"Call the palace guards," Oliver snapped, grateful his voice came out even. "Your trap worked—great—but I don't see how we can take that thing on our own." He hadn't even gotten a good look at it since it seemed to be clawing its way out of the puddle of gloom in the floor. Determining what it was, how big it might be, and what kind of magic it could use was impossible without having seen more of it. There was no time to wait either—he wasn't keen on becoming dinner for that creature. It was a wonder Maven had talked him into her little plan at all.

Maven nodded and snapped the spellbook shut before tossing it into her chair. She tapped the opal gem dangling from her left ear, which began to glow on contact—a communicator gem. "I'll send word."

The lights in the library flickered. With a harsh snap, Oliver's vision plunged into darkness. Total silence greeted him in the black void. Even the press of the door against his shoulder vanished. For a sickening moment, he was completely alone. Ice crystalized in his veins and his throat clenched with panic. He gripped his knife. "Arayna?"

Instead of getting an answer, a heavy force slammed into him, throwing him to the floor. A red blur appeared atop him and twisted his arms sharply, pinning them against his back. Long nails dug into his skin through his thick coat, and he clenched his teeth against a hiss. Pain exploded in his shoulder just as the world returned, still cloaked in darkness but no longer isolating him.

It was several seconds before his vision began to clear and he could make out the shapes. Across from him, Arayna wrestled against an invisible figure that pinned her against the door. Her expression twisted with rage as she kicked and clawed, but her efforts were wasted against the force. Maven and Nari had both disappeared, leaving only Maven's book behind in the chair where she had been sitting.

Choppy strands of crimson hair spilled over his head and tickled his nose, concealing the seating area from view. Laughter cut through the haze in his mind. The grip on his arms tightened. "Looking for something?" a woman's voice teased. Her breath fanned his ear.

Oliver jerked, fighting the urge to gag in distaste. He twisted against her hold; his gaze snagged on her face, and his chest tightened in fear.

Red eyes, deeper and brighter than the mess of tangled, clipped hair framing her face, stared back at him. A wolfish grin split her lips, dripping with malice and hunger. It wasn't her harsh features that snatched his breath away, nor the fangs poking out beneath her lips, but the ruby scales dotting her cheeks, glittering in what little light managed to sneak through the unnatural darkness. A matching set of long red horns stuck out from the top of her head. Ugly scars marred her face and neck—pale, ragged lines that stood out painfully against her tan skin. She reeked with the stench of blood and sweat, a war-torn monster in search of her next meal.

His fear twisted, morphing into horror that settled heavily in the pit of his stomach. The monster lurking in Maven's palace was a dragonborn.

"Stay here," the red dragonborn cooed. Her knee dug into his spine, and he clenched his jaw to keep back the painful cry that rose in his throat. She tipped her head, pointed ears twitching behind her curtain of hair. A murderous gleam lit her eyes. "As soon as *ahkirel* Stellae kills that Summoner girl, it can be your turn."

"Oliver!" Arayna shrieked. She thrashed against whatever force was holding her until, with one final jerk, she dropped to the ground. With a fierce roar, she tackled the dragonborn and threw her off Oliver's back. He pushed to his feet, caught between the icy fear in his veins and his concern for Arayna. The two wrestled, throwing punches wildly and pulling the other's hair. Arayna slammed the dragonborn girl's head into the floor, and she finally stopped thrashing, eyes unfocused and staring blankly at the ceiling. Breathless, Arayna pinned the dragonborn down.

"Go," she said. "There's a second one—no illusion can hide that stench from me for long. I think it chased Maven and Nari deeper into the library."

He nodded and grabbed his bow, readying an arrow against the frame. "You're sure you'll be alright on your own?"

Arayna grinned. "Even a dragonborn needs a little time to recover after you bust their head. I'll hold her here, but don't take too long."

Arayna's unwavering confidence was both an annoying and inspiring trait. Oliver had learned to become skeptical of it as they grew up. However, when he held her gaze this time, he didn't feel the usual tug of anxiety in his gut. Instead, he found a small smile pulling at the corners of his mouth. She trusted him, despite everything. It was only fair that he offered the same respect to her.

Turning, he plunged into the thick shadows surrounding the sitting area and headed deeper into Maven's library.

28

MONSTERS OF RED AND BLACK

THE LIBRARY WAS SHROUDED in the same illusory darkness that Oliver had been thrown into when the red dragonborn tackled him. It was thick enough that he could feel its presence against him—as frigid as the winter air beyond the palace, it skittered over his skin with a life of its own. He held his breath, afraid of tasting the smog or swallowing it. It shimmered with magic and danger, and it trembled with the ancient presence of a dragonborn. Their power was designed to inspire fear, to convince their prey that they could not escape. They were created by their goddess Selini to be the greatest hunters, born and bred to kill. It was all they knew.

Oliver had never fought a dragonborn before, blessed to have enjoyed a peaceful childhood until Eira stepped in. But Kase had. He killed one in self-defense when he was only eleven years old, a feat that would have been impossible if not for Smoke, the ancient and powerful dragon who had formed a strange attachment to him. Even later in life, he clashed with powerful dragonborn warriors to protect Calix, one of which Oliver suspected was the Golden Dragonborn Aurum, though Kase had never said. They feared Kase, or at the very least

233

detested him for his power over them. When he came upon the *séti xenakri*—the Protector's Sword which was expertly crafted for the autumn spirit Xenah eons ago—they hated him more, but he kept on defending what he cared about. Dragonborn or monster—it didn't matter what he faced.

Until it did, and he breathed his last. The thought rose unbidden from the depths of Oliver's mind. Yet even that bitterness which usually cleared his nostalgia in an instant could not remove the painful ache in his chest this time, nor the slithering fear beneath the surface.

For once, he wished for Kase to be by his side.

Oliver's shoulder brushed one of the bookshelves in the dark, and he jumped. "Maven?" he called into the darkness. The library hadn't seemed so big when he first entered, yet now it stretched endlessly around him in a maze of unnumbered rows. The more he wandered, the more lost he became and his unease grew. With one hand trailing along the shelf, he continued down the row until it ended. "Nari, where are you?"

The faint sound of Nari's voice echoed in the distance. He couldn't make out any words, but the strained pitch suggested danger. Pulling his hand from the bookcase, he charged deeper into the darkness.

Something snapped against him, sending a jolt of electricity shooting up his arms. In a burst of white sparks, he broke free of the maze into a mirror image of the sitting room he had left behind. Maven and Nari huddled against the farthest wall, shrouded in a protective bubble of magic. A figure in deep violet robes loomed over them, hurtling shards of crystals at the bubble. With each hit, it began to fracture. Nari gritted her teeth and planted herself between Maven and the figure, her staff lit by a brilliant glow like the palms of her hands. A thin stream of blood trickled down her cheek. It was *her* barrier, Oliver realized with a start. She was protecting Maven.

Not to be outdone by Nari, Oliver shoved down his fear and

pulled back his bowstring. The arrow struck the dragonborn in the shoulder, and he stumbled into the edge of the magic barrier with a pained grunt. When he whirled to face Oliver, his eyes flashed dangerously—a striking silver on black scleras—and his lip curled back in a vicious sneer. He had deep, black scales that matched his curly hair and the coiled horns of a ram atop his head. His skin was a sickly shade of white, almost ashen in the firelight.

He let out a low, rumbling growl, and his pupils narrowed to tiny slits, which heightened his dragon-like appearance. As he poised one hand over the arrow protruding from his expensive-looking robes, he strode toward Oliver, tall and confident. "I thought Ignis had dealt with you," he hissed in a thick Draconic accent—something gruff and heavy, lacking that lyrical lull possessed by other languages. "It is even more bothersome that you managed to find your way through my illusion." The arrow slid easily out of the wound with a sickening squelch, pulled along by a magic thread connected to one of his paper-white fingers. He heaved a great sigh as he fiddled with the arrow between his fingers. "I suppose I must handle everything myself." In one swift movement, the shaft of the arrow snapped in two, and he discarded the broken pieces at his feet.

"You dragonborn can't shut up," Oliver muttered as he snagged another arrow from his quiver and nocked it against his bow. This time, he felt the familiar tug in his chest as the bow's magic hummed to life. The smooth wood turned to ice beneath his hand as a pale blue spread across the surface of the bow's curves. He took aim and let loose.

The arrow pierced the dragonborn's form, but he evaporated into smoke on contact. Its prey gone, the arrow flew into the wall mere inches from Nari, who flinched as it made contact. Shadows shifted, swirling as if stirred by a giant claw. They rolled across the room and carried the echo of laughter with them. Oliver gripped the bow tighter, scanning the dark room for any sign of the creature. Maven and Nari were still tucked against the wall opposite him. They had the sense to keep their barrier up without being told.

The pool of shadows darkened at Oliver's feet. He leapt back and reached for another arrow just as the dragonborn emerged with threads of violet strung between his fingers. All it took was one pull, and the threads went taut—Oliver's legs were tied. With his balance yanked out from under him, he crashed into the floor. Pain exploded in the side of his skull, throwing black spots across his vision. The threads bit into his legs, tight enough that it was a wonder they hadn't drawn blood.

"Better," the dragonborn mused. With the toe of his boot, he kicked Oliver's bow out of his hand—it skidded across the floor until it hit the wall. Smiling coldly, the dragonborn smashed his heel on Oliver's hand.

Searing agony ripped up Oliver's arm, pricking his eyes with tears, but he choked back the scream that rose in the back of his throat. He wouldn't give a monster the satisfaction of knowing it hurt. When a cold blade settled against his throat, he only glared up at the dragonborn. Up close, the scattered round scales across his face and neck glowed with a dark purple rather than inky black, just like his whiteless eyes. They were inverse stars, glittering atop the ghostly pallor of his skin. Words of legend and war tickled the back of his mind, where his mother's songs of the dragonborn of old lurked. *A seer whose face resembles the night sky: black stars on white ink, and cold, unfeeling eyes that could see far past the bounds of men.* Familiarity twisted Oliver's gut, and he stared in horror at the face of the dragonborn with the growing realization that something was terribly wrong.

The blade pressed firmly against Oliver's neck, and the dragonborn hauled him upright with a fistful of his hair. "I'll only ask one more time," the dragonborn sneered. "Lower your barrier, Mage, or I take the head of this boy and crush you along with your magic."

For once, Oliver met Nari's eyes with confidence. She was shaking, glancing between Oliver and the dragonborn. Her hold on her staff had not weakened, nor had the glow of the protective shield, but her face had grown pale with exhaustion. Sweat beaded her forehead, and her eyes were underlined with dark circles. Even if she refused the dragonborn's request, there was only so long before her body gave out.

Maven, however, looked murderous. The fear in her face was gone, masked by a heated glare that burned with defiance. There was one thing you did not do and that was demand something of High Summoner Maven—a lesson she had practically branded onto Oliver's mind after he and Aviva had tried to discuss their growing concerns with her following Eira's theatrical appearance in the forest. Only now, he wasn't the receiver of her rage. It was the dragonborn who thought to challenge her. She summoned her red-painted staff and shouldered past Nari, ignoring the other girl's anxious look. "There's no need for threats," she said boldly, stepping out from the barrier like it was nothing. Power crackled in the very air around her. "I'll ask you this, dragonborn: who are you and why did you come for me?"

"I was sent by the goddess Selini to kill you." He smiled, but the grin stretched too wide across his lips and bared too many of his teeth to be considered pleasant or friendly.

Maven lifted her staff, the opal end pointed at his face. "Then you are a Head Dragonborn?"

"Aren't you clever?" The dragonborn withdrew his knife from Oliver's neck, though his hold on his head did not loosen. "I am Stellae, the second Head Dragonborn and the servant to Selini's Black Head, Nox."

"Your companion?" Maven narrowed her eyes.

"Ignis, the Red Head Dragonborn—the fourth among us."

Oliver's breath hitched. Not only was he bait for one Head Dragonborn's assassination plot, but he'd left Arayna on her own with another one. Moreover, Head Dragonborn weren't supposed to be able to leave the boundaries of Hybrid Territory, much less make it all the way inside the Summoners Palace. The magic border maintained by Maven's family—upheld by Maven herself—was supposed to prevent them from crossing over. The escape of Aurum, the top of Selini's servants, was one thing, but now there were three? It was only a matter of time before all five escaped. War would break out once more, and this time, it would spell the end for humanity.

Tears sprang to his eyes at the ache in his neck, his scalp burning as Stellae wrenched back his hair. Slowly, he reached for his hunting knife, strapped to his waist. His right hand still throbbed from being crushed by Stellae's boot, but his left was free and closer to the dragonborn. If he could just get ahold of his dagger, he had a shot at escaping.

"I see." Maven's staff brightened as she began to trace a spell in the air.

Stellae tensed, his attention snatched by the stir of magic in the air. Oliver smirked as his dagger settled in his hand, and he wrenched it from the scabbard. Twisting, he plunged the blade deep into Stellae's thigh. The dragonborn howled, but it quickly morphed into a growl. Before he could retaliate, silver threads surrounded him. They tightened against him, pinning his arms to his sides. His grip went slack, releasing his hold on Oliver. Finally free, Oliver yanked the knife back out of the dragonborn's leg—relishing another defeated scream from him—and scrambled to Maven's side.

As soon as the dragonborn was bound, the darkness surrounding them began to dissipate. The mirror sitting room shifted back to normal, as well as the maze of library shelves Oliver had run through. Arayna came back into sight, now wrestling with the red dragonborn, Ignis, instead of calmly holding her down. Somehow, Arayna was still winning. She barely spared them a glance even though the illusion had dissolved, and neither did Ignis.

Stellae grunted with effort as he twisted and struggled in his binds, teeth clenched in a snarl. The silver in his eyes flashed violet. He pushed against Maven's spell and burst free in an explosion of silver and purple flecks. Rage twisted his face, and he swung to face them with murder in his eyes. Mouth open in a bloodcurdling roar, he lunged for Maven's throat.

She twirled her staff and thrust the glowing end in his face. She slapped her free hand across Oliver's eyes seconds before the opal exploded in a brilliant flash of white light. Even with Maven shielding his face, Oliver's vision flickered dangerously. When the flash was beginning to die down, she grabbed his arm and pulled him out of the way. Stellae crashed into the ground, dazed and blinking furiously.

"Stellae!" For the first time, Ignis looked over. She threw Arayna into a nearby shelf, which toppled over with Arayna trapped beneath splinters and books. The dragonborn summoned a large battle ax and raced toward them with the weapon raised. Her crazed expression was so familiar that Oliver froze. She almost looked like…

In a flash, Nari appeared between him and the weapon, staff raised as she summoned another shield. The weapon bounced uselessly off of it, and Ignis cursed in frustration. Nari glared at Oliver over her shoulder. "You're welcome!"

"Is that all you know how to do?" He wrinkled his nose. "It's becoming less impressive."

"Shut up!"

Maven touched his arm. When he looked at her, she nodded toward his bow, which was still lying on the other end of the room. Ignis was busy hacking away at Nari's shield, her scarred face darkening with each strike that failed. Behind her, Stellae rose unsteadily to his feet, grimacing as he tried to stand on his injured leg. His eyes no longer stared piercingly; it was safe to assume he couldn't see them at all. There was little he could do in such a state; however, Oliver wasn't sure Ignis would be stopped as easily. Even with the blood caked to the back of her head, she was somehow steady on her feet. She was a monster, but it seemed she knew little of magic.

His bow was made to slay such creatures.

While Nari maintained their shield, Maven summoned another spell. This one bound Stellae and successfully pinned him down. He screeched in defiance, and Ignis looked over at him. For a brief moment, Oliver was unattended. He dove out from the protection of Nari's barrier and snatched up his bow. It crackled with magic, eagerly awaiting release. He turned, nocked an arrow, and aimed for Ignis. Ice crystalized beneath his grip. He let loose, and the frigid arrow soared.

It struck her in the shoulder, and she went down with a garbled scream. Crystals of ice exploded around the point of the arrow and quickly swallowed her in thick chunks. She kicked and thrashed, but the ice continued to crawl across her body.

The door burst open, and Maven's soldiers flooded the room with Kier leading. The six of them surrounded the two Head Dragonborn, weapons drawn and at the ready. Ignis bared her teeth up at the men, but they didn't even flinch. Sighing in relief, Nari finally dropped her shield and let her shoulders sag.

"Detain them," Maven said, striding forward. "I want to question them further."

"Yes, High Summoner." Kier dipped his head before turning to issue orders to the men.

As two of the men moved to lift Stellae from the ground in his binds, his gaze suddenly snapped up to them, focused and clear. "Not today," he murmured. His form wavered and dissolved, sucked up into his shadow beneath them. Maven's silver threads fell slack before disappearing, their target gone.

Oliver waited with bated breath for the monster to emerge once more, but he never did. Ignis seemed to realize it first, and she cursed at her partner in a slew of Draconic. He didn't return —not even for her. One of the soldiers—a Mage, Oliver guessed, from the delicate staff in his hand—placed a hand against her forehead. A glittering set of foreign symbols appeared on her skin. Her eyes fluttered shut, and the last of her protests was lost. Four of the six men hauled her away, her shoulder still encased in ice with Oliver's arrow sticking out from the middle of it.

Shaking, Maven collapsed against her staff. Kier rushed to attend to her, while the other remaining soldier fled the room— perhaps to find a healer. Nari looked to be in no better shape, but she remained on her feet until she made it to the nearest chair, which she flung herself into unceremoniously. Oliver shuffled over to the collapsed shelf, fighting against the growing panic in his chest as he shoved the debris aside. He finally cleared the last of the books, exposing Arayna's face beneath the mess. Blood trickled from her nose and a small cut across her forehead, but her eyes opened when the light hit her face. She smiled as they settled on him.

"I was pretty great, right?" she asked.

In spite of everything, he found himself smiling. "Just wait until I tell you who you were fighting."

She grimaced. "I don't want to know."

"Trust me, you do." He held out his hand.

This time, she took it, and he pulled her from the debris with an ease that didn't seem to match the weariness hanging over him. He blamed it on the thrum of adrenaline in his veins, and returned to scolding her as he plucked a stray splinter from her hair. She laughed, and for a moment, all was right once more.

29

WITH THE SUMMONER'S BLESSING

IMMEDIATELY AFTER THE ATTACK, Maven was whisked away by her physician and a tall, glamorous woman with the same wavy black hair and delicate face as Maven. The woman's fussing and fretting was never-ending, but there was a certain unmistakable gentleness in the way it was delivered. Oliver guessed she was the previous High Summoner and Maven's mother, Estelle Astraela. He never thought he would see her in person since she had always been a recluse, even during her brief reign, but had become even more so after Maven's ascent to power. There were some things that even a natural recluse could not ignore. A direct attack on her daughter by two Head Dragonborn must have been one such thing.

After they left the library and the sound of Estelle's chatter faded into the next room, Kier broke the awkward silence with a sigh. "Maven will be fine," he said, still looking down the hall where she had been led away. "I'm sure she's just exhausted and will recover with rest. You were all lucky to escape mostly unscathed."

Lucky indeed. Oliver's lip twitched. For such powerful warriors, renowned by myths and feared all over Anticuus, the dragonborn certainly didn't try very hard to complete their job. Moreover, they had gone about it in a painfully roundabout way, spreading mistrust and fear about the castle first instead of going straight for Maven, masquerading as an unknown beast that swam through the shadows when they could have done just as well with their natural forms. He frowned and cast his gaze to the floor, the same place Stellae had been before vanishing. Did they come with some other goal in mind?

"We have prepared rooms for the three of you to rest in as well," Kier continued, and he gestured for them to follow him out of the library. "I'm sure Maven will want to speak with you when she is well again. Please, follow me."

Usually, Nari would be the first to trail after Kier, eager to blab about her personal accomplishments or whatever other fancy had struck her in that moment. Instead, this time, she barely managed to haul herself out of the chair she had collapsed into. Unfortunately for her, Kier was already out the door before he noticed—or if he did, he pretended not to. Oliver couldn't blame him. It wasn't his job to babysit Nari.

She pouted like a wounded puppy. Oliver rolled his eyes because it was, after all, *his* job to babysit Nari in Ronan's place. After a quick glance at Arayna to make sure she was fine, and receiving an encouraging nod from her for his efforts, he crossed to where Nari stood sulking. He hooked his arm around her shoulders, ignoring her protests, and guided her out the library doors.

"You're welcome," he said, unable to keep the smugness from his voice. For all her boasting, she was reduced to the same tired mess as any other Mage after a long battle. Aviva could hold out better than this, but he decided not to mention that.

Nari turned up her nose at him in her usual air of haughtiness, but her cheeks colored in embarrassment. Her silence spoke volumes.

"This is supposed to be your Guardian's job," he continued to needle her. "I expect a good tip for this."

"No."

Arayna snorted with laughter from somewhere behind them. "Does Ronan even get paid? What do illegal Mages *do* to earn money?"

"I have money!" Nari interjected. Her face had turned red enough that she could easily be mistaken for a ripe tomato. Even her ears peeking out behind her disheveled hair were crimson. "I could still take on jobs while running errands for Aviva. It's not like the average person asks for certification once they realize you can do magic—they just offer you coins in exchange for work."

"You dodged the first question." Oliver lifted one brow, fighting the urge to smile at the way she squirmed beneath his stare.

"That's between me and Ronan, so butt out."

Kier cleared his throat. He stood at the other end of the hall, looking blatantly unamused by their antics. If Oliver squinted, he looked much older, like his brief interaction with them was chipping away at his life. "This way," he said and turned a corner.

They followed him the rest of the way in silence—save for occasional snickers from Arayna and Nari's harshly whispered interjections for her to knock it off. It wasn't too long before they reached the wing of the palace reserved for guests. Kier showed each of them to their own rooms, all of which were situated next to each other. He explained that a court healer would come to see them soon and asked that they wait until then. With a curt nod and a final promise to see that food was brought to them by morning, he left them to their own devices. Nari slipped away from Oliver's support as soon as she had a chance and squirreled herself away in her room without so much as a thank you. At least that meant she wasn't too shaken by the attack.

However, it left Oliver and Arayna standing awkwardly together in the hall while the light in the sconces danced, flooding the silence with the whispers of flame. The shadows stretched across the floor, and he couldn't help the unease that settled in his bones. Everywhere he looked, he could see the dragonborn's black and silver eyes staring back at him from the darkness; they were calculating, cold, and unreadable.

If it bothered Arayna the way it bothered him, he couldn't tell. Her ears twitched, but they were no longer stiff and alert. Her eyes wandered the empty hall, settling briefly on a tapestry that hung between two rooms across from them. It was too dark for him to make out, but she could no doubt see every detail of the art in the dim light. There was some good that came from her curse, some skills that would be missed when she was eventually freed.

He studied the doors across the hall, rubbing the back of his neck awkwardly. The touch sent a stab of pain shooting across his knuckles, but he ignored it. There was no discoloration or broken bones, just a bruise and the knowledge that he had been stupid to let himself lose his weapon so easily. Arayna, on the other hand…

He steeled himself before addressing her. "Are you hurt? I could still catch up with Kier and ask for a palace healer—well, ask for one to see you more urgently, at least. They can't all be occupied with Maven."

"Nothing I won't shake off," she said, voice swelling with pride. "I'm a lot tougher than a bookshelf. And a dragonborn."

"Right." He fidgeted aimlessly, tugging on his sleeves or anything else on his person until his hand slowly found its way to the bow strung across his back. As always, it was warm to the touch, zapping the tips of his fingers with the faint presence of magic. His heart sank as he ran his thumb along the smooth wood. Every word, every conversation he had with Arayna since Nari's forest had been forced until the attack. It was a stark reminder that she was his friend despite all the hardships. He missed being her companion—talking, laughing, teasing, and enjoying each other's company. A lump formed in his throat.

"Listen," he began. When she looked at him, he inhaled sharply and ran his fingers through his hair as an excuse to look away. "I'm sorry for everything. I'm sorry that I lied. I'm sorry that I didn't feel I could tell you the truth. I thought I was doing the right thing, what was best for you, but I was motivated by fear. I was being unfair."

Arayna chewed her lip, pointedly avoiding his gaze when he tried to meet her eye. Her ears drooped. "I'm sorry, too," she said. "I should have considered…" She stopped, and her foot began to tap irritably against the floor. Sighing, she hugged her middle and let her hair fall in her face, shoulders hunched so that she was as small as possible. "You have a right to be afraid after everything. I know you didn't make this choice selfishly. You're right, I am cursed, and I had always wondered why I hadn't already been lost. But…" Finally, she lifted her head. "Can we agree to work together on this?"

For a moment, he was lost in her eyes. They were a striking shade of blue like the rich array of flowers that sprouted around the edges of the forest back home, like the endless azure sky on a cloudless day—clear and bright and beautiful. They weren't the eyes of a monster, one that only knew how to kill. He found himself smiling, and a pleasant warmth bloomed in his chest. "I'd like that," he whispered, cautious that the moment would break if he spoke too loudly.

She grinned, returning to the familiar face of his friend, scars, wolfish fangs, and all. "Goodnight, Oliver." With that goodbye, she slipped into her room. The door closed softly behind her, but even it no longer seemed as uninviting.

Alone, he examined his bow, tracing his thumb over the

wood again. It snagged on a small, jagged crack in the material, and he winced. Sparks of magic snapped around the edge of the break, pouring out from the inside like blood from a wound. As quickly as it had come, his elation faded.

The bow was broken.

THE WHOLE PALACE erupted in panic once news of the dragonborn attack on their beloved High Summoner spread. The Mage that came to heal Oliver's wounds couldn't seem to get away fast enough, her eyes always darting around as if she thought the walls were full of dragonborn. He tried to reassure her, but it didn't seem to do much. Especially not after she had already been graced with the task of tending to Arayna in all her beastly glory. The poor Mage scurried off and disappeared the moment the sharp pain in Oliver's scalp diminished.

Guards were immediately dispatched to search for traces of Stellae. They looked high and low, but he was never found. It seemed he truly had fled, leaving Ignis behind to rot in her cell. Or perhaps he trusted that she would find a way to free herself —both outcomes Oliver found unpleasant to the point of sickening, but he tried not to think about it. A few days passed and Ignis still remained under lock and key, closely monitored by Mages and palace guards. He dared to hold an optimistic opinion that she would remain there until Maven decided otherwise. He could only hope Selini, the five-headed dragon Ignis served, would not take offense at the arrest of her servant. There was little to be done when she herself deemed it necessary to inflict her wrath upon someone personally—or so he assumed. He couldn't remember any story where she had ever acted on her own. It was always her servants being sent out into the world.

When there was a quiet moment, he pulled Arayna aside and

showed her the crack in the bow. It was no longer than his thumb and barely wider than a split in the wood, but the Mage's warnings rang in his mind. If it was broken, he would lose Arayna entirely.

She shrugged when he finished his explanation. "I don't feel any differently," she said. "Maybe this isn't enough to matter?"

"Everything matters with magic, Arayna," he snapped as he wrapped the break in the bow in a cloth like bandaging a wound. It had stopped oozing that glittering substance, but the thought of the crack spidering further up the wood left a bitter taste in his mouth. It was only a matter of time before it broke entirely, and he didn't even understand how it had cracked in the first place.

Stellae's face flashed through his mind again, and he shivered. Maybe it wasn't too far-fetched to assume the dragonborn had something to do with it. If he knew the secret behind it, would he bother to destroy it?

Before Arayna could continue the conversation, Nari emerged from the hall, beaming with pride and life once more. Her days of rest had done her well. She walked with a skip in her step, lighter than air as she joined them outside the ornate doors to the throne room. Maven had summoned them together —it would be the first time they had seen her since the attack, but if Nari was well again, Oliver assumed she would be too.

"Shall we go in?" Nari raised her hand to knock, wiggling her brows at them. In her white cloak, she looked deceptively pure, a wolf in sheep's clothing. Today, it seemed, she believed she had earned something for her efforts.

Oliver sighed. Even if he disagreed, she would march on in anyway. All she had done for the last several days was complain, eat, and sleep. She probably even complained in her sleep.

She knocked—loudly and decisively. Arayna frowned, cutting her eyes between Oliver and the door like she had wanted to say more before Nari intruded. All he could offer was a helpless shrug. They were again reduced to their role as stewards of Nari's will, hooked and dragged along like fish.

The doors swung open, revealing the luxurious throne room within. This time, bright sunlight streamed through the windows in swaths of luminant gold. Maven stood poised at the foot of the dias, hands folded in front of her and face graced with a gentle smile. She was dressed in purple robes like when he had first met her, draped in the same diaphanous cloak of the Summoners that resembled the sky at sunset. Gone was the bejeweled dress of a queen; she had returned to her role of scholar and magic-user, portrayed in even the way her shoulders settled. Her mother was nowhere to be found, having once more hidden herself away in the depths of the palace now that the anxiety had passed. When the doors closed behind them this time, Maven's shoulders relaxed.

"Thank you for your help." Maven dipped her head in a polite bow, black curls spilling over her shoulders like waves of ink. "I'm not sure I would have been able to overcome them on my own."

Oliver bit his tongue to hold back the laugh that rose in the back of his throat. They had played their roles as distractions quite well, but he was certain Maven didn't really need them. Her pleasant demeanor was difficult to read, a mask that disguised her true thoughts well. However, he was no stranger to the way magic users thought, especially those who were extremely talented.

He half expected Nari to give a haughty sniff, her back straight and her eyes glittering with mirth, and say something like, *of course you wouldn't have because it was thanks to my amazingness that we won.* But she didn't. Graciously—in a very practiced flourish—she mirrored Maven's respectful bow. "We are honored to have been of assistance to you."

Oliver met Arayna's gaze across the way. She grimaced, looking just as confused as he felt.

"As promised," Maven continued. She produced a sealed scroll from the air, raining sparks from her fingers as she took hold of the parchment. In small, measured steps, she approached Nari. "This contains a purification spell that might help you, but I'll warn you that it takes a great deal of magic to conjure it. Not many magic-users can use it—even I have trouble with it. Only you will know if you will be able to learn it and make use of it, but it is powerful enough to drive out the darkness. And…" With another wave of her hand, gold rings glittering in the sunlight, she produced a small brooch. Its gold face was stamped with the Summoner's insignia, edges rimmed like a coin.

Nari brightened, and a tiny gasp slipped through her lips. She bounced on the balls of her feet, wringing her hands eagerly. "Is that a Mage license?"

"An *apprentice* license, yes," Maven corrected. "I know your master has passed, but I believe she knew you still had room to grow. Whatever she was trying to teach you, you must learn it first before I can grant you your full title." Her silver eyes darkened, and she looked away. "This is the most I can do for now."

Nari accepted her gifts reverently with a childish gleam in her eyes. She was practically shaking with excitement. She held up the gold brooch to the light, basking beneath it like it was the sun. When she remembered her manners again, she pocketed the brooch along with the old scroll. "Thank you," she added quickly, less practiced and graceful than before.

Maven tried to smile again, but it didn't reach her eyes this time. "I didn't realize we would be facing two of Selini's disciples. I apologize for putting you through that."

Oliver's skin crawled with unease, and it took all his willpower not to look over his shoulder. He could almost *feel* the black dragonborn's stare drilling holes into his back, him breathing down his neck, his claws scraping across the carpeted floor. If this was how Eira felt in Aurum's presence, it was no wonder she was so quick to try to forget, and why she was determined not to let him get ahold of anyone else. But more important than that was the question looming over him, one that had clung to his mind for days as persistently as cobwebs.

"How did the Head Dragonborn get here?" he asked. "Isn't the barrier supposed to prevent them from crossing over?"

"It's strange that Selini would send two of her top generals." Arayna nodded, her brow wrinkled in thought. "She must be desperate to get rid of you."

Maven tensed. "The only explanation I can think of is that they wish to have the barrier spell broken by killing me, but even then they would still have to find the core and destroy it. With it gone, however, they would be able to march over the border and continue their conquest for complete control over Anticuus. As for how they got past that barrier themselves…" She chewed her lip and cast her eyes to the ground. Twisting her robes in her fingers, she remained in thoughtful silence for some time. The truth became painfully obvious, long before she admitted it. "I don't know," she whispered. "I intend to question Ignis further about it. I must do everything in my power to prevent more dragonborn from crossing over before a slaughter begins."

"You should know Eira believes the Golden Head Dragonborn has escaped as well," Oliver murmured, scrounging for the gentlest way to break the news. There was no point in being soft. No matter how he phrased it, it would shatter her. Upholding the barrier was her duty, and by letting three of Selini's most powerful warriors cross—not to mention any stragglers that had meandered over due to the flimsy rules of the original spell—she had failed.

"I see." She made a pointed effort to avoid his gaze as she

twisted the tiny opal ring. "I will discuss this with the Summoners Council as well."

The silence that fell was stifling, thicker than the air that polluted the illusory library Stellae had plunged them into. Maven's attention seemed to have wandered, and she turned to the windows, which overlooked the palace courtyard. Nari had gone back to staring at her brooch, more enthralled by it than the spell they had worked so hard for. Arayna stared blankly at the glittering chandelier above them. Because it was midday and sunlight poured into the room, it was unlit, but it still sparkled like the world's most expensive piece of junk.

Oliver's broken bow flashed through his mind, and his throat tightened. Steeling himself, he joined Maven by the window, throwing a careful glance back to make sure the girls didn't follow. They both paid him no mind, content to let their attentions wander elsewhere until Maven dismissed them. The Summoner didn't look up as he joined her side, so he drew in a calming breath to let his nerves settle. "I know you have other things on your mind," he said, keeping his voice low though he was aware Arayna's keen hearing would pick it up anyway. "But I wanted to ask if you know anything about the beast curse and how it might be revoked."

Maven shook her head, letting her hands drop back to her side. "I'm sorry, but if you have a chance, you might visit the archives in Calistie City. Beast magic stems from druid practices, and most of their records are stored in the Calistian Royal Library. You'll need special permission to enter though."

"Can't you grant it?"

She pursed her lips. "Calistian territories do not belong to me. I doubt my authority would mean much there. However, Aviva was descended from a druid family, wasn't she?"

"She didn't keep up with any of their practices and seemed to know very little about beast magic." When Arayna was little and first began to discover her ability to shapeshift, Aviva was in awe of such a power. She studied it at length by observing Arayna, but he doubted she had any secret knowledge about it—especially not after she had been secluded for so long.

Maven glanced at Arayna, whose ears were not so discreetly pricked in their direction, though her gaze was trained on the opposite wall in a poor attempt at feigning disinterest. "I can't encourage certain behaviors outright, but I have faith you'll find a way to uncover what you wish to know."

The air suddenly crackled with the presence of magic. Maven spun, summoning her staff, shoulders tense. Oliver followed her gaze to the empty space between Nari and Arayna, which had lit up in a brilliant flash of white and gold. Arayna leapt back, hackles raised and lip curled. Nari regarded the strange phenomenon coldly, unconcerned but no less intrigued.

With a loud crack and another blinding flash, two figures appeared in the throne room, and the light winked out of existence behind them. Ronan now stood at Nari's side, his white cloak caked in mud at the hem and his face haggard. The second figure, a familiar woman in a red skirt, collapsed at Nari's feet, shaking with exhaustion and heaving in greedy gulps of air.

Oliver put his hand to Maven's staff and lowered it, shaking his head. Confusion and concern swirled in his mind as he crept toward the thief. Last time he had seen her, she had gone off with Tobias and the others on her ridiculous quest for the Shadowslayer. Now, she was covered in mud and scrapes, and her hair was tangled, loose from its usual braids. She looked as if she had run halfway across the continent.

Eira didn't wait to be greeted. Her head snapped up the moment he was a mere step away, and she grabbed his arm with an iron grip. "It's Aurum," she breathed. "He took them away."

PART FOUR
DESPAIR

"Soon, the shadow learns his curse can be ended
if only he offers a sacrifice of power and blood.
Delirious with joy, he promises to return again
to the man he once was."

30
WHITE SCALES

EMPTINESS SURROUNDED CALIX IN A COLD EMBRACE. The first thing he noticed was the mental block between him and Stiria. The thread of their bond stopped at the base of a wall, one that oozed with a foreign presence. Panic clawed up the back of Calix's throat in a desperate cry that begged to be released. Without Stiria, his thoughts drifted, unable to cling to anything, and his heart hammered his ribs with fear.

He couldn't see straight. The world was spinning, a distorted array of wild colors and flashing lights, paired with the familiar ring of Aurum's cruel laughter in his ears. His head throbbed, and it took him several long seconds to realize his troubled vision was connected to his headache and the heaviness in his limbs, the blow to his head likely to blame. His back was slick with sweat, his hair plastered to his forehead with the same, and yet he shivered uncontrollably. But it wasn't his nightmarish visions that snapped him back to his senses or the fiery agony tearing across his skin or his separation from Stiria. It was the scent of blood. *Her* blood.

It was everywhere. His hands were sticky with the stuff, and he cried out as he tried to scramble away from the crimson stains. They clung to his skin, followed him, and refused to let go. He was sitting in a puddle of it, and the levels were slowly rising. He was drowning in it.

For the second time, he awoke with a start, unsure of when he had drifted off again. It was becoming harder and harder to keep his bleary eyes open, to distinguish reality from his freakish imagination. Everything hurt—even his lungs spiked with pain each time he took a breath. Biting hard on his tongue, he squeezed his eyes shut and forced himself to recall what had happened. Aurum struck his head, and darkness had overtaken him, but what about before that? He sat now in a dingy cell, breathing in the stench of blood and other fluids he would rather not dwell on. There was no arguing that Aurum must have brought them there, though why he kept them alive was a mystery. He hated to think what Aurum might be planning; death was certainly a far better alternative.

A weight settled against Calix's shoulder, forcing him to take in the present again. His back was pressed to the cold stone wall, his knees drawn up against his chest to keep himself as small as possible. He twisted, and his gaze settled on Kiara's head resting against him, her long hair spilling over him. It was tangled in his fingers. Though the scent of blood still hung in the air, it wasn't from his skin. It was her wound, a long, jagged cut across her chest.

His heart fluttered anxiously. He couldn't remember sitting with her. He nestled closer and leaned his head atop hers, straining for the sound of her shallow breathing. It was faint, barely audible above the pounding of his heart echoing in his ears, but still there. He twisted a small section of her long hair around his fingers in a messy braid. He lost count of the number of times he had done that while she slept. It was the only thing that kept him from losing himself, though the ache in his head said otherwise. He was slipping.

He wanted to shrink in on himself. Helplessness writhed in

the pit of his stomach, and he tasted bile at the back of his throat. She should never be the one bleeding to death, the one getting hurt.

"It's all my fault." He wasn't sure how many times those words had left his lips, but it never felt like it was enough. "I shouldn't have let this happen. Not to you."

No answer. Not even so much as a shift. She was perfectly still, cold against his side.

It was his fault.

An itch crawled through the skin beneath his scales, one he desperately yearned to scratch. He gritted his teeth against the urge and kept his hands busy braiding her hair—twisting and tucking and folding, a rhythm he knew by heart that soon soothed the compulsion. It all came back to him in a rush—this was what he had been doing since he first awoke in the cell, since he first assured himself that she was still alive. It was the only thing keeping him from tearing himself apart. One tiny braid at a time, he was grounding his sanity, biding his time until Aurum thought to return.

She stirred. "Calix?" she whispered, so hoarse he might have missed it above the blood roaring in his ears.

He startled and sat upright. "I'm with you. Are you alright? I–I don't know what else to do, Kiara. There's blood everywhere and..."

She sat up, her face contorting in pain. She groaned and kept her hands pressed firmly to the gash, but it was a meaningless action. Her wound had been wrapped haphazardly in Tobias's coat before he retreated to the other side of the cell. He had done it while Calix watched in stunned silence, the world shrinking to a tiny pinhole as his chest tightened with panic. His meager attempt at first aid was already soaked through. Aurum didn't intend for her to survive. It was a miracle she hadn't died yet.

"Don't move." He put his hand against her shoulder. She

flinched, and he quickly withdrew. "Please. You have to stay still."

Sweat beaded her pale, clammy face, but she managed a smile. With shaky hands, she reached for the pocket of her tunic and produced a small object humming with pleasant energy. There was a prideful gleam in her eyes when she held it up, one that almost brought life back to her face. It didn't last long before her head collapsed against his shoulder again and her fist thumped his chest, the object still tightly enclosed. "I'm not going to die that easily," she murmured, already fading again.

He squeezed her bloody hand—the tips of her fingers were like ice in his grip. At his touch, her fingers uncurled, revealing a pearlescent white scale, one that was giving off a constant pulse of healing energy. A scale from Faiera's back. It wasn't enough to close the wound, but it had been able to stop Aurum's attack from killing her.

A shaky sigh of relief escaped his lips, and he pressed the scale back into her hand before closing her fingers around it. He gave her fist another quick squeeze. "*Illémine*, you scare me."

He thought he heard a soft laugh, but her eyes had already fallen shut again by the time he looked at her face. His relief was soon shattered as she fell limp against his side. The scales of white dragons did hold great healing properties, but they couldn't sustain her forever. They were only stalling the inevitable. Without Faiera or a healer, she would die.

Dimly, he thought of his own wounds, how she had fled the icy depths of the mountains while he was unconscious and risked her identity for a healer. If she had experienced the same crushing fear as him, it was no wonder she'd behaved so rashly.

For her, he would fight Aurum barehanded. He would do anything to make sure she survived.

As the itch returned to his scales, he forced himself to focus on something else. He rolled his head back and took in the sad sights once more. The cell was small, barely wide enough for two of them to lay side by side without touching either the back wall or the thick metal bars that lined the exit. Tobias was huddled on the far side, shoulders hunched and knees pulled to his chest. His head leaned against the corner between the bars and the wall, and his eyes were shut with sleep. Though bruised and weary, he was in far better shape than Kiara, but even he deserved a moment of rest.

Two sets of footsteps echoed down the hall, bouncing shamelessly along the empty stone corridor. One was a confident stride, taking long, heavy steps—a telltale sound that sent shivers down Calix's spine. The other was light and quick, like a child desperate to keep up with a parent. Laughter pealed down the hall, but it wasn't Aurum's.

Tobias jolted awake, and his hand immediately flew to the empty place where his sword should have been. Confusion darkened his expression before he noticed Calix. His face hardened immediately.

A shadow passed over the bars, and the gleeful laughter trailed closer. Seconds passed before a small boy appeared in front of the cell, his round face stretched in a wide grin and his eyes shimmering with mirth—gold against pools of ink. He danced on light feet, stumbling and twirling and giggling away. His presence sent goosebumps shooting up along Calix's arms, and he huddled closer to Kiara.

The boy was unlike any creature Calix had seen—his skin was gray, yet full of life, and coal black scales covered his cheeks and the bridge of his nose. The same black shade stained his hands from his claw-like fingertips up to his elbows. His teeth were sharp like a dragon's, stark white against his ashen face, and two horns poked out from his spiky black hair. In place of ears, he had a crown of spines along the sides of his face, their shape reminiscent of a normal black dragon's. His skinny form was concealed beneath a black cowl that fell to mid thigh, exposing bare legs and clawed feet. A dragon's tail swished behind his back.

He was like a dragonborn who had failed to attain their true humanoid form. Selini would call that an *imperfection,* and yet he was loose, running the halls freely alongside Aurum, whose hands bore the blood of countless innocents who were deemed unworthy. Children like Calix, whose life didn't matter in the eyes of the goddess, all because he didn't suit her image of the dragonborn. Calix's lip curled. Pure disgust bubbled to the surface.

The dragon-boy sidled up to the bars, inky fingers curling around the cold metal as he pressed his face to them. There was life behind his eyes but little intelligence. "The master approaches," he sang, head swaying to a rhythm only he could hear. "Look alive—as well as you can."

"Get down, Trepi," Aurum snapped. He emerged from the corridor just in time to yank the boy from the bars and throw him to the floor. Trepi squealed as his back slammed into the ground, but he quickly righted himself and began to bound circles around Aurum as if nothing had happened. Aurum merely swept him aside with a stern glare.

For the first time, fear sparked in Trepi's eyes. He backed away from Aurum, head low, and finally plopped himself down against the opposite wall with his shoulders hunched. With the swish of his floor length cloak, Aurum moved in front of Trepi and completely concealed his small form.

Calix stiffened. Flashes of his previous encounters with the dragonborn raced through his mind, along with the phantom sting of every wound he had ever received from his desperate struggles to escape. These were the golden eyes that haunted them, that he fought so hard to escape from, that Kase gave his life to keep him away from. But here he was again, a bird in a cage trapped in the palm of Aurum's hand.

Against the icy fear building in his chest, against the small part of him that screamed to keep his head down, he met Aurum's gaze and held it. If he went down, he would go down fighting—to his very last breath, he would make Aurum's life as miserable as possible. He would be the greatest thorn in his side.

He expected Aurum's face to be beaming with hatred and amusement, but it wasn't. This time, there was a cold rage in the depths of his glare. It was no longer that boisterous, showy mask he put on before. Instead, the lines in his face appeared deeper, and the circles beneath his eyes were darker. Still, his smile was just as chilling. "How long has it been since you found yourself in a cell like this, Caeruleus?" he drawled, skimming his fingers along the metal bars that separated them. "Four years? Five years? How did you enjoy your taste of freedom? Was it worth the blood shed?" He chuckled to himself. "I ought to leave you here to rot. I wonder how long it would take for you to turn to dust."

"You can't leave me here." Calix forced a shaky smile, and with it came a nervous laugh that rattled like his bones. "The longer I live, the more I spite the goddess with my imperfections, and the more of a failure you are."

Something in Aurum's face twitched. Calix held his breath, waiting for him to strike out in rage and demand that he learn to hold his tongue when speaking of the great goddess Selini and her mighty Head Dragonborn servants, but he didn't. Beneath Aurum's glowing gold stare, Calix's skin crawled with unease. His silence was a greater punishment than his rage.

Tobias rose to his feet, slowly, carefully, as if he were afraid to draw Aurum's attention. "How about a deal?" he murmured in a shaky undertone. "Kiara will die if she isn't treated soon. Bring us a healer, and we'll do anything you want."

Calix sucked in a sharp breath and threw a glare at the impertinent swordsman. Words were his strong suit, but Calix could never understand what was going on in his head. Dragonborn didn't take deals—there was no way he was foolish enough to believe Aurum would be true to his word.

Aurum smiled. He was no fool either. "Ah yes, the Calistian princess. I suppose it would not be in my best interest to let the heir to the throne die. Then again, if I sent her dead body to the gates of Calistie City, how long before her enraged people brought war to Selini's doorstep?"

Hot rage ignited in Calix's core. He gritted his teeth against the urge to lash out, cradling Kiara closer instead. *Don't fall for his taunts,* he reminded himself in Stiria's place. Mechanically, he forced a deep breath—in and out.

Tobias's fists curled at his sides, but his face remained impassive as he regarded Aurum. "There's something you want more than war, isn't there? Something you would trade for. Heal Kiara, and we'll give you whatever you want."

A thoughtful frown settled on Aurum's face, but it couldn't disguise the malevolent glow to his eyes. At his feet, Trepi hissed, back arched like a cat and expression twisted in disgust. Aurum ignored him. "I would like to fight her again when she's full of life," he said. Turning to the dragon-boy, his voice hardened. "Trepidatio, fetch an acolyte from the temple. Preferably from Coae's wing. She houses the best healers. Be quick about it."

Trepidatio shot to his feet, mouth open in indignation. His gold-and-black eyes cut between Calix and Aurum, burning with hatred, but he snapped his mouth shut and gave a resigned sniff as he turned up his nose to the group. "Yes, Your Goldness," he said begrudgingly. As he dove toward the floor, his form shrank, growing wings and scales until he turned into a black dragon no larger than a dog. He flew off, grumbling to himself the whole way.

Once Trepidatio was gone, Aurum touched the cell door, his palm glowing with gold flecks of magic. The door swung open, creaking loudly on rusty hinges. "Caeruleus comes with me. The other two will stay here and wait for Trepidatio."

Calix shrank against the stone wall, prey beneath the monster's narrowed eyes. He shivered, still cradling Kiara's cold body in his arms. "That's your only request?"

"No." Aurum laughed, and his pitch black scales darkened suddenly. "I was already coming to get you. I'll collect on my part of our bargain later."

"Absolutely not," Tobias snapped, throwing himself between Calix and Aurum, arms raised to further block Aurum's view. "We stay together."

In a flash of light, a sword appeared in Aurum's hand, its wickedly sharp blade glinting in the dim torchlight. "He comes with me," the dragonborn growled, "or the deal is off and the girl dies."

The fear growing in Calix's chest suddenly blossomed, choking out all rational thought. The room spun around him, shrinking in until it was crushing him. He heaved in a shallow breath, desperate to fill his lungs, but it was never enough. Darkness pressed against him; it clawed at his legs, sank its teeth into his arms, and threatened to drag him into the depths. Even the itch in his scales couldn't ground him. Even the stench of blood beneath his nails couldn't pull him out. All he could see were those cold eyes—that brilliant gold that consumed everything else, backed by those coal-black scales and that confident smile.

There was nowhere to run, not when he was facing Aurum.

Kiara's head slipped from his shoulder and thumped against his chest. Startled, he glanced down at her, now sprawled across his lap. Her eyes were sealed shut, but they fluttered restlessly beneath her lids. Sweat beaded her forehead, and she too was fighting to breathe as the world slipped from her grasp, as her body slowly gave up on her.

It was his fault.

Swallowing hard, he gently lifted her and laid her down against the wall, careful not to disturb the crude bandaging of her wounds. He squeezed her hand one more time, grateful for the pulse of warmth from the white scale, and stood. Both Tobias and Aurum stared, one begging him not to go and the other confident he would.

"Calix." Tobias shook his head, shoulders trembling. His lips were sealed tight, but there was no way to completely seal the words behind them. *Don't go*, his eyes said.

Against the tightness in his throat, against the ice crystalizing in his veins, against the emptiness in his heart, Calix forced a smile. "I can't ask Kiara to die for me. Look after her."

He didn't have the opportunity to hear Tobias's response before Aurum grabbed his wrist and yanked him out of the cell. The door slammed shut behind him, and he was hauled away with his head hanging.

31

FAMILY

Aurum's flowing black robes trailed after him, collecting dust from the floors as he walked briskly down the hall. They no longer dripped shadows and rolled with smoke as they did when he masqueraded as the Shadowslayer, his Draconic features hidden beneath the blank white mask that left nothing but murder behind. His grip on Calix's wrist was icy, void of any natural warmth, but his hold was too strong for a corpse. Gold threads wrapped around Calix's arm so that even if he managed to pry himself free of Aurum's hand, he was still tied to him. That didn't stop Calix from trying. Glaring daggers at Aurum's back, he purposefully dragged one foot. His toe snagged on a loose stone, and he pitched toward the ground. His father used to let go when he fell, giving Calix the chance to slip away.

Aurum held tighter and hauled him back to his feet without a word. It was no longer the face of a scoffer, the Aurum who laughed as he cut his enemies down. He stared ahead with a solid determination, lips set in a stiff, thin line. The gold flecks in his eyes glowed with an eerie light, painfully bright against his black scales and beneath his disheveled black hair.

Calix set his jaw and looked at his feet, pouring his concentration into walking straight. Aurum's silence sent shivers down his spine. He hated that he was starting to prefer the flamboyant mockery. He risked another glance at the dragonborn's face and licked his dry lips as he weighed his questions in his mind. Anything to keep himself from drowning in fear since he was cut off from those who would be able to pull him from the depths. He watched for the twitch of Aurum's jaw, the shift that would signal he was preparing to lash out. When there was none, Calix scrounged for his voice. "Where are we?"

"A place you know well."

Heat rose to the surface beneath Calix's scales, and it took all his willpower not to scratch until the skin on his arm was raw. Aurum's answer was purposefully vague, but it was enough for him to glean something useful, something that forced his bloody memories to the surface. Ceremonial drawl, the relentless nip of cold, an embroidered ribbon of blue pressed into his hand, and Kase's echoing promises of protection. Things from the past, things best forgotten. He shivered uncontrollably and let his gaze drag across the cracks in the hard stone to burn away the gruesome image of Kase's body, empty and broken.

They had to be in Selini's territory.

The subtle roll of Aurum's laughter sliced through the numb horror that sapped the strength from Calix's limbs. He jerked Calix forward. This time when he stumbled, it was accidental, and the stone scraped his arms, jolting him out of his reverie. The fresh cut throbbed as blood gathered at its edges in glistening beads of crimson. He winced, but he barely had a moment to take in the sting before Aurum hauled him up again.

"This is your homecoming." The dragonborn's voice curled with hints of a devilish smile. "Shouldn't you be excited?"

"This place isn't my home," Calix spat, forcing himself to meet Aurum's golden eyes. Though they bored straight through to his soul with the ferocity he had feared since he was a tiny child, he lifted his chin and held firm. "It never will be."

Aurum stopped at the entrance to a dark, damp stairwell. In his shapeless black cloak, he loomed like a shadow over Calix. The only part of him that could be easily distinguished from the darkness were his startling eyes. "Do you still believe Kase is your home?"

Calix's heart skipped a beat. *Kase.* A light in his dark world, a brilliant, roaring flame who bled luminance into the darkest corners of Calix's life. When he smiled, when he laughed, the world was brighter—warmer. His strong embrace sheltered Calix from the monsters that chased him, and his hands were worn from holding his sword, but when he ruffled Calix's hair the touch was soft. His voice wavered when his sadness caught up to him and broke when he could no longer hold back his tears.

"I'm sorry," Kase had said once through a trembling smile. He had pulled Calix into a final embrace, one that was tighter than usual and lingered until Calix let himself believe it would never end. *"You have to go, but we'll meet again someday."*

Something trickled down Calix's cheek. His vision turned as muddy as his memory, hot and damp. He touched his face, numb as he stared at the wetness on his fingers. Tears. When did he start crying? Quickly, he sniffed and wiped his tears away, anything to avoid looking Aurum in the face.

Aurum's grip suddenly loosened. Startled, Calix risked a glance at him, holding his breath in fear of the twisted look he might find painted on his face. But it wasn't a look of disgust— or even hatred or barely concealed laughter—that he saw.

For a frightening moment, Aurum looked at him with pity. The decayed darkness in his scales subsided ever so slightly, making way for a golden sheen beneath the matte black. His eyes softened, and their depths swirled with something indiscernible. Pity. Sorrow. Calix never knew the great Golden

Dragonborn Aurum could feel such things. The bitter taste of disgust coated his tongue, and he forced himself to swallow the bile that crawled up his throat. *Pity* was the last thing he wanted from the monster who was bent on taking his life.

But... He snatched a glance at his wrist, now barely even cradled in Aurum's hand. His gold threads had gone slack as his mind had drifted, dimmer than the sconces lining the hall. Confidence surged through Calix along with a dizzying wave of adrenaline. With a harsh yank, he pulled free and stumbled away. He pivoted on his heel and dashed back the way he had come, relishing the wind on his face, the pounding of his feet against stone. It was almost enough to cut away the threads of fear, almost enough to convince him he could leave Aurum behind for good.

Ahead, the shadows congealed, forming a wall that stretched across his path. Aurum flashed in front of him, the pity wiped clean from his expression. Magic glittered on the tips of his fingers, and all it took was the flick of his wrist. Calix slammed into the opposite wall under the weight of Aurum's spell, the air snatched from his lungs. His head cracked against the stone, pain exploding in the side of his skull as stars flashed across his vision. He barely registered when the spell released him and he flopped limp and lifeless against the ground.

"I see now." Aurum's boots scraped the dirty stone floors as he approached. They were the only thing Calix could make out in the darkness, their scuffs blurring together in a web of imperfections. When he crouched, his cloak covered them in a curtain of black. "It's not Kase anymore. It's them." He chuckled to himself, voice tight with amusement. "Unfortunately for them, they're not strong enough to leave you like Kase was."

Calix wanted to scream that he was wrong, but his anger fizzled out before it could even ignite. Exhaustion pulled at his limbs, numbing even the sharp sting in his head. Even the press of stone against his body slowly faded as his vision pinholed.

Pressure built behind his eyes until he feared they would burst, but he held onto the feeling. *Ground yourself. Don't slip now.* Gritting his teeth, he pushed himself up on shaky limbs. The world rocked as he stared Aurum in the face. The glow in his golden eyes was blinding now. It only worsened his headache, but he didn't back down.

"Whatever you're trying to do, it won't work," he rasped. At Aurum's brief look of surprise, he found himself smiling through the blood pouring down the side of his face. For once, the image of the letters tickled his memory, and it spurred him on. Written in smudged ink and scrawled Draconic was the truth that he would twist into his weapon. "You know it, too. You failed, and that's why you never sent those letters to your *tenirel.* That's why you're here instead of at the temple."

Aurum's grip was icy as he grabbed the collar of Calix's tunic, pulling it flush against Calix's neck. When he yanked Calix to his side, the force cut off his desperate gasp for air. Choking, he scrabbled for his footing and wrestled against Aurum's hold, but his limbs barely even lifted at his command. Aurum didn't even look down as he continued dragging him back to the stairwell—feeble and small, that was all Calix was to him. Prey he could easily squash. And yet, he hadn't delivered the killing blow.

"You know nothing," Aurum hissed, shoulders tense with anger and eyes blazing. With a sharp tug, he threw Calix down at the foot of the stairs. The stone steps dug into his back, but he ignored the jolt they sent up his spine.

Calix wheezed, massaging the bruise in his throat. It tensed painfully when he swallowed, but he forced the words out anyway. Just a little more. "I know you're not as powerful as you want everyone to think you are. If you were, you wouldn't be wasting so much time."

Aurum summoned his sword again. He leveled the point at Calix's neck—so swift that a breath of wind whipped across

Calix's face. Seething rage rolled off him in waves, and his pupils had narrowed to dangerous slits of black, practically drowning in the golden sea. Yet something was off. It wasn't the look of malice that haunted his nightmares or the hungry glare that lurked in the shadows and sent shivers down his spine. There were weary circles beneath his eyes, and his usually tan complexion had become ashy. He had barely done anything that should have caused exhaustion for one of his status, but he was panting, out of breath already.

"Everything I do," Aurum said, "is for Unda."

With those heavy words hanging in the air between them, he raised his sword, eyes flashing, and brought the blade down on Calix's shoulder. Agony ripped through his whole body, choking out a guttural scream from his throat. He slumped at Aurum's feet in a puddle of his blood, drifting further away from himself as the ringing in his ears drowned out everything else.

32

THE ACOLYTE

THERE WAS NOTHING WORSE than being depended on. At first, something inside Tobias stirred with excitement, and he flushed with pride. He was someone whom Calix could trust despite everything.

Reality crashed down upon him a mere heartbeat later as he watched Calix being led away. The cell door clanged shut decisively behind him, and that twisted smile curled the corners of Aurum's mouth before the dragonborn turned his back on them. Fear squeezed his chest until he worried his heart would burst. If it weren't for the tightness in his throat, he would have cried out. He would have argued more.

He settled beside Kiara, leg bouncing anxiously as he waited for her to wake again. The coat he had hastily wrapped her wound with had turned even darker with blood. When Calix left, he had laid her upon the stone with all the same care and tenderness one might expect when reverently handling a corpse. She hadn't moved from where he had left her. Her eyes were tightly sealed, shoulders rising and falling in tiny, fragile breaths. Her cinnamon hair sprawled around her, loose from its usual ponytail but decorated with countless braids of varying sizes and neatness. For someone who was barely clinging to life, she looked deceptively peaceful. She might as well have been sleeping if it weren't for all the blood.

For once, he wished that creepy dragon would come back. Unconsciously, his gaze slid to the bars that allowed him a cluttered look at the hall. There was no sign yet that he had returned with an acolyte, and Tobias doubted that he was in any rush despite Aurum's order. What was more puzzling was that his dragon form was the same as the one he had seen at Unda's clinic—the same little black dragon that had performed as Lord Cassius Vyrn to frighten Kiara away from the others. Tobias had assumed he was nothing more than a mindless beast that Aurum had laid a spell on, but now he wasn't sure. The ability to shift into a humanoid form was a gift that only belonged to the dragonborn, yet the boy didn't seem like one. Tainted magic surrounded him, an aura that flickered and danced with the erratic rhythm of an insect's wingbeats. If anything, he seemed more like a dragon who had been transformed into a hybrid than a child born of Selini's people.

Tobias tapped his leg in the same anxious beat, and he rubbed the phantom pain in his palm from Aurum's magic arrow. What was the purpose of keeping such a creature around? A dragonborn shouldn't have any need for an errand boy. Even if Aurum did, he was a Head Dragonborn. He should have already had servants from the temple that he could call on. Did he keep the boy around for companionship? But what use would a monster have for the company of others?

By the time he caught the sound of footsteps racing down the hall, Tobias's head was spinning with questions. He barely looked up when the little black dragon fluttered up to the bars and shifted back into the gray-skinned boy, grinning ear to ear —or jaw spike to jaw spike, as he didn't have the ears of a human or a dragonborn. He pressed his face to the cell. His beady eyes raked over the scene, lingering long on Kiara. "I brought the acolyte." He threw back his head and cackled. "If the girl is still alive to be healed. Her death would please the master, yes. Very much indeed."

Tobias clenched his jaw to hold back his retort, but there was a sliver of truth to Trepidatio's words. It had been clear as day on Aurum's face: if Kiara died, he would win. The fact that he agreed so quickly to Tobias's proposition made his skin prickle, and he couldn't help but wonder if all he had done was doom her to a fate worse than death.

Seeing that his jabs weren't getting any reaction, Trepidatio huffed and dropped the bars. He stepped back to make room for a second figure—a petite dragonborn woman with multi-colored scales on her cheeks and forehead. Her face was delicate and unassuming. She wore a simple pale blue chiton that fluttered elegantly around her legs as she walked. A dark blue veil draped over her brown hair, held in place by a silver circlet. She furrowed her brow, pink lips pinched as she took in the scene. "Unlock the door," she said to Trepidatio, though her gaze was focused on Kiara. "There isn't time to waste."

"Of course, miss." Trepidatio twirled a keyring around his finger, his black claws darker in the dim light. He fitted the key into the lock, and it opened with an audible clink. He locked the door again behind the woman and stuffed the keys back into the folds of his cloak. "I will fetch the master. Work fast, or His Goldness will be disappointed in you." Giggling to himself, he scampered off.

Tobias stared at the woman, tense. A small part of him waited for her to reveal a hidden weapon, then to lunge and stab him until the life bled from his body. Instead, she watched him warily, one hand gripping the other to hide that she was trembling. Her eyes cut to the toes of her sandaled feet. "May I?" she whispered.

He shuffled instinctively in front of Kiara. "Are you a healer?"

The color in her scales changed. It was slow at first, starting in a handful before they all shifted like the turning over of leaves. What had once been a startling green turned to a mix of blues and reds, calming but not without an edge. "The girl will die if you delay," she said. There was no threat behind her words; they fell softly, a fact she was simply stating. Her eyes swam with sorrow.

"You are a healer, aren't you?" he tried again. "This girl is very important, and I'm not letting you get any closer if you don't answer me." Despite being under Aurum's orders, he didn't trust Trepidatio to bring a healer. He wasn't even sure it was fair to trust Trepidatio would know a healer when he saw one. Tobias himself was still having a hard time believing there were healers readily available in Hybrid Territory. As far as he was concerned, they had no need for such a talent. They threw themselves into battle without concern for the outcome, and if they died, they died serving a great and delusional goddess.

Yet this woman's frame was small. Though she wasn't thin, she didn't appear to have battle-worn muscles or any sort of threatening appearance. She was dressed delicately, clinking with jewelry each time she took a step, and hunched her shoulders to keep herself as small as possible. He knew it before she answered.

"I am an acolyte of the temple, and I serve the Blue Head Dragonborn," she said, touching a hand to her heart. A thin strip of blue cloth with silver snowflakes embroidered on it was tied around her wrist. "I can perform minor healing spells, yes. I understand your mistrust, but—"

"That's all I needed to know." Tobias stepped aside, keeping his head low. Her voice was shaky, but not in a way that suggested she was trying to hide a lie. He didn't know which wing belonged to Coae—a name he assumed belonged to one of the heads of Selini—but Aurum had asked for an acolyte. Even if she came with ill intent, she had no need to belittle her skill.

The woman's skirt shuffled across the dirty cell floor as she came forward and knelt beside Kiara. Gently, she peeled back the haphazard bandaging that Tobias had done, her eyes glistening with tears as her scales took on another softer shade of blue. Kiara stirred, but didn't wake. She gripped the white scale tighter as the acolyte held a hand over the wound. A circle of sky blue runes appeared beneath her palm, and a faint light enveloped her. The air hummed with the familiar presence of magic. The pain in Kiara's face slowly ebbed away as the wound began to stitch itself closed bit by bit.

"How cruel," the acolyte murmured. For a moment, her eyes narrowed, and she suddenly looked like someone else. Maybe it was the cut of her jaw, or the delicate curve of her pointed ears, or the hardened look in her stormy gray eyes—perhaps even the flush in her tan skin—but she mirrored someone he had seen before as anger and frustration culminated in the wrinkles in her brow. "The master won't approve of Aurum's actions."

Tobias frowned. "By master, you mean the Blue Head Dragonborn?" *The one who watches with cold eyes, the one whom Calix said has vanished.*

Behind her veil and her curtain of dark hair, he couldn't see her expression, but her shoulders tensed. "There is nothing he can do while you are confined to this place," she whispered, always soft. She ducked her head and lowered her voice further until it was so quiet he had to strain to hear it. "You must flee as soon as you are able."

"We can't leave without Calix."

"Calix?" She raised her head, eyes wide as they met his. Deep, dark red rolled through her scales, and the lines in her face suddenly seemed so much deeper, making her look even older. "You don't mean... Caeruleus, do you?"

Tobias bit the inside of his mouth as everything Calix had

said about his people rushed back to him. He swallowed hard, scrambling for a reply. The words slipped by, all of them too feeble to paint the argument he needed. Instead, he steeled himself and said plainly, "He's innocent."

To his surprise, the acolyte looked away, returning to her healing spell. "I know he is."

"You have to help him escape." Tobias shot to his feet, desperate to relieve the anxious energy building inside him. "If he stays, Aurum is going to kill him."

"There's nothing I can do. Any action I take puts the master at risk." The spell circle vanished, and she dropped her hand to her lap as the glow in her skin slowly subsided. She reached for Tobias's bloody coat again. With a shake, it was restored to its clean, unstained state. Sparks danced across the fabric, hinting to another touch of magic. She bunched the thick fabric and began to rip it into long pieces. Carefully and precisely, she wrapped the strips of fabric over the wound before fixing Kiara's tunic. Then she sat back on her heels. "I've done what I can, but my magic is limited. Too much strain will cause the wound to reopen, so please advise her to be careful."

Tobias frowned, still clinging to her vague mentions of the elusive blue dragonborn. "What risk is there for someone like him?" he asked. As far as he was concerned, dragonborn were always fighting anyway. It was hard to imagine there wasn't already infighting among the Heads, just like he expected that Selini fought herself at times. There was no way the five heads were always in agreement. Chaos was what the dragonborn thrived on. It was what they were born from. Why should it matter?

The acolyte sank against the wall, putting ample space between herself and the two. She ripped her veil from her head and threw it to the floor. Dark brown curls fell in her face. "I cannot force his hand," she muttered.

"You're saying he's afraid of Aurum."

A muscle in her face twitched, and her gaze lingered on Kiara. Finally, she sighed and folded her hands in her lap. "It's not my place to divulge my lord's emotions," she said. "But *I* am afraid. Of Aurum, and for the Blue Head Dragonborn."

Thousands more questions swirled in Tobias's mind, but he couldn't find the energy to piece any of them together—or to determine which mattered more. There were many myths about the Blue Head Dragonborn that he'd loved as a kid, and the idea of unraveling them now sparked some childish curiosity in him. Moreover, there was a chance at learning the truth behind the "*tenirel*" in the letters, and from there he could discover what Aurum was after. A bitter, more mature part of him wanted to curl against the wall on the far side of the room, putting as much space between himself and the acolyte as possible as he waited in fear for her to leave. There was a sliver of a chance that none of her words were true, though she seemed sincere. She was still a dragonborn even if she lacked the horns and hardened eyes of her people.

Another part of him remembered his promise to Calix, and he huddled closer to Kiara in resigned silence. Some of the color had returned to her skin, breathing life and security back into her peaceful expression. The pained furrow in her brow had relaxed into a strangely serene look. Each inhale no longer came with a shudder. Instead, she breathed evenly, though slow and drawn out as one deep in sleep. He couldn't help the awe that fluttered through his chest. Magic had the power to determine life and death. He had been a victim of the scale himself, saved only by Aviva's spells that stitched up the hole in his side. To be powerful was to hold the world in the palm of one's hand.

When envy reared its ugly head again, he swallowed hard and forced himself to focus on the grime stuck under his nails instead. If he tasted magic, he would never let go. He ran his thumb over his palm again, though the pain was long gone and there was no wound at all. Maybe it was a good thing Aurum had destroyed Aviva's last resort spell, her gift of magic to him. Magic was also a downward spiral, the end of which spelled ruin for the unwise.

The acolyte stirred, blue skirt shifting like waves crashing against the shore as she tucked her legs beneath its folds. Already, the hem was darkening from being dragged across the dirt-covered floor. "Are you close with Caeruleus?" she whispered, head low as if she were ashamed that she had asked. The scales on the backs of her hands had turned a mix of blues and greens—no doubt mirroring the pattern on her face.

Tobias hesitated, uncertainty creeping across his fleeting memories of Calix. They had spent most of their time together eyeing each other like two caged predators calculating who would lunge first. "I'm a victim of circumstance," he finally settled on, wringing his hands. "Kiara knows him better than I do."

"Kiara." The dragonborn tested the name on her tongue, lifting her head just enough to glance at the wounded girl between them. The words rolled awkwardly with her accent, too lyrical for the harsh sounds of Draconic. Even the languages of Calistians and dragonborn were at odds. "I see."

"Did you know him?" Tobias asked. He tensed as the silence stretched between them, heavy with tension he couldn't place.

Her smile was strained. "I wish I did."

It was then that something clicked in his mind. Huddled in the shadows, the lines in her face etched deeply in the flickering light, there was a glint in her stormy eyes that was unmistakable. If they were blood red instead of steely gray, he would have caught it sooner. She was nearly identical to Calix—albeit a softer version of the hard edges in his appearance, her face free of the scars that marred his. Age had worn away what he guessed had once been a youthful bloom. The realization dawned on him slowly, as distant as the sun rising in the early morning but no less blinding.

"You're his mother?" The confidence fizzled out of his voice the second the words left his lips, and his statement dipped off into a question that hung awkwardly between them. Too late, he regretted it, fearing he had assumed something unfair—and no doubt cruel, given the circumstances of Calix's standing with the dragonborn. His face warmed with shame. "O–or at least, you must be related to him. Sorry, it's just that you look so similar. For a moment, I thought…"

The acolyte laughed lightly. She shifted and collected her veil, dusting it off before she draped it over her head and situated the silver band atop it. It cast a soft shadow across her face, one that made her eyes glow. Though she was still smiling and the sound of her laughter was akin to that of tinkling bells, there was a deep, unending sorrow behind her eyes, one he didn't dare to claim to understand. Hopelessness, shame, despair… this was the face of a woman who had lost everything, who had failed to defend something precious to her. Mother or not, something inside her was broken.

"I am no longer his mother." She stood, pale blue skirt pooling around her like puddles of endless azure. As she moved to stand by the entrance of the cell, they shifted around her. "At one point, I suppose I was. But now, I can only be a servant of Selini's temple, a precious instrument of the Blue Head Dragonborn, dreaming that I'll never have to see Caeruleus again. Because if I do…" Her voice broke, shoulders trembling. "That would mean it is too late for him."

Her words crashed over him with the force of the ocean's full might and pried his eyes open to the truth. It took all he had not to stagger beneath the weight of what she had shared. In a mere moment, everything he had ever known about dragonborn was fractured all over again. There was *emotion* behind her words, sadness that was almost human. She opened the door to a world of possibilities in which the dragonborn were more than mindless, bloodthirsty monsters. Pity for her and her situation wrenched his heart so sharply that he struggled to breathe.

If even this lowly acolyte, the broken mother of Calix Caeruleus, could express such emotions, what did that mean for the other dragonborn?

33

THE ELF

Tobias was still reeling when the shadows shifted once more. The acolyte jumped back from the iron bars, smoothing her face into the blank expression she had entered with. The distant crash of a door reverberated down the endless stone corridor and swept past the tiny cell with a rush of cold air. Trepidatio's familiar chortle skittered along the walls, paired with his quick footsteps and the heavier, slower set that belonged to the Head Dragonborn. They appeared together this time, though Aurum was no longer draped in his matching black cloak. He wore a loose fitting tunic, proudly displaying a gold diamond-shaped pin on his belt that glittered with the faint imprint of Selini's five heads. Without the shroud of darkness, he stood straighter, his powerful form no longer disguised beneath the folds of his cloak. He wore his sword at his hip, hand resting against it casually. The sudden openness in his appearance sent a shiver down Tobias's spine. They were no longer looking at the guise of the ghost of Sheniir. Instead, he was openly calling attention to his true self.

Trepidatio slumped against the wall opposite the cell, chin in his hands as he sank to the ground. His eyes were empty as they wandered across Tobias's face. Cloaked in black as inky as his scales and hair, with skin as ashen as the dead, the child almost could have passed for the Shadowslayer too.

Tobias shifted closer to Kiara as his mind drudged up memories of the Calistian lord, one whose appearance had been a lie but no less convincing to the person it was meant to frighten. He couldn't help but wonder how many forms the dragon child could take. "Where's Calix?" he asked, but the words almost caught in his throat, too heavy to voice.

Aurum's face hardened. "Where he needs to be," he said. With the flick of his wrist, he cracked the door open. He met the acolyte's eyes. "Caekáti—now there's a fine healer and a loyal acolyte. One of his best. I trust your work is done."

She shrank beneath his gaze, little more than prey despite her status. "Head Dragonborn," she muttered. "The girl is healed, but she is weak. It would be best if—"

"She can speak?"

"Y-yes, Head Dragonborn."

"You're dismissed." Aurum's eyes flashed bright gold as the pressure of magic flooded the air. Glittering threads draped around his fingers, sparking like thousands of stars against the night sky. His next address came out in a string of Draconic words that rolled together so fluidly Tobias couldn't pick them apart from each other. They radiated power—enough that even he almost looked away in shame like Caekáti was doing.

Keeping her head low and her shoulders squared, she left murmuring apologies to the golden dragonborn. A quick glance back was all Tobias got before the cell locked again and she fled down the corridor.

Aurum clicked his tongue against his teeth and shifted to block Tobias's view of the acolyte's retreating form. "As promised, I kept up my end of our deal, so now it's your turn. Wake the girl. There's something I wish to discuss with both of you."

A sudden chill ran down Tobias's spine. Aurum's black scales glittered in the light, an unending pool of shadows set into his face. The scent of blood clung so strongly to him that even Tobias's human senses could catch it. The question rose again to the tip of his tongue, but he clenched his jaw to keep it down. Asking after Calix wouldn't get him anywhere—or worse, he would learn something he would wish he hadn't. Gritting his teeth, he turned to wake Kiara.

His hand had brushed against her shoulder when her eyes snapped open, still hazy with drowsiness. They settled on him, and her breath hitched. He pursed his lips, shaking his head when she started to speak. Careful to keep his movements small and unnoticeable, he nodded in Aurum's direction. She froze, taking stock of the scene. Understanding slowly dawned on her, returning some of the clarity to her gaze.

"Kiara." The dragonborn grinned through the bars. "Nice of you to return to the world of the living. Oh, or do you prefer to be addressed by your formal title?"

She shoved up from the floor with a determined shout, the flames of anger burning in her eyes. The sound cut off, and she doubled over with her arms wrapped around her middle while Aurum laughed. Trepidatio soon joined him with his childish squeal, and the echo of their laughter bounced around the empty space until it was dizzying, its volume increased tenfold as it repeated back to them. It twisted Tobias's gut into uncomfortable knots. If they felt confident enough to laugh, did they have no fear?

If they believed they had won, were they correct?

Kiara forced herself upright and flung the white scale through the bars. It hit Aurum between the eyes, bouncing harmlessly off the scales that covered his forehead and the bridge of his nose, but it shut him up. When he looked her way, his expression flattened. The aura of magic around him wavered, and the air suddenly turned thick with its static presence. Even Trepidatio had gone silent.

Kiara straightened under his glare, though she was breathing heavily from the strain. "Get to the point," she hissed. "You want something from us, so quit wasting time. Because when I get out of here, I'm coming for your head."

Aurum touched the place the scale had struck, amusement dancing across his face. "Yes, I'm so frightened. How shall I defend myself against a little girl, a scrawny hybrid, and a nobody from an unremarkable town? I fear you will be my end." He flung himself against the bars in a dramatic show, faking a wound to his heart.

Behind him, Trepidatio burst into another bout of laughter, kicking his bare feet as he rolled in an uncontrollable fit. "The little girl," he managed to eke out between breaths. "She can't do anything to His Goldness!"

Tobias clenched his fists until his nails dug into his palms, his face warm with humiliation. "If you're not afraid of us, why did you need to lock us up? You could have left us in Lumas. How do you know we would have gotten anywhere with what we knew? Unless… you *are* afraid."

Gold threads flashed as they slammed Tobias and Kiara against the far wall. Though thin as a spider's web, they pressed deep into his neck until they cut off his airway, drawing blood. Fear seized Tobias, and he fell slack beneath the magic's hold, forced to wait in agony as the seconds stretched and his vision turned dark, lungs burning.

Across from him, Aurum stood perfectly still, one hand raised to control the force of magic. It burned in his eyes, a glow so bright it was almost blinding. "I'm growing tired of your defiance. I've been patient. I've adhered to your demands, but do not forget who holds the power here. I taught Caeruleus the same lesson, and I'll teach it to you if I must: I am *not* afraid of you." The growl that sharpened the edges of his words rumbled deep in the back of his throat, a low sound that shook with rage he wasn't bothering to conceal anymore. He let the words hang before he released the threads and dropped his hand to his side.

Tobias and Kiara crumpled to the floor, both wheezing to catch their breath. The world was still spinning when Tobias tried to sit up on shaky limbs. Blackness tainted the edges of his vision, and his throat burned. Upon bringing his trembling hand to the place the threads had been, he came away with a familiar stickiness on the tips of his fingers. An overwhelming sense of regret slammed into him, threatening to knock him over. He couldn't help but think back to what Talia was always telling him: he should have kept his mouth shut. *Who am I to badger a dragonborn with my impertinence?*

Aurum's threats only seemed to fan the flames for Kiara. A storm brewed behind her eyes, waves that threatened to drown anyone who dared to prod her further. Her back was straight with confidence and defiance as she stood again, her hand pressed flat to the light wound in her own neck. Tobias was certain that if it weren't for the wall between them, she would have lunged for Aurum's throat already.

Such was the nature of Calistians. Like the dragonborn they sought to destroy, they were able to focus solely on the art of killing when they wanted. Yet Calistian warriors were still human at their core, and humanity was what kept them sane.

Aurum straightened the front of his tunic, swiping an invisible speck of dust from his shoulder. "Now that everyone has calmed down and remembered their place, let's move on to what I came to discuss. Answer truthfully, as I expect you to hold up your end of our bargain. Kiara would be dead if it wasn't for me."

She wouldn't have been in that state if it wasn't for you, Tobias wanted to remind him, but this time he managed to refrain with a sideways glance at her. If they continued to harass him, it would only be a matter of time before he got bored of his kindness act and killed them. It was better to play along. And if they kept their heads low, they might have a shot at learning what had become of Calix.

"It has come to my attention that you encountered a healer while in Lumas," the dragonborn said, resting a hand against the sword at his side—Tobias gritted his teeth against the reminder of its presence. "One who possessed power great enough to repel Trepidatio and to hide both himself and you from me for quite some time. Even now, I am unable to locate this magic user."

Tobias's breath hitched. He fumbled for an answer or misdirection, but his mind had gone blank. If they gave away Unda, Aurum was sure to kill him not just for his magic but for being an elf.

"There was no such healer in Lumas," Kiara answered smoothly, her expression thoughtful yet flat. The lie rolled easily from her tongue with practiced precision. It was so perfect that Tobias almost believed it.

Aurum's eyes narrowed, his pupils like slits that glittered in the torchlight. "I heard from Trepidatio. There was someone there with you."

"There was a healer, yes." Kiara leaned against the back wall of the cell and checked her hand. The blood had congealed on the wound in her neck. She dropped her hand to her side casually. "He used herbal remedies."

"Don't lie. No non-magic remedy could completely heal Calix's wounds in such a short amount of time."

Tobias held his tongue, not daring to even breathe for fear of stealing Aurum's attention. Tension crackled between the two, already thick with the truth they both knew. Aurum was no fool. He was the Shadowslayer who had dealt those blows to Calix. He was right. There was no way to lie their way out of this question. The only solution was magic.

Trepidatio crawled on all fours to stand at Aurum's feet, his half human form bent awkwardly to suit the motion. His empty eyes glittered like uncut gems, and his smile stretched so wide it was a wonder his skin didn't split. "I saw him," he sang in an eerie tune, his voice rising and falling to a rhythm no one else could hear. "He was there, and I scared him with my illusion. An elf, white as snow and brimming with magic, Your Goldness." He cackled. "I made him turn white with fear."

In the blink of an eye, Aurum's countenance changed. His entire face darkened, down to even the black of his scales. He turned sharply to Trepidatio, who now sat upright and beamed up at him proudly. The dragonborn didn't share his enthusiasm, however. Metal scraped metal as he wrenched his sword from its sheath. He slashed Trepidatio across the face, splattering black blood against the stone. Trepidatio shrieked, flung to the side with the momentum of the strike. He huddled against the wall, eyes wide and lips quivering with fear. As Aurum advanced, he pressed his forehead to the ground in a hurried bow.

Aurum grabbed him by the scruff and yanked him upright. Inky fluid dribbled down the boy's face, and he whimpered, casting his gaze to the side.

"You didn't say he was an *elf*," Aurum growled.

Trepidatio's throat bobbed. He shrank in on himself, shoulders raised and chin tucked against his chest. "Y-you didn't ask."

"I shouldn't have to." Aurum dropped him like a ragdoll and slammed the sword back into its sheath. "You should have killed him. When you see an elf, you kill it on sight. Do I make myself clear?"

"Yes, sir. Of course, sir." Trepidatio hurriedly folded into another low bow, his face pressed so firmly into the stone that it smeared blood from his wound across the ground. "I'll kill him next time. I'll kill him a hundred times until he's dead!"

"He's long gone," Tobias snapped. As Aurum's attention crashed back onto him, instant regret shot through him. His gut wrenched at the scene he had witnessed, and all hope of reasoning with the dragonborn went flying. If he attacked even his assistants, there was no chance of bargaining with him. He wasn't like Eira, someone who was easily distracted, who was vulnerable and scared, who folded at the slightest promise of ending their conflict.

But it was too late to turn back now. Not when the words had already slipped. He wet his lips to allow himself another pause, a chance to collect his thoughts, before he continued in a small voice.

"You won't find him in Lumas because you left Eira behind. She'll tell him that you're coming, and only an idiot would stay under those circumstances." He stood straighter and forced his voice to quit shaking, despite Aurum's penetrating stare threatening to burn a hole straight through him. "An elf who has lived that long is no fool. He knows you; he knows your tricks."

For several painful seconds, Aurum considered his words. The look on his face changed from one of cold calculation to the hungry grin of a predator on the hunt for elusive prey. "So Trepidatio was right. There was an elf in Lumas, one with power enough to heal, to hide, and to break Trepi's illusion."

Tobias flinched, struck by the realization that he had only confirmed what the little dragon boy had said. He glanced at Kiara, who was still pretending to be impassive, but even her mask was beginning to crack. His pity for Trepidatio morphed into disgust, and he couldn't help but wonder if their argument had been designed to trap him.

Trepidatio had yet to move from his position on the ground, his bloody face still pressed into the stone. Beneath his cloak, it seemed he was still trembling. Aurum ignored him as he approached the bars again with long, confident strides. He leaned in so that he was almost touching the cell door with his blackened scales, and the cruel smile on his lips curled higher. "He's an elf," the dragonborn said. "Foolishness is in his blood.

Even if he has fled, he won't stay away. He has no doubt grown attached to that human village—they always do. If I see Eira there, I'll tell her you sent me."

Cold dread dropped to the pit of Tobias's stomach like a heavy stone. Numbness hit him before he could register the implication of Aurum's words, and he was still mulling them over when Aurum left. It was only after he was gone that horror seized Tobias by the throat, its jaws poised to snuff the life from his lungs.

He had given Aurum the tools he needed to kill the last elf. More than that, he had given him reason to set his sights on Eira yet again. After all he had promised her, after all he had done to save her, he still couldn't protect her from the monster.

34

ESCAPE

As soon as Aurum was gone, Tobias took to pacing the length of the cell, muttering to himself with his face scrunched in a pitiful look that twisted Kiara on the inside. The dried blood from the small cut on his neck didn't even seem to bother him. He walked from one wall to the other, a constant rhythm of boots against stone and the scuff of dirt as he turned. She didn't know how he had energy to burn. Her legs had given out the moment the dragonborn was gone, and she'd collapsed again, taking the silent moment to finally breathe. But it was never enough. Her lungs burned as she fought to take in enough to fill them, and her shoulders trembled, barely strong enough to hold her upright. Tears welled in her eyes, hot as they slid down her cheeks.

She had *failed.* She had promised to protect Calix, but he was gone. It was her duty as a Calistian to protect any surviving elves from being discovered and killed, but she had led Aurum right to one. She hadn't been able to get Unda safely away from Lumas, and her last connection to home—the necklace—was destroyed. Even Faiera was separated from her, so far away that she couldn't feel the faint presence of her bond. It

292

might as well have been severed, from the emptiness in her mind.

The cut across her chest, though healed, suddenly ached. Heavy with exhaustion, she curled up with her back to the wall, her knees pulled to her core. Her tears spilled over before she could stop them, her throat tightening as she forced herself to keep quiet. She was better than this. She was stronger than this. She was the princess of Calistie. She didn't cry in front of others, and certainly not her enemies. Keenly aware that Trepidatio was still on guard outside their cell, she buried her face to make sure he couldn't see.

Tobias's pacing stopped. "Kiara?" His hand settled against her shoulder.

She startled, slapping his hand away on instinct. For just a moment, she couldn't register the concern in his eyes. Instead, she was looking at the face of someone else—the very same that Trepidatio had used to frighten her away from Unda's side. When she blinked, the moment was gone, but the rush of adrenaline still skittered beneath her skin.

Shame burned her cheeks, and she looked away, wiping her tears. "Sorry. I thought that…" The truth was there, on the tip of her tongue, just waiting to be shared. He already knew that she was afraid, yet she couldn't bring herself to say it out loud. Not when she could hear the dismissal of the court echoing in her mind. *You're just looking for attention,* they would say. *Don't be so dramatic.*

She had failed them, too. Rather than face the problem, she'd run away, fooled Talia into teaching her to become a Dragon Rider, tricked Calix into thinking she was better than she was, promising things she couldn't do.

Her breath hitched as the tears spilled over again. Another apology rose to her lips, but she feared that if she opened her mouth all that would come out was a sob. Pressing her quivering lips together, she lowered her head to hide her tears.

Tobias didn't press. He sat between her and Trepidatio so that his frame blocked the dragon boy's view through the bars. "Aurum took Calix away," he murmured after a long pause. "I should be apologizing to you. I'm the one that tried to bargain with him. I couldn't let you die and neither could Calix."

Another sob built up behind her clenched teeth. She pressed her fists to her eyes and waited until it passed. "We shouldn't have to trade lives around."

"That's the game," Tobias said. "It's always been Aurum's game, I think."

She almost couldn't bring herself to ask the question that was burning a hole through her very core, the only thing she really wanted to know. The answer could break her, but she had to hear it. Her heart squeezed with anxiety, but she forced herself to look Tobias in the eye. "Is Calix still alive?"

Tobias's brow furrowed, and he pursed his lips. His silence only echoed the anxiety thrumming in her veins.

When he made no attempt to answer her, Trepidatio snickered. He sat against the bars of the cell, twisting to peer owlishly at them over his shoulder. Black blood still oozed from the cut on his face, now smeared all over his skin from pressing it to the ground, but his wide grin suggested he no longer cared. "The hybrid is still alive, yes, yes. Master wishes to draw out his suffering as long as possible." Laughing to himself, he stretched the word *long* out until it became nothing more than a meaningless sound. "When he gets back from Lumas, he'll kill the hybrid first."

"Gets back?" Kiara echoed, leaning in. She shared a glance with Tobias, searching for the same spark of hope in his face. When she caught the tiny smile that replaced his thoughtful frown, she couldn't help but mirror the expression. She quickly flattened her mouth back into a frown before she shuffled past him to get closer to Trepidatio. "What do you mean?"

"His Goldness has gone to kill the elf." He squealed with

another fit of laughter, kicking his feet like a child who couldn't contain his elation. Flipping himself over, he pressed his bloody face to the bars and jabbed his finger between them, pointing one black claw at her chest. "I'm in charge while he's gone. I'll kill you till you're dead if you cause trouble for Master. I'll make him proud of me this time."

Aurum was gone. She could hardly suppress the urge to smile. That fool was so focused on eradicating the elves, so confident that she could do nothing, that he had left them in the hands of Trepidatio. He might as well have handed them the keys and begged for them to leave on his hands and knees. It was too soon to feel defeated.

"I see." Kiara let her shoulders droop as she hung her head. She sniffled again for good measure, glad for once that her face was already puffy and red from crying. It would disguise the glowing excitement that was building in her chest.

Trepidatio stood and straightened the front of his cowl, lifting his chin proudly. His ashen skin was ghostly in the flickering torchlight. "That's right," he said, mimicking Aurum's low drawl. His voice was too high-pitched for the sound, and it came out as a poor imitation. "Don't try anything funny. Just stay there and sulk."

Of course. That was exactly what she was going to do until she was certain Aurum had left. Though the dragon boy appeared to be lacking in sense, she assumed he still had enough to monitor them. Otherwise, Aurum wouldn't put him in charge of his prisoners. Trepidatio may have been able to cast illusions, but that didn't mean he was a formidable fighter. So, if there was any chance Aurum was still somewhere nearby, he would be alerted by Trepidatio the moment she and Tobias tried to do anything, and it would be over before it even began. Their best shot was to lay low until he was gone and hope that Unda and Eira would be smart enough to leave Lumas before the dragonborn arrived, like Tobias had proclaimed.

And to hope that Calix was still clinging to life as well. The thought of him alone made her chest ache. She didn't know what Aurum might have told him or done to him, but she knew none of it would be good.

She rose carefully to her feet, dizzy the moment she stood, and returned to where Tobias was still sitting against the back wall. His face was scrunched in thought, and he didn't look up as she sat beside him. The need to sulk seemed to have left him entirely. With a new problem to solve, the life had returned to his eyes. His knee bounced excitedly. Kiara couldn't help but be warmed with confidence.

IT FELT LIKE HOURS HAD PASSED, but still the torches lining the hallway outside the cell burned strong. Ghostly firelight danced along the cracks in the stone, hissing and spitting as it moved with the steady flow of air from someplace farther away. An open window, perhaps. Kiara tried to drink in the taste of fresh air, but it had already become stale with the foul stench of the dungeon.

Trepidatio eventually lost interest in staring at them with wide, unblinking eyes and shifted into the form of a small, onyx-colored dragon. He chased his tail, chirped and listened gleefully to the way the sound bounced around the hallway, and clambered up and down the walls—a bundle of never-ending energy. There was hardly a moment of rest between activities, and there appeared to be no rhyme or reason to what he chose to entertain himself. At one point, he flopped down across from the cell and began to chew his back foot, his forked tongue flicking between his talons to clean the dirt from them. He reminded her more of one of the bug-eyed lap dogs the court ladies carried around in small purses than a dragon. In that form, he seemed even less like a young boy. She wasn't sure which was the *real* Trepidatio.

When the little dragon's head began to droop, eyes falling shut despite himself, Kiara waited with bated breath until soft snores replaced the constant scrape of his tongue against his scales. Finally, she relaxed, shoulders sagging. She hadn't known she had been sitting so tensely, but every muscle in her body ached.

Tobias leaned in to whisper, "Do you think this means Aurum has left?"

The prickle of anxiety crawled up her spine. There was no way to know for sure, but it was possible the two were connected somehow. After Aurum had lashed out at him, she didn't think even Trepidatio would be so quick to fall asleep on the job until he was sure his master was gone. "Let's hope so," she answered in an undertone, watching for a sign that Trepidatio might have heard. He didn't move.

Tobias wiped a hand across his face. The movement left a smear of dirt behind. "He has the key. Unless you know how to pick a lock?"

She shook her head, though her face warmed. Attempts had been made, unsuccessfully. Some were as simple as trying to break into Talia's office to find her files on other students at the academy. She had been caught then. Never again.

"I miss Eira," he said, leaning against the wall. "I guess we need to figure out a way to get the key from Trepidatio."

"There was an acolyte here, right? Is there a chance she's coming back?"

"I doubt it. Her duty was fulfilled. Besides…" He stopped himself and clamped his mouth shut, brow furrowing. Despite his being an open book, always displaying exactly what he was thinking plainly on his face, it was sometimes like trying to read in a language she didn't understand. The words were there, but they were nonsense to her. Whatever had stopped him was a secret buried so deeply that even his thinking face couldn't give it away. Eventually, he cleared his throat, shifting his gaze away as he picked at a loose thread in the hem of his tunic. "She serves the Blue Head Dragonborn," he said. "That's the fifth, isn't it? The one Calix said had disappeared?"

"The dragonborn can be replaced." Kiara folded her arms, lips pinched. Calix had always been uncertain about the role of the youngest dragonborn. He told her at one point that he thought he had a dream—or perhaps a foggy memory—where a blue dragonborn had set him free, helped him escape Hybrid Territory before Aurum could take his life, but he refused to give his name. He had called himself Sefah, Calix said, which puzzled Kiara even more. No dragonborn would dare stoop to the level of the Calistian winter spirit. *It has to be an alias,* she told Calix then. *He's hiding something.*

Calix hadn't heard anything since, and she had nothing new to provide him with either. Even the Calistians believed the Blue Head Dragonborn from the time of the elves to be gone, but it didn't add up. If that were the case, he was the only one to be replaced since the current Heads had been named hundreds of years ago. It didn't sit right with her. Historically, Selini always replaced the Heads as a group, never one at a time.

So then why had no one heard of or seen the Blue Head Dragonborn in so long? Even with the barrier acting to prevent the dragonborn from crossing over, the actions of the other four were closely monitored by the Summoners—or they were supposed to be. The blue one had become a ghost.

"Well," Tobias continued, now twisting the thread around his fingers, "she said something about not forcing his hand. What if… the Blue Dragonborn is not on Aurum's side but is against him?"

Rather than one definitive emotion, a mix of several whirled through Kiara's mind all at once. It was dizzying to try to separate them. Instead, she clamped her jaw shut and took his suggestion apart. It wasn't unheard of for there to be infighting among the Head Dragonborn, and she would be stupid to assume that any group of individuals never fought. Though the *reason* was lost on her. Was there something the Blue Dragonborn gained by going against Aurum? Maybe he wanted power. Being the fifth Head Dragonborn meant he had little influence over the other four, though he still had an elevated position among his people. Maybe it was personal.

The storm of emotions swirling across the ocean of her thoughts darkened, leading closer to the eye at its center. It flickered with uncertainty, battered her with wrongness. There was something else that prevented the pieces from slotting together.

"The letters," she murmured, cupping her chin. "We still don't have solid proof that points to who exactly Aurum's *tenirel* is. If it's the youngest member, and you're saying he's against Aurum's plans, why would Aurum be writing to him like they're close to each other?"

"I'm just speculating." He mussed his hair, a twitch in his jaw betraying the frustration that rattled beneath his words. "I don't even know his name. Maybe Aurum was trying to convince him to support him or something. Or maybe he doesn't know they're not in alignment."

It did intrigue her—desperately, a small part of her yearned to scrounge for another crack that would break Aurum, and the idea of seeing him crumble excited her. But speculation would not fulfill her promise to Calix, nor would it get him far away from those that would kill him. As she released a tiny sigh, the prickle of excitement fizzled out. "Whatever the truth, it doesn't change that the Blue Head Dragonborn isn't coming to let us out. We're on our own." She waited for Tobias's reaction, but he remained intent on avoiding her face. His shoulders slumped slightly, and she took that to mean he agreed. When he said nothing else, she finished, "So, how do you suggest we get the key?"

His hand found its way to his chest, where he balled up a fistful of his tunic and clutched it tightly. It was easy to miss the cord around his neck when he wasn't making a grab for whatever pendant he was concealing. It was something he seemed to do when he was nervous—more so when his sword wasn't around. "I have a key," he said. "It won't fit the lock, obviously, but Trepidatio doesn't have to know that. He might be dumb enough to believe it's the real key."

"You think he'd come in here to take it?"

"Possibly."

"What then? Are we going to fight him? We have no weapons." The mere idea of a fight sent a sharp prick through her freshly patched wound. Pushing her shoulders back was enough to aggravate it. She doubted it would take kindly to a fight, especially not when she was at a disadvantage. Trepidatio may not have been the brightest, but he knew she was hurt. Her gaze slid to where her white scale lay discarded outside the cell. Aurum must have stepped on it as he left because it had broken into tiny pieces. Even the fractures had lost their glow.

Not far from the scale, Trepidatio stirred and groaned in his sleep. Still in his tiny dragon form, he tucked his snout under his tail, eyelids fluttering. Kiara stiffened until he fell still again.

If he got his claws in either one of them, there was a chance they wouldn't survive without a healer.

Tobias chewed his lip. There was a distant look in his eyes, like she was mere seconds from losing him to his thoughts completely, yet he seemed to like having a puzzle to solve. "Maybe a good, clean hit would be enough to knock him out?"

"With your bare hands? He's covered in scales."

"Right. Maybe we just need to trap him."

"Trap who?"

Kiara jolted out of their conversation at the familiar high-pitched whine of Trepidatio's voice. He had shifted back to the form of the half-dragon child, his grin so wide it was inhuman, and was staring at them through the bars again with a glitter of mischief in his gold-on-black eyes. As he stood, his cloak rustled, and the dragon tail that remained in that form swished around his bare feet.

Fear rattled against Kiara's ribs as she sucked in a shaky breath. Failure. If they let their intentions slip, their shot at freedom would be gone before they even had a chance to try. Stone pressed into her back before she even realized she had taken a step.

Tobias, however, steeled himself. With his fists clenched at his sides, he moved closer to the bars where Trepidatio lurked. "I'm surprised Aurum trusts you so much considering you've already failed your job as guard dog."

Trepidatio recoiled, lip curling to expose sharp fangs. "I am *not* a guard dog. I am Master's faithful servant, his closest companion."

"Really?" Tobias twirled the black cord around his finger, teasing Trepidatio with the key he kept hidden beneath his shirt. "That's interesting. We read several of Aurum's letters and they never mentioned you—unless, of course, you're his *tenirel?*"

Trepidatio's ashen face flushed an even darker shade of gray, but he guffawed, hiding his shaky hands behind him. "That *tenirel?* I'm better than him. Aurum loves me more! I'm his new," he said, emphasizing the word, "*tenirel.*"

Kiara glanced at Tobias, whose expression was still calculating. If Trepidatio had overheard their trick with the key, they had to find some other way to goad him into being trapped. Needling him for information while searching for a crack in his defenses was their best shot at killing two birds with one stone. She suppressed the last shiver of fear and pushed away from the back wall. "He writes you letters?"

"He doesn't have to!" Trepidatio chirped. He lunged at the

bars, gripping them so tightly his knuckles paled. He let out another laugh, but it was tinged with madness. "I'm always with him. I know what he's doing, and I support him, unlike that fake *tenirel* he writes to. I love His Goldness. I am his new *tenirel,* the only one he needs!"

"But he left you here." Tobias sighed and pinched the bridge of his nose, shaking his head. "And now you've failed your task. He's going to be very cross with you when he gets back."

Trepidatio's eyes widened as they drifted up to the cut across his face, now dried and caked with black blood like ink on a page. Gingerly, he touched the edge of the cut and sucked in a sharp breath, his gaze now watery. "H-he will?"

Feigning a heavy expression, Tobias tugged the black cord to expose a brass key tied safely to it. It swung like a pendulum, and Trepidatio followed it hungrily—confusion, anger, and fear all mingling together into a look of horror. A moment later, he blinked and squinted at the key. Then, he burst into another fit of laughter, one so fierce he doubled over against the bars to support himself.

"You stupid human!" he giggled between breaths. "That's not the key to your cell. The key to the cell looks like this." With the wave of his hand, he summoned a larger, heavier key, one that glittered gold beneath the torchlight.

The instant it appeared in his hand, Tobias made a grab for it. Trepidatio realized too late as Tobias's hand closed around the hefty key. He shrieked in defiance and pulled against Tobias, but Tobias held firm. Trepidatio grew more frantic the longer the game of tug-of-war went on, but it was only a matter of seconds before his hand slipped and he crashed to the ground without the key. Tobias immediately pulled back into the cell and made a break for the door before Trepidatio could get back on his feet. He slid his hands between the bars and worked the key into the lock. With a quick turn, the door opened.

He tossed the key to Kiara. "Go!"

She fumbled to catch it. It was heavy as it landed in her hands, and she quickly tucked it into the pouch attached to her belt. With a subtle nod, she dashed out the open door just as Trepidatio lunged for her, howling in rage. She sidestepped his attack, keenly aware of his claws, and skirted around him. She was almost free when a sharp yank on her scalp stopped her in her tracks. Pain skittered across her skull, and she gasped as she swung around.

Trepidatio had snagged a fistful of her hair, gripping it like a leash and pulling so hard that she bit her tongue to distract from the pain. Tobias emerged behind him and hooked his arms around Trepidatio's middle, lifting him into the air. As he pulled Trepidatio into the cell, the dragon boy screamed and kicked, tugging harder on Kiara's hair. She yelped and stumbled back.

"I won't let go!" Trepidatio screeched, wrapping the hair around his fist. "You can't leave. Master won't let you!"

Blinking away tears, Kiara fumbled for something sharp. Anything. Her head was spinning, burning with agony as he pulled harder on her scalp. She had to get away. She had to get to Calix.

When her fingers slipped beneath her belt, they snagged on something so insignificant she had forgotten about it—a blade her father had given her to open letters. It was too small for combat, but she had kept it reasonably sharp over the years. Sharp enough to free herself. Gritting her teeth, she wrenched it from its hiding place and flicked the folding blade out. She curled her entire fist around the tiny handle of the little pocket knife. Determination lit a fire in her chest, and she forced herself to meet Trepidatio's eye as she put the blade to her hair, taut between them. Warnings flashed through her mind, whispers spoken by her mother, her father, and other members of the court: young Calistian royals were not to cut their hair until they ascended to the throne.

But Calix was waiting for her.

She balanced the blade against her finger and sliced her hair, relieving the pressure on her scalp one small section at a time. Trepidatio cried out and made a grab for another section, but it fell slack in his hands before he could wrap it around his fingers. As she cut the last length, a weight disappeared from her and she stood up straighter. Uneven locks of brown hair fell over her shoulders, tickling her chin with choppy, short ends. All around her feet were tiny braids and delicate curls, glossy in the light.

Again, Trepidatio shrieked, but this time his words came out in a string of Draconic. He fought against Tobias's hold, but the man wrestled him into the cell. As he and Trepidatio hit the back wall, he cried around a face full of black cloak. "Shut the door!"

Kiara fished the key out of the pouch and threw herself against the cell door. The key slid into the lock, but she hesitated with a quick glance at Tobias, still wrestling against Trepidatio in his arms. Her heart stuttered, afraid to abandon him again when he had been nothing but helpful. "I'll come back," she promised.

The lock clicked the moment she turned the key, trapping Tobias behind bars with Trepidatio.

Carefully stepping over the discarded sections of her once-long hair, she pocketed the key and raced down the hall with Trepidatio wailing in defeat behind her. She didn't look back, afraid of what specters of the past she might see.

35

CONFESSION

Since she had been drifting aimlessly in and out of consciousness when Calix was taken, Kiara had no idea where he could be. A trail of blood droplets was her only clue. When she happened upon signs of a struggle in the hallway, she knew she had to be going the right way. She was no stranger to Aurum's cruelty when it came to Calix—he took special pleasure in making him suffer—but the splash of dried blood on the stone stairs was enough to twist her stomach into uncomfortable, heavy knots. Calix could take a hit despite his frame, but there was only so much he could take before he broke.

She snuck down the labyrinthine hallways, sticking to the grimy, shadow-covered wall whenever possible, though she never encountered anyone else. Once Trepidatio was out of earshot, the whole place fell into an eerie silence. There were no other guards or other personnel. She couldn't tell if Aurum was stupid or if he was keeping his cards hidden. Did he want her to let her guard down so he could spring some kind of trap on her even in his absence?

Choppy locks of cinnamon hair tickled her chin, reminding her of her sudden weightlessness. She walked straighter, shoulders back and head high, the way she was taught to stand to support the crown. Only now, she was so far from its weight that she couldn't picture herself ever wearing it again. Sweat slicked her palms as an anxious shiver traveled up her arms. It was ceremonial, nothing more. But she could already feel the burning stares of her parents boring into her back, and the onlookers from the court ready to tear her to shreds at the slightest mistake. First, she let herself get tangled with a hybrid, the enemy of her people. Now, she had lost all respect for her customs, cutting her hair into an uneven mess. She was grateful to be surrounded by stone. If she saw herself in a reflection anywhere, she knew she would break.

You had to get away. She steeled herself, remembering the painful tug in her scalp when Trepidatio had pulled against her, threatening to trap her again. *Your people are far away. Your hair doesn't matter when there are lives at stake.*

Clinging to her small pocket knife like a lifeline, she crept through the low torchlight. After she had ascended the stairs, she had found herself in yet another hallway that was a mirror image of the one she had traversed below. It was becoming increasingly difficult to determine the structure of the building and what it was meant to be. It was constructed of solid stone everywhere, lifeless without carpets or tapestries to break it up. She had yet to come across a single window—just constant lines of dimly lit torches settled in sconces along the wall. The longer she walked, the more obvious it became that there was a striking lack of doors. Even on the level where her cell had been, there hadn't been many. If anything, it was more like an enclosed maze than a functional structure, and she was nothing but a rat being drawn deeper into its center for the promise of something she desired.

What if Trepidatio had lied?

Her short hair scraped the back of her neck, its jagged edges itchy as they brushed her skin.

Was she being used?

Each step jostled the chopped ends so that they slithered across her skin. Some were still long enough to tickle her spine. Their uneven length, the disjointed places in which her hair touched her skin, grated on her nerves.

She had abandoned Tobias again and abandoned the last elf the way she had abandoned her duties—all for Calix. The more she walked, the more a heaviness settled over her chest and her gut sank. Aurum was an ancient creature, older than anything she could comprehend, and there was calculation in the glittering depths of his eyes when he had attacked her. He was baiting her, dangling Calix's unguarded position in front of her knowing she couldn't refuse. He *was* luring her in.

But for what purpose? What did he gain by abandoning his post, leaving his incompetent pet in charge, and risking the escape of his prisoners—all to kill one elf?

Wind caressed her face, a gentle brush that beckoned farther down the hall. It toyed with the open flames around her, and their flickering cast long, haunting shadows across the ground. Wind. A breeze. The tantalizing scent of earth. The gentle whisper of a distant presence. It was the first time anything had broken the stale, trapped air inside the maze. Pocketing her little knife, she raced down the hall, wincing at the strain placed on her wound. Her bandages loosened, but she ran anyway, limping awkwardly to keep from agitating the cut.

At the end of the hall, a door appeared out of the darkness—solid wood reinforced by two metal bars that ran across it horizontally, glinting in the torchlight. A small rectangular window was overlaid by a grate, but it offered a peek inside. It was just above Kiara's head, but she pushed herself up on her toes to get a tiny glimpse of the other side.

The room was circular, constructed of stone and without windows like everything else. It was completely dark save for what little light filtered through the hole in the door. She strained to pick out anything in the deep shadows, but the room was eerily still and silent as death.

"Calix," she whispered, hoping for a sight of him.

A small form crumpled against the wall shifted, and the light snagged on a set of iridescent blue scales, edged with dried blood.

It was enough. She dropped back onto her heels and fumbled with the handle. The door rattled—locked, of course. Panic clawed at her throat as she glanced around for a key, but all she could see was gray stone and blood stains where Calix's body must have been dragged. Her heart twisted. That was how Aurum liked to leave him: dangling at the edge of death but never dead. It was a sick game, one he loved more than his mission. If he even had a mission anymore.

She bent down to examine the keyhole, heart hammering in her chest. The size and shape itched with familiarity, and she narrowed her eyes as she reached slowly for the pouch she had stuffed the other cell's key into. This time, it was warm in her hand, crackling with an inkling of magic. As she lifted it toward the keyhole, the teeth shifted, morphing the body into a different key entirely, though its weight remained the same. When the prick of magic energy died down, she held her breath and inserted it into the lock. It fit, and when she turned, the lock clicked.

Relief soared through her chest. She flung the door open, almost forgetting to pocket the key again as she raced inside. Light spilled into the room from the hallway, banishing the inky darkness that lurked all around the room. Calix was huddled in a broken heap in the corner by the door, where he had left a series of frantic claw marks in the wood, which were red with the blood that caked his nails.

"Calix!" She dropped to his side and gently rolled him over to get a better look at him. Unruly fringe of dark brown hair hung in his face, just as choppy and uneven as her own now.

They stirred with each faint breath, and his eyelids fluttered. When she touched his cheek, his skin was feverishly warm—a stark contrast to the icy stone walls wrapped around them. The back of his head was crusted with dried blood, swollen around a wound that was completely hidden by his hair. The front of his cloak was cut and damp with blood.

She sucked in a breath. "You're hurt," she murmured, though the words fell flat as the reality crushed her. Any longer, and he would have died.

He winced at her touch and let out a soft groan. His eyes snapped open, vibrant red like always, but it took him a moment to focus on her face. They widened before he pushed upright and flung his arms around her neck, tensing as he pulled her in closer. "How did you get here? And—" His fingers slid up into her hair, and he jerked away, gripping her shoulders. Shock and confusion lit up his eyes as he searched her face, brow furrowed tightly. "What happened to your hair?"

All at once, it slammed into her again. Even though his bloodied fingers pressed into her arms, she could feel herself drifting. Weightless. Insignificant.

She hung her head as fresh tears welled in her eyes, blurring her vision into obscurity before they dripped onto her lap. The ends of her hair brushed against her face again. She swallowed against the lump in her throat. "I cut it," she said, and the words scraped her as they left, hoarse and broken. It was foolish. *She* was foolish. She sniffled and scrubbed the tears from her face before forcing a shaky smile at the pity in his eyes. "Trepidatio wouldn't let go, so I cut it. Mama will be furious. If I ever make it home, that is."

For a moment, Calix sat with her in silence. His grip loosened before his hands fell away, one returning to his lap while the other reached tentatively to her face. His fingers, calloused and dirty, were impossibly gentle as they brushed her cheek, sweeping a lock of hair behind her ears—one that was still half braided and slowly unwinding. "I know you, Kiara. I know the crown is a heavy burden for you, but right now, you can be free of that, can't you?"

"I can't keep running from my duty forever." She jerked away from his touch, ignoring the hurt in his eyes. "I am the heir to Calistie's throne. I am bound to my people. I have an image to uphold, one that is sacred and is supposed to convey peace and power. I *broke* that image, Calix. I've ruined myself. I may as well have spit on the throne and stomped on the crown. That's what it is to cut my hair before I'm crowned. That's what I've done."

"Peace and power?" Calix echoed, bitterness creeping into his voice as he curled his lip. Scoffing, he touched the wound in his shoulder. "How can you convey an ideal that doesn't exist? Aurum is plotting something, and if he gets what he's after, there won't be a throne for you to ascend to." He took her hands again, squeezing them gently so that the warmth of his palms settled into her cold fingers. "You did what you had to do. I need you here, Kiara. Not worrying about something far away, something you left behind. I need you with me, otherwise..."

The tears welled again, but this time her face warmed beneath them. "Let's focus on getting out of here. You're trying to hide it, but I know you're in pain."

He looked away and scratched at the exposed scales on his arm. "I'm just glad you're alright."

She smiled slightly, but it quickly fell. Grabbing the hem of his torn cloak, she started to pull it off. He let her, though he winced as the thick fabric fell away to expose the wound in his shoulder. Crimson blood dried against his tunic, plastering it to the edges of the thin cut. It didn't appear to be as deep as the one Aurum had given her in Lumas, but the sight still pulled at her heartstrings. Without Faiera and the scale she had thrown away, she couldn't ease his pain.

"We should get this patched up before we try to move," she

said, helping him out of his tunic, keenly aware of the scars etched into his bare skin. When the wound healed, it would just be one more. The thought made her chest tight.

She grabbed the little knife. Her knowledge of first aid was flimsy at best, but she tried to recall the hazy memories of someone dressing her wound while she had been barely conscious. She cut his cloak into workable strips and began to wrap the pieces across his chest and shoulder, careful to pull it tight but not restrict his movements too much.

His jaw clenched, but he said nothing, merely holding still until she sat back and released him. When she was done, she pocketed the knife while Calix twisted to admire her handiwork. His movements were stiff, his face contorting each time he aggravated the wound, but it was the best she could do. Slowly, he pulled his tunic back on.

"It's temporary," she said. "Our window of time is small, so we should move."

She rose to her feet and steadied herself before hauling him up with her. He sagged against her with a shuddering wince, his arm curled protectively around his middle. "Sorry," he murmured. "The room is spinning. Everything hurts."

"We need to get back to Tobias. I locked him in the dungeon with Trepidatio." Kiara hooked her arm around Calix to support him. He leaned into her, still light enough that she could walk but heavy enough that it wasn't long before her shoulders ached. One step at a time, they trudged out of the tiny room and plunged into the dim torchlight.

"You never answered my question," he said. His breath caught in his throat as he missed a step, nearly sending them both to the ground. Kiara steadied herself against the wall, clenching her jaw. He murmured a quick apology, cheeks flushed. "H-how did you get to me? I didn't think Aurum would let you."

"Aurum left," Kiara muttered. She straightened, forcing

down the flutter of anxiety that threatened to grow again. "We accidentally let slip that we met an elf. He went mad and left in a hurry. This is our best chance to escape—this place is totally empty, aside from Trepidatio."

"The elf!" Calix pulled away, pressing a hand to his forehead as he screwed his eyes shut with a wince. He stumbled into the opposite wall. His skin turned clammy and pale. "That's right. He said… He said…" Shaking his head, he shoved away from the wall, swaying unsteadily, and pressed down the hall. "We need to get out of here."

Kiara hurried after him and took his arm. He stopped, staring at her with wide, uncertain eyes. His lips pinched, and he quickly looked away. As he moved on, she walked at his side, careful to keep pace with his unsteady limp. "What did Aurum tell you?"

His silence spoke volumes, as loud as the roar of thunder in a harsh storm. Fear propelled his steps. She had seen it before in the set of his jaw, the way he carried himself, and even in the halting way he walked when he was injured. It wasn't just his wounds making him so uncertain. Something else was holding him back. Aurum must have struck a nerve, no doubt gloating over his victory and cutting Calix to the quick. Or, if Calix struck right, it was possible he had been able to extract something of value from the dragonborn. Aurum was no fool, but he loved to talk. Old Calistian scrolls, reports from a soldier who had clashed with him before, said that it was one of his greatest weaknesses. He couldn't resist talking about himself, and the letters they had found were proof of that.

"Calix," she prompted, careful to keep her voice gentle.

He whirled to face her. The scar across his face seemed deeper in the thick shadows, cutting lines that made him appear ghostly and fragile, more corpse than living being. "We're being set up to become pawns in a different game—one attended by the goddess herself. We have to leave before it's too late to get free."

Kiara shook her head, confusion clouding her thoughts in fog so thick she couldn't even find the words to reply. Eventually, she managed, "What are you talking about?"

"The *tenirel*," he said. "I know who it is, and I don't want to be caught up in this war."

36

ONE CALLED TREPIDATIO

TREPIDATIO'S SHRILL WAIL STILL RANG in Tobias's ears long after Kiara was gone. The boy thrashed in his hold, kicking and scratching. His claws dug into Tobias's arms, drawing fresh blood and leaving a vicious sting behind. Tobias gritted his teeth against the yelp that rose in his throat like bile. He clung tighter, desperate not to let go even though the door was shut and locked. He still didn't know if Trepidatio could magically produce another key or shift into a form that was small enough to escape the cell. The only thing he was certain of was that he had to buy Kiara enough time to rescue Calix.

And trust that they would return for him.

As he squeezed Trepidatio around his middle, the boy's form began to shrink in his arms. The soft brush of his cloak turned into the rough scrape of scales, and he grew colder and more slippery. Panic cinched Tobias's heart, and he adjusted his grip too late. Trepidatio, now back in his small black dragon form, dropped to the floor and skittered to the bars. He flung himself against them with a hiss, scrabbling against the metal—reduced to a caged animal. The scrape of his claws was worse than his defeated howling, but it seemed he was trapped. Tobias released a breath. At least Kiara could focus without Aurum's shifter pet trailing after her.

The only downside is I *have to deal with Aurum's shifter pet.* His hand, dripping with the blood that oozed down his arm, itched for the familiar grip of leather against his palm, the weight of his sword. Without it, he was defenseless against Trepidatio's claws and fangs, and his scaly hide provided him with better defense as well. So long as he remained in his dragon form, there was nothing Tobias could do.

The little dragon whirled to face him, a snarl curling his lip. Tobias pressed against the wall to put as much distance between them as possible. His mind was spinning. There had to be some weakness he could exploit. In size, he had the upper hand, but the small space would work to the dragon's advantage. There was no cover, no place for him to run. There were only walls and layers upon layers of dirt and grime.

Dirt. Tobias glanced at his hands, now a mess of red and brown. Something wriggled to the front of his mind, an inkling of wisdom from his sister's dragon books that he used to steal after she went to bed. Taking away a dragon's senses was one way to weaken it.

Trepidatio lunged, jaw parted, teeth gleaming. Tobias shot to the floor, scraping up a handful of dirt into his hand. Rolling over, he came face to face with the dragon, who prowled forward with his tail swishing behind him like a cat. The second time he lunged, Tobias flung the cloud of dirt into his face. Trepidatio's pupils shrank to narrow slits, and he squeezed his eyes shut with a pathetic squeal, crashing into the ground. He blinked furiously and scratched his eyes with his talons, but it only smudged the dirt more.

Tobias kicked his underbelly while he was down. The little dragon shrieked and flailed blindly, but Tobias danced out of his way. A tiny smile edged the corners of his mouth. It wasn't so bad as long as he stayed out of range of Trepidatio's short limbs.

The dragon, however, flared his wings and took to the air. For a moment, he flew blindly in circles, lashing out at the very air that moved around him. Then he fell silent and tilted his head. Tobias stiffened, but it must have been the hammering of his heart that betrayed him. Trepidatio flung at him again.

Before Tobias could move, an arrow pierced Trepidatio's wings, throwing him to the ground. The moment he hit the stone, ice exploded around the sizable rip in the thin membrane, quickly encasing the little dragon's side. He squealed again and fought against the magic's hold, but he was pinned down. Blinded and trapped, he flapped his other wing in a desperate last-ditch effort. Not even that was enough to free his little body.

Tobias stared at the arrow and the familiar ice trap as muddled confusion washed over the thrum of adrenaline in his veins. Footsteps echoed down the corridor, and he turned just in time to see Oliver emerge from the darkness, a fresh arrow nocked on his bow and the same tight-lipped frown on his face as always. His only greeting was a quick nod. A second later, Eira and an unfamiliar young girl joined him, all panting as if they had run forever to get to the cell. Immediately, Tobias's gaze locked with Eira's. The tight coil of fear squeezing Tobias's heart loosened and fell away, and he smiled despite himself.

"I can't believe it. You came for me?" He took a hesitating step at first, hanging back in case it was another elaborate illusion. When Eira bent to examine the lock, her tools in hand, and expertly cracked it open, his hesitation fell away. Her grin was reassurance enough, and the glitter of pride in her eyes could belong to no one but her. He raced out the door of the cell and pulled her into an embrace, grateful for the way her startled gasp tickled his neck. She was there. She was real. She was safe and away from Lumas.

Stiffly, she patted his shoulder. "Well, consider us even. You saved me, I saved you. We're good now."

"Yes." He pulled away, clearing his throat as his face warmed. She was looking at him with that annoying smirk—he cast his eyes to the floor instead, focusing on the scuff where Trepidatio had been pacing just moments before. "That's all. Glad to know the debt is settled."

The other girl made some noise in the back of throat—one that screamed impatience—and rolled her eyes almost as dramatically as Oliver. She was dressed in the white cloak of a Mage, a staff with a familiar glittering orb on one end in her hand. Even without an introduction, he began to fit the pieces together. Oliver had successfully found Aviva's apprentice, Nari. "This is nice," she said, "but Eira said there were three of you. What happened to the others? And…" Her face twisted into a mix of confusion and disgust as she nudged the discarded lengths of Kiara's hair with the end of her staff. "I'm not sure what to make of this."

Tobias slammed the cell door shut, his gaze lingering on Trepidatio, who was still struggling against the ice. "Aurum took Calix away. Kiara went to find him while I dealt with Trepidatio."

"Consider him dealt with. Let's go. This place gives me the creeps." Nari grimaced, shivering.

"And Aurum?" Eira asked. She spared a quick glance at the little dragon as well. "He doesn't seem to be around." Her expression fell and her attention snapped back to Tobias. "Don't tell me—"

"Lumas," Tobias interrupted. The pain in her expression was more than enough to dredge up all the regret he had buried. He couldn't bear to hear her piece it together in words—he had sold out Unda. "We have to return to Lumas."

Oliver's amber glare hardened. "That's more than I agreed

to. Let's find Calix and Kiara and get out of here. You can continue discussing your fool's errand later."

"It's not just some errand," Tobias snapped, bristling under Oliver's constant scrutiny. "The last living elf is in Lumas. We can't let Aurum kill him." It was easy to remember why they had gone their separate ways and why he didn't miss butting heads with such an arrogant man.

Oliver narrowed his eyes as a muscle in his face twitched. Something was turning in his mind, weighing Tobias's words against another one of his ready-made arguments that somehow always made him look superior. For a moment, it almost seemed like he wouldn't argue this time. Tobias didn't dare to let relief wash over him until he heard acceptance from Oliver himself. Oliver was never one to roll over—he always had to have the last word.

With a sigh, he pinched the bridge of his nose. "Why do you care about this all of the sudden? You weren't alive when the elves were slaughtered—none of us were. You don't owe them anything. Protect your own and stop trying to spread yourself so thin."

Tobias burned, fingers curled so tightly against his palms that his dirty nails dug into his skin. It was irritating—Oliver's calloused words, his cold expression that whispered anyone would be an idiot to argue, and his unwillingness to move on any subject. He always dug his heels in, desperate to prove he was better than anyone who dared disagree with him.

But this time, there was a slight pinch in his face, a furrow between his brow and a tightness in his jaw that said something else. Beneath his hard exterior, there was a person still, one who was wrestling with his own fears. Whatever it was, it made no room for the elf he didn't know.

There was an unspoken final line to his argument, one that echoed in Tobias's mind even without it being voiced. He had said it before so long ago, when they had argued back in the tavern in Faruu, when he nearly broke down beneath the weight of grief.

Hadn't Kase spread himself too thin trying to protect more than he could?

Even so, Tobias swallowed his pride. Instead of a retort, he sighed and released the tension in his shoulders. "It's not wrong for me to care about other people. Unda was kind to us when he didn't have to be. I can't let Aurum kill him because of some petty grudge, but you don't have to go."

Off to the side, the Mage scoffed, boots scuffing the stone as she meandered toward the cell door. Behind it, Trepidatio was still flailing against the ice, but a sizable crack had splintered the surface of it. Nari slammed her hand over the lock. Light flashed in the palm of her hand. Instantly, the locks clicked into place, trapping Trepidatio inside. He screeched and scrabbled harder against the ice, but even he had to know his fate was already sealed.

Nari turned, smiling in satisfaction at her work. "Your little conversation is all well and good, but we should get moving. I don't know about you, but I'd rather talk outside in the fresh air. This place reeks."

"Wait. Where's Arayna?" Tobias squinted into the darkness, waiting for her to appear. All he saw was Oliver's scowl.

It was Nari who rolled her eyes this time. "She stayed at the Summoners Palace with Ronan. There was one last thing Maven wanted to take care of, so we split up."

Her answer only left him more confused. "Who's Ronan?"

"We should go." Eira didn't wait for anyone else to agree before she snatched up Tobias's arm and took off back the way she had come. Her grip was like iron, harsh as it clamped around the cuts from Trepidatio's claws, but he found it strangely comforting to know she was there.

"Calix and Kiara went the other way," Tobias said, guiding her back before they had gone too far. This time, as they sped past Trepidatio, he caught a glimpse of the dragon's form changing again. His wings shrunk and disappeared, limbs growing longer and turning ashen gray, still tipped with black claws at the ends of his hands and feet. Tears glistened on his cheeks, but the scream that scraped out of his throat was anything but pitiable. It haunted Tobias as it bounced along the corridor. His skin crawled. He took Eira's hand and broke into a sprint, hoping the others would match his speed.

Anything to put distance between himself and the enigma that was Trepidatio.

"You can't keep me here!" the dragon child screeched, his voice cracked and broken as it began to give out. "I'm the only *tenirel* Aurum needs. I'm the only one who can understand his vision, and I won't let you destroy it!"

The pressure in the air plummeted. Tobias's ears popped, suddenly filled with a shrill ringing as a painful stab ripped through his eardrums. He jerked to a stop, hissing as he threw his hands to his ears. Lightning raced across his skin, lifting the hairs along his arms. Magic flooded the air, thick and crackling with energy. It left a metallic tang on Tobias's tongue when he inhaled sharply.

Nari's expression fell, her eyes wide with fear. "Get down!" she snapped, spinning on her heel to face the cell they had left behind. She slammed the end of her staff into the ground, and the orb exploded with light, conjuring a shield around them just as a hoard of shadows burst from the dungeon where Trepidatio was. They parted like water around the shield, floating harmlessly past everyone inside.

When the darkness cleared, Tobias glimpsed the front of the cell laying haphazardly against the opposite wall, broken clean off. A huge muzzle emerged from the tiny room, curled to expose rows of sharp teeth. Beady eyes fell upon them, set into a head that barely fit into the small space. The huge black dragon threw back its head and broke through the stone above them as easily as if it were made of paper. Rubble rained down around him, but it bounced harmlessly off his thick plates of armored scales. His jaw parted as he unleashed a roar that shook the earth, resonating deep in Tobias's bones.

There was no denying it. Trepidatio was a monster, one that turned Tobias's blood to ice.

37

AURUM'S BLACK DRAGON

Exhaustion caught up to Calix long before they even made it to the stairs. Kiara's presence became a distant thing, flitting in and out of his awareness like the touch of her arm wrapped around him. He hated that he was so weak, stumbling along beside her and supported by her strength, not his, but his head throbbed. Everything had become hazy and distorted. Even his vision kept drifting, blackened at the edges as the threads of consciousness came undone.

Her silence was haunting—as jagged as the uneven lengths in her hastily chopped hair that spilled around her face and over her shoulders. From the thoughtful frown on her lips, he knew she was still mulling over what he had confessed, what Aurum had poured at his feet. *Everything I do is for Unda,* he had said, a memory so hazy Calix almost convinced himself it hadn't been real. It rang with agony though, the same pain that burned in his shoulder even now. Blood clung to his clothes, to his hands, flooding his nose with the stench of it. It had long since dried, matted to his tunic and sticky with a haphazard scab. Each movement jarred it, igniting the flaming agony anew.

Kiara stumbled, bumping the wall as she fought to steady

herself. Sweat beaded her brow, her skin clammy and pale. She was trembling with exhaustion. Despite Aurum's promise, her wound was clearly still aggravated. Something pulled sharply at Calix's chest, a mixture of pity and helplessness. He couldn't do anything for her, and she only suffered because of him.

"Almost to the stairs," she rasped. "Shouldn't be too far after that."

"And the exit?"

"I… don't know. We have to meet up with Tobias first. But I'm hoping the key will show us the way once we're all together."

They had barely made it to the top of the winding staircase when the ground shuddered. Below, an explosion echoed through the corridors, one that shook the dust from the low ceiling and threw Calix and Kiara against the wall. Calix staggered, struggling to find his footing while the floor rocked beneath him. His wounded shoulder slammed into the stone. Fiery agony ripped across the wound. He gasped, vision flickering darkly. His blood roared in his ears, drowning out the sound of Kiara's voice. It wasn't until her arm hooked under his and hauled him back up that he realized she was waiting for his answer.

"Magic," he offered with a wheeze. "Something must have happened with Tobias and Trepidatio."

Her brow wrinkled. "Yes, but are you okay?" she asked, slowing each syllable the way someone did when they were forced to repeat themselves too many times. Normally, it made the back of his neck hot with shame, as he already struggled with languages and didn't need to be reminded. Coming from her, however, all he got was a little flutter in the pit of his stomach.

"You have to stop asking," he murmured. "You're never going to like the answer."

The ground rumbled again. This time, Kiara steadied both of

them against the wall, her arm wrapped so tightly around Calix's middle that he struggled to take a deep breath.

"We have to keep moving." Kiara stepped down to the next stair, sticking to the wall on one side with him leaning against the other.

He followed her, stepping when she stepped and pausing when she stopped. His blood stained the stairs, and he cringed at the sight of the crimson droplets trailing up to the little room where Aurum had locked him away. He couldn't remember the walk after their fight, just that he was dragged across the unforgiving stone and flung lifelessly into the room. Had Aurum been silent? It seemed like the perfect time to gloat or to laugh, but he couldn't recall either of those things—only the screech of the door's hinges and the click of the locks. When he'd come to, he'd crawled to the door, scraping the wood with his nails until his fingers bled. Aurum didn't gloat then either.

Again, the ground shook. Kiara's foot slipped, and she pitched forward with a yelp. Gritting his teeth, Calix grabbed a fistful of the back of her tunic, narrowly snagging it with the tips of his fingers, and hauled her to his side. Somewhere ahead, a dragon bellowed, the sound trembling as if it had scraped its throat raw. It wasn't the high-pitched whine that Trepidatio usually unleashed, nor was it the deep, rumbling bass of Smoke's voice. The unknown sent a shiver racing down Calix's spine.

Kiara stiffened against him. "Do you think... Tobias did something to upset Trepidatio? I thought he was mostly harmless but—"

"We need to hurry," Calix said, pulling away from her. It was agony, each step jolting the wounds in his body, but he couldn't stand the thought of slowing her down. With one hand pressed to the curved wall, he limped down the stairs one at a time, halting when his vision swam with darkness.

Together, they reached the bottom, their long shadows

stretched down into the darkness by the flickering torches—most of which had gone out during the commotion. The final step was cracked, splattered with blood where Aurum had thrown Calix against it. He jerked away, the back of his head throbbing with the sharp reminder of the attack. Kiara followed without stopping to look at the spot. No doubt, she had already seen it, already dealt with the sickening thought that Calix had fought a losing battle in the corridor—yet he never learned. He was headed toward another one.

But he kept walking, one step at a time, into the darkness with Kiara beside him. It didn't matter what waited for them. While she was there, he would keep fighting, keep living, keep surviving. No trap set by Aurum was going to get the better of him, and nothing the goddess or her servants promised would convince him to become a pawn in her war game.

Kase didn't die for me to lose here. Not when my new family needs me.

"All I have is my letter opener," Kiara said, exposing the tiny folding knife. Its blade was polished silver, sparkling in the torchlight. It was more of a decoration than a weapon, and the darkness in her pale blue eyes said she knew it too. It was certainly no dragonslayer.

Calix glanced at his tattered, bloodstained clothes. He had no weapons with him, and without being able to feel his connection to Stiria, he couldn't call on the dragon's power either. Against any other foe, he might have charged in bare-handed, but only a moron would take on a dragon that way. He tried not to think about how that was exactly what Tobias would have to do if he really was caught up in this fight alone.

Before he could answer Kiara, a blinding light burst into view at the end of the corridor. It cast four shadows across the ground before Calix was forced to look away. Another shudder ripped across the ground, and a crack spiderwebbed through the stone overhead. Magic crackled in the air, so thick Calix could taste it when he inhaled. It was coppery, like blood, and sparked on his tongue, a fire that lived and breathed a life of its own.

With a loud crack like the rumble of thunder, the ceiling split. Calix tensed and lunged for Kiara, throwing her out of the way of the rubble. It crashed to the ground where they had been a mere heartbeat before, splintering the floor with sharp spikes of rock. Sunlight broke through the darkness in lazy streams. Calix blinked furiously and shielded his eyes with his hands as he sat up. When the light glinted off a mound of black scales, his breath snagged.

Standing at what used to be the far end of the hall, now a mess of rubble and stone, was a massive black dragon the size of a sturdy oak tree. Its eyes glinted gold on black, bleeding a darkness from the cracks in its scales that made Calix's skin prickle with the encroaching touch of dark magic. It threw back its head and gave a loud cry, one that pierced Calix's ears and rattled his bones.

Around him, Aurum's stronghold turned to dust. Calix sank into the sand where solid ground had once been. He scrambled to his feet and offered a hand to Kiara. The labyrinth disappeared, opening up a desert wasteland with nowhere to hide from the dragon's destruction. Dirt and sand stretched on for miles beneath the early morning sun, broken only by the swell of hills that paled in comparison to the black dragon's size. They were at the mercy of the dragon—Trepidatio himself.

Calix took a step and sank into the thick dust. Aurum had already told him that he had imprisoned them in Selini's territory, but it had never felt real in the endless corridors of cold stone and dim torches. Now, standing beneath the hot sun, surrounded by miles of open land, his heart sank, nerves set ablaze by a spark of fear. He *was* in Selini's territory. This was the desert of Senn.

Cold hands grabbed his shoulder, nails sharp enough to dig

into his flesh as they closed tighter and tighter around him. He jumped, and the vision disappeared. It was Kiara's hand against his shoulder, nothing more than a gentle touch though her expression was stern. "We need to move," she said. "Before he spots us."

"Our cover just dissolved." He gestured frantically to the knee-high layer of sand swirling around them, gray like the stone it had once been. Even the torches had melted, their ghostly flames forever extinguished.

She chewed her lip and glanced at Trepidatio. He had yet to look their way, his beady eyes focused on something at his feet. He bent down and sniffed around in the dirt, digging for something—or someone. Whatever he was searching for with such single-minded focus had to be what had caused him to take this monstrous form.

It had to be Tobias.

Calix was still standing frozen when a streak of white flashed across the sky, followed by a brilliant swish of azure blue. The prickle of magic sank beneath his skin, snapping a single thread back into place in his mind. All at once, a rush of cold air slammed into him, paired with the gentle call of a familiar voice, one that slid down the thread as fluidly as water rolling downhill. If it weren't for the sudden chill in his bones, a welcome sensation that quickly drove out the desert heat and the burn of his wounds, he could have cried as the streak of azure whisked toward him. Iridescent scales glinted in the sunlight, and a pale blue mane of wild curls toyed and danced in the wind.

Found you, Stiria's voice called, close enough to touch. Seconds later, the blue dragon zipped by, mouth open, and snagged the collar of Calix's tunic with his teeth. Without stopping, he curved expertly and dropped Calix into the saddle strapped to his back.

Wind raced past them, nipping Calix's face as he ducked low

against the dragon's neck, digging his fingers into the leather saddle. The tears that welled in his eyes were ripped away by the rush of air as they sped through the sky, and he laughed in spite of it all. Burying his face in Stiria's mane, he allowed himself to relax for just a moment. *I missed you, my friend.*

They circled the ground where he had been standing as the white blur—Faiera—slowed to allow Kiara to swing onto her back. Faiera took to the skies, spiraling as she shot up. Only when she reached the same height as Stiria did she unfurl her wings again to catch the breeze. Calix grinned at Kiara as their dragons flew side by side. She beamed back, her clipped hair billowing untamed around her. He hadn't known how empty he could feel without Stiria's constant presence nor how much he would miss soaring through the skies. Power surged through him. The touch of Stiria's magic settled in his fingertips, begging to be released. Whole again, not even Trepidatio could stop him.

We have your weapons, Stiria said as he swerved, this time headed straight for Trepidatio's massive black form. *All of your things are still packed away in the saddlebags. I saw the fortress collapse on the others. We need to draw the dragon's attention away so Nari can get everyone out safely.*

You brought others. No wonder Trepidatio is so angry.

Thank Eira. She was persistent. Though it was Unda that sent her on her way.

The name made Calix's fingers curl, his mind whirling with bitter confusion and the heat of frustration. Again, he was met with the hazy image of the blue dragonborn who had helped him escape so long ago. *He's not an elf. He's a dragonborn, Stiria. He has to be.*

Don't worry about him right now. Focus on the enemy in front of you.

Stiria flew directly over Trepidatio's head, which was almost as large as the blue dragon. Calix fumbled for his weapons, strapped to the side of the saddle where he had packed them back in Lumas, back when they thought they were only running from Cassius. His hand closed around the middle of his bow, and he flinched. Flashes of memories flitted through his mind—his black arrow piercing Kase's murderer and Kase himself falling to his demise. He hadn't touched it since, not when his hand was still sticky with that blood.

But this was different. Trepidatio was still digging, snuffling the sand and whining as he searched for his unseen prey. There was still time.

Steeling himself, Calix unbuckled the bow and snatched one of the arrows from his quiver. Slow, deep breaths—in and out again. He nocked the bow, pulled the string to his cheek—gritting his teeth against the ache in his wounds—and waited for Stiria to circle back. He searched the dragon's thick armor, and his gaze latched on the narrow gap just below his spiked jaw. He held steady. As soon as Stiria's flight evened out, he let loose. The arrow pierced a chink in Trepidatio's armor.

It was such a small thing, little more than the first strike of an axe to the trunk of a massive tree, but Trepidatio threw back his head and roared. Eyes wild and glittering, he swung to face Calix. His lip curled. He tensed.

"Go higher!" Calix flattened himself to Stiria's neck again, burying one hand in the dragon's fluffy mane.

With one strong push of his wings, Stiria soared upward just as Trepidatio snapped at the empty air where they had been, narrowly missing the tip of Stiria's tail. Faiera circled behind Trepidatio, stark white clashing with black scales as she lunged for the back of his head. Her talons expertly found the cracks in his scales, raking the soft flesh beneath. She tore off one of his larger scales. Trepidatio screeched again, a low rattling sound that shook with rage and pain. He swatted at her with his talons, but she dove out of the way and whisked past him to join Stiria.

Trepidatio may have been large, but he had sacrificed his

agile movements for a size he didn't know how to control. Black blood oozed from the wound Faiera had left him with, leaving inky droplets in the gray sand beneath him. A large scar marred his face as well, eerily similar to the one that cut across Calix's own. The mark hadn't been there the last time he had seen Trepidatio.

Roaring again, he turned, his tail sweeping across the dirt and sending a huge cloud into the sky. It ripped up a layer that had been covering a small, glowing orb and the four figures hidden inside, all huddled around a Mage's staff. Trepidatio's eyes were pinned on Calix, however, his old prey forgotten. Lip curling, he took another clumsy swing at Stiria, but missed by the length of an entire other dragon. The flicker of fear in Calix's chest was finally beginning to fade. In its place, something playful danced.

Kiara and Faiera were still in the air beside him. He motioned to her, signaling toward the group below. She nodded, and the two shot toward the ground, disappearing behind Trepidatio as he closed in.

Calix reached for his bond with Stiria, twining the thread around himself.

Stira's scales flashed with a pale blue light. Shards of ice formed around him, shimmering with flecks of magic in the bright sunlight. With the jerk of his head, the spikes launched at Trepidatio. Some bounced harmlessly off his scales, but a few hit the mark in the open wound left by Faiera.

Trepidatio howled and lunged at the two. His gaping maw was pitch black like the blood that poured down his back. It reeked with the stench of decay, like Aurum's scales. Stiria snapped his wings against his sides and dove for the ground. Calix clung to the saddle as his stomach dropped, squeezing his eyes shut against the wind nipping his face. Stiria's talons scraped the sand when he unfurled his wings, and Trepidatio's jaws closed around nothing but air again. He was no match for Stiria's speed nor his wit.

"You should have stayed a little dragon!" Calix jeered, nocking another arrow on his bow as they soared past Trepidatio's face. His pupils were narrow slits, and his nostrils flared. Calix waited as Stiria swerved until he steadied their flight, now poised directly beside Trepidatio, who watched warily with one big, wide eye.

Calix dragged the string of the bow back to his cheek. Everything burned, but his blood was singing. "You would have been a smaller target," he muttered. He let loose.

The arrow struck Trepidatio in the center of his golden eye. He reared back with another bone-rattling roar and struck blindly with one set of claws. His huge black talons sailed through the air, and Calix's heart skipped. He pressed flat to Stiria's back as the dragon spun out of the way, but he wasn't fast enough. Trepidatio's claws connected with his side, their tips snagging Calix's leg, and threw them out of the sky. Calix's stomach dropped as they plummeted toward the ground, the air ripped from his throat so that he couldn't even scream at the agony tearing up his leg. All he could do was cling to Stiria, who flailed for control of the winds again, and pray the ground would be forgiving.

Instead of the harsh scrape of sand and the crack of his skull that he was expecting, Calix collided with something soft—a net that crackled against his skin. It stopped their descent mere paces before they crashed into the ground. He pried his eyes open to find himself surrounded by a web of blue and gray threads. They vanished in an instant, and he and Stiria dropped to the ground unharmed.

A little to his left, a girl heaved a great sigh. She tossed her hair, her face the picture of pride, and twirled a Mage's staff in one hand, still lit with the same blue glow. "You're welcome."

Shakily, Calix slid from Stiria's back. The moment his leg

took his weight, it exploded with pain. The ground rocked beneath him, and he leaned against Stiria's side with a hiss, biting the inside of his cheek as he stared at the blood pouring from the gash across his calf.

Kiara was at his side in an instant, taking his arm and easing him to the ground, where she bent over his wound. Some of the color had returned to her complexion, and the makeshift bandage peeking out beneath her tunic had been removed. It wasn't until the Mage girl shoved her out of the way and hovered a glowing hand over his own wound that he realized why. Instantly, the pain dissipated as his skin began to stitch itself back together, guided by the blue threads of her magic. When she was done, she sat back and sighed again, jaw clenched and gaze settled on anything but his face.

"This is a one-time thing," she said. "If it wasn't a request from Her Highness, I'd never use my magic on a *half-breed*."

Calix's chest tightened. "Thanks. You are…?"

"Apprentice Mage Nari," she snapped. She stood, tossing her short dark hair again before she stalked off to rejoin Eira and Tobias, who were watching Trepidatio with wary expressions. The dragon was still wailing in agony, swiping blindly at the air —though it looked more like he was throwing a fit than searching for a foe to attack. He might as well have been wallowing in the sand.

A little farther back was the final figure, standing rigid and alert beside Faiera with his enchanted bow in hand. His hardened amber gaze was trained on his prey, his lips pinched in an eternal frown. His attention flicked to Calix, who stiffened beneath the force of his stare. If it weren't for the hard lines in his face, for the bright, angry glow in his almond shaped eyes, he could have been mistaken for his late cousin. But Calix knew better than to hope he could find Kase's strength in Oliver. He had proven long ago that he didn't care whether Calix lived or died.

Oliver gripped his bow tighter. "We need a plan," he said. "If we want to stop that thing, we have to work together."

"He's hardly a threat now. Maybe we should let him go?" Eira fiddled with her gloves.

"If we let him go, he will return to Aurum, and Aurum will come after us. Besides, what if Trepidatio disguises himself like he did in Lumas? What if he opens another portal and traps us again?" Calix shook his head. His skin prickled beneath his scales, and he clenched his fists to keep from scratching at it. "I won't take any chances."

Eira wouldn't meet his eye, but she kept quiet. He could only hope she would see it his way. Pawns were everything to Selini. Letting one survive could cost their lives. If he wanted to overcome the goddess and her Head Dragonborn, he couldn't afford to be soft toward Aurum.

"I have something in mind," Tobias interjected. Like a timid animal, he could always sense the buzz of tension in the air. When he stepped forward, it dissipated instantly as all eyes turned to him instead. He hesitated at first, but there was determination in the set of his jaw and the way he pushed his shoulders back. "I think I know how to stop Trepidatio."

Calix peered at the huge black dragon over Stiria's back, keenly aware of Kiara crouched beside him and the others gathered around him in a semicircle. It made the hairs on the back of his neck stand on end, but he relished the oddity of the sensation. He never expected to return to Selini's territory—certainly not with so many people who were willing to stand with him. Even Nari's harsh words and Oliver's presence couldn't sway his heart. It was everything Aurum would hate: they hadn't left him to die, nor were they going to fall to something like Trepidatio.

Despite himself, despite the raging monster behind him, he grinned as he turned to face the others. "Let's hear it."

38

THE SEA OF SAND

Tobias's first plan tried to rely heavily on Stiria's ability to create illusions to allow a swift and painless escape. He had only seen the dragon make minor changes to Calix's appearance, but the blue dragons were rumored to be able to do so much more. Calix was quick to correct him by saying that Stiria was still young and his mastery of illusions had not yet bloomed enough to cast anything big enough to distract Trepidatio. He also reminded him that Trepidatio was not someone to pity. Though Tobias had some reservations after watching the black dragon, he couldn't find the words to argue. Then came the backup plan.

Oliver, Kiara, and Calix took to the skies on the backs of Stiria and Faiera, each armed with a bow and a look that could kill anyone. Stiria shot toward Trepidatio's blind side, twisting and spiraling through the air since his only passenger was Calix. They weaved through the skies in graceful patterns, quickly capturing Trepidatio's attention with shouts and little icicles fired at his face. Faiera dove around to his back, where Oliver and Kiara both aimed for the weak spot the white dragon had opened up. Trepidatio spun and snapped, his growl so low it shook the earth.

It was like Calix had explained: his size was his downfall, though he was still smaller than Smoke and the Venen, the dragon they had fought at Sheniir. He was disoriented, used to being small and quick. He was still trying to fight like a little dragon.

"Remember, we need to ground him. That's our best shot of getting a good attack into that spot on his neck." Tobias turned to Nari and Eira who were crowded around him.

The apprentice held her staff in a white-knuckled grip, her gray eyes focused on the dragon in the distance. Dust swirled around them, stirred by a heavy wind whipped up by his movements. Both squinted against the dirt in the air, and Eira shielded her eyes with one hand, Kiara's black knife clutched against her palm. They were both shaky, clearly still rattled by Calix's insistence that killing Trepidatio was the only way.

Tobias cleared his throat to catch Nari's attention. She startled and turned to him, brow furrowed in a thoughtful look that almost mirrored Aviva's. "Nari, you know a binding spell, right?"

She pushed her shoulders back. "I've never fought something this big, but I can manage."

"But can you do it?"

She sighed, making a show of rolling her eyes before facing him again. "Like I've said the last hundred times you asked, yes! Do you question *every* Mage this much?"

"You're not a Mage," Eira interjected. "You're still an apprentice."

Nari gritted her teeth, but she was already summoning a thick rope of glittering blue, similar to the threads she had created for the net. They were surprisingly sturdy for something made entirely of magical energy, but she had been confident enough to catch Calix and Stiria with them. It wasn't too much of a stretch that they would be enough to tie up Trepidatio's legs and sweep them out from under him. "Do you want my help or not?" she snapped.

In his brief minutes spent with Nari, Tobias had learned the best answer was silence. He gestured for her to lead the way, making sure to keep his expression flat as she paraded past him, the rope wrapped around her shoulder and down her arm. Her ego seemed like such a fragile thing, and he didn't want to be anywhere near her when it finally exploded.

She walked a few paces out from where they had huddled behind a mound of sand, meager cover between them and the wrath of such a beast but it was better than nothing. When she was close enough that the tip of Trepidatio's tail nearly grazed her legs as it swooped past, she drove the end of her staff into the ground and thrust the hand covered in magic rope toward the dragon while the other clung to the body of her staff.

Without a weapon, Tobias could do nothing but stand and watch, holding his breath every time Trepidatio's teeth and claws narrowly missed the dragons flying circles overhead. He couldn't bargain with a raging creature who couldn't even speak his tongue. He couldn't talk his way out of this—if anything, his talking had been one ripple in the pond that led to such a massive tidal wave of rage. It was his goading that first ticked off Trepidatio. The little dragon's words were still ringing in his ears even now.

I'm the only tenirel *Aurum needs. I'm the only one who can understand his vision, and I won't let you destroy it!*

Was he at odds with the *tenirel* in the letters? It was almost too cruel to kill him, not to mention he seemed to know so much more than they did and was more likely to spill something than Aurum himself. If they kept him alive, could they get information out of him? But if Aurum truly cared for him like he claimed, how long would it be before he came to get him?

Tobias couldn't help but remember the way Aurum had

attacked him, slicing his face and leaving him to bleed out on the floor at his feet. It was difficult to tell if he held the same attachment to Trepidatio that the dragon held for him, which twisted his statement about being Aurum's *tenirel* in all kinds of foul ways. There was something more going on, but Tobias had no one to peel back the curtain.

And if they couldn't calm Trepidatio, was there really any choice? If they tried to run, could they escape? Calix was insistent that killing him was the only way, but Tobias couldn't bring himself to agree so readily. Even now, it twisted his insides.

"Get down!" Eira yelled, breaking his reverie.

He dove to the ground, getting a face full of gray sand. Trepidatio's tail swung toward them, thick as a tree trunk. Nari didn't move, but she had told them she wouldn't be able to until the spell was complete. Eira planted herself directly in the tail's path and, as it came toward her, plunged the black dagger into the cracks of the scales. Trepidatio immediately ripped it away, tearing the soft skin free of the knife. His inky blood splattered the sand as he whirled around, but his good eye was still searching for them when Stiria flew in front of his face and snatched up his attention again.

Eira swiped the blade through the air, shaking inky droplets from it. "Hey, Unda was right! This thing is nice. It practically overflows with magic."

Tobias pushed to his feet. "You just wanted me to hit the dirt."

Her mischievous grin said it all. He glared at her and spat out a mouthful of dust. It left a strangely sweet taste on his tongue and crackled with the remnants of whatever spell had caused it to fall apart.

Nari suddenly jerked back as the rope launched from her arm. It slithered through the air like a snake, somehow never ending as it wove around Trepidatio's legs. With his rage focused solely on the dragons, he never noticed until Nari grabbed the rope and tugged. It snapped tightly around Trepidatio's legs, binding them together. He screeched as he toppled over, unfurling his giant wings. Stiria slashed the thin membrane of one side from the bone down to the end before he could take off. With one last howl, Trepidatio went down. He crashed into the ground with a force that rattled the earth and sent up a wave of sand into the air. Tobias shielded his eyes as it rolled over them, carried by a strong gale that had almost enough force to knock him over.

Grit and wind washed over him, and he waited until it settled before he dared to look at the monster they had brought down. Stiria and Faiera descended gracefully, landing just outside the remnants of the dust cloud. Oliver quickly slid from Faiera's back, his bow in hand and always at the ready. Nari ripped her staff from the earth and shifted to a defensive stance. Eira held Kiara's knife aloft, her expression sharp and dangerous.

When the dust settled, an eerie silence fell over the sea of sand. Confusion twisted Tobias's gut into uncomfortable knots. Trepidatio was never silent.

The chaos cleared, but there was no large dragon hidden beneath the shroud. There was nothing at all but a huge imprint where he had landed. Even Nari's ropes had vanished, leaving faint sparks of blue behind that soon winked out.

Oliver crept to the edge of the dragon-shaped mark in the ground, searching the dirt for some sign of him. "You didn't tell us he can turn invisible."

Tobias frowned. "He can't. But he can change sizes—" All at once, it hit him, and he jerked his gaze to the sky. He squinted against the blinding sun as he skimmed the cloudless azure for a tiny black spot fleeing the scene.

"There!" Calix pointed to a small speck flying just a few feet off the ground, wings beating unevenly as Trepidatio fought to keep himself aloft with one so injured. He left a trail of black blood behind him, dripping from wounds all over his tiny body. Yet somehow, with every uneven wing beat, he was getting farther away and shrinking into the horizon that led deeper into the desert.

"I've got him," Oliver muttered. He drew his string back and took aim, but the sharp crack of wood made him freeze up and drop his tension on the string. Panic flitted across his expression, his target forgotten as he gingerly touched a sizable split in the middle of the bow. He cursed. "Kiara?"

"No arrows," she said, gesturing to her empty quiver strapped to Faiera's side.

"I've got one." Calix leapt off Stiria's back, ripping the last arrow from his quiver and nocking it against his bow as he took aim. A black arrow, Tobias realized with a start. One that screamed familiarity, dragging up an image he had almost forgotten.

Uriah's body, his heart pierced straight through with a black arrow that had come from the shadows, a gift from a figure they had never seen while they were at Sheniir. Killed before they could understand his secrets.

Tobias opened his mouth to stop Calix, uncertainty wriggling beneath the ice-cold fear crystalizing in his veins, but it was too late. Calix fired the arrow in a straight shot for Trepidatio, but it never made the mark. The little dragon opened a shadowy portal, the same kind that had brought Tobias and the Dragon Riders to Aurum's stronghold, and disappeared inside. It shut behind him immediately, sealing out Calix's arrow, which went down somewhere far out of sight.

The stillness in the air was stifling. The longer it went on, the more Tobias found himself wishing someone else would speak up, but everyone was too busy staring in defeat at the place where Trepidatio had escaped, the end of his bloody trail. He would no doubt flee to Aurum, tell him they had escaped, and it was only a matter of time before the dragonborn came back for them.

Yet, that wasn't the cause of the icy coil around Tobias's heart, squeezing so tightly that he couldn't breathe. When Calix turned, their eyes met, and Tobias stiffened. Red. His eyes were red, staggeringly bright against the backlight of the sun. Beyond him, at the other edge of the desert where it slowly turned to green, rolling hills, a huge temple overlooked the land. Half hidden behind its pillars, Tobias could have sworn he saw a five headed dragon watching them, her blue head staring directly into his soul. This was Selini's territory, the place where her people roamed free beyond the border that separated them from the rest of the world.

But all he could think about was the black arrow sticking out of Uriah's chest.

His tongue was dry, stuck to the roof of his mouth, but somehow he forced it to move. "You're the one," he said. "You killed Uriah, didn't you?"

Calix's eyes widened, his narrow pupils turning to slits as his expression twisted with fear. The vision of the goddess behind him disappeared, and he was alone and fragile again. It didn't change the truth. For whatever reason, he had killed Uriah.

Instead of confessing, instead of arguing, instead of attacking or running away, Calix's brow furrowed, though his hands were trembling, curled so tightly around his bow that it was a wonder the wood didn't break. "Who's Uriah?" he breathed, so small it was easy to miss.

"Your black arrow," Tobias snapped before he could stop himself. As soon as Calix flinched, regret washed over him. He took a deep breath before he continued, forcing his voice to even out. "We found one just like it in Uriah's body at Sheniir. You were there, weren't you? Why did you kill him?"

"You killed Uriah?" Oliver whirled to face Calix, his panic

forgotten as he reached for his hunting knife in place of his bow.

Calix raised his hands and took a measured step back until he was pressed against Stiria, who curled his tail protectively around him and curled his lip slightly. "I—I did kill someone at Sheniir, yes. I thought it was Aurum, but Aurum is still alive."

"So you admit it!" Oliver advanced, the knife in his hand now. "I knew you were no good. I told Kase you couldn't learn, that you were still a monster, but he didn't *listen*. Now he's dead because of you!"

"I shot him because he murdered Kase!" Calix raised his voice until it broke, quivering with the beginnings of tears. His eyes flashed dangerously, but he quickly looked away, one hand pressed to the bloody mess in his shoulder. "Whoever you thought you knew, forget him. I shot and killed a monster that day, and I have reason to believe he was connected to Aurum. I thought understanding the Shadowslayer would explain it to me, but there's still so much I don't know."

The pieces slotted together all too well. Tobias tasted bile on his tongue, bitter and thick, but he swallowed it back down. It burned his throat, yet he couldn't find the energy to even cringe at the sensation. They had already seen the kinds of illusions Aurum could create with Trepidatio and how he could disguise himself as the Shadowslayer. It wasn't too difficult to imagine Uriah had never been real at all. The thought made Tobias's gut sink with an overwhelming hopeless feeling.

If Uriah had always been some kind of pawn, if he had never been a person of his own, then they had always been in the palm of Aurum's hand. Since the day Kase and Tobias met him in the cave, they had been pawns in his game, playing right into his hands. It clicked—why Eira had been so deep in the cave, despite that there was only one entrance, why she always knew where to find them long before Uriah ever "betrayed" them, why he was so adamant with the Summoner's rules, why they had never seen him and Aurum in the same place.

Why he spoke of his little brother in the same way the letters whispered of Aurum's *tenirel.*

In the hands of someone truly powerful, there was nothing magic could not do. Defeating him would be impossible.

Suddenly, Tobias couldn't even fathom going to Lumas. He let the subject drop as he turned his back on Calix, setting his sights instead on the temple looming over them in the distance. Though he could no longer see the vision of the five headed dragon, he could still feel her eyes on him, always watching and growing closer the longer he remained in her territory. She knew, and it wouldn't be long before they were discovered.

He was stupid to think he ever stood a chance against a Head Dragonborn. Every step had only pushed him farther into the clutches of the goddess, and he had been foolish enough to drag everyone else down with him.

39

THE FALL

Lumas was a peaceful town. It was the perfect place to build a quiet life. Despite being on the outskirts of Calistie, so close to the frigid Aurora Mountain Range that very few chose to live there, it had a way of picking up news. From there, Unda could keep his eyes and ears open for clues about Calix's journey, for gossip about Aurum and the spread of dark magic, for whispers about the Shadowslayer ghost. Not only that, but he could repay his never ending debt to the kingdom of Calistie in small ways. In Lumas, people needed him. He was their healer, their guide, their precious secret. He was their *elf*.

His peace was too good to be true.

The full moon was high in the sky when he came down from the mountains, but its silver glow was weak compared to the flames that engulfed the little town. Horror seized Unda by the throat, blurring his vision with hot tears as ice crystalized on the tips of his fingers. The wax seal from the ghost's camp forgotten, he sprinted back to the town. Snow crunched beneath his boots, the powder thick and heavy and stained black. The tang of burnt wood and flesh lingered in the air, and he swallowed against the scream that rose in throat as he ran.

Magic crackled in the air, nothing but its residual touch, but it was enough to force the ice higher up his arms. Faint gold threads drifted through the air, still glittering and warm. There was no denying it, but he burned with the need to.

He sped across the snowy plains, pumping his legs and arms until they ached. His heart twisted painfully, and he missed a step. Too late, he tried to catch himself, and he pitched into the mud face first. It scraped his nose, stung his eyes, but he shoved himself up. Already, frost was spreading across the ground beneath his touch. He gritted his teeth and sealed the pool of magic in his chest, one that was steadily leaking through his bones. If he lost control now, Aurum would find him. He couldn't risk being found, not when he was so close. Not when he had worked so hard.

But when he lifted his head, all he could see for miles was destruction. The roaring flames were hot on his skin despite the distance. Their tongues climbed higher, almost tall enough to lick the stars. It was a sign—nowhere was safe. Destruction would always find him. Everything he touched would be destroyed by Aurum.

Nothing but ashes remained of Lumas, and when the flames finally dissipated, they would be all that was left.

A sob tore from his throat, so raw it scraped his insides and shook him to his very core. The ice inside him exploded, covering everything in a wide berth around him in a white sheen. Tears spilled down his cheeks, hot and cold at the same time. As another cry racked him, he pressed his face to the dirt, his fists curled around a handful of soot and snow. It did little to cushion the sharp sting as his nails dug into his skin.

It was foolish to think Aurum would never learn of an elf in Lumas, that he would have forgotten his grudge, that he would never come to lay waste to the town in search of the elf.

An elf who didn't exist because he was nothing more than an illusion—a disguise who had fooled countless people.

A lie that had destroyed countless lives.

Unda screamed until his throat was raw. He beat his fist into the dirt until each hit rattled his bones, until his skin burned with contact, until the ice he made ripped it apart. A sharp, familiar tug yanked his chest, its talons sinking deep into his heart until he couldn't even breathe. He tasted salt on his lips, wet with his tears and grimy with mud.

When his tears began to subside, he sat up. By then, the flames had gone out and the touch of Aurum's magic had dissipated, but the silence they left behind was worse. Nothing but the howl of wind and the ringing of his own screams in his ears filled the void, and nothing would for a long time. The scar over his heart ached again, an old wound that would never leave him be. Like the silver sword at his side, it was a ghost from ages past, one that would walk with him for eternity.

Shakily, he lifted his hand, blackened with dirt and soot. At some point, he must have dropped his illusion. The weight of the horns on his head returned along with the cold touch of the scales dotting his cheeks. One finger was clear as ice and tinged blue, but it curled when the others did. He swallowed hard and looked away from the painful reminder.

Consequences. There were always consequences. He couldn't run from them nor deny them anymore. He had already tried—that was Lumas, his perfect utopia, his escape from the temple, his chance to make things right.

Aurum's letters flashed through his memories. Perfectly penned but never sent, they were left to rot in "the Shadowslayer's" camp until they were discovered by Calix and the others. Each one began the same way.

Dear tenirel.

Something hot and heavy slammed into Unda, a blow that nearly sent him spiraling. Rage. Anger. Hate. They flitted through his mind, taunting him with the promise that each one could set things right, but he knew better. As he drew in a deep breath, he collected everything—the anger burning deep in the scar in his chest, the sadness weighing heavily over his limbs, the fear slithering up his spine—and let it all go in a long exhale. The itchiness in his eyes began to subside along with the painful twist in his gut.

He had wasted enough time. He had destroyed enough in his efforts to heal and provide. He had lied and twisted and hid and pretended long enough.

It was time to return to the temple. It was time to accept that he was Unda, the Blue Head Dragonborn. It was time to accept that he was Aurum's beloved little brother.

And that it was his duty to end Aurum's violence.

24/3/T/xx-80

The following letter has been preserved and translated from Draconic. It is only one of many, but I believe it is more than enough. My hope is that it will help High Summoner Maven better understand what we uncovered in the Aurora Mountains.

— TOBIAS, KEEPER OF THE RECORDS

Dear tenirel,

I don't know what to say to you anymore, so I suppose I will stop trying to withhold things from you. I miss you, tenirel, painfully, obviously, abysmally. The days are long, and I can't help but watch them blend as they used to. They've become nothing but sand in the hourglass again, even though you asked me not to let them slip through my fingers. I'm sorry. I've let them slip again.

Weaving myself back together is tedious, and it distorts life in all facets. I know you won't understand as you've always rejected the veticaabe with such disdain, but it is like trying to wake from a long dream, though never quite breaking the surface. That, at least, I know you will understand. The scar tries to pull you back under every day, doesn't it?

I was shot. The horror that gripped me was so surreal, and the pain didn't even last long before everything was gone. You have always been quiet about your time under, but I feel fair in likening the experience to yours. I wish you were here to speak of such things with me. This is an area that I am unfamiliar with myself, but you know better than me. You are a miracle. I am sorry for the agony you had to go through to achieve this, but I will always be here to keep you from repeating that.

And even if you were to fall under once more, I would put you back together. That is my promise. It always has been, and it always will be.

I will immortalize you and myself. And when there is nothing else, there will be the two of us. Things will return to what they were—I swear they will, so wait for me until then.

First, I must rid myself of this sickness so that you can stand to look at me again. I have a helper now, a little thing fittingly named Trepidatio for he is fear and brings fear and is quite fearful himself. He keeps me company and aids my search. But I wish you would take his place. He will never be you. I'm sorry that I tried to fill the hole you left behind. It was wrong of me, but the sickness compels me. I must be rid of it so that you will return to me again.

The spellbook proved useful yet puzzling. The process is slow and tedious, and the world does not abound with magic like it used to. Collecting what I need is a process of great agony. Wait for me. I won't give up. Please wait for me, no matter how long it takes. I need you to wait for me.

If the goddess asks how the search goes, inform her that my trap has worked wonders. The blood of that man drew the hybrid out of hiding immediately, and he is already so broken that it won't be long before he is a better sacrifice than he was before. Forgive me for the delays. Cleansing these black scales is time consuming. No matter how I look at them, they never shine gold, and the darkness eats away at me.

Do your stitches still ache? I'm sorry. I'm sorry for all that I've done. I'm sorry that you never look at me the way you used to. But I will make it right. I will always make it right, over and over again. I will always be your ahkirel.

Please wait for me. In this time while I cannot protect you, rely upon your sword. I know you use it well enough. It doesn't need much guidance to kill (remember that you are allowed to kill. There doesn't need to be a reason. You can kill. You can always kill. That is what the sword is for).

Do you watch me in the pool? I wish to make you proud again. Everything I do is for you so that we can return to the way things were. Please wait for me. I will make it right.

Most of all, I love you. Never forget that I do this out of love. I need you, I always have, and I love you dearly. You are my tenirel, and I am your ahkirel.

Wait for me.

Drekisn diem a, Aurum

END OF BOOK TWO

The saga continues in book three
OF ICE AND SHADOWS

ALSO BY ROBIN WINCKLER

The Legends of Anticuus series

The Wrath of Winter

Of Spellbooks and Thieves

Of Scars and Scales

Of Ice and Shadows - coming soon!

~

If you enjoyed this book, please consider leaving a review. It helps more than you know!

ACKNOWLEDGMENTS

When I began this series, finishing it (like… truly *finishing* it and getting it into the hands of readers) seemed too distant to even think about. Now, we're one book away from the end of the trilogy! This series has grown with me, and I'm excited to see how far it has come and how far it will go. Hopefully, you are as excited for the next book as I am! But before I close out this book, I want to say a few thank yous.

To my family: thank you for your continued support along this journey! My book would not have reached as many people as it has without all of you, and I would certainly not have made it to this point either. Also thank you to my dog, Pippin, for impatiently shoving my computer out of my lap and generally making it very difficult to write. He's here to look cute, and he does it well.

To everyone who made it through the long wait and returned for book two: THANK YOU! (I don't use caps lock lightly either). I'm truly grateful for everyone who shared my enthusiasm for this series and came back for more. You keep me going when writing is difficult or overwhelming.

To my friends who cheered me on from the sidelines and listened to my many attempts to unravel my old drafts, my critique partners who helped me find the places that needed some extra polishing, and everyone who stopped to ask me how the book was going: I'm so thankful for your support!

To the people who helped make publishing possible such as my cover designer (Sarah Penney) and my editors (Laine and

Aria Nichols): thank you for your work on this story! It wouldn't be as beautiful or as polished as it is now if not for you.

Finally, thank YOU for reading! I hope that you will look forward to book three! Aurum said it best: wait for me until then.

ABOUT THE AUTHOR

Robin Winckler is a YA fantasy author with a love for magic, dragons, adventure, and all things high fantasy. She will graduate in May 2025 with a degree in English, which she hopes to use to grow her writing skills. When she is not writing, she can be found drawing, reading, or playing with her beloved dog, Pippin.

instagram.com/author.robinwinckler
threads.net/@author.robinwinckler
patreon.com/authorrobinwinckler